Maggie stopped abruptly. A massive black horse stood in the middle of the road, blocking her way and taking up far more space than an average animal would. Her eyes lifted slowly, past the huge and sleekly muscled legs of the horse to the breeches-clad, equally well-muscled legs of the rider. Past a gloved hand and a rich, russet coat that was fitted perfectly to broad shoulders. Then, for a long moment, her breath caught in her throat. . . .

As she stared, the man reached up and tipped his hat, revealing steel gray eyes and wavy hair the rich brown of the earth. "Good day, madam."

English, she thought at the sound of the deep voice. *And aye, patrician.*

This man from a medieval castle's wall would be English. She blinked, lifted her chin, and coolly asked, "Can I be of help to you?"

He did not reply immediately; instead, he fixed her with an unsettling, steely gaze that very nearly had her hand lifting to touch her flushed cheeks. . . .

By Emma Jensen
Published by The Ballantine Publishing Group:

CHOICE DECEPTIONS
VIVID NOTIONS
COUP DE GRACE
WHAT CHLOE WANTS
ENTWINED
HIS GRACE ENDURES
BEST LAID SCHEMES
FALLEN

FALLEN

Emma Jensen

IVY BOOKS • NEW YORK

An Ivy Book
Published by The Ballantine Publishing Group
Copyright © 2001 by Emma Jensen

www.randomhouse.com/BB/

Library of Congress Catalog Card Number: 00-193204

ISBN 0-8041-1955-4

Manufactured in the United States of America

First Edition: April 2001

10 9 8 7 6 5 4 3 2 1

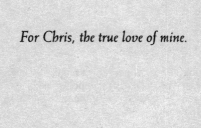

For Chris, the true love of mine.

Scarbro Fair

O are you going to Scarbro Fair,
Savoury sage rosemary and thyme;
Remember me to a lass who lives there,
For once she was a true lover of mine.

And tell her to make me a cambric shirt,
Savoury sage rosemary and thyme;
Without any seam or needlework,
And then she shall be a true lover of mine.

And tell her to wash it in yonder dry well,
Savoury sage rosemary and thyme;
Where water ne'er sprung nor a drop of rain fell,
And then she'll be a true lover of mine.

And tell her to dry it on yonder thorn,
Savoury sage rosemary and thyme;
Which never bore blossom since Adam was born,
Or never be a true lover of mine.

When she has finished and done her I'll repay,
Savoury sage rosemary and thyme;
She can come unto me and married we'll be,
And she will be a true lover of mine.

Now he has asked me questions three,
Savoury sage rosemary and thyme;
I hope he will answer as many for me,
For once he was a true lover of mine.

Then tell him to find me an acre of land,
Savoury sage rosemary and thyme;

Between the salt water and the sea sand,
  And then he'll be a true lover of mine.

And tell him to plough it with a ram's horn,
  Savoury sage rosemary and thyme;
And sow it throughout with one peppercorn,
  And then he'll be a true lover of mine.

And tell him to reap it with a sickle of leather,
  Savoury sage rosemary and thyme;
And bind it all up with one peacock feather,
  Or never be a true lover of mine.

When he has done and finished his work,
  Savoury sage rosemary and thyme;
He may come and have his cambric shirt,
  And then he shall be a true lover of mine.

PROLOGUE

O chionn fhada anns an Eilean Sgitheanach . . .

Och, but I forget myself. In English, then, for while my tale finds its heart west of the Highlands, it springs from southerly discontent. 'Tis not unusual, to find Scottish troubles come from England, but this one came twice. 'Tis a tale of three impossible questions, two stubborn souls, and one love as enduring as towering cliffs and timeless ballads.

But see now how I've gotten ahead of myself, and behind. So I'll begin again.

A long time ago on the Isle of Skye . . .

The Isle of Skye, 1746

Not so many years ago, a man might have come to this spot, all but blind in the dense mist, and thought he had come to the end of the world. The Englishman stood with one foot solid on cliff rock, the other held to land only by the edge of his heel, and wondered how long he would fall. Forever, perhaps. Or no longer than a heartbeat.

"If I were to help you o'er the edge, none would know it."

He smiled as the voice came through the mist, followed by the slight, beloved form. "True," he agreed easily, "and I suspect few would weep." He stepped away from the cliff to gather a handful of coarse woolen

1

cloak, gently drawing her to him. "Would you weep for me, my love?"

Ah, she was lovely, her skin glowing pearl-like in the mist. He dreamed of that softness each night, even when she was curved warmly around him, of running his fingers over the curve of her brow, through the fire-touched silk of her hair. They were dreams he was not prepared to let go.

"Oh, aye, I will weep." Her voice stirred him, as always, soft with its Scottish lilt. "Sooner, I think, than I'd expected. You are leaving. Nay." She ran one small hand over his chest, as if testing its very soundness. "You've already gone."

He cursed quietly, but did not deny the fact that he was leaving. His task on the island was done and only a fool would remain. "I am still here and asking you now, as before, to come away with me."

She stiffened in his arms. " 'Tis a harsh thing you ask of me."

"I ask only that you leave a place."

"Aye, and half of my heart." It grieved her, more than she could have imagined, that he still did not understand. "Ask of me . . . Ask of me a shirt without seam."

"A shirt? You wish to sew for me?"

"You were not listening. A shirt," she repeated, "without seam or thread."

He stared at her blankly. "Why would I ask that of you?"

"Promise me, then. Promise me a plot of land 'tween sand and sea."

"You are making no sense, love. What you ask is not possible."

"Aye," she said softly. " 'Tis impossible."

They stood breast to breast and she knew, with complete certainty, that he felt her heartbeat. They were too well bound for it to be otherwise. The loss of him already felt like a bleeding inside, a quietly steady pulse that had thundered with her steps as she walked over the moorland to join him.

'Twas too much, too much to think they could be separated.

His skin was cool where he rested his forehead against hers. She raised trembling fingers high to his face, to the bold cheekbones and slashing brows she loved so well. The mist had dampened his hair so it lay sleek and dark against his head, its earthy color lost in the night. There was the fire of anger in his eyes, in his touch, and she knew he was lost to her, even as he held her in his arms.

"You will not forsake me," he said slowly, his voice low and ragged at the edges. It was the same desperate roughness that had coaxed, driven away doubt, and called out her name as they lay together at night. "You will not. . . ."

"Nay." She lowered one hand and withdrew the sprig of thyme from her pocket. Gently, so he would not feel, she slipped it into his, silently begging forgiveness for what she was about to do. "I'll not ever be doing that."

⊰ 1 ⊱

*'Twas an unsavoury life he led, our lad, in an
unsavoury land, where an angel wouldna tread.*
                    —Dubhgall MacIain MacLeòid

London, 1812

If there was one bit of dramatic nonsense Gabriel
Loudon, the Earl of Rievaulx, loathed more than Sunday
sermons, it was ghost stories. He loathed the familiar de-
vices, the predictable ends. Most of all, he loathed the
undercurrent of every sorry tale that said, "This might
be true; you cannot prove otherwise."

His feelings on the matter had been different once. As
a child he had loved to sit with his grandfather in front of
the fire while the old man spun tales of ghoulish glory, always about the long-departed Loudons who stalked
Scarborough House's dim halls on midwinter nights.
The earl had punctuated the tales by occasionally and
suddenly tickling the back of Gabriel's neck, where the
boy's hair already stood on end, with his gnarled fingers.
Gabriel had clung to his grandfather's knee in terrified
delight during the telling. And each night he had reluctantly crept off to bed, a taper gripped in each small fist
as he navigated the dark paneled halls on his shaky way
to bed.

His grandfather had been gone for fifteen years now
and, despite countless bantering promises to the contrary, had never made a reappearance in the ancient

house he'd loved and lovingly passed on to the son of his own long-dead son. Gabriel had grown into adulthood, a strong and handsome replica of so many past earls whose stern visages lined the galleries, and he had come to hate ghost stories.

Each and every one reminded him of the ghosts for which he himself was responsible.

At the moment, he was being subjected to a spectral tale of the sort that meant the least to him but set his teeth on edge nonetheless. God help him, it was yet one more involving the spirit of some blighted Highlander, and it was interfering with Gabriel's own earthly pleasures.

The men at the table behind him seemed to have lost interest in their game of vingt-et-un some time past, and had taken to exchanging ghostly tales loudly and with excruciating detail. As lax as Gabriel's own concentration on his cards had become in his boredom, it was completely ruined by the hiccuping narrative nearby.

Around the cavernous room, coins clinked as they changed hands. Men groaned with their losses; women cackled or squealed as groping hands found purchase. All the sounds of a true and busy gaming hell, ordinarily splendid to Gabriel's ears, but now appropriated and spoiled by the quintet behind him.

"It rosh again, the skreel of pipes among the fallen stones. . . ."

So far, this speaker had risen his skirling pipes three times, and mentioned his ghost, a one-armed chieftain, only once. Gabriel had been ready to turn and demand just how a one-armed Scot could play the bagpipes at all, but he wasn't really interested and there was no fun to be had in baiting drunken cretins. Beyond that, the table had eyed him fishily when he had taken his seat an hour earlier. As tempting as it might be, Gabriel saw no reason to ruin his own comfort by upsetting theirs.

He recognized most of the gathering. That in itself would ordinarily have been enough to send him running, but he was pleasantly drunk and winning. The misfortune of knowing many of his fellow gamesters was a mere annoyance. Sadly, the clientele of the Red Hollow had become rather patrician of late. When he had stumbled upon the Tavistock Street gaming hell some six months earlier, it had been filled with smoke, prostitutes, and tradesmen of the sort whose wares would never make their way into Mayfair shops.

The lightskirts were still present; Gabriel had removed one from his lap not ten minutes past. The smoke was still there, too, hovering like fog, obscuring the same scarred paneling and tattered, grimy brocade drapes. What had changed was that the room was now liberally peppered with far cleaner brocade waistcoats, adorning far cleaner gamblers. Apparently other members of the ton had discovered the place more recently. While Gabriel had kept its splendid existence very much to himself, someone else had not.

There was still a scattering of glowering toughs about, hunched at corner tables with their dice and dented tankards, but most had been hastened off by the new arrivals and by the cudgel-wielding proprietor, who had scented a far more profitable living in serving the blue bloods. And making certain their pockets were not picked by nimble fingers or their corseted sides pricked by lethal blades.

Gabriel supposed he would have to seek out the next hell soon enough. He had eschewed "Polite" company and insipid Society gatherings since returning from the Continent nearly a year ago. He certainly had no desire to share his formerly prime entertainment space with Society men now. For tonight, however, cards were cards, gold was gold, and the whiskey burned pleasantly on its way down. He would tolerate the nasal cries and intermittent bursts of spilled snuff.

Yes, he knew many of the men present, including several of those at the table behind him. They knew him. And were clearly not pleased with the acquaintance. As best Gabriel could recall, he had not fleeced any of these particular creatures at the tables, bedded their wives, or insulted their tailors. Of course, enough whiskey did dull his memory on occasion, but never fully erased it. His years in the service of King and Country had sharpened him too well for that.

It was likely nothing more than his reputation, then.

Gabriel had never asked to be dubbed the Archangel by his peers, had certainly never striven to epitomize the absurd sobriquet. And he couldn't really be bothered to care that it was gone, nor that his ignominy had swelled to the point that it had followed him even to this disreputable spot.

At one of the increasingly infrequent visits to his club, an erstwhile friend had seen fit to commend him, drunken wastrel that he had become, on his good fortune in not being shunned outright. How tolerant was the ton of its own, the fellow had murmured. Gabriel knew tolerance bloody well had nothing to do with it. The overfed capons who perched in the club's overstuffed chairs were terrified of him.

He also knew it hadn't always been so. But as it happened, this was neither the place nor time to contemplate his inelegant tumble from grace. Especially when those denouncing him were doing so for all the wrong reasons.

He did not dispute their right to scorn him; he just rather
wished they would do so on the correct grounds.

He shrugged, and drained his glass in a swallow. He
had all the time in the world to go yet another vicious
round with his demons. He had other matters to attend
to at present.

"Another?" he asked, surprised, of his companion
who had apparently recovered sufficiently from the last
hand of cards to deal the next. It seemed foolish to hope
the man would take the scowled hint and withdraw, but
if there was one pithy proverb Gabriel had heard ad nau-
seam, it involved the eternal existence of hope.

Clarence Fullerton coughed and waved a shaky hand
in front of his waxen face. The ever-present smoke
wafted for a moment, then settled again. A more poetic
man might have been reminded of Hebridean mists that
drifted over a man's face like a woman's cool, gentle fingers in the night. Gabriel chose instead to draw a thin
Egyptian cheroot from his silver case. He dragged the ill-
smelling candle over the table toward him, scarcely
noting the hot tallow that ran over his hand in the
process. As he bent his head, bringing the cigar to the
flame, he darted a hooded glance at his opponent.

Fullerton, for all his twenty-odd years, looked like a
schoolboy who had been fed a tadpole. He tugged re-
peatedly at his wilted cravat, and his eyes, beneath the
Byronic tangle of gold hair, were distressed and a bit
glazed. The carafe of poor-quality port he had purchased
explained the glaze. Gabriel suspected the rising pile of
debt markers in the center of the table went a long way
toward explaining the distress.

Gabriel could see Fullerton counting his losses as best
he could with his fogged brain. Fifty quid in gold, another

three hundred in paper promises. It was pocket money to the earl, but for the younger man it probably represented a quarter's allowance, if not a great deal more.

Fullerton shakily lifted several chits between his fingertips, let them flutter back to the pile. His chin went up, if only a trembling notch. "Another, yes."

His eyes were desperate now, an hour after the first hand, and Gabriel knew desperation went badly with cards. So did idiocy, and Fullerton had that in abundance. Only a fool would have slapped down a deck in front of a man a decade older and aeons ahead in experience. But there was an eager spark in the younger man, one Gabriel found amusing. It reminded him of the man he had once been.

He was nothing like this boy now. At thirty-two, he'd lived one lifetime of good sport and goodwill, and another of which he couldn't be nearly so indulgent. The Fallen Archangel. But that had been Fullerton's goal, he imagined, to face the notorious earl—the earl being in a drunkenly subdued state, of course—and leave with his skin intact, perhaps even a few extra quid in his pocket.

Idiocy.

Gabriel drew deeply on his cheroot, then released the smoke in a slow stream. It surrounded Fullerton's face, making him blink anew, then rose. A more righteous man might have seen it as a halo of sorts over the gold curls. Gabriel simply watched it dissipate into the rest of the haze. He drew again, short puffs, then set the cigar on the edge of the table. It rocked for a moment, dropping ash on Fullerton's slack leg.

Gabriel idly sifted through the pile of markers with one finger. "Not a good night for you, it seems."

He saw the younger man's throat work convulsively.

"Nothing another hand or two won't set aright, my lord."

And winged swine, Gabriel thought, were landing atop Parliament even as they spoke. "Perhaps not," he agreed, "but I find myself disinclined to play further." He scooped the chits into an untidy pile, shoved them into his waistcoat pocket. "Good night, Fullerton."

"But sir . . ." Fullerton watched, wild-eyed, as Gabriel rose to his feet. "You cannot . . . I do not wish to cease!"

"We so seldom get what we want in life, Fullerton. For my part, I do not wish to go on."

"Lord Rievaulx, please. I entreat you. As a gent—" The young man broke off, blinked miserably. "As a gentleman," he managed finally.

Gabriel said nothing for a long moment. Then, "Fortune is such a curious thing, is it not?" He reached into his pocket for his recently gained spoils and casually tossed a coin to a hovering whore. She grinned, displaying more gaps than teeth, and scuttled off toward the taps. Gabriel gave Fullerton a bland salute, then gestured to the cheroot smoldering at the edge of the table. "Have a cigar, puppy."

As he wove his somewhat unsteady way across the floor he got a fleeting glimpse of Fullerton dropping his golden head into his hands. There was nothing quite so pitiful, Gabriel thought as he got a good grip on the wobbling bannister, as a witless ass who indulged his drunken despondency in public.

He could feel eyes on his back as he ascended the stairs. The ghostie quintet, he imagined, among others. None of whom would be in the least sorry to see the back of him. And still for all the wrong reasons. He thought one or two might gather up Fullerton and share some oh-so-righteous indignation. Bully for them.

He clipped his shoulder against the door frame at the top of the stairs, scraped his hand against the rough wood as he donned his hat. It was only when he stumbled over the threshold and actually had to employ his silver-headed stick to regain his balance that he realized just how sodden he was. And with seriously inferior whiskey, more was the pity.

The brute of a doorman waited only long enough to make certain he wasn't going to change his mind and weave back down the stairs, before shutting the heavy door with a resounding *thunk*. Gabriel tugged the very corner of his coattail free and stepped into the street.

It was quiet there, eerily so. The famed London mist that began to creep in with the midnight hour was heavy now, and invasive. Gabriel unconsciously rubbed a hand over his chest, over the healed saber wound that ached in damp weather.

The Hollow's door thumped again behind him, disgorging more patrons. Gabriel leaned against a convenient wall and squinted into the darkness, trying to get his bearings. He supposed the best option would be to wander in what he assumed was the direction of Drury Lane and Covent Garden. He would be able to get a hackney there, or he could simply walk the mile back to his Curzon Street house. There he would go facedown into his bed, one way or another. One way was directly; the other way would involve some superior whiskey en route. It didn't much matter which. He had nowhere to be the following day, nor the one after, nor the one after that, stretching on rather further than he could stand to contemplate at present. A man's days had a way of dragging on a bit when he was summarily retired from the military. Nights were worse. . . .

He glanced down the alley as a landau came rolling

toward him. Decidedly grand for such a venue, it looked very much out of place. It also looked very familiar. Gabriel didn't need to see the ornate crest emblazoned on the door. He knew precisely who had just arrived in front of the Red Hollow.

The vehicle rolled to a halt. The driver climbed down from his box, but the landau's door was already swinging wide. A tall figure clambered to the stones. He was far better dressed than Gabriel, carrying a far shinier walking stick. He leaned heavily upon it as he stared up the dark street.

"Rievaulx?"

Gabriel levered himself away from the wall with a sigh. "Good evening, Oriel. Splendid weather we are having, is it not?"

Nathan Paget, Marquess of Oriel, and fellow former member of a military intelligence unit so clandestine it had not even had an official name, snorted. Then demanded, "Do you require assistance in getting into the carriage?"

"As a matter of fact, I do not, and damn you kindly for asking."

Lord Oriel's sigh was far more eloquent than Gabriel's had been. "Sometimes I don't know why I bother."

"I am far less concerned with the *why* than the *how*, as it happens."

"Ogilvie told me you might be found here."

Gabriel scowled. "I specifically did not inform him of my intentions. Sometimes I do not wish to be found." In truth, his failure to tell his formidable butler of his intended whereabouts had more to do with carelessness than design—and Oriel well knew it. He was the only person who ever came looking for the Earl of Rievaulx these days. "So, you found me. . . ."

"On the verge of toppling into a pile of refuse, or so Carver informed me."

"On the verge of deciding just what entertainment would suit the remainder of the evening." He gave Oriel's driver a wry if unoffended salute. "In fact, I believe I haven't had nearly enough to drink this evening. Since you obviously wish to speak with me, why not join me inside. I'll even buy the rotgut."

He knew there was a better chance of getting the man to enter Princess Caroline's boudoir these days than a place like the Hollow. Oriel certainly did not disappoint in his response. He sniffed, wrinkled his very patrician nose. "You must be jesting."

Gabriel chuckled, then reached out to touch his friend's sleeve. "Get back in the carriage," he said gently. "Standing on these stones cannot be doing your leg any good."

"Rubbish." But Oriel did return to the landau, his limp more pronounced than usual.

The coachman was waiting at the door. "A moment, Carver," Gabriel said, then to Oriel who was climbing inside, "I'd meant to do this tomorrow, but now will suffice."

He emptied his pockets on the carriage floor. Hampered somewhat by his wavery vision and uncooperative fingers, he sorted among the mess for his coin purse and Fullerton's vowels and tore the latter into large pieces. Then, emptying the coins into the pile, he dropped the torn paper into the pouch. He would keep the fifty pounds. Nobility, what he still possessed of it, had its limits. Fullerton could use the lesson. Beyond that, the puppy had still been sober when he'd lost the coins. Gabriel had already been three sheets to the wind.

Handing the pouch to Oriel's driver, he sent the man

into the Hollow to deliver the shredded gift. "Fullerton. Look for the child with golden curls and an empty port bottle," he instructed dryly. Then, as Carver hurried into the hell, he joined his friend in the carriage.

Oriel was sprawled across the facing seat, fingers tapping a rhythmless tattoo on his extended leg. War had been hard on him, too. But unlike Gabriel, he had found love and happiness on his return, had been able to accept them when they were offered in the form of a clever Scottish spinster with a sharp tongue and an expansive heart. Of course, Oriel had never fallen past the point of redemption. He was, had always been, noble as Caesar, solid as stone.

"I trust you didn't come after me to scold yet again," Gabriel muttered despite knowing perfectly well that such sullenness was beneath even him.

Oriel's brows rose. "I never scold. I merely suggest that drinking yourself into a stupor is perhaps not the best use of an evening. And no, I came after you—"

The coachman stuck his head through the open door and announced to Gabriel, "Done, my lord."

"Done. . . ?" Oriel repeated. "No, I daresay I don't want to know. Let's be off, Carver."

Gabriel glanced back as they pulled away, just in time to see Fullerton stumble through the hell's portal. The young man stood in the street, haloed by the meager light spilling through the door. It was probably no more than the shadows, but Gabriel imagined he saw a glimmer of hope along with the slack jaw.

"Idiot," he muttered, then turned his full attention to his erstwhile rescuer. "Where are we going?"

"My house," was Oriel's bland reply. "I'd thought to go to Brooks's, but I daresay you've had enough enjoyment for one evening."

Gabriel snorted. "Just as well you think so. Last time I strolled down St. James's, Pickering spat on me."

"You made his daughter an offer that had nothing to do with matrimony, if memory serves, at my *wife's* party."

"Well, the girl would hardly have told Pickering about that. And she kept patting my thigh under the supper table. I was merely responding appropriately." He waited for a sniff from that patrician nose, but of course none came. He and Oriel had known each other nearly all their lives, had forged a friendship so strong that nothing—certainly not the disapproval of some stiff-lipped Society asses—could dent it. Sighing, he faced the inevitable. "You'd better tell me why you came looking for me tonight. What sin of mine has been brought to your attention this time?"

"I shudder to contemplate what you've done of late, but I'm more concerned with what you can do."

"I can see to myself, thank you."

Oriel ignored him. "I need you to go to Skye."

Had the man requested that he swim to Calais, Gabriel couldn't have been more surprised. "Skye? Good Lord, why? Have Isobel's brothers escaped again?"

The feckless pair seemed to spend all their time removing themselves from their Skye home where Oriel frequently banished them and trotting back to the guest quarters of his London house. The marquess's mouth tightened. Gabriel, who had assumed it was at the mention of the junior MacLeods, felt his own jaw dropping not a moment later when Oriel announced, "Wulf sent word that L'Écossais has been traced to Skye. I can't go after him, not as I am now; we all know that. You can."

A shiver, half dread and half excitement, rippled up Gabriel's spine. *L'Écossais.* A grimly familiar name to their elite corps. *L'Écossais. The Scot.* Little was known of the man save his nationality and the fact that he had been a fulcrum for a network of French spies. Without anyone ever seeing his face, he had managed to drum up a surprising amount of support for the enemy, both in Ireland and in his native Scotland.

L'Écossais. The Scot. An opportunity to make right even one of the terrible blunders . . .

Gabriel shook his head, grunted. "Let Wulf go after him. Or Rotheroe."

"Wulf needs to be in Spain. Rotheroe is a cyphers man, no use here. You are the only choice."

In his head Gabriel began the familiar and helpless recitation of the names from their defunct corps: St. Wulfstan, Rotheroe, Rievaulx, Oriel. And the dead: Brandon, Brooke, Montgomerie . . . His chest constricted agonizingly.

"Montgomerie wasn't your fault, man," Oriel said gently, intently, always a mind reader at the worst times. "Nor were Brandon or Witherspoon or Brooke. Their blood isn't on your hands."

Perhaps not, Gabriel agreed silently, but it was certain as hell he had their souls on his conscience. More ghosts. "Don't ask me to do this," he muttered. "Don't ask me to do anything."

"Too late."

Gabriel fully agreed. It was too late. "No."

Oriel shrugged. "It's your choice, of course."

"Of course."

"Well, I'll take you home, then. No use in plying you with my brandy if your mind is already set." The marquess lifted his own cane toward the trap. "By the by, what was it you gave Fullerton back there?"

"A second chance, I suppose," Gabriel replied, then,

hearing his own words, "Bloody hell." He sighed. "You can wipe that damned smile off your face. Contrary to what you might believe, Oriel, you do not know me better than I know myself."

"I never claimed to," was his friend's easy reply. "I do know, however, that you will appreciate the whiskey on Skye."

Gabriel gazed at his oldest friend, his unwavering comrade, and cursed fluently.

⊰ 2 ⊱

Thyme is for healing,
clove for love.
Rosemary is for remembrance.
Sage leaf makes wishes come true
and heather makes the rain fall.

Skye, three weeks later

Maggie MacLeod picked her way carefully over the sharp rocks to the edge of the cliffs. She'd passed the last quarter hour sheltered by an outcropping of boulders some hundred feet away, waiting for her resolve to harden and the last of her neighbors to pass by on their way to the village road. She did not particularly want witnesses to what she was about to do and so had waited patiently, exchanging warm greetings with Fen MacDonald and Tavis Tolmey, with Lachtna Norrie and Jeannie MacDonald as they went by. Now she was alone, and ready.

Spring had taken its time in coming to the Highlands and the Western Isles and the wind was still fierce, especially where she stood overlooking the Cuillin Sound. Far below, whitecapped waves churned and beat hard against the rocks. It was not a welcoming spot, even on the best of days, but Maggie needed to be right where she was.

She had been back on Skye for a month now, after three years in England, and came to the cliffs whenever time permitted. She had always been drawn to the spot, even as a child. Some ten years back, a concerned Calum MacAuley, the local innkeeper, had stood up in church

18

and offered to build a fence just for her safety. He had been fondly laughed back into his seat by the congregation. Even then, everyone knew that Maggie MacLeod would merely climb right over the top. There was something, though none could say what, drawing her there.

Maggie found contentment easily and in many places; it was in her character. But she had never found happiness away from home. Skye, with its wild beauty and quiet people, had called to her relentlessly during her time away. Now, face turned to the wind, she could describe each crevice in the ancient cliff rock without looking, could recite the varying colors of the wild thyme and heather stretching behind her toward the village road. She had dreamed of this spot so often while in England that, had she not been able to come home, no detail would ever have been forgotten.

The villagers tended to avoid the cliffs where they sloped away from the high road, kept away by daily tasks, the dangerous winds, and by the eerie legends surrounding the place. Many claimed that a pair of ghostly lovers walked the narrow path near the edge. Maggie had never seen them, nor did she believe the tale. Oh, she had a deep, fond place in her heart for island lore, certainly, but it didn't extend to ghosties and ghoulies and things that went bump in the night.

She did not come to the cliffs in search of wandering spirits. She certainly never came at night when the wind and damp made the path dangerous. No, she came during the day when her tasks permitted, for a bit of peace and solitude. In the past several days she'd come for some respite from the odd restlessness that had been plaguing her.

It was time now. Maggie unfolded her hand and studied the man's glove she held. It was creased from having spent so many months at the bottom of her trunk. She had taken it out every so often, doing her best to smooth the wrinkles from the buff doeskin. It had long since lost the faint scent of its owner's inexpensive snuff, not so long since lost the ability to bring hot, shameful tears to her eyes.

"Good-bye, Peter," she whispered harshly. Then she cast the glove over the cliff edge, not caring whether it hit the water or landed like a broken creature on the rocks. If legend was to be believed, it would not be the first item of fine English clothing to land there. Nor would she be the first Skye woman to stand at that spot, heart cold.

Sometimes she did think fleetingly of the ill-destined lovers and wondered how much of the tale was true. A grain, no doubt, as with most legends. The rest would be the product of long winter nights and too many tankards of nutty ale.

She was far better off thinking of her herbs. She had taken advantage of the rare sunshine to collect rushes from the fen on her way to the cliffs, remembering only to bring one empty basket with her. The other, the one filled with herb sachets and tisanes for her neighbors, was still sitting just outside her cottage door, waiting to be drenched by the coming rain. And now she had wasted precious minutes dreaming at Scavaig Point.

It wasn't like her to be careless. Yet, in the past several days, she had blundered about like some hen-witted creature, leaving her tasks scattered behind her as if by a mischievous wind. Only that morning, she had nearly sent herself tip over tail when she'd stumbled over a collection of empty bottles left in the middle of the parlor floor. Heaven only knew when she had put them there, or why. And, in retying the garter come loose in the flailing, she had noted that one of her stockings was white, the other gray.

" 'Tis howling at the moon you'd be at next, my lass," she muttered, exasperated with herself. Then, "You'll be fine now."

It was time to be heading home. Her task was done. There were bannocks to bake, household accounts to attend, and the day being Friday, ale to water down. It was not yet teatime. With any luck, her father would only have downed half the pitcher. Much as Maggie loved him, she did not think the neighbors would care to be regaled with Burns's finest, bellowed jovially from the top of the hill till the wee hours. The wind, after all, had a way of carrying such things much farther than they ought to go.

Time to be off, then. Taming the rippling of her worn cloak, she reached into the second pocket and withdrew a dried sage leaf. Closing her eyes for an instant, she whispered *"For true love"* to herself, then tossed the leaf. The wind lifted it, twirled it into a merry spiral, and carried it over the cliff edge. It was a silly act, she knew, wishing on sage, and chided herself for it. As if she could have stopped the urge.

She stepped back from the cliff's edge, shook off the moment of fancy, and breathed deeply. She could smell the tang of brine and, behind it, the clean scent of rain. Of course, the angry-looking clouds blowing in overhead bore a clear message, as did the faint rumble of thunder in the distance. But she preferred to gauge the weather by the scents carried on the air. The eyes and ears were easily fooled, not the nose.

Her smile widened as she bent over to collect her basket. She had caught a faint whiff of camphor and winter savoury moments earlier. It grew stronger now.

"If you're thinking to sneak up on me, Lachlann MacDonald," she said without turning around, "you'd best think again."

She heard a snort of disgust, then her neighbor's familiar laugh. "How do you do it, Maggie, lass?"

"Magic," she shot back, still, after four weeks, reveling in being able to speak Gaelic again after so many years of English. "Beaten off that cold, have you?"

"I have. And I'll tell you now it was my own manly will that did it, and not your noxious camphor salve."

Lachlann took great delight in mocking her healing craft, despite the fact that he was always on her stoop asking for some salve or other. In deference to his pride, she hid her grin before facing him. He had propped his long, work-hardened form against a tumble of boulders some twenty feet away, trying not to look as if he had been caught trying to scare ten years off her life.

" 'Tisn't very sporting of you, creeping up on me here," Maggie teased. "I might have gone sliding into the sea. Then where would you have been next time a cold crept up on *you*?"

"Ach, you've the feet of a goat here. 'Twould take more than a wee fright to send you tumbling. Besides, I was waiting for you to come away from the edge."

"Generous of you." Maggie walked over to sweep shaggy black hair from his forehead and inspect the blossoming bruise there. "Dare I ask?"

He grunted. "Leave off, Maggie Lìl."

She smiled. It was clear Lachlann had imbibed a bit more than he should the night before. He managed the village's low doorways well enough ordinarily. His impressive height only vexed him when he'd had too much ale. "Will I mix you something for that bruise? Or for the ache I'm sure you have inside your hard head?"

"Nay, you will not. I'm taking no chances that some crazed concoction of yours will have me dropping dead at your feet." He glanced down as if pondering the possibility. A slow, satisfied smile spread over his face. "Ah, Maggie . . . Dare I ask?"

She followed his gaze and sighed. She was wearing a pair of her father's brogans, and had laced them in a pattern that would take a mathematician to solve.

"Best not. A fit of the brain, I think. 'Twill pass, if I don't take it into my head to wander off into the sea or some such nonsense first. And don't you be grinning at me as if you were so clever. I've yet to walk into a cross-beam."

Lachlann grunted, but took her basket from her hands cheerfully enough. "Collecting rocks, are you? This weighs the earth."

At nearly six-and-a-half-feet tall, with arms like oak branches, Lachlann hefted fifty-pound bags of oats as if they were feathers. " 'Tis but a bit of bark," Maggie teased.

"Bark? I'd say the whole tree." Lachlann balanced the basket easily with one hand while rooting about with the other. Maggie slapped his fingers away. "What sort of bark?"

"Some birch. And cherry, from the fallen tree at the Norries'." She glanced up as the first drop of rain fell. "I wanted to gather them before the deluge. I don't suppose you have your wagon nearby."

"I don't. I was over at Tolmey's, helping him repair his wall. Seemed easier to walk."

"Well, you'll be walking home in the rain, then." The coarse wool of her hood scratched as she pulled it over her head, but it was better than being wetted through.

"Carry my back-bending load to the high road and I'll send Tessa over with fresh shortbread tonight."

"Done." He offered his free arm and she fell into step beside him. "So," he asked after a moment, "what is the cherry for? A love potion, is it?"

She poked him in the ribs. "Only for you, you big oaf. And I'll see you dosed just as Sileas Wilkie walks by."

He shuddered at the mention of the young lady who all but stumbled over her own toes whenever their paths crossed. "I'd sooner take a *Sasunnach* hag to wife."

"I vow that could be arranged. There's always an English traveler or two about come summer. Mayhaps the next one will have a maiden auntie in tow."

Lachlann snorted. "Or a whey-faced son for you. Mayhaps I'll gather a bit of cherry bark for my own evil use. Beware next time the sea spits one up among us."

Maggie managed a smile. She didn't want to think of any Englishmen. Still, the thought of one landing on the isle had its wicked appeal. The Sound crossing left many a traveler looking as if they had been sucked in and out of the belly of some great beast. They usually lost the green tinge just in time to be laid low by the special mustard that Calum MacAuley put out just for English visitors. Were he not such a sweet fellow ordinarily, Maggie would have taken him to task for the act. As it was, she merely cajoled him into slipping a curative dose of mint into whatever meal the afflicted visitor could be coaxed into eating next.

Needless to say, MacAuley's inn got very little repeat custom from the south.

Lachlann was rooting among her basket again. "Have you anything in here to repel Tearlach Beaton? I don't like the way he's been sniffing about you since you got home."

Maggie thought of suggesting mustard, but there was no need. "Good of you to bring it up, lad. I remind you that Tearlach is your friend and you like him very well indeed, as do I. You cannot go about intimidating any young man who flirts with me a wee bit, Lachlann. I'm not a child anymore and I'll do my own refusing." And she would, from now on.

All she got for her mild tirade was a shrug. "I wouldn't have to, Mairghread, if you'd but give some thought to yourself instead of everyone else. You can't go on forever this way, turning away everyone's care for you. 'Tisn't your nature, you know."

"Rot," she muttered. "I'm hard-hearted."

"You're not that. Anything but." Lachlann all but dragged her to a halt, and ignoring the mutinous set of her jaw, added softly, "Ah, Maggie. You've a beautiful heart to go with that face of yours, meant to be shared with better than the likes of Tearlach Beaton, much as, aye, I hate to say it of a friend."

If only he knew, Maggie thought sadly, how she had offered everything to one man. And had her heart—if only her heart—tossed right back at her. Lachlann didn't know. No one did. It was her secret, and if the memory grieved her, so be it. She'd avoided a public scandal, come home reasonably whole, and would take better care from here on out.

Letting out her breath in an exasperated huff, she announced, "Well, take your piece of my heart, then, and leave me be."

"Oh, Maggie, lass." Lachlann drew her arm tight against his side. "Fine, then. Come walk in the rain with me."

He whistled a low, lilting tune as they picked their way over the rocky earth. Maggie recognized the air easily:

Dubghall MacIain's "Home to Skye." It was among her favorites, certainly one of Lachlann's. He, too, was obviously happy to have come home to Skye, even if his absences were far more frequent and never anything close to as long as hers had been.

"How was Aberdeen, then?" she asked. "We expected you to be gone a full sennight and more."

Lachlann snorted. "I'd have been home as soon as I could spin on my heel if I'd been able. One night there was plenty. I'll not be selling my cattle to Skene any longer; the price he offered was an insult. I'll be off to Glasgow come the first of May."

"Ah, too bad, that."

He merely shrugged, much as Maggie would have expected him to. He took his duties as seriously as any man, and took the inconveniences of them better than most. So Aberdeen had been a waste of time; Glasgow beckoned. He was back to whistling.

The rain was falling in earnest as they neared the village road. Beyond, rocks and heather rose to the large copse of oak and hawthorn that more than one local resident insisted was enchanted. It was true that the greenery sprang up in the midst of the hard earth hill where little else save the hardiest heather had ever grown. But as far as Maggie was concerned, Nature always found a way and had somehow found Her way to a fertile spot. Fairies had naught whatsoever to do with it.

The odd, fingertips-on-her-skin sensation was nothing more than the rain, she decided. And when her eyes snapped back to the center of the copse at some movement but saw only gently shifting leaves, she credited the wind. Still, she paused at the edge of the road, her fingers clenching in the rough wool of Lachlann's sleeve.

"Pick up your feet, if you please." He shook wet hair from his eyes. "I'm drowning here."

But Maggie was staring intently across the hollow, waiting for whatever motion had caught her attention again. The shadows seemed to have taken on the form of a horse and rider for an instant. She was still for a full minute, but saw nothing, heard nothing but the rain pattering softly on the earth—and Lachlann's grumbling. She released his sleeve and stepped forward, across the road and right off it into a patch of scrubby heather.

"Och, Mairghread, what are you about now?"

Maggie glanced back, blinked. "I don't know," she admitted vaguely. "I thought I saw . . . felt something."

"Felt something? Sweet Jesu, you are addled." Lachlann strode forward to slap a broad palm over the better part of her face. "You're not overwarm."

Maggie shoved his hand away. "Up there, in the copse."

He peered in the direction she was pointing. "There's naught there, lass."

"Aye . . . Aye, I know." But there had been, she thought. Perhaps.

"Will I come the rest of the way with you?" Lachlann was staring down at her now, a tolerant and faintly amused smile on his face. "I'll flatten any goblins with this rock basket of yours."

Maggie quickly tugged the basket from his hands. "Off with you. Rest assured I'll not walk into a tree in my addled state."

"Maggie . . ."

"Nay. Truly, Lachlann, I am fine, and I'll be glad of a bit of time to myself before getting home. Tessa will be restless with the rain keeping her in. We'll have no peace till it passes."

Lachlann looked ready to protest, but Maggie pressed, "Go see to your work. I'll send Tessa with the shortbread later."

"Fine, then." He shrugged, then affectionately chucked her under the chin. "Don't you be stopping to talk to any fairies on your way."

In moments, his long stride was taking him quickly down the road. Maggie headed in the opposite direction, but not after a last look at the copse. Naught. By the time she rounded the bend that led toward home, she was thinking on other matters entirely. Old Mr. Beaton would be needing his tisane soon; the Norries would have some savoury. Tessa loathed comfrey tea, but she had been coughing a bit. . . .

Maggie stopped abruptly. A massive black horse stood in the middle of the road, blocking her way and taking up far more space than an average animal would. She suddenly felt the imaginary fingertips at her neck again. Her eyes lifted slowly, past the huge and sleekly muscled legs of the horse to the breeches-clad, equally well-muscled leg of the rider. Past a gloved hand and a rich, russet coat that was fitted perfectly to broad shoulders. Then, for a long moment, her breath caught in her throat.

The face was narrow, blunt-boned, lightly tanned beneath the curling hat brim. It was a face from a tapestry, she found herself thinking, a visage from an era long gone: fierce, boldly molded. A patrician face, with its firm, wide mouth, high cheekbones, and lofty brow.

As she stared, still oddly short of breath, the man reached up and tipped his hat, revealing steel gray eyes and wavy hair the rich brown of the earth. "Good day, madam."

English, she thought at the sound of the deep voice. *And aye, patrician.*

"Good day," she replied, finding the words among the Gaelic scrambling through her head. English. This man from a medieval castle's wall would be English. She blinked, lifted her chin, and coolly asked, "Can I be of help to you?"

He did not reply immediately; instead, he fixed her with an unsettling, steely gaze that very nearly had her hand lifting to touch her flushed cheeks. Then, "I wouldn't think so, but I thank you." He tipped his hat again. "Good day, madam."

"G—" But he was off, wheeling his behemoth of a horse to canter away down the lane.

Maggie stood where she was, rain pattering onto her cloak, heart pounding against her ribs, until he was out of sight. Then, a bit shakily, she continued toward home. A sportsman, she wondered, seeking cheap land on which to hunt Highland game? A guest of the Clanranalds—a cousin? A wandering knight . . .

"*A bhoirionnaich gun chiall!*" she scolded herself aloud. *Silly girl*. Who he was mattered not at all. Not at all.

She reached her cottage minutes later and promptly hurried round back. Her second basket was just where she had left it, drenched and no doubt ruined. The bottles inside would have protected her herbs, though. It had been a day where a basket lost to carelessness fit right in. And it was easily replaced.

Her sister accosted her the moment she set foot in the cottage's rear door, a whirling mass of coltish limbs and unrestrained auburn hair. Thirteen-year-old Tessa, dirt-smudged as always and, as expected, clearly restless from rain-enforced time inside, began tugging at Maggie's cloak even before she had put down the basket. It was more hindrance than help.

"Have you heard?" the girl demanded, her hands tangling in the wet wool. "There's a *Sasunnach* here, up from London. Tearlach says he's the devil, of course, but Elspeth MacDonald spied him and says he has the face of an angel. Is he important, do you think? What on earth is he doing here if he can be there?"

"Tessa." Maggie resolutely ignored the thump of her heart and wearily removed first her sister's hands and then the sodden cloak. "Hang this by the fire and check the water in the kettle for me."

"But, Maggie—"

"Now, if you would, please. We'll talk when I've seen to matters at hand."

Tessa talked anyway. All the way out to the hearth and back with the kettle which, Maggie discovered soon enough, was almost completely empty. "Imagine, Maggie, we come home, as far from London as one can get without leaving the Isles and *blap*"—she slapped the oak table— "we've an Englishman in our midst almost before we've unpacked."

She paused to cough once. Maggie counted to five, then handed the copper kettle back. "You'll fill this, please, and put it back to boil. You need a cup of tea."

Tessa muffled another cough and rolled her MacLeod-green eyes. "Not comfrey! Oh, very well." Much to Maggie's relief, the mention of comfrey had somehow turned the girl's thoughts from the mysterious Englishman. "Calum says the seals are back beneath the cliffs. Wee pups, too. So I went to have a look last night. I saw them, you know."

"The seals? In the dark?"

"Not the seals. *Them*."

Maggie sighed. "You did no such thing."

"I did, I tell you! They were at Scavaig Point. He was

all dripping with seaweed and she was crying, hands around the dirk in her chest."

"Tessa, enough! We'll talk later about what you were doing out on the cliffs after dark. For now, let's see to that cough."

"I saw them, Maggie. 'Tis a sign, of course, a *Sasun-nach* here. . . ."

Wearily, Maggie handed her the soggy basket. "Dig out the licorice, then, if you won't have the comfrey. Carefully!" she added when the girl slung the basket in a cheerful arc.

Tessa skipped across the flagstone floor toward the pantry, the sound of glass jangling in her wake. Maggie willed the water to boil quickly. She needed a cup of tea herself.

The loud pounding at the front door a minute later had her jumping, brought the sound of broken glass this time in its wake. And no wonder she and Tessa were startled, Maggie thought as she hurried from the kitchen. No one used the front door here. Family and visitors alike always came through the back.

She hauled open the heavy door, took a wide-eyed look at the tall figure on the stoop.

"Good day, madam, I . . ." A pair of familiar steely eyes blinked down at her from an impressive height. "Well, I'll be damned."

⊰ 3 ⊱

As I walked o'er the darkling leas,
Sing ivy leaf, Sweet William, and thyme,
I spied a bonny lass thro' the trees,
She was once a true love of mine.

Gabriel had thought her beautiful on first viewing, standing in the road with her face tilted into the rain and her eyes cool. Now she all but took his breath away.

Outside, in the rain, her colors had been hidden. Free now from the cloak's hood and from a few of its pins, her hair glowed a burnished auburn. It framed a face so lovely it made his very eyes ache. Pale as cream and a perfect oval, it was a vision from a Raphael painting. Vividly green eyes, wide-spaced and slightly tilted beneath winging dark brows; a delicate nose; a generous mouth the color and texture of a damask rose.

"I'll be damned," he repeated, and watched as one of her brows lifted.

"Is it the kirk you'd be seeking, then?" She paused, translating, "The church?"

An angel's face and an imp's tongue. Gabriel knew what a kirk was, even if he had long since stopped believing. But he didn't think that was information he needed to share. So instead he said, "I am looking for the MacLeod household."

"You've found it."

"Ah. I am Rievaulx."

If the name meant anything at all to the woman, her expression did not show it. She certainly did not look impressed. If anything, her lovely face registered faint distaste. He was used to that.

She was polite, however. Stepping back from the door, she gestured him in. "Come in from the rain, Mr. Rievaulx."

He did, removing his hat and knocking its crown in the process against the low door frame. Nearly everything he had seen so far on this cursed island had been small and damp. Including the woman in front of him.

Perhaps she wasn't so small, really. The top of her head, had she been standing chest to chest with him rather than a deliberate several arms' lengths away, would nearly reach his jaw. And the dampness was now little more than tendrils of hair curling around her face. But he could still see her standing in the rain. It was an image he didn't think himself likely to forget.

Something had stopped him as he'd ridden by the rowan copse, had him hauling his mount to a halt and secretively watching a woman swathed in a cloak and rain. She'd been with a brute of a man. Gabriel had ignored her companion, but he'd been unable to take his eyes off her. Something stronger than will had sent him out into the road for a glimpse of her face. And something just as strong had had him wheeling away once he had.

"Thank you"—there was no ring on the hand holding the door—"Miss . . ."

"Margaret." Almost as if it were an afterthought, she added, "MacLeod."

Isobel's sister. He ought to have known, really. Isobel was no beauty, but she was vibrant. The MacLeod brothers were a handsome if annoying pair. There was something of a family resemblance in the auburn hair and green eyes, but Margaret was far more than handsome. And now, standing mere inches from her in the little hall, he had discovered that she smelled like autumn, like the spice of mulled cider.

She closed the door behind him with a thump. "I'd guess you're soaked through. I'll take your coat."

Gabriel knew his friend's wife had come from relatively humble beginnings, at least in comparison to Oriel's status and wealth. But the MacLeods' father was a gentleman, and limited as his means might once have been, he would certainly now be living well enough on Oriel's generosity. He could certainly afford to clothe his glorious second daughter in something far finer than faded gray wool, and to employ some servants. Gabriel had had to settle his own horse in the small stable.

As if reading his mind, Miss MacLeod reached for his hat and announced, "You've caught us at a bit of a disadvantage. Our maid is away and I haven't even a fire in the parlor."

No questions about who he was or why he was there. Gabriel was finding the Skye people to be an inscrutable lot. No one asked questions; everyone was stonily polite. This was as much of a welcome as he had received, and still required a very loose definition of the word. He had a very good idea that his English voice and clothing had everything to do with his cool reception by the other Islanders he had encountered. But Margaret MacLeod had lived for years in England. He didn't imagine she was holding his birth against him. Perhaps she was just a very good judge of character.

He sighed as he handed over his greatcoat.

"I apologize, Miss MacLeod. I had assumed you would be aware of my arrival. Lord Oriel is an age-old friend and Lady Oriel was to send an introduction ahead of me."

A smile flitted all too briefly across her lips. "Was she?

Well, with the post as it is, I expect I'll be getting that letter after you've gone again." She hung his coat and hat in a crowded cupboard and gestured him toward an open door. "Any friend to Nathan and Isobel is welcome. If you'll come into the parlor, I'll bring some tea and coals for the fire. My father ought to be home soon. He'll be happy to hear news of Town."

Before he could stop her, she was gone, leaving him in the cold little room which seemed to grow colder with each minute that passed. Women like Margaret MacLeod raised the temperature of any space just by standing within it. Gabriel wondered if she knew the chill she'd left him in. Then he wondered if she'd done it on purpose. He expected she was used to being ogled and panted after.

If this was indeed a message, he would heed it. His purpose for being on Skye did not leave room for any sort of dalliance, especially not with a friend's sister-in-law. Gabriel knew he'd fallen a good number of profligate notches from glory, but he hadn't lost any of his brains. He was very good at controlling his desires. Or rather, he corrected wryly as he removed his flask from his pocket and surveyed the minimal decorations of the parlor, he had once been very good at controlling his desires. There hadn't been much call for control in the past several years.

He certainly hadn't bided his time before coming to this house. He had meant to, had intended to settle himself into whatever lodgings he could find, review his plans yet one more time, then pay his call. But the tiny room he'd been given by the sullen keeper of what was apparently the only inn for miles had been even colder than the one he occupied at present, and the meager refreshment offered had been wholly unappealing, from the tough-looking, unidentifiable meat to the unnervingly green mustard. So he'd promptly made what sense he could of the fellow's muttered directions and gone in search of the home of James MacLeod.

He needed more time to ponder just what he'd found in the man's daughter. He wasn't used to being disconcerted by women, even inordinately beautiful ones, and it chafed. Fire in her hair and ice in her eyes. He already needed to regain some measure of command. And he wanted to breathe in that soft scent again. He decided a good way to do both was not to stay where she had put him.

He tossed back a measure of brandy and returned the flask to his pocket. Then he followed the scarred yet highly polished wood floor and the sounds of movement, past a half-dozen doors, to the rear of the house. Soft voices, lilting with that unmistakable Gaelic tinge, came from behind one sturdy panel. Gabriel didn't knock.

Margaret, who'd had her back to the door, spun around at his entrance. She was quite alone. A pin flew from her hair to ping against the stone floor. A quick blush stained her cheeks. "Sir . . ."

He glanced around the kitchen. Everything was worn and spotless, from the floor to the massive, scarred wood table. A fire burned cheerily in the hearth, a hissing kettle above it. The warm air smelled incredibly appealing, enticing, a heady combination of spices Gabriel couldn't even begin to identify. Bunches of herbs, silver and green and lavender, hung from hooks on the walls and ceiling. More were spread over most of the room's flat surfaces, vying for space with colored glass jars, contents unidentifiable by sight. And in the middle of it all was this cool goddess—albeit a vaguely embarrassed and annoyed-looking one.

"I'd meant you to stay in the parlor," she was saying a bit stiffly. "The kitchen is no place for guests."

He offered what he hoped was an appeasing smile. "I did not want you going to any bother, Miss MacLeod."

She narrowed her glorious eyes for a moment. Gabriel waited for her response.

Instead, there was a loud snort from nearby. Then the empty doorway into what might have been a pantry erupted in a burst of auburn and blue. "Oh, Maggie's a fine one for bothering. If she hadn't a middle name already, 'twould be that."

The girl, quite obviously a MacLeod, came to a halt on the opposite side of the table. Gabriel's first thought was that someone ought to tell her that staring so intently was rude. His second was that she was destined to break more than her share of hearts a few years along. She shared Maggie's glossy hair and green eyes. Her skin, no doubt, was just as lovely, when it was not liberally smudged with dirt.

James MacLeod, Gabriel mused, had produced rather spectacular offspring. It was apparent that Oriel's tight-lipped if affectionate use of the phrase *blighted gnome* to describe his father-in-law must have more to do with character than appearance.

"So you're the *Sasunnach*."

Gabriel had heard that word countless times since riding north of the border. He optimistically assumed it meant "Englishman," and nothing worse. The girl was one of but a handful of people who had said it without looking as if it left a bad taste in the mouth.

"I am a *Sasunnach*, yes," he replied crisply.

"Well, you don't look like the devil to me. I've a mind to suggest Tearlach find himself a pair of spectacles. But then, you're nothing of an angel, either—"

"*Cuist!*" Margaret stepped in, removed a blue glass jar from the girl's hands, and gestured her toward the far side of the kitchen. "Mr. Rievaulx, this is Tessa, the youngest of the brood. Tessa, you'll take a damp cloth to your hands and face and then you'll greet our guest properly."

The girl grumbled, but obeyed and splashed some water from a basin in the direction of her cheeks. She was back at the table in moments, dropping into a seat with enough force to rattle the crockery. Propping her chin on slightly less grubby fists, she gave Gabriel a thorough once-over.

"We've a *Sasunnach* ghost here. His Skye lover pushed him off a cliff. I've seen—"

"Tessa!"

"What, Maggie? Oh, very well. What sort of name is Ree-vo, my lord? Italian?"

"French, originally," he replied.

"You don't look French."

Gabriel took that as a compliment. "The Norman blood is fairly well diluted by now," he informed her dryly. "As a matter of fact, I am more Scottish than anything else."

The girl gave another impressive snort. "With a name like that?"

From the corner of his eye, Gabriel watched Margaret. He could sense her indecision. Just when he was certain she was going to send him back to the cold parlor, she gave a small shrug. "Sit down, then, Mr. Rievaulx," she said, "and have some tea."

Perhaps it wasn't polite to sit while she stood, but Gabriel decided it was expedient. So he took a seat across from the little inquisitor. It seemed the Scots reserve had missed at least one Scot. "Rievaulx is my title, not my name."

"Oh." Name or title, Tessa seemed only marginally more interested than her sister had when she'd heard it. "What sort of lord are you?"

"I am an earl sort, as it happens."

Margaret was moving from hearth to table and back now, bringing a plate of sweetly aromatic scones first, then a steaming teapot. The cups, Gabriel noted, were good, old china, delicately formed. His hostess's form was just as fine: softly rounded, elegant beneath the shapeless, worn wool. Gabriel was very good at seeing beneath unrevealing clothing.

"An earl, hmm." Tessa's sniff was not quite on a par with her snort, but it was eloquent. "My brother-in-law is a marquess. He'll be a duke someday. That beats an earl twice."

"Yes," Gabriel agreed wryly. "It does."

"Well, an earl's plenty grand enough anyway. Have you a great castle?"

"A castle?"

"All English lordlings seem to have castles or some-such. Nathan has a great monstrous hall. Are you not so important, then?"

"Tessa! Enough!" Maggie was back, fluttering her apron at the girl. "Go dig your worms or climb a tree. You'll not be pestering M . . . Lord Rievaulx, nor plaguing him with your impertinence."

"Really," Gabriel offered, distracted by her scent, "it is not—"

"See? He doesn't think I'm impertinent. Do you think I'm impertinent?"

"Well, I—"

"Tessa." Maggie's voice lowered warningly.

The girl gave a dramatic sigh worthy of the London stage. "Och, but you're bossy this morning. Fine. I'll go

in a minute." She half rose from her seat, leaning her
weight on the table, face solemn and eyes alight. "Have
you six names, Lord Rievaulx?"

"I beg your pardon?"

"Six names. All English lordlings seem to have 'em.
Silly waste, if you ask me."

"Tessa!" Margaret scolded yet again, brandishing the
teapot now. "Watch your tongue!"

"Well, they do and it is. Nathan has a passel he doesn't
use." The familiar green eyes slewed back to Gabriel.
"Do you?"

"Four, and my family name." Oddly enough, Gabriel
was feeling very nearly amused, and very nearly comfortable, as if he was somewhere he actually ought to be.
Novel, he decided. "Does that count as a passel?"

" 'Tis at least two more than anyone here." Tessa
looked at him expectantly.

"Gabriel Charles Augustus Lorne Loudon."

Loudon.

Maggie set cup to saucer with more force than she'd
intended. Both Tessa and their guest flinched. "Your tea,
sir . . . Lord Rievaulx." She handed him the cup, glanced
down at her own to avoid the hard silver gaze that she
couldn't help but feel saw more than it should.

"Best keep that list to yourself," Tessa announced,
breaking the frozen moment. Then, "Maggie says you're
a friend of Isobel's. Are you to stay here with us?"

No! Friend of her sister or not, Maggie didn't want to
ask him. She didn't want him in her house. There was
something of her brother-in-law in this man's bearing
and in his demeanor. Both were aristocratic, austere, arrogant as only men of their station could be. And perhaps a bit haunted by experience. But while Nathan
made her want to talk to him, to offer him herbal tisanes

and a sister's affection, Gabriel Rievaulx, with his aristocratic voice and arrogant mouth, simply made her feel taut and uneasy.

Ten minutes into their acquaintance and she was already judging him. *For shame, Mairghread,* she scolded herself, but nonetheless breathed a silent sigh of relief when he replied, "I am staying at the inn."

"Have you tried Calum's mustard?" Tessa asked. Maggie winced.

"I haven't. I don't care for mustard." He spoke to Tessa, but Maggie could feel his attention on her. "Why should I keep my name to myself?"

"Because of the Campbells and MacDonalds, of course." With that, the girl pushed herself away from the table. Tessa, silly, splendid creature that she was, did drama well. "I'm off, then, but I expect I'll see you again." She gave a charming smile, dipped into a perfect, graceful curtsy. "Good day, Lord Rievaulx."

"Good day, Miss Tessa."

And she was gone, pounding up the back stairs, leaving Maggie alone with their disquieting guest.

"Miss MacLeod . . ."

"Margaret will do. Or Maggie. We don't stand on ceremony here, Lord Rievaulx."

No, they didn't. Life was easier in Scotland. Less pomp, less rules, less formality than in England. Maggie expected the earl to look awkward—or even just a bit uncomfortable—sitting at a battered table in a country kitchen. He didn't. Perhaps the wool coat and linen shirt were finer than most seen about, the large hand gripping the china cup slightly less rough, but the man looked very much at ease.

Maggie hated to pry. It wasn't in her nature. But she needed to know what had brought an English earl to her island. And when he might be expected to leave. "Skye seems an unlikely spot for a holiday, my lord."

He had accepted a scone, dipped into the clotted cream, and now took a slow, thorough bite. "I had some family business in Argyllshire," he said eventually. "Skye wasn't so great a distance and Isobel always speaks so highly of her birthplace. I'd promised her to come have a look and bring her greetings to her family."

Maggie could well imagine her sister, blissful in her marriage but always just a bit homesick, urging a friend to visit Skye. It wasn't nearly as easy seeing this man making the trek, either for the sights or to appease anyone. But then, she didn't know him. Agreeable natures came in all sorts of packages. Even hard, inscrutable ones. Just as hard natures could be cloaked in pretty faces and words. Which was all well and good, she thought, but it would take a fair amount of convincing to make her believe this man wasn't as hard inside as out.

She would survive perfectly well without that experience.

"How are you finding the inn?" she asked politely.

"I only arrived this noon. So far, it seems . . . adequate."

As long as he avoided the mustard, Maggie thought, and ruthlessly quashed the little voice that was berating her for leaving anyone to Calum's mercies.

"I would have arrived on your doorstep sooner, but I fear I was given very poor directions. I owe my arrival to heavenly intervention rather than the innkeeper."

"Ah, that would be Calum MacAuley," Maggie replied, not thinking when she added, "and no surprise."

One of the earl's dark brows arced upward. "Why do I doubt that has anything to do with his intelligence or sense of direction?"

Maggie wasn't about to launch into a diatribe, personal or Islander, against the English. "Calum has his quirks. And as for divine intervention, I daresay the Lord would steer most people to the kirk rather than our doorstep. Give your credit to Lachlann MacDonald's good path. It leads right to us."

A faint clatter from the yard had caught her attention. Her father was home, and she decided she'd best head him off and see what sort of shape he was in—for all their sakes.

"Excuse me for a moment, my lord," she murmured. Rievaulx nodded, stood gracefully when she did, and if he were annoyed to be left alone in a cottage kitchen, his expression certainly didn't show it.

Maggie found her father just outside the rear door, struggling to manage the latch while his arms were full. He was juggling his coat, which he had probably forgotten to don on the wet walk home, several bottles, and what appeared to be a cylinder of rapidly unfurling Edinburgh newspapers.

"Ah, good lass, Mairghread!" he crowed as she deftly divested him of the bottles. "Bit of a habble, here, y'ken." The Highland brogue and cant deepened in direct proportion to how much liquor James MacLeod had imbibed. Maggie, with practice born of experience, guessed at a half-dozen tankards.

He knocked his muddy boots loudly if ineffectually against the stone stoop and planted an affectionate kiss on her cheek. The ale fumes were less potent than some Fridays, but enough to wrinkle Maggie's nose. "Tell me there's a fire going," he said, shaking out his unworn coat. "I'm a wee bit dampish here."

By all rights he ought to be chilled to the marrow, but the liquor would have given him ample if illusionary warmth. Maggie shook her head in fond exasperation.

"There's a fire and pot of tea in the kitchen, Papa. And a guest to go with them."

"Aye?" Jamie's famed MacLeod green eyes brightened even more. He loved visitors. "Anyone interesting?"

"Oh, aye, to be sure," was her wry reply. "The Earl of Rievaulx, as a matter of fact. English." She sighed at her father's undimmed grin, resigned. "He's an old friend to Nathan and very grand. You'll want to put this on." She trundled him into his coat, glad to see it was relatively dry and one of his better ones, purchased from Nathan's tailor—on Nathan's credit. "And you'll give me that shirt you're wearing before you leave the house again."

Jamie paused long enough to survey the rumpled expanse above his worn tartan waistcoat, then rubbed thoughtfully at his stubbly chin. "I've but worn it twice, Maggie, love."

"Aye, and slept in it twice, too. Don't try to fool me. I know you slept on the parlor sofa last night."

"That Tessa," he grumbled. "Can't keep a whit from her eyes."

"Nay, you can't. Lively night at MacAuley's, was it?"

" 'Twas indeed."

"And today?"

"Just a few pints with the lads. Heard there was an Englishman about and we had to toast his speedy departure. Of course, I had no idea at the time that he was *our* Englishman."

The *our* didn't sit well, but Maggie smiled nonetheless. "You couldn't have known." She ran a loving hand over her father's wild gray hair, smoothing it as best she could. "Well, come and meet him. And remember that Nathan cares for him."

So far, his eagerness to meet their guest had superceded the fact that the guest was English, but Maggie wasn't taking any chances. Jamie, despite having dragged his five children over half of England in search of employment he could keep, had no great affection for the place or the people. That was no real surprise to anyone. He had been ousted from one secretarial and two teaching positions when his habit of drinking a dram or two more than he should came to his employers' attention.

Of course, his one sorry attempt at thievery could very well have landed him in jail. Instead, the man from whom he had stolen was now married to his eldest daughter and, no bones about it, was supplying the funds that allowed Jamie to return to Skye and the dubious gentility to which he had been born.

Now he was striding toward the kitchen with all the grandeur of a king, and only the slightest weave or two along the way.

Rievaulx was already on his feet when they entered. "You must be my estimable host," he announced, bowing in Jamie's direction. "An honor, Mr. MacLeod. I am Rievaulx."

Bowing had been just the right move. If there was anything Jamie could not resist, it was being treated as a gentleman. Well, Maggie amended, if there was *one* thing he could not resist, it was claret, but genteel regard came a fair second. Quite the laird of the manor now, he waved the other man back into his seat. The image was marred somewhat by his slept-on-the-sofa, a-few-pints-with-the-lads appearance.

"Welcome, welcome, m'boy. Do sit down."

And the earl did, as easily as if the invitation had been for a bottle of brandy at a St. James club, rather than plain fare in a cottage kitchen.

"Know anything of the Turf, lad?" her father was asking even as he took his own seat, waving what was at least a sennight-old edition of the Edinburgh paper. Clearly the talk at the tavern had centered around the southern races, and once Jamie got his ale-affected mind on a subject it stuck until washed away by the next series of pints. "I've a mind to take myself south for a bit of entertainment soon."

With his son-in-law's money, Maggie mused wryly, and no more sense or luck than his own sons.

"Not a great deal . . ." Rievaulx replied, and Jamie's face fell. "About Scotland's tracks, at least. I've heard there are some quite Newmarket's and Epsom's equal, but I'm a York man, myself."

"Are you?" Jamie regarded him with renewed interest. "My cousin's filly had a good run there last year. Name of Lass o' Lochalsh. Did you see her, perchance?"

The earl took a mouthful of tea Maggie had poured for him, blinked at its strength. "I did not."

"Missed that particular race, did you?"

"I'm afraid I was on the Peninsula for much of last year."

"Ah, like my son-in-law. Marvelous man. Something of a hero, I gather, but far too modest to speak of it." Jamie's eyes narrowed cannily. "Don't suppose you'll tell me what you lads were doing there."

He supposed correctly. Maggie watched the earl's eyes cool and his formidable jaw harden. Whatever had happened to her brother-in-law in Portugal had left him with a permanent limp and badly damaged vision. It appeared Rievaulx had fared better, at least physically, but it was clear he wouldn't be speaking of the Peninsula easily, if at all. Instead, he replied, voice cool, "Nothing worth remembering now that I am a carefree civilian again. Perhaps I'll make it to the York Turf this year. My estate is to the east, on the coast."

"Not Yorkshire, surely?" Jamie tended to place every English peer within fifty miles of London.

"Near Scarborough," Gabriel answered, and Maggie's heart thumped.

O are you going to Scarbro Fair? Savoury, sage, rosemary, and thyme . . .

"Good lad," Jamie said cheerfully. He tossed the paper aside. "How long is your visit, sir?"

"A few days. A fortnight at most."

"Aye, well, you'll find my sons' room a comfortable enough place to rest your head, tho' not what you're used to, I'm sure."

"Papa," Maggie began nervously.

"Actually, Mr. MacLeod," the earl cut in smoothly, "I have already arranged to stay at the inn."

"So we'll unarrange it." Jamie shook an admonitory finger at his daughter. "Rare for me to beat you to the invitations, lass. I'd have expected you to have seen to it as soon as Lord Rievaulx arrived."

Maggie closed her eyes for one tense, weary second. Then, " 'Twas careless of me, to be sure," she managed, resigned.

"I don't wish to impose," was the earl's quiet response.

"Rot! Not a bit of it! We'll just go have a word with Calum. I'm sure he'll understand." Jamie was on his feet again. Maggie could all but see the doorway of the tavern reflected in his eyes. The prospect of having Lord Rievaulx in tow clearly delighted him, despite the fact that he'd been toasting the man's departure not an hour past. Turf aside, he was readily attached to any potential drinking companion, especially one who might be counted upon to foot the bill. "Come along, lad. No dawdling."

The earl rose to follow Jamie. The half bow he gave

Maggie before leaving was all that was polite. As was his smile, even if it did put her in mind of a tiger with a peacock supper in mind.

It seemed Lord Rievaulx was going to be their guest for a spell. And there wasn't a thing Maggie could do about it.

⊰ 4 ⊱

Sage Water for Soothing Bruises

Take three handsful dried sage, one each chamomile and St. John's wort. Boil with a full kettle of water for half an hour. Strain, discarding the herbs and keeping the water. Add a pint of honey and a handful of thyme. Bring three times to a boil. Remove from fire and let cool before applying to the afflicted area.

Keep in mind, 'tisn't meant for a bruised heart.

Gabriel woke to watery light. It took him far too long to remember where he was, to place the narrow bed and mismatched furnishings. Too much time away from the life of the Ten, he decided. His reflexes were still passable, but his mind was dull as duck teeth.

Dull as duck teeth. That had been Brandon's expression. Razors, swords, eating knives with nicked edges— all had been dull as duck teeth more often than not on the Peninsula. And Brandon had always been mildly offended if good-natured when his companions laughed at his quaint Northumberland colloquialisms. Cheerful, open-faced Brandon, whose family dairy farm had been no match for the lure of military service.

Gabriel had considered stopping in Northumberland on his way north, to pay his respects to Brandon's parents and the sweet neighbor girl, Jenny, who had penned countless letters telling her beloved of the wet and wind and new babies in the village. He'd avoided the county entirely, going a good fifty miles out of his way to do so. He hadn't been able to pay the visit. The thought of facing grieving parents, a heartbroken sweetheart—or,

49

even worse in a way, a sweetheart who had eventually become the happy wife of some other young farmer—was more than Gabriel could stomach. More than that, he had no idea what he could possibly have said.

I am sorry for your loss. Billy Brandon was a good soldier, a good man. Lovely farm you have here. Cows, are they? I do apologize for being half a minute too slow to keep your son from dying. Bloody shame, that.

The faint lingering contentment from the first truly good night's sleep he'd had in months vanished like smoke. Sitting up, he scrubbed his hands hard over his face, then raked them through his hair. He didn't need a mirror to know how rough he looked. It was little wonder the tiny tavern had emptied within minutes of his arrival the night before. Even the fact that he had been in the company of a local had not helped. Clearly the few patrons had wanted nothing to do with a scraggy Englishman whose once sharp stare was dull as duck teeth.

The innkeeper hadn't seemed overly upset with his defection to other lodgings. The fellow had been just as surly as before, except for a brief period when he'd been nearly convivial, urging a plate of the same gray meat with its accompanying pot of green mustard. That offering, which Gabriel was on the verge of accepting, had for some reason necessitated a hushed and lively discussion between the innkeeper and MacLeod at the end of the bar. The food had disappeared. The innkeeper had gone back to glowering.

Jamie MacLeod, Gabriel had learned in the following hours, was exactly as his son-in-law described him: a damnably likable fool. He prattled about the Turf, he pontificated on Whitehall, he told ribald jests that had gone out of fashion with doublets, and drank like a trout. He'd talked extensively about his friends and neighbors, leaving Gabriel with a headful of absolutely useless information, said nothing about Maggie save calling her a "splendid lass," and leaned on Gabriel's arm like a sodden sack of flour all the way back to the cottage several hours later.

They had arrived back to find Gabriel's portmanteau dumped unceremoniously by some mysterious hand on the back step and a very disapproving Maggie waiting in the kitchen. She'd clucked her tongue and shaken her lovely head—at both of them, Gabriel thought—and, refusing his offer of assistance, disappeared with her father up the stairs. Gabriel half expected the pair of them to come bumping back down. MacLeod, despite being as gnomelike as Oriel asserted, wasn't a lightweight. But Maggie clearly had a thread of iron in her.

He had waited for her in the kitchen, planning a discussion full of polite charm and half-truths. She hadn't reappeared. Instead, Tessa had bounded into the room, asked him yet another endless series of questions about his home, horse, and boot maker, loaded a tray of food, shoved his portmanteau into his hands, and showed him to an upstairs bedchamber. All as if this was a regular turn of events in the house. Knowing what he did of the various male MacLeods, Gabriel decided it might well be.

He had devoured the herb-crusted capon and nutty bread, eyes closing in pleasure with the first bite, downed the contents of his flask, then climbed between worn-to-softness, lavender-scented sheets, and readied himself for his usual fitful sleep. He'd slept like the dead.

Wincing now at that poor choice of similes and the return of Brandon's wide face to his thoughts, he shoved back the bedclothes and readied himself for the first day of his proverbial search for redemption. He had only the vaguest ideas of how he was going to track down his quarry now that he was here on Skye. And, tenuous as his connection to the MacLeods was, he knew it was more than possible that L'Écossais might become suspicious of his presence on the isle—assuming the man was there to begin with—and disappear forever.

Gabriel Charles Augustus Lorne Loudon, Earl of Rievaulx and holder of various and sundry lesser titles and inglorious sobriquets, had never been one to contemplate failure. Which was, he supposed wryly as he availed himself of the ewer and basin, why his failures clouted him so hard. When he was sober enough to acknowledge them, at least.

He wondered if the Scots served ale with breakfast.

Maggie set the second pan of shortbread on the windowsill to cool and took a moment for herself. Her father was still asleep and Tessa had already been fed and ushered out for her morning rambles. Through the little kitchen window Maggie tranquilly watched a family of wrens flitting over the scrubby yard and in the branches of the single stunted apple tree. The morning mists were lifting, hinting at afternoon sun. If there was time, she would carry her oilskin-lined basket down to the strand and gather some Irish moss from the sea.

For now, there was bread to bake and herbs to sort. Her eyes lit on the spray of early wildflowers beside the dried sage. Tearlach Beaton had brought them. She had sent him off with a hyssop mix for his father's bad chest and her best friendly smile. She feared Lachlann was right; Tearlach had been hovering a bit since her return. She supposed there would be a time when she'd need to address the matter. For the moment, she was choosing the weak option of ignoring it, hoping it was nothing more than the casual flirtation of a virile young man and would shift to another pretty face with the next change of wind. She couldn't contemplate more than that. The idea of hurting an old friend pained her, but she knew Tearlach Beaton wasn't the man for her. Part of her wished he were. How easy it would be to spend her life with someone she knew and loved, like Tearlach, like Lachlann. And how cowardly.

She could do it, wrap her heart up and tuck it away, marry for comfort rather than love. Never be wounded again, or shamed. Never have to worry about the sweet, dangerous effect on her senses of knowing eyes in a warrior's face . . . She shook her head in annoyance. She had far better things to contemplate than the various men who seemed to thump through her life like careless bulls.

She'd grown so very talented at sending unwanted thoughts away and she made good use of that talent now. Deliberately humming to herself, clearing her mind of its purposeless thoughts, she checked her steeping herbs. Chamomile, St. John's wort, sage. Sage to soothe the skin . . . sage for wishes. The ancient ballad slipped easily onto her tongue. It was one of many names and no certain origin. Maggie found herself quietly singing the version her mother used to hum while tending the garden. *Savoury, sage, rosemary, and thyme . . .*

"Remember me," the voice came from behind her, deep and melodic, though the words were spoken rather than sung, "to a lass who lives there, for she once was a true love of mine."

Startled, Maggie spun around. Their guest was there, leaning against the solid frame, looking, if possible, even more dangerous than the day before. He was dressed for London, in his expensive coat and fine breeches, but wouldn't have looked out of place in the shadows of Old

Edinburgh. His cravat was loosely tied, giving Maggie a glimpse of a sleekly corded neck; there was a hint of relaxed muscle beneath his pale waistcoat. His sable hair waved back from his brow, displaying a few threads of silver and a small scar at his hairline.

He was stunning. He was also just that little bit frightening.

Just a man, she told herself sharply when her heart thumped, *who will take himself away south again soon.*

" 'Scarbro Fair,' " he said. "My nurse used to sing it to me at Fair time."

Hiding her suddenly short breath behind a cool tone, she regarded him, hands on her hips. "Good morning, Lord Rievaulx. I didn't expect you for hours yet."

One dark brow lifted. "There was no reason for me to stay in bed."

Something in the gray eyes sent a faint ripple through Maggie's blood. She ignored it. "Keeping pace with my father and his ale has felled many a foolish man."

"Do you scold all of your guests first thing in the morning, Miss MacLeod?"

If anything, Lord Rievaulx seemed amused. Still, ashamed suddenly, Maggie bit her lip. This wasn't at all like her, this sniping. It wasn't at all like her and she couldn't begin to explain it. Sighing, taking her hands from her hips and lifting them in apology, she offered, "If I do, I don't mean it. Sit down, my lord, and have some breakfast."

The mention of food had him smiling, a quick, flashing grin that disappeared almost immediately, but not before Maggie felt its full force. In that instant, the warrior had given way to the courtier and it was a powerful shift. Her breath caught in her throat again, another little hitch that was as unexpected as it was unwelcome. *English,* her head said firmly. *Simple as that.* She drew a steadying breath as he crossed the room.

He paused at the table, resting one large hand on the spindle back of a chair. "Your staff has not . . . returned?"

"Our maid will be gone for a spell. She's with her ailing mother. I manage without her. And Andy MacAuley will have seen to the stables already. He does a bit of work here early before helping his father with the inn. 'Twas he who brought your things last night."

She decided not to comment on the fact that young Andy had left the single portmanteau out on the steps. She certainly hadn't brought it in. There had been enough to do, she'd told herself at the time, with cooking and preparing a room, that hefting her guest's baggage would have to wait. Especially a guest she hadn't invited. Later, as dinner grew cold on the stove and there was no sign of the men, she'd managed to forget about the portmanteau entirely.

"So who am I to thank for last night's marvelous fare?" He was still standing. And, abruptly, he was charming. "I haven't enjoyed a meal so much in many weeks."

"It was cold," Maggie said shortly.

"It was delicious."

"Well." Letting out her breath in a quiet, defeated huff, she waved him into his chair. "I do the cooking, Lord Rievaulx. I enjoy it. And I thank you for the compliment."

"It was no more than you deserved, Miss MacLeod."

"Maggie."

"Maggie." Hunger apparently won out over decorum, for he lowered himself into his seat. He filled the little chair; Maggie heard it creak and heard, too, the rough slide of his boots over the floor as he stretched out his long legs and made himself comfortable. "I would sell my sorry soul for whatever's in that pot."

"You would be making a poor bargain, then," she shot back. " 'Tis sage water for a friend's bruised head. There's oat porridge, though, with fresh cream."

His expression made it clear that porridge was not his usual breakfast choice. He did give a faint smile, however, when she set the plate in front of him. In deference to his English sensibilities, she served the stuff hot, with a generous dollop of honey.

He did glance a bit dubiously at the dark tea she poured. Unabashed, she gave him a serene smile. Her brother-in-law preferred coffee, too, but Maggie was having no part of that silly affectation in her home. A cup of good, strong tea was the best start to any day. Especially the day after a night drinking in her father's company.

The little ripples of nerves the earl's presence engendered were being smoothed away now by familiar tasks. If she had to play hostess to this man for a few days, she decided, she would. And she would do it well. She could do that.

Maggie was gratified to hear Lord Rievaulx sigh in pleasure with the first bite of food. Considering his journey, he was unlikely to have had a decent meal in days. Taking further pity on him, she drew several eggs from the morning's collection and heated a pan.

Gabriel watched her work. There was an alluring grace to her movements as she crossed the flagstone floor, collecting a cloth here, a pan there. This morning, beneath her apron, she was wearing a dress of mossy gray-green wool. He could see it was several years out of fashion and had no doubt once been a more vivid green. It suited her, though, both color and style. And worn state. The soft fabric, bound just beneath her breasts with a slightly frayed ribbon, molded itself to her delightful curves as she moved. Gabriel had never envied a piece of cloth before.

Damn but she was pretty, he thought, more in exasperation than pleasure. The warmth of the kitchen, the fragrant steam from the pot, Maggie MacLeod—all were making him feel decidedly heated. She had her back to him now as she worked at the stove. Her lush auburn hair was knotted atop her head, but several tendrils had come loose to curl against her cheeks and the back of her neck. It would be the most natural thing in the world to rise to his feet, to come up behind her, wrap his arms around her slender waist, and press his lips to that spot at her nape. . . .

He blinked, losing the reverie as she cracked a pair of waiting eggs into the hot skillet, then glanced at him over her shoulder.

"Have you any plans for your stay here on Skye?"

None he could share, of course. "I know little about the island," he replied evasively. "I am hoping you . . . your family will be so kind as to educate me during my visit."

He wondered if she would have looked more enthusiastic if he had suggested a barefoot trek over broken glass. She was polite enough, however, when she said, "We'll be of whatever help we can, my lord."

She moved with a smooth efficiency, tipping the eggs onto a plate and quickly tossing thick slices of cured bacon into the pan. In minutes, the steaming plate was in front of him, as tantalizing to his eyes as to his nose.

"Why don't you sit down, Maggie? Stop moving for a moment."

She merely gave him a patient smile and went back to the stove. When she lifted the lid of the steaming pot, the sweet scent billowed through the room, filling Gabriel's head. She stirred in a generous amount of honey from an earthenware jar, added a handful more of fragrant herbs, and he wondered at the use of the stuff as a balm for anything. It smelled far more like something to be swallowed and savored than applied. But then, he thought, there were great pleasures to be found in warm honey on heated skin. He imagined Maggie's skin, bared and warm and flushed. And just as clearly, imagined the new depths to which he would sink, seducing his only friend's sister-in-law. Gabriel didn't think he could stomach one more ignoble tumble; he was fairly certain he wouldn't be able to stand losing Oriel's friendship.

But a man could dream. Even if he couldn't touch.

With no small amount of irony, Gabriel decided that if he couldn't feast on the tempting Margaret MacLeod, he could at least take advantage of her cooking. While she stirred, he dug into his meal. After several minutes, he broke the relatively companionable silence to ask the first of what he knew would be many questions about Maggie's island and its denizens.

"Tell me," he said, "why Tessa suggested I keep my name to myself while I'm here. It would seem everyone I meet would learn it sooner or later."

"People will learn your title," was her response. "Not the rest."

"Ah. Do Islanders have an aversion to 'Gabriel' for some reason? 'Augustus'?"

Maggie turned to face him fully, her lovely mouth compressed. " 'Tis the others. But you'd know why."

"As a matter of fact, I wouldn't."

She tilted her head and studied him for a moment as if doubting his honesty. Then she sighed and sat down, but not, he noted, before drawing her chair farther away from his own seat. "Both Lorne and Loudon," she said, fingertips toying with a crevice in the scarred tabletop, "are Scottish names."

"They are, yes—"

"And both connected to the Campbells."

"Of course. John, the Duke of Argyll, is a distant cousin."

"I'd not be mentioning that while you're here."

No clearer on the matter than he had been at the beginning, Gabriel demanded, "For heaven's sake, Maggie, tell me why."

She shook her head and gave a sad smile. "You really don't know of the feud between the Campbells and MacDonalds. Nay? Well, 'tis too old and too full to explain all of it, but there's been bad blood smoldering and much blood shed over the centuries. You must have heard of Glencoe."

When he merely looked at her blankly, she explained. "Alasdair, the head of the MacIan MacDonalds of Glencoe, was slow in declaring his fealty to King William in 1692. So a company of Argyll's men—Argyll was only an earldom then—went to Glencoe under the command of Captain Robert Campbell. Alasdair admitted them, fed and boarded them for nearly a fortnight. Gamed with them at his tables. Then, in the dead of night, the Campbells murdered the MacDonalds in their beds— women and children as well as the men. Those who escaped the massacre were forced to flee in the winter cold. Few survived to tell the tale." Maggie folded her hands primly on the table. "So there you have it."

Gabriel was uncertain just what he had. "What has this to do with Skye?"

"Och, you really are ignorant of the clan way, aren't you? There are scores of MacDonalds on Skye; MacDonalds of the Isles, to be precise, but connected to all members of the clan. No Campbell is welcome in MacDonald territory, regardless of where he hails from."

"You are jesting."

"I am not. 'Tis the way of the clans. What's left of us, anyway."

Awed and very mildly offended, Gabriel pressed, "And the MacLeods? I was under the impression Skye was your domain."

"We share it with the MacDonalds. There's been bad blood there, too, but we've peace now, have for many years. I've MacDonald cousins, MacDonald friends."

"And a distant Campbell in your home."

Maggie shrugged as she rose from the table. "You're a friend to kin. I'll certainly not hold your ancestry against you, but I can't say the same for others here. If I were you, I'd keep to calling yourself Gabriel Rievaulx while you're on Skye. There's enough French blood in Scots history that none will think less of you for it."

"No less than they do already of my being English."

She faced him fully, eyes cool as green glass. "All we've had from the English has been harsh control, deceit, war, and death. People see that when they see you. And best remember your Duke of Argyll and his Campbells are more English than Scot. You've two strikes against you."

Gabriel gave a weary sigh. "How old are you, Maggie MacLeod?"

"I'll be two-and-twenty come August. Why?"

"So young, yet with the bitterness of a hundred years. I cannot imagine it is all a matter of your Scots loyalty. Has an unfortunate Campbell done you some grievous ill?"

"Nay," she said shortly. "This has nothing to do with me."

"Doesn't it?" Gabriel studied her for a moment through narrowed eyes. "I have offended you."

"You haven't. Of course you haven't." But her tone didn't match her words.

"Mmm. I suppose it was a rather intimate question. Do you not care for them?"

"Intimate questions?"

"Yes," he confirmed, unable to keep from admiring the soft flush that had spread over her skin. When she didn't answer, merely waited to clear his place, cool and polite, he offered, "Am I keeping you from something? Is there an eager young man waiting to take you strolling through the leas, perhaps?"

That got a response, and a tart one.

"That, my lord," she said crisply, sliding his plate almost from beneath his hands, "is a personal query, and nay, I don't much care for them."

He held her gaze for a heartbeat, then leaned back, crossing his arms over his chest. "Campbells and personal queries. I'll be certain not to forget either." He gathered his thoughts. Smiled at her. "You can see for yourself I'm hardly a bad sort. Can we declare a truce in this house—call me a dear and incurious friend to kin rather than a nosy descendent of the enemy?"

He watched her features—that lush mouth—shift. "You are who you are, Gabriel Loudon. None can argue that. Now, will you have something more to eat?"

"I . . . No, thank you."

She nodded briskly, then leaned in to take his bowl and cup. Gabriel lifted a hand to help, but his fingers drifted as if by their own will toward a curling strand of loose auburn hair. He might have imagined her breathy sigh. He certainly didn't mistake the fact that his own breath suddenly felt a bit thick in his throat.

A sudden, quiet hiss had Maggie spinning about, had

Gabriel reaching by habit to his side, toward a weapon that hadn't been there since Portugal.

Behind them, massive shoulders filling an open window, was the sort of man Gabriel had always associated with the north of Scotland: brawny, grim-faced, and probably possessed of the same intelligence as the famed Highland cattle. This one's size alone would intimidate most men; his scowl would cow the devil.

Gabriel was intimidated by very little. Planting his hands on the table, he rose to his feet. He and the brute outside, very likely Maggie's companion from the day before, kept their eyes on each other. Neither spoke.

Maggie broke the silence. "My lord, this is my neighbor, Lachlann MacDonald. *A Lachlann, seo* . . . this is—"

With a growl, and without waiting for the introduction to be completed, the man vanished from the window.

"Well." Gabriel's expectations of the general Skye population were low, and they were being met.

Beside him, Maggie sighed. "I am . . . If you would . . . excuse me, sir." And she disappeared, too, out the door, leaving Gabriel standing in the middle of the kitchen.

Lachlann was waiting for her in the yard, a storm brewing behind his blue eyes. Maggie decided she'd best set her own roiling thoughts aside and meet her friend's before they erupted. "What can you be thinking?" she demanded in Gaelic. " 'Tis like a great, brainless hound, you are, growling and glaring at my guest. He's done you no ill. You've never even met him!"

Lachlann's formidable jaw was set stubbornly. "I haven't, nay. But there's something about him, Maggie, something I cannot like."

This had her rolling her eyes. "You've only just seen

him through a window, Lachlann! Have you taken a turn to sorcery, then, looking inside a man's mind?"

"I've no need to see into his mind. His eyes are enough. I don't care for the way he was looking at you."

"Lachlann!"

"Well, I don't. Did you have to make him so comfortable here, Maggie?"

"And what were we supposed to do, leave him to Calum's care?"

"Aye."

Maggie counted five, tried a reassuring smile that felt weak. She could only imagine how it looked. "He's a friend to Isobel and Nathan. What would you think if you were to arrive in London and they left you to stay at an inn?"

"Now, that's a daft question, isn't it? What would I be doing going to London?"

So much for patience. "Come meet him."

"I'd sooner eat mud."

"Oh, Lachlann." Maggie sighed. "Fine. I have your balm cooling. You can come back for it later and see for yourself that the man hasn't ravaged me."

" 'Tisn't amusing, Mairghread." Lachlann shoved his hands into the waistband of his rough trousers. "I'll stay out here. Just in case."

"You'll do no such thing. My father is here, and Tessa is about somewhere. Even should Lord Rievaulx fall into a mad, fevered delirium and try to strangle me, I daresay they are ample protection."

"Not amusing, either."

"Och, Lachlann, if you won't come in and be civil, go home!" She started to push past him toward the door, but a massive fist wrapped around her arm, halting her.

"Maggie, he's English. Nothing good comes with an Englishman to Skye."

Sighing, Maggie reminded herself this was a dear friend and that his care was a blessing. "What is all this, Lachlann? You think I'm not strong enough to resist a bonny face and clever words?" She hoped he would take the hot flush in her cheeks for temper rather than shame. He didn't know about Peter. He might have guessed some small part of what had happened, but he didn't know. "Trust me when I say I'll not end up wandering the cliffs with a dirk in my breast."

"Damn it, Maggie! They've no more morals than pigs, the *Sasunnach*. And you've no defenses against such."

She snorted. "When Scotland gains her freedom and someone makes you king, you can make such foolish pronouncements and folk will call you sage. But for now, you're just a Skye freeholder, Lachlann, and you've no right to judge, or hurt me so."

She watched as his handsome features jerked. "Ach, Maggie Lìl." The ice was gone from his eyes now, replaced by remorse. "I'm sorry." Defeated, he turned toward the garden wall. "I'll go. You know you've just to send Tessa running should you need me."

"I know." Maggie reached out, brushed her fingers down his sleeve. "And I know you mean well, Lachlann. Thank you."

He was barely out of sight when her knees finally gave way and she sagged against the wall. It took a few deep breaths and one good curse directed inward, but she managed to straighten at last, to lift her chin and face the kitchen door she'd shakily closed behind her.

It was all nonsense Lachlann spoke, she told herself firmly, no more than centuries of Scotland's hatred for the English which had been burned into the blood and stoked by nights of grim tales at the hearthside. As if she could be so moved by a pretty face to make a fool of herself over a man. Again.

Testing, Maggie raised fingertips to her face. Her skin felt cool enough. For shame, she scolded silently, letting Lachlann's words get to her so. It was nonsense, and an unfortunate comparison to a miserable legend.

Oh, but there was a bit of a problem. Maggie pressed one hand into her annoyingly jittery stomach and ruthlessly stifled the memory of the warmth she'd felt in that instant when she and the Englishman had been nearly jaw to jaw. She wouldn't think on it, she vowed. And, if the fates were smiling kindly, she wouldn't repeat the experience. Or be reminded that she hadn't felt such a quick, heated flush in Peter's arms.

The Englishman hadn't even touched her. She'd gone warm from tip to toe and he hadn't even touched her.

He wouldn't be doing so, either.

Maggie brushed her damp palms roughly down her apron and squared her jaw. She had plenty to do and never enough time. There was bread to bake and herbs to sort. There was carrageen to gather and tisanes to deliver. Yes, she decided, that was it. She would trade her household tasks for those away from home, at least for an hour or two. The herbs and washing would still be there when she returned. With luck, her scattered mind would have gathered itself and would be waiting for her, too.

There was no sign of the earl when she stepped back into the kitchen. Perhaps it was somewhat less than hospitable of her to just disappear, but she wasn't going to allow herself to feel too guilty. Her father could see to the other man, whenever he decided to make his own appearance. Stripping off her apron, Maggie hung it behind the door and reached for an already loaded basket.

"Making your escape?"

For the second time that morning, Maggie's heart gave a skittish lurch. And again, she felt a hot blush rising in her cheeks. She managed a single, not quite steadying breath before turning to face Gabriel.

"I've errands to do," she informed him, hoping she did not look as much like a fleeing rabbit as she felt. "But I can certainly put them off till later."

Something glinted in his eyes. Amusement, derision—Maggie couldn't tell. Her chin went up instinctively.

"Why?" he asked, that patrician drawl giving the single word weight it should not possess. "Don't let me interfere with your daily tasks."

As if he hadn't already, simply by being there, turned Maggie's quiet life somewhat upside down. "You are a guest, sir. I would not have you feel . . . unwelcome."

"Perish the thought." His smile did not quite reach his eyes. "Then, if you'll wait just a moment, I'll fetch my hat."

She blinked at him. "Your hat?"

"Of course. I am accepting your kind invitation and accompanying you on your errands."

Trapped, not quite knowing when she had lost complete control of matters, Maggie waited. He was back in a minute, expensive hat in hand.

"Shall we?" Reaching out, he took the basket from her. "Lead on, Margaret MacLeod."

And not knowing what else to do, she did, leading him toward the cliff road.

⊰ 5 ⊱

There's Rosemary, that's for remembrance;
Pray, love, remember . . .
                    —Shakespeare, *Hamlet*

There were clouds hovering on the horizon, but Gabriel assumed any rain would wait until night if it came at all. It was a fine day for deception.

He stole a glance at the woman walking by his side. Even without really knowing her at all, he doubted Maggie had ever told a falsehood in her life, let alone lied her way into someone's home and trust. He didn't think she would be pleased to know how he had lied thus far. He thought she would like the truth even less. There was little doubt in his mind that, while the MacLeods were not likely to be in support of Napoleon, they wouldn't shed any tears for dethroned Georges.

Scotland was full of Jacobites, men and women loyal to the Stuarts who believed Bonny Prince Charlie, grandson of the deposed King James, had been the rightful heir to the British throne. To them, the Hanovers were usurpers, wrongful and unfit for the throne. Even seventy years after Charlie's flight back to the Continent, nearly a decade since the last in the royal male line had died, Stuart supporters peppered the British Isles. Here, in the northernmost climes of Scotland, Jacobites would still outnumber Royalists by a good ten to one. Of course, there was every possibility that sympathy for the Stuarts had little to do with it any longer. The Royals, especially

67

the current crop, were quite capable of alienating their subjects with no help whatsoever from history.

Add to that already inauspicious mix the fact that Scotland had strong ties to France. It always had. And, perhaps most importantly, there was a tradition of Highland loyalty whose depths Gabriel knew he did not even begin to comprehend. All of this would make him a very unpopular fellow indeed should it turn out that his quarry was, in fact, one of Skye's own.

He was going to have to tread very carefully. Maggie's loyalty to her island and heritage was obvious. He suspected there was nothing she wouldn't do for her family, little she wouldn't do for her Skye friends and neighbors. Gabriel needed the MacLeods' help and cooperation. If they hated him in the end, so be it. For now he needed them to welcome him as a guest and friend of the family. Unless they did, and very visibly, there was little chance of other people trusting him enough to let down their guards. Someone was sheltering a traitor in the neighborhood. Or, just as likely and more insidious, a neighbor *was* the traitor.

Not for the first time, Gabriel cursed the task he had taken on. There just wasn't enough information, and what little he did have was old and not necessarily reliable. He couldn't be expected to work this way. He needed time and military intelligence and the assistance of another trained mind. . . .

Excuses. He had plenty of those. He also had the blood of good men on his hands and a chance, finally, to make some small amends.

Eyes narrowed against the ever-present wind, he scanned the view spread before him. The earth, more gray than green, stretched downward toward what he could only assume was the village: a scattering of buildings and one wide, rocky road. Beyond, the land was dotted with grazing cows and the occasional stone cottage.

Some piquant impulse had him pausing above a small ruin. One wall stood almost intact; the others had long since tumbled inward and would soon be lost to the fingers of flowering vines and velvety moss. Nature reclaiming its own. "What was this?"

Stopping beside him, Maggie replied, " 'Tis the old *Eaglais Chaitliceach*. The Catholic church."

A far cry, certainly, from the lavish cathedrals of England's history. "Are there still many Catholics on Skye?"

"Some, to be sure," Maggie answered after a long moment. "My grandfather converted to Church of Scotland; my cousins at Sconser are still Catholic."

"And there's no fighting over it?"

"Ach, why? We've always had better matters to bash heads over: stolen flocks, stolen wives, stolen whiskey. 'Tis an easily riled, easily contented people we are here on Skye."

"So what happened to the church?" he asked her, thinking of the Rievaulx Abbey ruins that lay so close to his lands, of the rich, glittery spoils that had made their way into his family's hands during the last King Henry's anti-Catholic tantrums. "The carvings, the silver. . . ?"

She shook her head with a wry smile. "The wood could have gone to a newer kirk, or to a cow byre, I suppose, and any silver would have been in the priest's hair. 'Twasn't St. Peter's in Rome, my lord, nor even York Minster. From all I know, I'd say 'twas a drafty little village kirk like all the others, a pile of stone where being nearer to God meant no one minded the gaps in the roof."

Gabriel watched the wry smile curve her lips. The

fresh air had brought a bloom to her skin, brightened the vividly green eyes. It was all there in her face: the love of her home and community, the knowledge of its faults and foibles. For a fleeting moment, he wondered what it would be like to be a part of something so free of pretense. Maggie must have been miserable during the time her family spent away, though Gabriel suspected she had done everything in her power to hide it.

"You're happy here," he commented. It wasn't a question.

She looked surprised. "I am, of course."

Yes, he thought, she would be, and the matter would be as simple and solid as the remnants of the old church below. She was just the sort of woman who would give her affection and acceptance as it was warranted: to a place, to the people there. And she wouldn't be wary, looking for betrayal or hidden motives in anything or anyone. It was yet one more grace he was finding in her character. He supposed he could ask for advance pardon for taking advantage of that character—*Forgive me for what I am going to do*—but as he didn't believe in any benevolent higher power, and asking Maggie's forgiveness now for harm he might later do her would put something of a strain on their relationship, he held his tongue.

"You have always lived here?" he asked instead.

"Except for a few months in Edinburgh and three years in England, aye."

"And how do you find Edinburgh? I've always thought the Highlands squeezed a good amount of their essence into the city."

The smile she gave him was reminiscent of that one would give a slow child. "Have you indeed? I've always thought England had squeezed a great deal of its essence into Edinburgh." She tempered the words with another smile, blithe this time. " 'Tis a grand place in its way, but I had a terrible time of it, trying to find a rosemary plant without soot on it."

"And soot does nothing for bruises?"

For a moment he thought she might take offense at his poor jest. Apparently she didn't.

"Nay, to be sure. Everyone knows soot is for carbuncles."

Gabriel laughed, something he hadn't done much of in a very long time. Then asked, "Do you care for all of the bruises on Skye?"

"Only the ones I see," was her quick reply.

"A weighty task, Miss MacLeod."

" 'Tis what I do," she said simply.

Gabriel studied the gently rolling hills, tested the tinge of sea in the air, and thought it would not be such a bad place to spend one's life. If one were not accustomed to modern entertainment and action, of course. He expected he would go mad within a fortnight.

Less, if this woman slipped any more deeply into his head and under his skin.

They were at the outskirts of the village now, such as it was. In his brief stop at the inn on his arrival, he had seen only one street and perhaps two buildings that could be shops. "How on earth do you amuse yourselves?" he demanded, eyes sweeping the little tableau.

She laughed. It was an intoxicating sound. "Much as anyone, I imagine."

"Maggie, really. In Town, even in York, we have clubs, mills, theater. Balls and soirees."

"And I'm sure they're grand, indeed." Now he thought she might be humoring him. "We have *ceilidhs*—parties with dancing to fully rival your lofty balls. You'll come to tonight's if it suits you. Too much whiskey on Fridays usually gives us a good fistfight, and we haven't to pay as you do at your mills. Young Elspeth MacDonald's quarrels with her betrothed are as lively as anything you might find at the theater."

She pointed at a red-painted wood door. "See, there's MacAuley's. 'Tis as much a club as your White's, I daresay. The food is hearty, ale plentiful, and you might like to know there will no doubt be a good bit of wagering on whether you pass your stay on Skye unscathed."

"Why would I not?"

Her shrug was blithe and graceful. The fleeting, capricious smile that went with it would have had half the young bucks in the ton fawning at her feet. It certainly wiped away that faint frisson of unease that he'd felt at her words. "Oh, Englishmen don't fare well on Skye. But then, you've been told that already."

"So I have," he murmured. "Indeed I have."

"Well, watch where you put your feet and hands, then, and come along. I've several stops to make and no time to dawdle."

Charmed, and distracted, he followed her supple form as she marched away from him down the slope. "For what it's worth," he informed her, matching his stride to hers, "the most important bargains and accords in English government are made behind the doors of the St. James clubs."

"Oh, politics." She blew out a dismissive breath. "We're not political here. Neither the MacLeod nor MacDonald clan of the island went to Culloden Field. We simply go on as we are, knowing trouble will come from the south whether we court it or not."

"Culloden," he repeated on a sigh. "Of course. All noble thoughts and roads lead to Culloden Field."

"Careful, lad. More than a thousand good-hearted Scots died there over the British crown."

"Charles Stuart was nothing but a foolish pretender."

"Bonny Prince Charlie had his claims," she shot back hotly.

"Careful, lass. You might be mistaken for a woman with political views."

Oh, she was beautiful when she laughed. " 'Tis my history, *Sasunnach,* not politics."

"And you know your history well?"

"Well enough. 'Tis like an English child's fairy tales, I imagine, given to us each night by the hearth and bedside."

Gabriel studied her profile as she walked. Perfect, he thought, but her mouth had taken on a now familiar firmness. "You have a very low opinion of England."

"Not in the least," she replied promptly. " 'Tis a lovely place, what I've seen of it."

Clever girl, he thought, but evasiveness was his domain, not hers. "A low opinion of the English, then. Is it a matter of principle?"

"A matter of history, more like."

"Given to you at bedtime like a lullaby." He thought to ask whether it was her history or her island's, but held his tongue. He hadn't had much success the first time he had tried to learn a personal detail. He would wait. "Scarborough Fair is English, you know."

He whistled, something he hadn't done in a very long time. And wondered if he'd imagined the quick stiffening of her jaw at the sound of the familiar melody. He stopped whistling. "Scarborough is a good enough place."

"I'm sure it is," was her immediate response. "I expect you'll be missing it soon enough, and eager to get home."

Before Gabriel could open his mouth to reply, Maggie

had spun away up a flagstone path toward a tiny cottage. " 'Tis the Beatons'," she called back. "Mr. Beaton has a weak chest and won't take a whit of care for himself unless we all join forces and go at him like woodpeckers."

A tiny, white-haired woman with a face like a walnut answered the knock. That face broke into a wide smile on seeing Maggie. She looked at the basket, gave Gabriel a thorough perusal as he hurried up the path, and let out a long and musical stream of Gaelic. Maggie answered briefly in kind. The woman cackled, nodded, and disappeared inside.

"Are you coming, then?" Maggie tossed over her shoulder, and entered.

With nothing to do but follow, he did.

Old Mr. Beaton was seated by the fire, a hoary head visible above the folds of one of his wife's copious wool throws. He wasn't looking well, Maggie noted sadly, his cheeks sunken in his seamed face. But the smile he gave her was quick, bright, and set his faded blue eyes twinkling.

"Ah, 'tis the clever Maggie with her magic basket," he said in Gaelic. "And with a young man, no less. The English, is he?"

"He is, and not such a very bad sort." She bent down to kiss the parchment cheek. "He's a friend to Isobel's husband."

"Well, he's welcome, then." Offering a greeting, still in Gaelic as neither he nor his wife knew English, he waved Gabriel into the facing chair. The younger man took it, albeit stiffly. "You'll not be marrying this one, Maggie, and flitting south like your sister, now, will you?"

The very thought made her laugh, even as it brought a flush to her cheeks. "Pigs will fly first!"

"Mmm. I've a lively hog out back, lass, so watch your words."

"I'll keep that in mind. Now, did you take the tisane I sent off with Tearlach this morning?"

"To be sure I did."

Over his head, his wife shook her head and held two fingers less than an inch apart to show how little he had taken. Maggie swallowed her sigh. "I've more with me."

"Och, I'm fit as a fiddle, lass. No need to fuss over me. Between you and Tearlach, I feel like an old rooster surrounded by pecking chicks." He chucked her chin with a bony finger. "What do you have for my troublesome son?"

"Peppermint and good wishes," Maggie replied quickly. She'd had quite enough talk of young men, especially when one was sitting not five feet away and the other was Mr. Beaton's son. Smiling a bit desperately now, she left the old man to stare at Gabriel and carried the herbs to Mrs. Beaton, who was preparing a steaming kettle. As the older woman set the familiar concoction to brew, she gave Maggie a conspiratorial wink. "He's a bonny one, he is."

"I would hope you think so, after fifty years of marriage."

"Oh, so clever. Not my bonny man, but yours. You're a dear one, Mairghread, but you cannot go on as you are forever."

Maggie sighed, checked the tisane. "So Lachlann was just telling me. Are you two in league perchance?"

"Nay, though it might help. So, are you going to keep your Englishman?"

"He's not mine to keep, Mrs. Beaton. 'Tis a free man grown, he is, subject to his own whims. And I'd not have him in any case. I've no desire to tie myself to a toplofty Englishman, nor any man."

And she hadn't. Not any longer.

"You're but waiting, lass, with your eyes off to the distance. Take care you don't miss what's right under your nose." When Maggie merely gave a tight smile, Mrs. Beaton relented. "You think I'm a foolish old woman, but I know your heart, Maggie Lìl. I'll leave you be, though. Tell me how Isobel is doing with her toplofty Englishman. Is there good news to celebrate?"

"None yet, though I daresay it won't be long. They're both eager to fill the nursery."

Their talk turned to the rest of the MacLeod siblings, then to the Beatons' three children. Cait was married to a MacKenzie and lived near Dunvegan. Peadar had left the islands for the lure of Inverness and seldom came home. Tearlach had his own land to tend just over the Sound, near Glenelg, but stayed near to hand when his father was unwell. Maggie listened with half an ear to Mr. Beaton, and darted a glance or two in his direction. He was solemnly talking to Gabriel in Gaelic. Gabriel, for his part, was listening, occasionally offering a polite if vague nod when his host paused. If only he knew he was being cheerfully and deliberately lectured on the merits of hog dung for raising root vegetables.

She waited until Mr. Beaton was sipping contentedly at the tisane before collecting her basket and preparing to leave.

"You bring your young man back anytime you like," Mrs. Beaton offered, one of her hands now linked with her husband's.

"Aye, he doesn't seem such a bad fellow," the old man added, winking. "Proud, but a woman always sees to that." To Gabriel, he said, *"Tha Mairghread ag ràdh*

*nach e dùtaich snog a tha anns a' Sasann. S' beag orm na
mucan na h-ùrach."*

Gabriel blinked, then gave the short, polished bow
Maggie was beginning to associate with every coming
and going. "Thank you," he said stiffly.

"Tapadh leat," Maggie translated.

Mr. Beaton did not quite succeed in turning his chuckle
into a cough. Maggie saw the earl's impressive jaw jerk
up a visible notch. Tossing the old man a frown he would
know she did not mean, she got Gabriel out the door.

His face was an inscrutable mask as they made their
way along the rough road. He said nothing, but took the
basket from Maggie's hands. He ought to have looked
silly, she thought, carrying a fraying reed basket. He
didn't.

For a brief second, Maggie wondered if he had a heart
a woman could touch. There was something about him
that made her want to reach out, smooth the faint and
often present scowl from his face, but she sensed he
would turn any care away. He was a hard one, this man
with the archangel's name, and it would take more than
a friendly touch to get beneath the granite surface. Ah,
but mightn't a woman find something special there.

Then, inwardly scolding herself for entertaining such
utterly absurd thoughts, she announced, "We're to stop
by Lady Malcolmson's next. You'll be happier there."

"Oh? Why is that?"

"She knows English." The widow was, too, elegant
and clever, far more likely company for the earl than
anyone else in the little community, but Maggie saw no
need to mention that to him. He would discover it soon
enough for himself. "And she has seen the world far beyond our little corner."

She waved to Muire MacAuley, who was hanging

wash behind the tavern; exchanged greetings with Lach-lann's married sister, who was tending the little garden in front of her cottage; and paused so young Georàs MacGaa could tell her all about his pet lamb. Everyone they met studied Gabriel as if he were some exotic—and slightly smelly—foreign creature. He didn't seem to notice at all.

"Maggie," he asked at last, as they neared the pair of ancient oaks that flanked the entrance to the Malcolmson grounds, "for what precisely did I thank Mr. Beaton?"

"Oh, he was just bidding you welcome should you come again."

The look he gave her made it clear he was not entirely fooled, but he let the matter go. And a good thing, too. She wasn't certain how she would have explained the old man's informing Gabriel that Maggie thought England an awful place because the pigs were earthbound.

She didn't think England an awful place. She'd told the truth there when Gabriel had asked. Nor did she dislike the English, at least no more than the average Scotswoman. Even raised as she had been, with the village legend of a faithless Englishman and his spurned Skye lover, she'd grown to adulthood more romantic than wary.

And look where that had gotten her.

She wasn't going to flog herself yet again. Not now, anyway. She was going to get through tea with Edana Malcolmson, make certain her family and guest were fed and comfortable, then she was going to go to the *ceilidh*, where she would find a quiet corner and listen to the fiddles.

Beside her the earl was whistling again, and again it was the familiar tune. She felt the lure of it like a tiny hook within her. *O are you going to Scarbro Fair . . .*

" 'Tis a saddening song," she said before she could stop herself.

"Is it?" He paused, clearly running the words through his head. "More foolish, I'd say. The silly demands that keep sillier young sweethearts apart."

Not silly, Maggie found herself thinking. *Impossible.* And wondered why it bothered her that this man didn't seem to comprehend the difference.

Soon they were turning onto the Malcolmson drive. In front of each oak at the entrance was a stone gatepost: squat obelisks with carved eagles crouched atop them. Maggie had always thought the posts ridiculous, made all the more so by the size of the trees behind them. But there was more than a touch of the grandiose about Edana. The pair of affectations flanking the dirt road was silly, to be sure, but hardly unforgivable.

Maggie and Gabriel walked up the drive that might have been grand if it were longer. As it was, they had only to walk twenty yards or so to reach the house. Built of the same native granite and sandstone as the lowliest crofter's hut, the glorified cottage sat solidly on rising ground. Only the neatly arranged flower gardens and pair of fat pugs wheezing on the stoop indicated that anyone other than a simple Islander lived inside.

MacGillechallum, Lady Malcolmson's butler, answered Maggie's knock. If the earl found anything odd about a red-haired, massively bearded, tree-sized butler, he gave no indication. When MacGillechallum grunted and thrust out a ham-sized fist, Gabriel merely handed over his hat and stick with the subtle lift of one brow.

"She's in back," the butler grunted, then stomped toward the rear of the house. Maggie knew to follow. She was used to the man, knew he had been a stonecutter in his younger years and had never quite adapted to house service. She had no idea why he had left his trade for this; she rather suspected he was a bit in love with his mistress.

Maggie herself was not quite so fond of Edana Malcolmson. She didn't dislike the woman, really. It was more of a vague disapproval. The gateposts had something to do with it, certainly; there was no call for such ostentation in their little corner of Scotland. But Edana's resplendence did have one advantage; she was fascinating to Tessa. She had been across continents and oceans from Calais to Cairo to the Indies with her late husband. She had collected tales and objects that left Tessa wide-eyed and uncustomarily tongue-tied. In a place where visits to towns as close as Inverness were a rarity, Lady Malcolmson was Marco Polo, Grace O'Malley, and Christopher Columbus rolled into one pretty package. And if the tales were interspersed with lessons in decorum, French, and fashion, Tessa rarely complained.

In exchange for these informal sessions, Maggie provided the lady with various herbal washes, ointments, and sachets. She sat through the occasional tea, trying to ignore the pointed glances at her plain, well-worn dresses and uncoiffed hair, and resisted the urge to slop the expensive bergamot blend into her saucer.

She could smell the tea as they entered the little room in the rear of the house that Lady Malcolmson used as her sitting room. The simple wooden floor was covered by a profusion of lush silk rugs from the East, portraits of exotically dressed gentlemen and masks with animal faces decorated the painted walls, and nearly every flat surface was covered by jeweled boxes, small totems, carved amulets. In the midst of it all, Edana reclined on an embroidered chaise, the chatelaine at home.

"Well, Maggie. What a lovely surprise. And with a gentleman in tow. Even better."

Introductions made, tea dutifully poured, Maggie took a seat near the window and sat back, ready to leave the others to chat about Almack's or the Bois de Boulogne or whatever the titled discussed. She didn't plan on their staying long, but she didn't want to incur Edana's displeasure, either, by failing to give the lady an early and up-close view of their guest. Edana's pique was a formidable thing, and would inevitably result in Tessa being forced to do circuits of this room with a heavy book atop her head, or something similar.

"So, my lord, what brings you to Skye?" Lady Malcolmson demanded, leaning forward in her seat. Her eyes locked on Gabriel's; one hand reached up to toy with the cross dangling just above her bodice.

He returned her smile and settled in. This was just the sort of woman he'd tended to seek out since his return from the Continent: lithe, catlike, and easily entertained. The lack of a visible husband was another among Gabriel's list of splendid attributes. He knew Lady Malcolmson just by looking at her. And it was more than the carefully coiffed blond hair, the welcome in the sharp blue eyes, or the fashionable white dress that hinted at what little it didn't display. A man would always know just where he stood. No surprises.

He repeated the story he had been telling: family business, time to waste before the Season reached its zenith, a promise to Isobel Oriel. He had a feeling he could have told Lady Malcolmson the truth and she wouldn't have batted a lush lash. Why he was there would be far less important than the fact that he was there. Gabriel assumed life on Skye was deadly dull for this woman, with her cultured voice and display of exotic curios.

"And the MacLeods have taken you in, of course," she drawled, waving a languid hand toward Maggie. "Margaret tends to us all, you know. She can't help it. Can you, dearest? It's rather like a holy vocation."

Across the room, Maggie was sitting ramrod straight in an oddly carved little chair. Basket at her feet, hands clasped in her lap, she was the pastoral to the other woman's palatial. She was also, Gabriel decided, a bit annoyed. Her soft voice betrayed nothing, however, when she replied, "We cannot all be adventurers, Edana, but I hardly think myself nunlike."

"Well, I am beginning to think myself so. I have been cloistered here forever, it seems. I am accustomed to travel, Lord Rievaulx, but relied so on the company of my late husband. The quiet weighs upon me."

Yes, he rather thought it would. "Have you no plans at all to travel?"

"I might have, as it happens. But life has a way of toying with the best laid schemes, does it not?" The lady gave an elegant shrug, clearly not expecting an answer. "Rather like rain on a hunt day," she said with mock melancholy, and promptly turned the conversation to more cheerful climes.

They talked of the weather, of Gabriel's travel north, of Isobel and her marquess husband. All the while, Gabriel knew he was being examined and not, he thought, found wanting. Yes, Edana Malcolmson would be bored and restless in this place where her late husband had no doubt settled her. Knowing restlessness well, Gabriel understood.

He found himself staring at a particularly ugly wooden figurine of a horse, on the table at his hostess's elbow. The thing had rolling eyes and bared teeth and would have looked less out of place in an abattoir. Following his gaze, Lady Malcolmson smiled and said, "My only local piece. It's a kelpie, a guardian of the water."

"Charming."

"Isn't it? And it comes with a delightful tale. Do you enjoy ghost stories, Lord Rievaulx?"

"I don't, as it happens."

"Ah. Pity. I should very much like to have shared it—"

A muffled thump from outside the door had Lady Malcolmson turning toward the door, a quick frown marring her elegant brow. She smoothed it almost immediately and gave a silvery laugh. "My life is not so *very* quiet, perhaps." She slid one leg off the chaise, giving Gabriel a good view of nicely turned, silk-sheathed calf. Apparently the visit was over. And not, Gabriel thought, because the lady wished it.

"We should be going," Maggie said from her place. "I've yet to stop by Clodagh Norrie's."

"From my home to that hovel. Goodness, dearest, what a road you travel." Lady Malcolmson, both slippered feet on the floor now, leaned forward and gave Gabriel a wry, conspiratorial smile. "Maggie is so much better a person than I. But then, I suppose we cannot all be angels."

"No," he heard himself say gruffly. "We cannot."

He rose with the ladies, watched as their hostess gracefully rearranged several yards of crimson silk wrap. "I trust you will be at the *ceilidh* tonight, my lord."

"I will."

"Marvelous. Our little gatherings are in desperate need of fresh faces." She accepted a small, green glass jar from Maggie with a regal thanks and opened the door. The behemoth was waiting to show them out. "Until tonight, then, my lord." And to Maggie, "Splendid girl for bringing him to me. You never come empty-handed."

Maggie was striding away from the house even before the door had thumped shut behind them. Gabriel caught up with her easily. "Where now?" he asked as they reached the path.

"Clodagh Norrie's," was the tight reply. "She is a weaver and has terrible pain in her hands. I've an ointment for her."

"Maggie—"

"Do you mind walking right along the cliffs? 'Twill save time."

"No," Gabriel said, "I don't mind at all."

And he didn't. He wanted to have a look at the local shoreline. What little intelligence on L'Écossais Oriel had passed on included the information that an intercepted communiqué had mentioned Barra, an isolated island nearly due west of where Gabriel now stood. From there, a vessel could easily sail to Ireland, or even all the way to France.

His gaze skimmed the horizon as they walked, settled on the towering rough peaks of some dark rock.

"What is that?" he asked, gesturing.

" 'Tis the Black Cuillin Range."

"Ugly."

Maggie halted and gazed thoughtfully at the scorched-looking expanse. "To a stranger, perhaps. To me, they're glorious. Created by a spear from the Sun, so legend has it."

"Oh?" Gabriel wasn't much more fond of folklore than ghost stories, but it seemed so natural to the place—and to the woman—that he found himself wanting to hear the tale.

"Aye. The *Cailleach*, or Hag of the Beare, was said to hold the maiden loved by Spring. Her power was so great that Spring could not fight her. So he called to the

Sun for help in vanquishing the mighty *Cailleach*. The Sun's spear missed her, but split the earth where it struck and sent up such a fiery mass that the Cuillins were formed."

"It sounds a bit like the myth of Persephone held in Hades. Did Spring get his maiden back?"

"I've no idea." Maggie's smile was wry. "I would imagine so. The *Cailleach* tends to lose in these tales."

"That makes you angry?"

"Not angry, nay. But the true genesis of the *Cailleach* wasn't as a screeching, evil witch, but as an old woman born over and again in the form of a young woman. The Celts believed she controlled the seasons."

"And the screeching witch persona?"

"Created by the Church to purge her image. She's neither mother nor virgin, you see, so she holds no place in Christian tradition."

"Spoken with the heartfelt zeal of a true pagan."

He had meant no offense and she seemed to take none. "Heartfelt . . . Well, I've a fond spot in my heart for our *Cailleach*. 'Tis balance, really. How foolish we would be to think we can have summer without winter, spring without fall. She understands, and gives us all of it, again and again and again, in cycle. Like all things gone by, the seasons repeat." She broke off then, blinked, and shook her head. "Enough. Clodagh will be waiting. Come along, before the wind rises."

Awed a bit, intrigued, and somehow touched, Gabriel walked with her. "You tell a good tale, Miss MacLeod."

She waved away the compliment. "I only repeat what's been told to me time and again."

"Ah, but with the deftness of one who enjoys the telling. It draws the listener in. Not everyone can do that."

"Nonsense. Anyone can tell a fairy tale."

"I can't," he replied simply. "I don't know any."

She stopped, turned to regard him with a mixture of surprise and, he thought, sympathy. "Did no one spin tales of knights and dragons for you as a boy?"

He thought of his grandfather, whose stories had been ghoulish and gory, well intended, but utterly lacking in hope or happy endings. "No."

"Ah. Well, 'twas always a bit of a scrabble at bedtime, the five of us gathering round our father for a story. He'd bounce the ones who sat on his feet." She smiled at the memory. " 'Twas usually Geordie and Rob. They weren't above a bit of shoving to get there first."

Gabriel stored away this little piece of information—the most personal Maggie had given him as yet—and could well imagine the scene: five red-haired children gathered in front of the simple hearth, jostling for the seat of honor atop Jamie's worn slippers.

"I have no idea what sort of sibling I would have been," he said truthfully. "My parents were content with me alone."

"Of course they were," was Maggie's response, quick and wholly polite. Gabriel smiled wryly. His parents hadn't been content so much with him as the fact that there was no further need to live under the same roof once the son and heir had made his dutiful entry into the world. "Have you cousins?"

"Oh, yes. I have cousins." Ones who had been none too pleased when he'd returned home from the Peninsula after months of being presumed dead. He'd had to oust one from the earldom and the bulk of the man's immediate family from Scarborough House. They'd dug in like leeches and had been just as hard to remove, trailing their newly inked family trees and careful accountings of

Gabriel's wealth in their sticky wake. "Not a fairy tale among the lot."

"Well," came the gentle offer, "I've plenty to spare."

Gabriel looked into her face and saw it all: beauty, innocence. A head full of myth and magic and a heart full of affection for friend and family alike. He couldn't imagine anyone for whom he was less suited, or any woman who had been more dramatically, unfortunately appealing.

"I'd best stay with what I already know," he said more gruffly than he'd intended. "I would no doubt do untold damage to your story."

She nodded, turned away. "As you wish."

They began walking again. "I should like to see the cliffs, though." He wouldn't forget his reason for being on Skye.

"And so you shall."

She was right. They came suddenly, dramatically, the earth seeming to have been sheared away by a great, jagged knife. Fearless, Maggie stood on the edge.

"Mind your step," she told him. " 'Tis a long way down."

And it was. Gabriel stood, one foot on solid earth, the other half over the edge, and peered down. Water teemed at the base of the cliffs, battering against barely visible rocks with fierce and elemental power. When he glanced back at Maggie, she had her face turned into the rising breeze, eyes closed.

"You love this place," he said. And he didn't just mean the cliff edge, although something told him the very spot where they stood held some powerful lure for her. Truth be told, he felt it, too.

"Aye. Too much, mayhaps."

He wasn't certain he understood that, but couldn't ask

her to explain. He'd been the one, after all, to shore up the brief sag in her cool wall. And wisely, he told himself. Best to have something solid in between them.

Still, he couldn't resist asking, "What would you do if you could no longer live here on Skye?"

He waited, expecting her to take him to task for prying—or not to reply at all. She did neither.

"Now, that, my lord," she said, "is an impossible question."

"There's no such thing as impossible questions, Maggie. Trick ones, but not impossible."

"Fine." A wayward strand of hair whipped across her face and she shoved it back. It was a futile gesture and she quickly gave up, leaving the auburn strands to riot in the wind. "Answer this for me, then. If I could find an acre of land 'twixt sand and sea there"—she pointed down, past the cliffs, to the pale crescent of the sandy cove—"would that count as living on Skye?"

"What sort of question is that?"

"My sort. Answer it, if you please."

"But it's impossible—"

"Just so," she agreed with a faint smile, and turned away.

Simmer's a pleasant time,
Flowers of ev'ry colour;
The water rins o'er the heugh,
And I long for my true lover.
Ay waukin, O.
                        —Robert Burns

As the fiddle music swept cheerily through the Tolmey cottage, Maggie felt Gabriel's presence behind her like a hovering storm cloud. Perhaps it had been a mistake to bring him to the *ceilidh*, but she couldn't have seen leaving him behind and Jamie certainly wouldn't have heard of it. Beyond that, Gabriel himself hadn't seemed reluctant to come. He had not precisely done handsprings at the prospect of attending a small country fete, but then, even after a mere two days of knowing him, Maggie would have been astonished to see him show much passion over anything.

That was the aristocracy, she thought. Boredom and disdain apparently came with the blue blood. True, her brother-in-law wasn't a bad person, but Maggie still found his stern reserve a bit intimidating. In the midst of the careless, boisterous MacLeods, Nathan rather put one in mind of a granite mountain: hard, implacable, quiet.

Here, in the middle of a lively spring *ceilidh*, Gabriel was much the same. It was almost as if he expected to have a dismal time, and was ensuring as much by standing near the wall, wearing a kasimir coat and an aristocratic frown.

They'd arrived late, delayed by Jamie's insistence on fashioning a cravat knot that would have foiled the cleverest London valet, and Tessa's insistence that shoes were nothing but a hindrance at a *ceilidh*. Then they'd had to wait for a short and fierce burst of rain to stop lashing the windows. Walking a mile on a fine spring night was one matter; doing it in a downpour was another. By the time they'd arrived at the Tolmeys', it was late, Jamie had loosened his cravat to allow his one-for-the-road tankard to go down easier, Tessa had mud up to her ankles, and Gabriel had grown quite silent.

Jamie had tottered off toward the liquid refreshments as soon as they'd arrived. Tessa had disappeared to compare adventures with the other attendees too young to mingle yet too old to be held or settled to sleep in a back room. Leaving Maggie alone to entertain their guest. He'd shown no inclination to eat, dance, or gossip. Not that Maggie was so eager to participate in any of those activities, but there was little else to do. She had intended to sit quietly near the music, perhaps with someone else's baby cuddled in her lap, and watch the festivity. Instead, she was standing with a man who wasn't asking her to dance—not that she would have accepted, she told herself firmly—or making much of an effort at conversation. He was studying the assembled revelers with an inscrutable expression on his face.

Maggie glanced around the room at her friends and neighbors. She was sure it was nothing compared to one of the grand balls Gabriel attended, but it was a good enough way for anyone to spend an evening. She had been looking forward to the *ceilidh*. She had missed these lively, welcoming little gatherings during her time away. At a Skye *ceilidh*, all that mattered was that the music and drink flowed freely, the gossip was mostly true, and the food mostly edible. No one worried about wearing the right cravat or choosing dance partners carefully so as to make the best match, and while some of the girls wore their best dresses and ribbons and pinched their cheeks pink to catch the attention of Lachlann and the other young men, there was no pomp. There was simply a community of friends and family feeling and looking content.

Maggie had coaxed her father into a freshly laundered shirt, Tessa into shoes and a dress that didn't look like it had been up and down a tree. She herself had chosen a finer dress than those she wore daily: plain, pale yellow, with modest sleeves and a pin-tucked bodice. Isobel was forever sending her fashionable clothing from London, an endless array of lush fabrics and plunging necklines. Maggie knew they were restrained by London standards, but not one was suited for a Skye evening, let alone a day of tromping through heather or collecting carrageen from the sea. So she folded them carefully away; Izzy scolded fondly, and sent more.

She tapped one slippered foot in time to the lilting reel. Skye had a long history of the finest music: the MacCrimmon pipers of Borreraig and the MacLeod fiddlers of Torrin. Her cousins were down from the north with their instruments and were sawing away now, fit and fiery and talented enough to be playing for a king. Rumor had it that a trio of MacLeod fiddlers had, in fact, played a Skye air for Bonny Charlie during his brief time on the island, with Calum MacAuley's grandmother on the harp and old Mr. Beaton's mother sitting at the spinet. The story went that the prince, so moved by the music, shed a heartfelt tear. Sile MacAuley caught it in a handkerchief and her grandson had that piece of linen still, framed behind glass on his tavern wall.

There was no royalty in attendance tonight. There were farmers and crofters, fishermen, and hardworking women. They were boisterous and cheerful and having a marvelous time. They were also giving the single noble visitor a wide berth.

Maggie knew that would be different if Gabriel weren't so forbidding. Perhaps no one would welcome him with the same effusion as they would another Highland Scot, but her neighbors weren't unfriendly. They were simply wary, and she didn't blame them.

"Looks like that Border fellow Hannah MacKenzie up and married," Tavis Tolmey muttered nearby. He'd been courting Hannah before she'd met her Borderer on a visit to cousins in Glasgow. "Damned dog."

"Looks like Campbell stock to me," was old Fen MacDonald's dour pronouncement. It might have carried more weight had Fen not thought everyone not from his corner of the island resembled a hated Campbell.

"Haven't seen him blink once," commented Tavis's brother Stephan. "Eyes like a bloody statue."

Everyone seemed to have an opinion. Calum MacAuley declared, "Rude bugger. Wouldn't touch my victuals."

"Clever lad," from a bright-eyed, pink-nosed Jamie. Then he hiccuped. "And rich as Croesus."

"He's lovely," one young lady breathed. Others had merely nodded and gaped. Some of the young men had grunted and flexed their fists.

Every comment was in Gaelic. English speakers weren't common among the local residents, but neither were they so very rare. It seemed none were going to use the language now. Except Maggie.

"Do you dance, my lord?"

She'd darted a quick glance at Gabriel. He was scowling. She didn't blame him, really. Being examined like an insect could not have been pleasant, but a bit of forbearance would serve him well. It wasn't every day that a little village in a remote corner of Scotland saw a stranger. A bit of gawking was to be expected. Beyond that, if his expression was still indicative of his mood, he was going to have a truly miserable evening.

The music slid seamlessly into a jig. A handful of couples swung enthusiastically onto the floor.

"Not like that," was Gabriel's dry retort.

" 'Tis a Skye jig. They'll play a country dance soon enough. I daresay you've done something similar at a few of your grand English balls. You'll keep up well enough."

He turned that cool gaze on her. "Forgive me. I ought to have asked you before this."

Maggie felt a blush rising fast and hot in her cheeks. Embarrassment that he thought she'd been hinting was only part of it. Just as much was due to the sudden thought of putting her hand into his.

"You mistake me, my lord," she said hurriedly. "I don't care to dance. But I would be happy to introduce you to any lady you choose. There's always need for an able man on the floor here."

His eyes briefly scanned the crowd. Then, "I am not a dancer. But I thank you for the offer."

Oh, that stung a bit. He'd summarily slighted everyone present with that dismissive glance. Including her. Maggie firmly quashed the sting and forced a smile. He was a guest, she reminded herself, friend to Isobel, and she would make him feel welcome regardless of her own opinions.

Oh, but his hands were large, wide of palm and long-fingered. They would certainly engulf hers. . . .

"Maighread!"

She saw Tearlach Beaton weaving his way through the crowd, pleasant face wreathed in its customary smile.

"I'd begun to think you'd tumbled into the sea or somesuch," he informed her in Gaelic. "I've been waiting to tell you my father's right as rain this evening, thanks all to you."

"Ah, I'm glad. Have you met—"

"Come and dance with me, Maggie MacLeod. I don't care to meet your guest, thanks all the same."

Maggie rolled her eyes. "All of you, looking at him as if he has marks of the plague on him."

Her friend grinned and tossed fair hair from his brow. "Stink of London, more like. Oh, cease with your scowling. I'll bid him welcome if you'll come and dance after."

Maggie sighed. "Very well." Then, in English, "My lord, this is Tearlach Beaton. You've met his parents. Tearlach, Lord Rievaulx."

"Sir," the earl said politely, hand extended.

Tearlach took it. *"Ceud mìle fàilte, Sasunnach,"* he welcomed him. Politely.

The two took each other's measure, eyes locked, shaking hands with bone-bending force, the universal and not necessarily polite behavior of men who aren't at all certain they are going to be friends. The fact that they spoke different languages didn't affect the message in the least.

The pair couldn't have been less alike: the earl dark, grim, and severely elegant, and Tearlach fair, ruddy-faced, and genial, comfortable in the rougher clothing of a successful farmer. They were of a height, though, and no doubt in complete agreement that they weren't overly impressed with what they were seeing in the other. Maggie shook her head in exasperation. Like little boys. All of them.

Tearlach broke the handshake with a wry smile. "Surly sod," he commented without malice.

Maggie wasn't about to translate that into English for the earl's benefit. "He's a friend to Isobel and Nathan," she said yet one more time, thinking it better to remain silent on her own opinions of Rievaulx, "with ties to Argyllshire. Isobel badgered him into visiting us here. He'll be gone soon enough."

"Aye, well, I suppose we can bear him until then." Tearlach reached for her elbow and gave her a cheerful, familiar tug. "Come and dance a jig with me, bonny lassie. I see Edana making a bee's line for your Englishman."

"Perhaps she's coming to have a word with me," Maggie said tartly.

"Not likely. 'Tis Edana, after all. Now come along."

Maggie turned to Gabriel as Tearlach tugged again. "Will you excuse me, my lord? I need to . . . I'm off to . . ."

"Dance?" was the bland response. Accompanied by yet another of his clipped bows. "By all means. Dance."

She saw Edana reach Gabriel's side just as Tearlach pulled her into the center of the lively jig.

"So what do you think of our little *ceilidh*, Lord Rievaulx?" The lady waved a hand toward a far wall where a crowd of drunken young men were ogling a cluster of sweet-faced young ladies. In a nearby corner, a red-faced fellow who bore a frightening resemblance to the Hanover clan was pinching the ample bottom of a woman who, though pretty, looked to be of an age with his mother. "You arrived just in time to see us all at our end-of-the-ball best. Does it not remind you of Carlton House?"

Gabriel contemplated his response as he contemplated Lady Malcolmson. She was dressed in a tawny dress that looked very fashionable, very expensive, and just a bit risqué. The sleeves were minimal, the bodice more so, and Gabriel felt his mouth curving in an admiring smile.

There was something catlike about her, and it was more than the heart-shaped face and husky voice. She was sleek and sly and just that little bit smug. In his better days as a much younger man, he would have found her difficult to resist. But he would have. More recently, he would have taken her to bed as quickly as possible, with as little conversation as possible. Now . . . Now he found himself admiring her and even liking her. He had always, noble days and not, appreciated a sharp mind behind a comely face.

"You have brought London right into this room with that suggestion."

She tipped her head in a graceful nod. "I thought perhaps you could use a friendly and familiar image."

He glanced around the room again. He wasn't sensing any real hostility—unless he counted the surly MacDonald friend of Maggie's who was propping up a far wall. And he didn't count the surly MacDonald. But neither was there much of a welcome. Clearly Lady Malcolmson saw that, too.

"They will thaw, you know," she said airily. "And if they don't, the devil take them."

He'd thought much the same before, many times.

"The devil take them," he echoed.

"I trust you've read Dr. Johnson's memoirs of the time he passed here on Skye."

"I haven't. I wasn't aware he had visited."

Lady Malcolmson clucked her tongue. "You are a poorly armed *touriste* indeed."

"And you make it seem as if I have blighted the good name of so many who've come before, madam."

"You are far from the first Englishman to visit the island, my lord," she said blandly. "Many come for the pleasure alone. But I imagine you are far from our average visitor, as well."

Gabriel gave a noncommittal hum. His reasons for being on the island and in this room had nothing to do with pleasure, of course, although he expected he was the only person present who could say so. He felt the weight of the flask in his pocket, recently filled by his generous host, and decided the celebrations called for a good swallow.

He didn't think he'd ever seen anything quite like this gathering. Dozens of people were squeezed into the little cottage, elbow to elbow, with only a square of floor the size of one of Scarborough House's cupboards cleared for dancing. Children darted about the room, stood on their fathers' feet to be danced, slept soundly not ten feet away from the enthusiastic fiddlers. Filled plates and sloshing tankards were passed over people's heads into waiting hands.

It was as hot and noisy and crowded as any London ball. The great difference, however, was that to a person, everyone seemed to be having a marvelous time. In a fleeting moment, Gabriel could almost comprehend why.

Across the room, Maggie was smiling as she clasped hands with the blond Beaton fellow. The man was grinning, thumping about like an ox with its hooves on fire, shouting out cheerful phrases that had the other dancers laughing, Maggie blushing, and that Gabriel couldn't understand.

"He'll never get himself a wife if he proposes like that."

Gabriel's gaze snapped back to the lady at his side. "I beg your pardon?"

"Tearlach. He's just promised Maggie his undying affection and second-best cow if she'll have him."

The laughter swelled with the music.

Gabriel relaxed his tense jaw, decided there was really

no need for him to comment. "You know the language," he said instead.

"Of course I do."

"I suppose if one lived long enough in a place like this, one would learn easily enough." He knew he wouldn't be on Skye long enough and cursed himself, not for the first time, for not thinking of the language problem before he thundered off on Oriel's noble commission.

"Of the five languages I speak, I would say Scots is by far the most difficult," Lady Malcolmson commented, just a bit archly. "But I am curious: tell me, my lord, just where you think me to be from."

He hadn't given it much thought. "Edinburgh? The Borders, perhaps. Someplace far more cultivated than this."

Her laugh was as husky as her voice. "I was born," she said cheerfully, "in a two-room cottage not half a mile from the house I inhabit now." At Gabriel's raised brows, she informed him, "I married a stranger, and well. But I am a Skyewoman, my lord, with the vagaries and the ties and the language. I shall take your surprise as a compliment. It is so very gratifying to know I should still look the part should I go to London or Paris again. I have so enjoyed my times among the Beau Monde."

Unbidden, Gabriel's gaze slid across the room until it settled on a mass of auburn curls. Maggie had threaded a pale yellow ribbon through her hair. She didn't have the skills of a seasoned Society miss, or a lady's maid; the ribbon was barely visible. But Gabriel had seen it immediately—one small salute to fashion and to the evening being special—and that teasing glimpse of sunshine through the fiery silk of her hair had sent a warm little thrill through him.

"Yes, she is beautiful, our Margaret." Lady Malcolmson was watching him with amusement in her topaz cat's eyes. "A bit prone to selflessness, I fear, and moments of sadly Madonna-like placidity, but a lovely creature nonetheless. Tearlach's proposal is but a jest. She won't marry him."

"She should," Gabriel said flatly.

She should. That is precisely what women like Maggie did: they married nice local boys who would give them nice homes, nice children, nice cleaned game for the dinner table, and no sensual, winner-takes-all games on the way to the altar.

The song had ended; the couples left the dance floor or stood waiting for the music to start up again. Maggie came toward him, cheeks flushed, the familiar halo of burnished curls loose around her face.

Nice bedamned.

"Good evening, Edana," she greeted the other woman.

"Maggie. Lord Rievaulx and I were just speaking of you." When Maggie merely waited, a pleasant half smile on her face, Lady Malcolmson continued, "He seems to feel you ought to marry Tearlach Beaton."

"Does he?" There was a sharp edge to Maggie's green eyes now, and a quick flush high on her cheeks that Gabriel would wager good money was anger. But as always, she was cool and calm when she replied, "Well, we all have our opinions on the matters of other people's lives."

"So we do." Lady Malcolmson rested one hand briefly on Gabriel's arm. "I am very much afraid I cannot stay and chat, but I do hope you will call on me, my lord. I am usually to be found at home."

"Certainly, madam."

She gave one of her catlike smiles, straightened Maggie's hair ribbon in lieu of a farewell, and drifted off into the crowd.

The fiddlers launched into a Scottish reel. Gabriel

thought he'd be able to manage it. It seemed rather important just then.

"Would you do me the honor, Miss MacLeod?"

"I was under the impression you did not care to dance, my lord," she shot back.

"I could say the same of you."

Her lovely lips compressed, but she gave no retort.

"You will dance with a sweetheart, but not with a guest. Is that it?"

Maggie took the concept of hospitality very seriously and Gabriel felt no compunctions about playing on that. Selfless, Lady Malcolmson had called her. Too much so, Gabriel was fast deciding. She slowly extended a hand, looking far from eager.

He took it. And resisted the urge to determine just how silken the skin at her inner wrist was. The touch of her hand against his was enough. He felt a spark like one off a flint, felt the unthwartable tightening of his loins, and silently willed his body into submission.

"So you don't deny it," he murmured as he led her into the set.

"Deny what, my lord?"

"That Beaton is your sweetheart."

An expression he hadn't seen before flashed across her face. A combination of anger and hurt, it startled him. "I don't speak on such things at all," came her wintry reply. "I wouldn't consider it seemly." Then she whirled away with the steps of the dance.

There was scant opportunity for talk during the reel. Too much movement, too many other people bowing and weaving and getting in the way. Gabriel ignored them as best he could and watched Maggie as she moved. It was a pleasure and a torture all the same.

He held her hand longer than necessary when she

came back to his side again, waiting until she looked up at him before letting go. His eyes were hooded, deep, and she blinked before she could be drawn in. Bad enough that her pulse was skipping more merrily than her feet. She didn't need to add an addled head to the mess.

"Forgive me; I am inquisitive," he said simply. When one hand rested briefly in the small of her back, she caught her breath.

What he was, she thought hazily, was wicked. He must have known the effect he was having on her senses.

Just beyond his shoulder she saw Ina MacDonald and Stephan Tolmey chatting in the corner. They were shoulder to shoulder, and for an instant their fingers met, twined. It was a stolen moment, love being silently declared in the midst of a crowded room, and it was so piquant that Maggie wanted to cry. But she wouldn't, of course. It was too public. And it was silly, after all this time, to feel any hurt at the sight of happy lovers.

She was simply muddled, annoyed that Edana and the earl had been discussing her and Tearlach as if they had the right, thrown by Gabriel's proximity and undecipherable mood. She was tired and a little sad and the rain, pounding again outside the windows, didn't help.

At least the dance made chatter difficult. She was regretting having accepted at all. Her heart was thumping fit to rival a Highland tattoo, and she could do without the heady feeling that came with her echoing pulse.

Just a man, she told herself yet again, *who'll be gone soon enough.*

Not quite soon enough, perhaps.

She tried to keep her mind on the steps of the dance and off the fact that each time Gabriel held her hand, she felt it all the way to her toes. It was a relief when the music ended and she was able to tug her fingers from his to clap for the fiddlers. She'd thought to disappear, to curtsy and thank him for the dance and vanish into some corner. But as the dancers moved from the floor, he gestured her ahead of them.

"I need a drink," he muttered. "Allow me to fetch something for you."

"Thank you, nay," she replied. "I . . . am fine as I am."

He gave her a tight smile. "I would suspect that is an understatement. I, however, am thirsty. Take pity on me, Miss MacLeod, and point me in the right direction."

Resigned, she led him instead. He accepted a dram of whiskey from Mrs. Tolmey, tossed it back. She saw his eyes fall on the lovers in the corner. "Well," he commented, "there's a pair who would clearly rather be somewhere else."

Maggie disagreed. "I would say they just want to be together. The where doesn't matter."

"Of course it does, but you are possessed of a romantic heart, Maggie MacLeod."

"And you are not," she murmured before she could stop herself.

It was a twisted grin that Gabriel gave her. "I am possessed of none at all."

Maggie wondered if he truly believed that. Then she wondered if perhaps she shouldn't believe it completely.

He paused with a second drink halfway to his lips. Then he narrowed his eyes and glanced around the room. "Good God, what is that noise?" he demanded. "Do you hear it?"

How could she not? Somewhere between a wail and a bellow, it resonated through the cottage.

Maggie closed her eyes for a weary moment. " 'Tis my father."

"Is he in pain?"

She shook her head. She wished she could keep the earl out of this familiar familial mess, but didn't see how. "Nay, not yet."

"Not . . . ?"

"He's being a bagpipe," she said simply. *And will have a fierce pounding in his head come morning,* she added silently. But her father never thought about such things when he was drinking. Morning, to him, like all consequences, was something at least a few hours away.

Jamie was holding court in the center of the room, his wobbling baritone swelling and receding with the imaginary bellows he pumped with his elbow. "*Nnnnnnnnnnn,*" he sang. "*Wahhhhhhhhhh, nnnnnnnn, ahhhhhnnn!*"

Tessa was at the edge of the delighted audience. " 'Awá Tee the War'?" she said cheerfully.

"Nay," Maggie sighed. " 'Tis 'All My Endearing Young Charms.' "

"Ah." To Gabriel, the girl announced, " 'Tis a slow march."

"So I gathered."

Behind Jamie, Maggie could see Fen MacDonald and Calum MacAuley marching solemnly in a small circle. Both had their eyes closed in concentration. For his own part, Jamie was listing to starboard and getting closer to the floor with every pump of his arm. Maggie edged up beside him and slipped one arm around his waist. He wheezed into silence. Then boomed, "Maggie, lass!" blasting her with whiskey fumes. "I've always said any man can play the pipes if he but puts a bit of weight into it." He pumped his elbow in demonstration.

"So you have, Papa."

"Not difficult a'tall. All in the arm and the lungs . . ."

He opened his mouth to bellow again. Maggie suggested, "Why don't you play us home, darling. We'll march over the heath."

"Home? Nay, nay. We're off to catch the will-o'-the-wisp, the lads and me!" He waved at Fen MacDonald, who'd stopped his circling and was now merely marching in place. "Fen says they're dancing to the west."

Maggie eyed Fen tiredly. "Does he now?"

The old man nodded. "I saw them, I did. Last night." He scratched his bald pate. "Or was it the night before?"

"In English!" Jamie yelled suddenly, pointing now at Gabriel. "For m'guest. He's not such a bad sort for an Englishman. Are you, lad?"

"Papa," Maggie chided.

"I have my moments," she heard Gabriel say evenly.

"Bollocks," said Fen. "Toads and kippers!" His knowledge of the language was fair, his use of it creative.

"He saw the will-o'-the-wisp," Jamie informed Gabriel cheerfully, the Highland brogue that appeared only when he was sotted making him nearly as hard to understand as Fen. "Fairy lights. Coming o'er the midnight sea to Skye."

"Did he row his dinghy out to catch it?" Tessa wanted to know.

Calum snorted. " 'Twould have been a daft man to row anything into the Sound this sennight past. The tides have jumped something fierce."

"Bunkum," said Fen.

Jamie nodded and gave the man a consoling pat on the back. "So we're off tonight to have another go."

Maggie bit her lip. "It's raining again, Papa. There will be no fairy lights tonight."

"Nay?" Tottering over to the window, pulling Maggie with him, Jamie pressed his nose to the glass and gazed mournfully into the night. "Well, bother."

"Bollocks," said Fen sadly. "Toads and nonsense."

The party, suddenly, was over.

Fortunately, the rain let up enough for them to make their way home. Gabriel supported Jamie with a strong arm around his back, matching his steps to the much smaller man's weaving ones with a steady patience. All the while Jamie wheezed and hummed his piping finest. They paused once so Jamie could adjust his imaginary bellows. Apparently they weren't working properly, as he ended with a long, mournful note.

"Are you all right, sir?" Gabriel asked solemnly. "Can you carry on? Walking," he added quickly.

"Oh, aye. Aye. Tho' perhaps you ought to sit down, lad. You're listing something fierce. We canna have you falling."

"No, that we cannot." Gabriel took a bit more of Jamie's weight on his arm. "We'll rest a moment here." He turned to Maggie. "The task falls on you again, Miss MacLeod, to tell a tale."

"Of what?" she asked.

"Of the fairy lights, of course. I find I am most curious."

"Oh, nay—"

"Go on, Maggie," Tessa urged. "I would do it, but I cannot seem to get it right."

"Please," Gabriel said simply, and that was that.

"Ach, very well, but 'tisn't much. Long ago, so the story says," Maggie began, "the Chief of Clan McKay needed fire so his people would be fed. Seeing fairy flames dancing in the night, he followed and grabbed the smallest one when it lagged behind. The fairies were so outraged that they vowed forever to taunt mortals with their light. No man would capture it again, they swore. And none has." She stopped, met Gabriel's even gaze, and flushed.

"Will-o'-the-wisp," he muttered. "Fairy lights."

" 'Tis an ancient tale," she declared, defending it, "and not such a bad one."

"I did not say it was. Do you think me so hard to please, Maggie?"

For an instant, a warm and fleeting moment, she wondered what it would be like to try. She resolutely banished the thought and replied, "I hadn't thought on it, my lord."

"Probably wise," she thought she heard him say, then he hefted her now snoring father over his shoulder and struck off toward home.

"Which room?" he asked Maggie once they were inside.

"Top of the stairs, first on the right."

Tessa ran ahead to turn back Jamie's covers.

Gabriel nodded. "Good night, Maggie."

"Good night, my lord."

She watched as he carried her father up the first steps. Jamie opened bleary eyes. "I was goin' to chase the will-o'-the-wisp, I was," he slurred sadly to the back of Gabriel's coat.

"So you were, sir," came the even reply. "I promise you there will be other chances."

"Aye, so there will. Good lad," Jamie mumbled, knocking Gabriel's hat over the bannister when he slung an arm up to pat the younger man on the head.

Maggie picked it up. Without thinking, she stroked the lush felt as she watched the pair of them go.

⇥ 7 ⇤

The Old Ones tell of thyme in hand to bring the faeries
and thyme in the air after murder most foul.
'Tis said he bore the scent of wild thyme, our lad,
as he made his way through lands where angels fell.
                                    —Dubhgall MacIain MacLeòid

*The fairies were so outraged that they vowed forever
to taunt mortals with their light. No man would capture
it again, they swore. And none has.*

What nonsense. Gabriel narrowed his eyes against the
wind and flattened himself as best he could against
the cold rock beneath his belly. *Fairies. Will-o'-the-wisps.*
There was no doubt in his mind that what the farmer had
seen was a very real light on the cliffs. So here he was,
prone at what felt like the end of the earth, waiting.

Gabriel had spent many a more uncomfortable night.
In Spain, on his way to Barcelona with a communiqué
for Brandon, he'd passed a good thirty hours hiding
from enemy soldiers in a mountain hole meant for a creature half his size. And that in December. In Portugal, a
crucial missive from Montgomerie and Rotheroe folded
uncomfortably in the toe of his boot, he had traveled the
three hundred miles from the southern port city of Cadiz
to Lisbon in the deep bowels of a merchant ship, sharing
his makeshift berth with salt, sea, and the occasional rat.

He shouldn't have been bothered at all by his present
situation. He was home from the war with all his limbs
and most of his wits intact. He was out in the almost too
fresh air, well bundled in his wool coat and breeches, hat
pulled low over his forehead against the encroaching sea

breeze. But there was something prodding at him, an unease that niggled and nagged and had the fine hairs at his nape rising.

Mist and wind, he told himself, and the inevitable softening that came with far too much drink and too little activity.

Midnight, the old man had said at the *ceilidh* the night before. The dancing lights had appeared then. It would be very near midnight now. From his vantage point near the cliff's edge, partially sheltered by rocks and heather, Gabriel squinted into the dark and damp. He thought he might have seen . . . Yes, there it was again, that faint flutter of light, perhaps twenty yards away along the cliffs. It flashed weakly, almost lost in the mist for which Skye was so famed, then appeared again. Gabriel couldn't detect a pattern, but the movement could well be deliberate.

Pulse quickening, muscles tensed, he moved as stealthily as he could. Staying flat on the ground, using his bent arms, he pulled himself closer to the edge. He could hear the water far below, pounding and hissing. The beach would be a half mile to the west; beneath him would be only rocks and white water. He couldn't see much of anything, but stared intently toward where he knew the rocky, inhospitable little island of Soay lay, perhaps three miles into the Sound. If this was, in fact, his quarry, waiting for a signal from the ship that would bear him away from the Isles, Soay would be the first contact. Barra was too far away for light to carry.

So that was it. L'Écossais's transport would come from Barra to Soay and signal from there. L'Écossais had only to wait until it arrived, then make his way to the little island in the Cuillin Sound. From there he would sail to Ireland or France or wherever he chose.

Gabriel didn't think any beacon short of one from a lighthouse would pierce this fog. If someone was waiting for L'Écossais on Soay, there would be no contact tonight.

He would follow the light here on Skye. With luck, he would be following his quarry right to wherever the man was lodged. That would make his job infinitely easier. He would be able to return in his own time and, in his own way, make the traitor simply disappear. No mess, no struggle, no witnesses.

Rolling away from the edge, coming up into a ready crouch, he looked to where the light had been. And waited for it to reappear. And waited. Finally, after several minutes of staring into the dense darkness, he made his way forward, cursing. *Never take your eyes off your opponent.* The first rule of combat and he'd already blundered.

He assumed whoever had been there with the lantern would be walking back toward the village, toward any of the cottages and outbuildings that made up the community. So he headed for the cliff road, the one he and Maggie had taken only the day before. Even in the seemingly impenetrable dark, he found the path easily and quietly.

Three days on Skye, and Gabriel felt as if he'd been there for aeons. But then, small places, peopled with families whose roots ran deep as ore, had a way of doing that to a man. He'd survive it, he thought sardonically. And he wouldn't give the place another thought as soon as he left.

Ah, but Maggie . . . In a mere three days, she had made him feel at home in her home. Her hospitality might have been reluctant, but he didn't think she could help herself. Each warm, oat-laced meal, the cider from the stone jar in the pantry, the ever-present scent of cloves that hovered around her—each little detail served to draw him in that little bit more. It had been a long time since Gabriel had had to notice details. The most he'd bothered with of late had been making certain that barmaids didn't short-change him before he was ready to stop drinking. Now he was noticing too much. The way firelight picked out certain gold and copper lights in her hair, sunlight others. That the only mark or freckle on her beautiful face was a single dark spot beside one winged brow. That her stockings, when her quick movements gave him a glimpse of her shapely calves, were sturdy lisle rather than silk.

He'd never wanted to caress cotton quite so much.

There, he thought wryly. She'd done it again. Slipped into his mind when she absolutely shouldn't be there. He needed his full attention on a matter that would no doubt horrify Maggie should she be privy to his task and plans. He didn't think she would take too kindly to his fantasies about her, either.

He imagined there were lightskirts to be found on Skye. There were lightskirts to be found almost everywhere in the world. He would very discreetly ask Jamie MacLeod, gentleman to gentleman. He suspected his host would enthusiastically lead him toward drink and other jollity. Or Edana Malcolmson would probably welcome him into her bed with open arms. Either way, he needed to slake this damnable thirst and leave the serene, inviolate Margaret as untouched as he'd found her. Not for the first time, he cursed what few scruples he had left. Damned nuisance, the human conscience. If he could simply toss his over the convenient cliff—lock, stock, and sorry memories.

He had given so much of his integrity away over the past year—tossing it, really, hand over fist with each coin that bought the basic pleasures. And he hadn't cared. The cards and rotgut and willing women had been enough. All he'd needed to satisfy were his base desires.

It had been a very long time since he'd wanted something he couldn't just buy or take, even longer since it had mattered. And it pricked like a tangle of thorns. He wanted Maggie MacLeod and he couldn't have her. . . .

His attention had lapsed. He'd stopped scanning the dark path intently as he went, and the figure looming suddenly toward him from the night had him giving a muffled curse and scrabbling for the second time in as many days for a weapon that wasn't there. Then, deadly and quick, his military training clicked into place. He swept out his left hand, getting a lethal grip on the individual's throat. There was a strangled yelp, then the figure went wild, flailing and flapping its arms in a futile attempt to get away.

It took Gabriel a moment to realize that whoever it was was a good head shorter than he, at least four stone lighter, and had all the fighting skills of a landed flounder. A single thrust of his shoulder and flick of his wrist had his opponent flat on the ground with his knee planted firmly in the heaving chest.

"Who are you?" he demanded, loosening his grip very slightly.

He felt throat muscles working jerkily beneath his fingers. "A-Andy," came the croaked response.

"Who?"

"Andy MacAuley."

The voice was the combined growl and squeak of an adolescent boy, and Gabriel suddenly had a very good idea of just who he was pinning to the ground. "The innkeeper's son?"

"Aye, my lord . . . sir."

Cursing, he released the boy, who stayed right where he was, flat on his back, gasping. If Gabriel wasn't mistaken, young MacAuley was a mere pup, no older than Tessa. At least he was one of the ones who spoke English. "What in God's name are you doing out here at this time of night?"

"W-waiting, sir."

Now Gabriel's senses went on alert again. "Waiting for what?" he snapped, leaning in.

Andy swallowed audibly. "I canna tell—"

"*For what?*"

"For the *Sasunnach* . . . the Englishman."

Gabriel sat back on his heels, mind racing. Was it possible that Oriel's intelligence had been wrong? That L'Écossais wasn't a Scot after all, but an Englishman familiar with the Highlands. . . ?

"I've seen him, you ken," the boy was insisting. "Right here. Her, too."

Her? An island woman lured into helping Napoleon's cause? Possible, but for the moment, Gabriel was more interested in the man. "What does he look like?" he demanded. "Do you know him?"

"Know him? I . . . Nay, though . . . Nay. Only to see. And he's a grim sight, he is, with seaweed wrapped all about him and his head a bloody mess."

"Seaweed . . . bloody mess . . ." This was beginning to sound vaguely and unpleasantly familiar. "You're speaking of the local ghost," he said flatly.

"Aye, to be sure. Two, really. The *Sasunnach* and M—"

"Enough." Gabriel did not want to hear more. The only things worse than fairy tales, after all, were ghost stories. "Where's your lantern?" Gabriel needed to know if it was MacAuley he'd seen on the cliff edge. If not, whoever it was would be long gone.

"I haven't one." There was pride in the youthful voice. "I don't need a light. Besides, 'twould only let the ghosts—"

"*Enough*. Go home, boy."

Young MacAuley pulled in his unwieldy limbs and sat up, but made no move to leave. "Tessa's spoken of you. You were at war with her brother-in-law. She said a great many things."

"God help me," Gabriel muttered.

"She says you remind her of the dead *Sasunnach*. The one who walks here."

In one of those twists of weather that only someone born to such climes would accept as normal, the heavy clouds overhead parted suddenly, and the moon shone weakly through. Gabriel could just make out the boy's skinny frame, knees drawn up to his chest, could see the whites of wide eyes.

"Is it true, sir?"

"That there are ghosts walking the cliff here? Of course not!"

"Oh." Now the boy sounded disappointed. " 'Tis a shame you don't believe, you being a *Sasunnach* and all. But that wasn't what I meant. I wanted to know if you'd been to war. With Isobel's husband."

Gabriel sighed. This was not how he had imagined his midnight foray. He was tired, frustrated, and not particularly inclined to have a lad-to-lad chat with the unpleasant innkeeper's son. God only knew what the Islanders fed their young to make them so pesty. "I have been to war," he answered finally. "With Isobel's husband."

"He's a hero, Tessa says."

"Yes. He is a hero."

"Are you?"

Gabriel flinched. He couldn't help it. Not that the boy would see. "No," he muttered. "I'm not."

Undaunted, Andy pressed, "Was it fierce? My cousin Lon joined the Glasgow Highland Light Artillery and sends the grandest letters from the south. They're training him to use a bayonet and fire cannons and march round the big square in time to the pipers. 'Tis a right grand life." The boy hugged his legs closer in excitement. "I want the war to last long enough for me to join up."

"God forbid."

"Sir?"

Gabriel had had more than enough. "War is dirty, dishonest, and about as grand as a goose egg," he said sharply. "Grow up and buy cows or sheep or some rooty vegetables instead, MacAuley. Find yourself a nice island girl. Get married. Spawn."

"Sir!" was the horrified response, and Gabriel nearly smiled, remembering his own opinion of settling down when he was this fellow's age. Odd, it seemed he didn't feel quite so strongly about it now, and he couldn't remember when that had changed.

"Go home, MacAuley, before your charming father finds you missing."

"Ach," the boy said dismissively, "I go out near every night."

Gabriel tucked that bit of information away for later use. "Be that as it may, this is no place for a boy your age at this time of night."

He rose and loomed, waiting to be obeyed. There was a bit of grumbling, but Andy finally shoved himself to his feet. "Sir." Gabriel heard the shaky intake of breath.

"You might flatten me again, but I thought I'd ask anyway. What are *you* doing out here?"

"Thinking about ghosts." Half-truths, Gabriel thought cynically, were such a nice departure from out-and-out lies.

Apparently Andy took him at his word, for he nodded his head emphatically, sending overlong hair flopping. "I come most nights, but I've only seen them a half-dozen times, mayhaps, and never up close."

"Count yourself fortunate for that."

"Sir?"

Gabriel waved off the question. He didn't care to explain just what an up-close contemplation of ghosts could do to a man. "Tell me, MacAuley, do you see anyone else out here at night?"

"Not usually, though sometimes Mr. MacLeod comes tottering along. Worries me, it does, seeing him like that. He does go along three sheets to the winds most nights—" The boy broke off abruptly. "Begging your pardon, my lord."

"Why? It was my estimable host you were calling a drunk," Gabriel said mildly. "Not me."

"Aye, but he's Maggie's da, and you'd be fancying Maggie."

"Nonsense." Oh, he fancied her indeed. He just didn't care to hear the words from a thirteen-year-old pup. "Did you see someone—"

"If you're thinking to make her promises and then break them, you'd best think again."

Gabriel watched as young MacAuley suddenly grew another several inches, stretching, no doubt, right up onto his toes. It might have been charming if it wasn't so silly. Maggie could add one more name to her list of loyal swains. "I have no intention of doing any such thing."

"Well, good. Otherwise you might well be seeing the cliffs from the bottom. Like the other *Sasunnach*."

As far as threats went, this one lacked some force. But Gabriel didn't doubt his being a man around Maggie made him suspect to all and sundry. Being an Englishman made it all that much worse. Fortunately for him, his purpose for being on Skye wasn't as easily identified as his sex or accent.

"I'll bear that in mind, MacAuley."

"Aye. Good." The boy lowered himself to stand flatfooted. "Ah, sir . . . You won't be telling my da you saw me here, will you?"

"Would he beat you?"

"My da? Not likely. He'd lecture something fierce, and I'd almost rather a beating."

"I see. Well, then, let's make a deal, shall we? I'll keep your midnight rambles a secret if you'll do the same for me."

"But you're a man grown. And a duke, no less." The boy sounded incredulous enough that Gabriel opted not to correct him. "You can do as you like."

"Yes, I certainly can. But you know Maggie. She takes care of everyone. It would worry her to know anyone was out along the cliffs at night. She would lecture something fierce. . . ."

"And you'd almost rather have a beating." Andy laughed. "You know, Maggie comes out here more than anyone else. My da wanted to build a fence to keep her safe."

Curious, Gabriel thought. He couldn't imagine Maggie daydreaming on the edge of the earth. She wouldn't allow herself the time. "Did he?"

"Nay. Everyone knew she'd just climb right over the

top. But she would fash herself over knowing we were out here."

"Our secret, then?"

"Oh, aye!"

"Good lad." Gabriel gave the boy a light shove, sending him on his way. He wondered if Andy escaped his chamber in the same way he himself had left the MacLeod house: handholds between the stones of the wall. Some had clearly been chiseled deeper, no doubt by the MacLeod brothers. They were an indolent pair; such an act had probably been among their greater exertions.

He recalled how very daring such escapes had seemed in his own schoolroom days. He'd come home on holiday from school at fourteen to find an ivy trellis in place beside his window. How convenient, he'd thought, gloating over the gullibility of the household. It had taken him until adulthood to realize the thing had been ordered by his grandfather—to keep him from falling and breaking his young, fool neck on those dark nights when youthful wanderlust had him prowling Scarborough House's grounds and environs.

The moon was gone behind the clouds again now, but he would find his way back to the MacLeods' easily enough. He took a last look at the cliff edge, barely visible through the thickening mist. He blinked. For the briefest instant, he'd thought he saw a figure there. And not just any figure, but a slight one—in a skirt that was being lifted by the wind. But there was nothing there now.

He shook his head. Nothing.

He would be back in daylight. Now that he'd found L'Écossais's night watch spot, he needed to see it in the day. If he could, he would bring Maggie and perhaps get one unguarded minute from her. . . .

Beautiful Maggie, with her fire-touched hair and shadowed eyes, was drawing him, strongly enough that he was staggered by the strength of the pull. There were plenty of beautiful women in the world, in Scotland. By all rights, she should be but one more. Somehow, she wasn't.

He wasn't certain just what intrigued him so much about her. Her quietness, perhaps, that innate calm he thought was probably necessary to keep her from running mad in the midst of her devil-may-care family. There was, too, an ever-present hint of sadness about her, although he'd be damned if he could find anything for her to be sad about. He'd never seen a simpler life than hers. But the suggestion was there and Gabriel didn't know many men who could resist a little bit of melancholy in a beautiful woman. The challenge to try to replace it with flushed delight was just too appealing.

Damn, but he would have liked the chance to try.

It had been a long time since he'd engaged in an internal battle of ethics against desire. He was, he decided as he crept up the cottage path, sorely out of practice.

There was a tiny light burning in the upper hall. Opting for a simpler way into the house than chinks in a wall, he made use of the parlor window. Once in, he silently removed his hat, coat, and boots and stashed them behind the door. He had a very good idea who was treading down the stairs. All he had to do was wait.

Maggie resignedly set her candle on the kitchen table and pulled her soft wool wrap around her shoulders. She hadn't been able to sleep. Moving quietly so as not to wake anyone else, she'd wandered downstairs. If she was to be awake, best to get some work done.

She lit the fire under the kettle and prepared a pot for

tea. It was a shame she had seen to the minimal household accounts the day before. The task would have occupied her mind, held off the thoughts for which she had neither patience nor desire. All she could do now, in the middle of the night, was sort herbs. They were already neat in their bundles or bottles, but it was the time of year when her stores were at their lowest and it would serve her well to know how much of each she had left.

A few minutes later, cup of tea at her elbow, bottles and bundles spread over the table, she set to work. Chamomile. There was plenty of that. Mint oil. Not as much, but mint was easily gathered in spring. Sage . . . Thyme . . . *Savoury, sage, rosemary, and thyme.*

She had known the man for three days—just three days. How was it that he filled her mind, lodged there like a wine-swelled cork? She knew better. She knew what feeling for a man could do. And still she was thinking of Gabriel.

"Ah, Mairghread," she muttered. "What happened to you?"

Glancing down at her hands, she discovered she had crushed a palmful of dried thyme. Annoyed, disgusted with herself, she poured the crumbled herbs into a jar and pushed away from the table.

"Isn't it a bit early for breakfast?"

Her heart lodged in her throat and she slapped her hand there as if to keep it from bursting out. *"Dia s'Muire,"* she gasped. "You've just stolen ten years of my life!"

Gabriel leaned in the doorway. "Ladies who creep about kitchens in the dead of night cannot complain about being startled."

" 'Tis my kitchen and I was hardly creeping." She thought he must be cold, stocking-footed as he was, with only a shirt over his breeches. For her own part, she was feeling decidedly warm. "What are you about, down here at this hour?"

He sauntered into the room, sniffed at the collection of herbs on the table. "Smells like you. Ah, why . . . I couldn't sleep. Neither could you, I assume."

"Aye, waukin' O," she murmured, moving instinctively for another mug and for a bit of distance between them. "Will you have some tea?"

"Thank you. What did you say just before that?"

"Aye, waukin' O. 'Tis from a Burns song."

" 'Wokkin'?"

"It means sleepless. 'Sleep I can get nane.' "

Gabriel accepted the tea and settled himself at the table. It irked Maggie how very comfortable he looked, as if he belonged and wouldn't soon be taking himself back to London's velvet-draped drawing rooms.

"And what was keeping Burns nane sleeping?"

"Stomachache," she replied tersely.

She was not about to tell him that Robbie was waukin' still and weary from thinking on his dearie. It sounded silly outside the song—and was altogether too personal for her peace of mind. She'd spent too many aching, sleepless nights to walk open-eyed into another. Deciding now that if Gabriel was to be prowling downstairs she ought to take herself back to her chamber, she began clearing the table.

"What are you doing?" he asked, reaching out to snare a sprig of dried rosemary.

"Cleaning so I may go to bed."

"I thought you were wokkin."

"I was busy. You can't sleep."

"Maggie—"

"There's shortbread in the blue jar if you're hungry."

"Maggie." He came up from his seat suddenly, so

quick and smooth that she could only draw a sharp breath as his hand covered hers, pinning it to the table. "Don't go."

They faced each other across the scarred wood. The flickering candlelight cast his features into sharp relief and shadows, making those cutting cheekbones stand out all the more. Above them, his eyes glinted silver. And that mouth, the poet's mouth in the warrior's face, called to her. In that instant, she wanted to reach up to trace his lower lip with her fingertip, just to touch for a moment.

She hastily pulled her hand from beneath his. "I should . . . go."

"Why?" He was still leaning on the table, hands braced between a bundle of wild thyme and one of fragrant heather. "Haven't you decided by now that I'm not going to harm you?"

Harm came in so many forms, she thought. Aloud, she said, "I'm not afraid of you, my lord—"

"Gabriel."

"Aye. Gabriel, with the angel's name. I really don't know you at all."

"Sit down," he said, coaxing and commanding at once with his gaze, "and I'll tell you whatever you want to know."

Oh, it was tempting. There was so much she wanted to ask him. What kept him awake at night while others slept. If he dreamed. If his dreams were of a sweetheart waiting for him back in England—some pale, delicate nobleman's daughter who embroidered and painted and could play a Burns tune on the pianoforte but had been well sheltered from the Scottish bard's earthy, heartfelt words.

She wanted to ask why he was there, on Skye. Why he was really there. Men like the Earl of Rievaulx didn't come to the ends of the earth to see the sights. They came to find something. Or lose something. But she wouldn't pry. She knew too much about longing, and about flight.

"Are you not sorry to be missing the Season?" she managed lightly.

He blinked at her. "Sorry?"

"Aye." Not wanting to sit again, she busied herself with tidying the table as she spoke. "I'd have thought you'd be in Town, for the Parliamentary session and the social whirl."

She glanced up, startled, at his sharp, humorless laugh. "Is that where you think I belong?" he demanded.

"Don't you? 'Tisn't unexpected, to be sure, but Skye hardly seems your sort of place."

"You mean I am hardly Skye's sort of person."

She paused in the midst of binding up the thyme. "I didn't say that."

"Mmm. I would wager everyone else nearby has."

"Well, I wouldn't presume to speak for anyone else. But you seem to be all that a gentleman of your place and status is meant to be."

"Ah, Maggie. You could do a man serious damage, speaking of him in such gracious terms." He reached out, took a sprig of thyme between his fingers, and rubbed it into dust. Then he met her eyes and shrugged. "You might be surprised to know with how little grace my estimable peers have been known to speak of me."

"That," she murmured, "is your business and none of my concern."

"Are you always so damnably virtuous?"

She winced at the language, flinched inwardly at the truthful answer. *Not at all.* She could only imagine what he would think of her if he knew the truth. "I like to believe I go about my life with merit."

There was a long moment of silence. Then, "My God," he murmured, "Lady Malcolmson really was dead on, wasn't she? You are a pious creature."

"I am not—"

He cut off her hot retort. "You are careful, inviolate, and that little bit saintly. Or is it angelic? No saint would look as you do."

"Sir!"

"Ah, and now I have offended you. I cannot believe you are unaware of how lovely you are."

"That is just my face," she shot back, thoroughly rattled now.

"I would say it's more than that." She didn't see him move, but in an instant he had her wrist circled in his fingers. "Aren't you at all curious about the darker side of life, Maggie MacLeod?"

Her heart was going like thunder. She was convinced he would feel her pulse rioting under his grasp. "Why are you doing this?" she whispered.

He tugged gently, steadily, until she was leaning on the table. The candle burned between them, its flame reflected in his eyes. He shoved it aside. It wobbled for a moment in its well-worn stand, nearly toppling into the scattered herbs.

"I haven't the vaguest idea." His voice was rough at the edges and her pulse fluttered again. "I know better. Damned but I know better. Go ahead, then," he said, and Maggie wondered if she was imagining the challenge in his tone. "Send me away. No doubt you'll want me out of your house."

To be sure, she thought, she should want him gone. She certainly wasn't going to be spoken to as if she were . . . As if she were naive. Simple. *Innocent*.

The irony wasn't lost on her. Here was a man who saw

her as an innocent, when she was nothing of the sort. Even more remarkable was the fact that he, by simply holding her hand across a table, was engendering thoughts and feelings more sinful than any she'd ever known.

Maggie shivered. "You'll release me, please."

He did, but not before sliding his thumb across the sensitive skin at her inner wrist. She shivered again. "Well?" he demanded. "Shall I pack my things?"

"If your conscience tells you to, aye." She dragged her gaze from his, looking instead at the tabletop. "But as long as you don't touch me again, I won't be telling you to go. You're a friend—"

"To Nathan and Isobel," he said gruffly. "And so I am. I'll stay."

"As you wish." There was a ripple of dried candle wax on the bundled heather, reminding Maggie of the blaze he could have set. She gathered the herbs with trembling hands. "I'll bid you a good night, then, my lord."

"Gabriel."

She sealed the last of the bottles without answering, returned them to their shelves.

"Mairghread."

She stopped halfway to the door but didn't turn. "Aye?"

"Angels fall on Skye, too, you know."

"So do bold Englishmen," she said evenly, and left the room.

⧗ 8 ⧗

As I roved out by the sea side,
(Ev'ry rose grows merry in time),
I met a sweet girl,
And I gave her my hand,
And I says, "Will you be a true lover of mine?"

Maggie's steps dragged a bit as she approached Edana Malcolmson's house. She wasn't sure she was up to a session of the other woman's languid insights and unintended—or not—insults. But Tessa had apparently shattered one of Edana's Italian glass vases during an ill-fated lesson in dancing, and Maggie felt some recompense was in order. She had a bottle of her lavender water and several rose sachets in her basket.

MacGillechallum, glowering and rumpled looking, eventually answered her knock and gestured her into Edana's sanctum. The lady was there on her chaise, garbed in a lush silk dressing gown that could only have come from some exotic Eastern locale, bottle of amber liquid near to hand.

"Ah, Maggie." Edana waved her into a seat. "What a nice surprise. Brandy?"

"Thank you, nay."

"I thought you would refuse." Edana tipped a measure into her glass. "But one can always hope."

A dark, heavy scent wafted through the room from a little brazier. It made Maggie think of things she had never seen: minareted palaces, gold-tiled fountains, ruby silk sheets. Insistent and heady, the perfume was making her a little dizzy. And it was making her think of Gabriel.

Memories of the warm little interlude with Gabriel had been slipping through her mind all morning. Each time she ruthlessly shoved them away, they sprang back: the feel of his hand on hers, his face in the flickering candlelight. The certainty that if she hadn't moved, had given in to the compelling pull of him, he would have kissed her with that wicked mouth. Even now, the swift tug of longing startled and frightened her. How easy it would be to give in, to allow herself just one small taste of these things that called to her—that she barely understood. How sweet and easy.

And how patently, completely self-destructive.

She shook her head, dispelling the thoughts, and looked up to find the other woman studying her with cat-like eyes. "Dare I ask?" Edana queried, lush mouth curving.

"Ask. . . ?" Maggie waved a hand sharply in front of her face, annoyed with the pervasive perfumed smoke, annoyed by her own weakness and the other woman's elegant smugness.

"You seem to be engaged in a weighty inner debate, my dear. I daresay it is a fascinating one."

"Capon or mutton for dinner," Maggie said evenly. "I cannot decide." She then bent down to open her basket, determined not to stay any longer than decorum demanded. "I've brought you some things. Not worth near the value of your vase, I'm sure, but . . ."

Edana took the bottle and sachets with a smile and set them on the table beside the brandy. "You really must avoid undue modesty. It does so remove the bloom from one's visage. And the vase doesn't matter. I'll get another when next I am in Venice."

"Are you planning to travel, then?" It was an old subject, Edana's leaving Skye, but Maggie was determined to be gracious.

"I am, as it happens. Soon perhaps. I'm tiring of this place."

That was even older. Edana had been tired of the island since she'd been old enough to understand there was a world beyond it.

Maggie, as always, it seemed, wanted nothing more than to shelter herself among the familiar walks and faces. She wanted that precious feeling of perfect equilibrium back—the one she'd had for a few fleeting minutes between casting one blithe-tongued Englishman's memory over the cliff and meeting another on the high road.

The thought of throwing her fate to the winds and the English Channel was not one she had any desire to contemplate.

"Paris first, *je pense*," Edana was saying. "Everything begins in Paris. Then Italy, top to toe . . . Are you leaving so soon?"

Maggie had tidied her basket and now held it in her lap. "I must. I've a roast to prepare. I merely wanted to stop by to deliver . . ." She gestured to her offerings on the table, so rustic among the lacquered boxes and odd little carvings.

"I very much look forward to using them." Edana watched Maggie rise. "So you've decided against the capon and mutton, I assume."

Maggie set her jaw, determined not to blush. "I have."

"Well, then, best get to it." Edana stretched a silk-clad leg, but didn't rise. "But first, you must tell me how you're getting on with your guest. I cannot imagine Lord Rievaulx is the easiest man to manage."

Only as easy as the tide, Maggie thought with a tiny

shiver. She said carefully, "We welcome all guests. And we don't see so very much of this one."

"No, I suppose you don't. Lord Rievaulx seems to be occupying himself well enough about the island. I'm certain he and I shall cross paths again soon enough. You will give him my best when next *you* see him, won't you?"

Maggie didn't much care for Edana's cool certainty, cared even less for her own vaguely angry response to it. "I will."

"Good." Edana reached for her glass again. "Dare I offer you some advice?"

"On. . . ?"

"Oh, life, I suppose. You don't mind, do you?"

Minding had never seemed to keep Edana from stating her opinion in the past. Maggie sighed. "Of course not," she said a bit tightly. "I know you wish me only the best."

She did sarcasm poorly, always had. Edana nodded, clearly none the wiser. "Of course I do. And I merely want to comment that you haven't seen much of the world. There is a naivete to you. . . ."

"Oh, to be sure."

"No, no. It is most charming. But you really must make a point of looking at things more than once, darling, at people more than once. One is very seldom what one seems at first glance."

An enigmatic offering, Maggie thought. And as appealing as day-old bread. "I expect you're absolutely correct, Edana. Thank you."

"Oh, it is my pleasure." Something in the other woman's eyes told Maggie that her spurious thanks hadn't been misread. "We doughty Scotswomen must see to keeping life on the correct path, mustn't we? After all, we certainly cannot depend upon the menfolk to do so."

Edana laughed at that, a jesting, trilling sound, but as far as Maggie was concerned, there was altogether too much truth in the thought.

Gabriel fingered the pouch of coins in his coat pocket as he pushed through the inn's door. Inside the tavern, a split pine fire burned cheerily in the stone hearth, dispelling the damp and chill of the evening. Two old men were seated around a small table, hunched over their tankards and what sounded like rolling dice. MacAuley stood near his taps, face set in its perpetual scowl, arms crossed over his barrel chest.

His scowl deepened at the sight of Gabriel. The two patrons glanced up. Gabriel recognized them both. Fen MacDonald muttered something that sounded like "rat sticks." Old Mr. Beaton lifted a gnarled hand in what seemed to be a welcoming wave.

"What can I do for you?" MacAuley grunted.

"Whiskey," Gabriel replied, returning Beaton's wave and striding unhurriedly to the bar. He removed the pouch from his pocket and slid a shilling toward MacAuley. "And whatever you gentlemen are having."

The innkeeper grunted again, but was quick enough to pocket the coin. He poured Gabriel's whiskey and one for himself. "The *Sasunnach*'s bought you a wee one, lads."

Fen MacDonald was on his feet in a creaky instant. He tottered over, three tankards in hand. "*Ta,*" he mumbled in Gabriel's direction, then as soon as MacAuley had poured, returned to his table. He said something in Gaelic; Beaton raised his hand again with a smile.

"Gracious sod," Gabriel muttered, then, "The third is for . . . luck?"

MacAuley merely tossed back his drink. Gabriel gestured for him to pour himself another.

His question was answered when his host suddenly rolled through a nearby doorway. Jamie had disappeared soon after supper and it was evident he'd come straight to his "club." His nose was a cheerful pink, his gait unsteady, and he was whistling a lively tune.

"Gabriel, lad!" he exclaimed happily. "What a pleasure." He weaved his way to the table, peered into his tankard, and grinned broadly. "A pleasure indeed. Come sit! And you, too, Calum. 'Tisn't as if you'll see much custom tonight."

Gabriel took out another coin. MacAuley's heavy black brows drew together. Then he shrugged, grabbed a whiskey bottle in each hand, and made his way over to the table. Jamie pulled up two more chairs and the party, albeit not the merriest, commenced.

"The lads and I were just talking about you," MacLeod announced.

"Were you indeed?"

"Aye. Calum here has a nephew in the army and I was telling him how you'd served at Wellington's side in many a bloody battle. He didn't believe me. Now you can set him straight on the matter."

Jamie beamed. There was nothing like a bit of one-upmanship, Gabriel thought wryly, using another person's achievements. Especially imagined ones. MacAuley was studying him through narrowed eyes.

"My corps was rarely in the general's company," he said, noting the innkeeper's self-satisfied nod, "but I joined Wellington's encampment twice in Portugal. He was gracious enough to have me at his table for dinner each time."

The truth of the matter was that he and the duke had passed several endless nights as the battles of Bussaco and Badajoz loomed, poring over crucial communiqués. He'd been fed, certainly, but he couldn't have told what the fare had been if his life depended on it. They had been tense times, gritty and dark, and possessed of none of the gentlemanly magnificence that people who had never served in the military always seemed to envision.

"Aye?" MacAuley was leaning forward in his seat now, as was Fen MacDonald. Jamie had been translating Gabriel's words into Gaelic for Beaton, and the old man lifted his tankard in Gabriel's direction. "He's a right sharp lad, is Lon. D'ye think he'll be meeting Wellington?"

Not if he remained in Glasgow with his troop, marching in endless circuits of the town square, Gabriel thought dryly. But since he'd agreed to keep Andy MacAuley's confidence, he said aloud, "If he's sharp enough, he just might."

"What o' Willy Whyte?" Fen demanded.

"Aye. He's up 'n' joined the Gordon Highlanders," Calum declared, plying the bottle all around. "And Angus MacKenzie."

"Duncan MacGaa," Jamie added.

"Eoin MacGillechallum!" Beaton piped up, joining in the spirit of things. With each name, the men took salutary draughts of their whiskey. In the interest of camaraderie, Gabriel followed.

Calum thumped the table with a meaty fist. "Pol Tolmey."

"Nay, nay." Jamie shook his head. "He joined that troop of traveling actors from Aberdeen."

"Oh, aye," Calum agreed sadly. The bottle went around again.

Oriel had told Gabriel he would enjoy the famed Skye whiskey. He'd been right. The stuff was a rich gold in color, even richer in taste. Where Irish went down like silk, Scotch burned like fire, and it was a marvelous sensation.

Gabriel tossed back the remains of his dram. It was time to turn the conversation to his own ends. He hadn't come just to drink himself blind, after all, no matter the countless times he'd found some peace and no small amount of enjoyment doing just that.

"Have many of your young men left for the wars?" he asked the others.

"Oh, aye, hundreds," from Fen. He began to tick the number off on his fingers. "Duncan MacGaa, Willy Whyte, Seumas—"

"Y'think we never leave the island?" MacAuley demanded of Gabriel. His belligerence was dulled somewhat by the whiskey. In fact, he appeared almost benevolent when he leaned forward with the empty bottle in hand and rapped the neck against Gabriel's wrist. "Do you, then?"

"Not at all," Gabriel replied smoothly. "In fact, I know better. I have been acquainted with Geordie and Rob MacLeod in London."

"And fine lads they are, too!" Jamie tapped his tankard. "A wee drop here to toast my sons, Calum!"

The second bottle was opened, the MacLeod boys duly toasted.

"So you're a roving lot," Gabriel encouraged.

"To be sure and we are. Tavis Tolmey was in Fort William but January last for a sennight. Came back with a nasty little itch . . ." MacAuley actually winked, ". . . but a hell of a story."

"Not near as good as those you tell of your jaunts to Inverness," Jamie said. To Gabriel, "Every month Calum trots off to the mainland. Visits every pub there, he does, and won't take me with him no matter how sweetly I ask."

" 'Tis business," was the gruff retort, "and no occasion for o'erindulgence. Ask Lachlann to take you to Aberdeen or Glasgow. He goes often enough."

"Aye," Jamie said mournfully, "but he willna have me, either. Says I prattle."

"Well, Edana willna have me on her jaunts, either." MacAuley waggled his brows. "But she says 'tis because I dinna talk!"

This got a round of laughs from the table. "Everyone knows Edana willna have you a'tall." Jamie ignored his friend's scowl and helped himself to the remains of the second bottle. "We most of us have taken a hop off the island at one time or another, lad," he informed Gabriel. "But we always come back. This place gets into your bones, and no matter the reason, we always come back."

"And the rest of the world comes to us," was MacAuley's dour comment. "Whether we wish it to or no." He shrugged. "No offense, lad. You're no' such a bad sort."

"None taken." Gabriel watched as Jamie did his hiccuping translations. "I daresay strangers stand out rather like sore thumbs."

"Oh, aye. Sore thumbs. 'Tis a rare visitor who can come to Skye and not be noted even before his feet touch the land. Unless *we* wish it otherwise, you ken. See that there?" MacAuley was pointing to what appeared to be a framed square of fabric behind the taps. " 'Twas a right famous visitor, that one. Bonnie Prince Charlie cried into that hankie, he did, the day after Flora MacDonald sneaked him o'er from Uist dressed as a lady's maid." He gestured to old Mr. Beaton. "Sim here's ma was there, too."

Beaton tilted his head and let out a quick stream of musical Gaelic, eyes fixed on Gabriel as he did.

Jamie translated, "They hid Charlie so well his own ma wouldn't have found him. But he left again, went on to France, and Scotland has never been the same since."

"Being soundly trounced in battle has a way of doing that to a place," Gabriel remarked.

"True enough." Jamie listened again to the older man. "He says 'tisn't your fault, but little good comes with visitors to our corner of Skye, Charlie among them."

"No? Is that spoken from experience? Did he meet . . . er . . . Charlie?"

The old man raised a hoary brow when Jamie asked him the question. "Nay," came the reply after he answered. "And he thanks you kindly for making him feel as old as he is."

"I did not mean—"

"Ach, lad, he's but teasing you. He wasn't but a glimmer in his ma's eye back in forty-six."

Beaton gave Gabriel a gentle smile, eyes bright in his seamed face. Then he lifted the hand he'd had cupped on the table throughout the conversation. Four oddly shaped white cubes sat there. He then reached into his pocket and withdrew several old-looking coins, which he tossed down.

"Sim wants to know if you'd care to have a go with the knucklebones." MacAuley grinned. "You game, *Sasunnach*?"

Gabriel took a closer look at the cubes. They appeared to be real bones. Knucklebones, he could only assume, probably from a pig. There were no marks on them. He'd never been one to shirk from a challenge, however. "Tell me what to do."

"Are you certain?" MacLeod asked, eyes twinkling. "Sim has a heaven-sent touch with the bones."

"I'll have to hope for the luck of the devil, then, won't I?"

It was MacAuley who explained the game. It was very simple; the bones were tossed like four-sided dice. The flat side of the bone was valued at one, the concave side three, the convex side four, and the twisted side six. Highest point total won the hand. Except, MacAuley informed him, when a roll came up one of each. That was *an righ*, the king, and beat everything else.

"One toss, one crown wager."

Gabriel glanced at the coin Beaton had placed on the table. It appeared to be as old as the man himself, with the face of the present monarch's grandfather on it. It seemed an odd thing, an old English coin, to be in the possession of a man who, by all reports, had never left Skye. But money, like the worst of gossip, Gabriel thought, had a way of sending itself in strange and distant directions. A silver crown was nothing to Gabriel, but he assumed it was a great deal of money indeed to the old man.

"I don't think—" he began.

Beaton rapped his hand on the table and said something short and sharp.

"He says you need to do this, lad," Jamie translated. Beaton shoved the bones toward Gabriel.

He picked them up, rolled them in the palm of his hand. They felt smooth, cool, and not quite balanced, as if they were ready to toss themselves. He removed a shiny new crown from his coin pouch and set it beside Beaton's. Then he threw the bones. They clattered over the table, one bouncing off Jamie's tankard, then came to rest in a crooked line.

"Four, three, six, four," MacAuley read them. "Seventeen."

Beaton nodded as he gathered the bones and shook them in his cupped hands. He closed his eyes for a moment, then tossed.

"Six," MacAuley said. "Six . . ."

Gabriel relaxed, ready to concede.

"One and three."

Sixteen.

He opened his mouth, ready to refuse the win, to demand best-of-three. But the three men were all lifting their tankards to him. Beaton cheerfully slid the coin across the table.

"I can't take this," Gabriel muttered to Jamie.

"Of course you can, lad. You won it fair and square."

Gabriel watched as Mr. Beaton scooped the bones into a small cloth pouch. The old man then drained his tankard and rose a bit unsteadily to his feet. "*Beannachd leibh,*" he said to the seated trio. Then he gestured for Gabriel to rise.

"Would you see him home, Gabriel?" Jamie asked. "He's not as steady on his pins as he used to be."

"It would be my pleasure." Gabriel rose and offered his arm. Together, he and Beaton left the tavern, the others' farewells following them out the door.

Neither spoke during the walk, but Mr. Beaton whistled along the way, a sweet air that Gabriel didn't know. At the cottage door, the old man smiled, tipped his chin in a cheerful bow, and reached for the latch.

"Sir." Gabriel reached toward his pocket and half withdrew his coin pouch, intending to return the crown.

Beaton shook his head sadly and clucked his tongue.

Gesturing for Gabriel to put his money away, he drew his own pouch from his pocket. He then tipped the knuckle-bones into his palm. As Gabriel watched, he gave them a good shake before bending slightly and tossing them onto the stone stoop.

Gabriel knew it would take him a few games to master which side corresponded to which value. But there was no mistaking this roll. One of each side faced up.

"*An righ,*" Beaton announced brightly. "Eh?" He gestured for Gabriel to gather the bones. He tossed them again, and again one of each side appeared.

Gabriel couldn't imagine how one could load a bone to cheat. It must have been skill, then. He felt the silver crown in his pocket and wondered why it was so important to the old man that he keep it. He had fistfuls of newer coins, with newer king's faces on them. Beaton must know that.

"Sir," he began. "Why. . . ?"

Beaton shook his head once more, then muttered something that sounded like "George," then, "Charlie Stuart." The rest was a short, sharp Gaelic phrase.

"I don't understand," Gabriel snapped.

He didn't know if the man's shrug was a response, or a hitch of aging limbs as he climbed the step. "*An righ Charlie,*" he repeated, and clapping Gabriel on the shoulder, disappeared into the house.

Gabriel shook his head. He wasn't certain what had just transpired, and didn't know if it really mattered. He would think on it later, when the effects of the whiskey had waned. He debated returning to the tavern, but decided against it. He'd learned enough for one night. He would come back before midnight if the mist wasn't too thick, wait near the cliffs to see if anyone appeared.

There were still a good five hours before then, at

least one more of daylight. He would go back to the MacLeods', perhaps catch Maggie at work again in the kitchen.

Something had him pausing as he crested the first rise, had him turning west. There, walking purposefully on the narrow path was a cloaked figure. It could have been anyone, his mind told him, but he knew it wasn't. He knew that form, that walk.

He caught up with her just as she reached the end of the path.

"Maggie."

He saw her start. She swung around, dislodging her hood. Her eyes were wide in her pale face, lips parted. "You'll be the death of me!" she gasped. "Sneaking up as you do." She narrowed her eyes and sniffed. "I'd not come any closer to the edge if I were you. You've been at Calum's whiskey. For shame, wandering the cliffs in your state."

She'd clasped a hand over her chest and he resisted the urge to cover her fingers with his. Instead, he joined her. "If you were to push . . ." he said dryly.

"None would know it." Sighing, shaking her head, she reached for his arm.

He allowed her to draw him away from the edge. "Would you miss me, Maggie?"

She rolled her eyes. "Lord save me from tipsy fools."

"Too late. But you didn't answer me."

"Oh, aye," she said, her voice light with blithe irony. "I would weep and wail and tear at my breast."

He gazed down at those inviting swells, imagined his hands there. "Well, I am beginning to think I would miss you, Maggie MacLeod." His gaze lifted to rose-soft lips, to vivid green eyes, shaded now, and heard himself urging, "Tell me about the ghost lovers who walk here."

He captured the hand she'd rested on his sleeve. She tugged; he held firm. "Oh, 'tis all nonsense, and I daresay you'd be the first to agree."

"Of course. Still, I've become curious. So tell me."

"Not now."

"Why are you so reluctant to speak of it?" he asked.

Now her eyes widened in surprise and denial. "I'm not reluctant."

"You talk easily enough about mountain witches and fairy lights. Why is this tale so different?"

"I . . . 'Tis sad, and silly, and . . . such a waste." She impatiently shoved a wayward auburn curl from her forehead with her free hand and scowled. "Why are you pressing me on this?"

"I would think that would be obvious." He stared down at her, not particularly caring that his smile probably resembled that of a ravening wolf. "I want to know about the clever Englishman who found a way to melt the resistance of a hardheaded Skyewoman."

"She pushed him off the cliff in the end," was Maggie's quick retort. "He'd betrayed her."

"Ah. She must have hated him."

"She loved him."

So simply stated, without sentiment, as if Maggie were giving him an immutable law of nature. He shrugged. "Different sides of the same coin, they say. So what happened to your vengeful lady after she dispatched her lover?"

"She stabbed herself in the heart with a dirk."

Gabriel let out a low whistle. "Decisive lady. Did she have a name?"

"I'm sure she did, but it's been lost to time and shame. As she died by her own hand, she was buried in an unmarked grave."

"Ah. A tragic tale to equal the rest of them. And now the pair are destined to an eternity of walking the cliffs. Is that it?"

"You're mocking me," Maggie snapped.

"I'm mocking the cliché. Now I can understand why you don't wish to repeat such an old chestnut. It requires a fresh touch."

He knew he could spend the rest of his life fighting this urge. He might even win. But the lure of Maggie MacLeod was an astonishing, breath-stealing thing. *Just a taste,* the devil in him taunted. *You can just have a taste of her.* Now. He leaned that scant bit closer.

"The reason I don't care to repeat the tale," Maggie announced coolly, holding her ground, "is that there's no love worth dying and killing for. Tales like ours make it seem like there is."

When he did not respond, she glared up at him and demanded, "Do you believe love is worth dying for, Gabriel? Do you believe love is worth betraying all you hold dear and know to be true?"

He stared into the impossibly beautiful face, the perfect features shifting with some powerful emotion. "No. No, I don't," he answered huskily, "but sometimes, and consequences bedamned, a man finds himself living in a moment he knows he would kill for."

"I can't see you believing any such thing. Not you."

"Oh, yes. I do. And I'll be damned," he muttered, repeating the first words he'd spoken to her. It seemed so much longer than four days. "I will be damned."

He didn't doubt that for an instant. But he needed this moment as much as he'd needed anything in a very long time. He drew her toward him.

"Gabriel—"

"Hush. Just let me . . . Please, once."

One kiss, he thought, would be enough. Enough to get her out from beneath his skin, out of his mind. He lifted her chin with his free hand, tilted her face toward his. And he knew, even as he felt her quickened breath on his own lips, that he was a blackguard and a fool.

9

To Bring Love, take:

One clove
Two apple seeds
Three sprigs rosemary
Four vanilla beans,

Bind in a fresh handkerchief with a ribbon
and wear close to the heart.

Sweet. So sweet. Maggie had never thought a simple touch could reach so much of her at once. The whisper of his lips over hers, the airy skim of his hands up her arms, both set her to shivering inwardly from her fingertips. She sighed with the wonder of it, then caught her breath when one of his large hands spread over her back, drawing her closer. He caressed the corner of her mouth with the tip of his tongue, feathered the touch to her jaw, lower over her throat to the point where her pulse beat, hot and thready.

She let her head drop back, let her arms go still at her sides. She could feel his breath, warm against her neck, feel every inch where the fabric of her bodice brushed against his chest. It would have taken a thin and persistent breeze indeed to slip into the space between them.

Just then a gust of wind came up from the sea, wrapping her skirts tightly around her legs and his. With it came a bit of sense to her head, and even as she thought to stop this, to pull away from the bewitching lure of this man, his gentleness swept away. His hands clenched, hard without bruising, on her arms, and his mouth covered hers again.

There was a fierceness to the kiss now, a flaring heat as

his lips pressed, urged, parted hers. That first sweep of his tongue had her eyes springing wide. The second had them drifting closed, closing off sight as every other sense exploded. This time, she tasted the spice of Highland whiskey, smelled the heady combination of pine smoke and male skin, and felt every inch of her body go to flame.

"Och, *Sasunnach,*" she breathed against his mouth, one hand rising of its own will to clench in the soft wool of his coat. She was frightened, driven by unfamiliar need, and completely uncertain of what she wanted to say to him. "I shouldn't . . ."

"Lie down with me," she heard him murmur. "Lie down with me here, Mairghread. I want to touch the very center of you."

She felt his hands, urging, drawing her down. One shifted from her arm, sending a path of sparks as it clasped at her ribs. His thumb brushed the sensitive underside of her breast, and she swallowed a husky gasp. His strong fingers and stirring words were drawing her down, drawing her in. . . .

She was struggling suddenly, her hands batting at his arms. It ached to pull away, ached like a wound, but she had to. "I can't . . . I . . . can't."

"Shh, sweetheart."

She saw him as if he were standing in moonlight. He was hazy, except for the glint in his eyes. "You'll go," she whispered mournfully. "You can't help it. You'll do what you came to do and you'll go."

"Maggie."

She blinked. Felt the salt air and wind, saw his face so close to hers. His eyes were fierce. "Gabriel."

"Yes?"

"Oh, Gabriel." She drew a steadying breath, then let it

ease out. "I thought . . . for a moment I was . . . Oh, no matter." She tugged against his grip. "You'll be leaving Skye soon."

"Yes." His mouth tightened, a new expression flitted over his face, gone before she could identify it. "Yes. I will leave."

She nodded once, and again. "You'll let me go now, please. I need to get home."

"Maggie. Mairghread. It's good between us. You know that."

"Your touch stirs me, Gabriel, warms me. I know that. But I don't know you, save for the fact that your heart isn't here. Nay." She held up her hand, stilling his reply. "I'm not offering you mine, nor am I expecting any empty declarations from you. I understand quick heat and desire, better than you think, probably. You think me naive and perhaps I am. I've certainly none of your worldliness. But I know the human body, and I understand the urges within."

"I . . . God." He dragged off his hat and ran a hand through his hair. She could see the tautness of his jaw, the barely banked fire in his eyes. "I should apologize. I must apologize. It is wrong of me to want to . . . love you. To ask you to let me."

"Love is the province of the heart, Gabriel," she said sharply. "You just want the shell around mine."

"Oh, Maggie. I didn't mean—"

"Don't. It's better with honesty."

He did step away then. She held her arms stiffly at her sides before they could lift to draw him back. It had been sweet, the kiss. Too sweet.

"Very well. But I'm making no promises—"

"I told you I didn't expect promises." Maggie blinked

hard to clear the tears that had sprung suddenly into her eyes.

"Let me finish." Gabriel didn't touch her, but he leaned forward until his face hovered close above hers. "I'll make no promises that I won't keep trying."

"*What?*"

"I want you."

"You shouldn't," she shot back, twisting her shaky hands into her cloak.

That earned her a wry smile. "How could I not? You are the stuff of a man's dreams, my dear. But if you mean I shouldn't try to have you, you're very probably right."

"Well, then—"

"I do far too many things I shouldn't. But I will promise you this . . ." He raised one finger, ran it along the underside of her jaw, lifting her chin and making her catch her breath yet again. "I'll only take what you freely give to me."

She closed her eyes for a precious second, then pulled away. "That's it, then. We're done with this."

Gabriel gave a soft snort. "So you say." Then, "You're not angry with me?"

It didn't occur to her to lie. "Nay, not angry. Disappointed, a bit, but more by myself. I should have known . . ." Maggie bit her lip and started to turn away.

He snared her arm before she could turn fully, then released her as quickly. "What happened to you, Maggie MacLeod?"

"I beg your pardon?"

"Was it a man? Did he break your heart?"

She gaped at him, cursing as telltale heat rose in her cheeks. "Why would you ask me such a thing?"

"It was a man." His eyes narrowed speculatively.

"Did he want you as much as I do? Did you hold him at wing's length, too?"

"My lord! For shame!" Flustered now, and suddenly angry, she snapped, "We're far more liberal here in Scotland than you English, but I'd like to think 'tisn't at the expense of respect!"

With that, she gathered her skirts and stalked away from him, heading toward home. She'd come to the cliffs, as usual, to find some peace. She had hoped to get Gabriel out of her mind, even if only for an hour. Considering how her safe little world had been spun on its axis of late, it should have been no surprise that he had followed her right to the edge.

He caught up with her before she reached the village road. "Maggie." His fingers brushed down her arm as she kept walking. "Maggie, stop. This isn't something you can run from."

She came to a jerky halt and rounded on him. Any hot words died on her tongue. With his hat gripped over his heart, earth-brown hair tousled by the wind, and eyes dark with desire for her, Gabriel took her breath away.

"It won't just go away because you wish it to," he said softly.

She nodded, not trusting her voice, and turned again toward the road.

He was right. She knew he was right.

She had no defenses against what he did to her. Oh, the kiss. It hadn't been her first. Nay, she had pressed lips and so much more with Peter in Hertfordshire. And she'd liked it well enough until it had ended so very badly.

But this time had been as different as land and sea. Gabriel's touch on her skin had registered beneath, so deep beneath that her legs had gone unsteady. There had been, too, those odd, vague moments when there had been a remembering—a sense of not being where she was.

What nonsense, she scolded herself, quickening her pace and trying not to listen to his footsteps behind her. She had been standing on the cliff's edge, in twilight and plain view of anyone who might chance along, allowing herself to be kissed by an inscrutable, arrogant *Sasunnach*. Kissing him back.

She'd been speaking only the truth when she'd told him how well she understood human passions. And she knew how very hard they could be to deny. It was a road she didn't want to travel again. Couldn't afford to travel again. But, oh, how bitterly sweet it was to feel longing again.

Gabriel was striding by her side suddenly. "I don't want it to go away, Maggie."

Something shifted around her heart, ached anew. "I do," she lied, voice surprisingly calm, and wondered what would be harder: having him near, or watching him go.

Gabriel studied her face as they walked. It was pale and stirringly beautiful, serene. The only indication that they'd been wrapped in a fiery embrace not five minutes earlier was the soft, kiss-bruised look of her lips.

Angel, madonna, saint. It was all there before him. He supposed he ought to feel guilty for having grabbed at such innocence. He knew he ought to feel low as a snake for wanting so much to despoil it. And that's what it would be. He wanted to do more than possess; he wanted to devour her, and there was no chance she could walk away from an encounter with a man like him anything but ravaged.

He felt a sharp, deep twinge of regret. But more powerful than that, he felt ravenous.

When she stopped abruptly and turned to face him, it was all he could do to keep from hauling her back into his arms. But she had hers crossed over her chest, an unmistakable if not especially effective barrier between them.

"When will you be leaving?" she demanded.

"Are you telling me you wish me to go now?"

"What I wish," she replied coolly, "is that you would stop meeting questions with questions. And, aye, I can't help thinking it would be best if you were to go."

"That is hardly the same as wanting me gone."

"Oh." She blew out a short breath and raised her eyes heavenward. "The conceit of men!"

Something oddly hopeful sparked in Gabriel's chest. "I don't suppose it would help my cause to assert the weakness of my sex."

"Weak as the stone under our feet," she shot back. Then sighed. "Ach, Gabriel. There's your burden, then. God didn't make you an angel, but the devil did well at making you a man."

He couldn't have said it better if he'd tried.

Maggie tilted her head and regarded him evenly. "What would you do if I were to turn you out of my home?"

"Take a room with MacAuley," he said promptly.

She shook her head. "God help us all."

This time, when she struck off, her gait was slower, her bearing less tense. Gabriel fell into step alongside her, sensing a reprieve. Not that he'd expected her to send him away. Not Saint Maggie.

But then, his little saint had nearly singed him with her fire. Her response to his kiss—before she had gone vague and skittish on him, of course—had all but sent him to his knees. She was an innately warm woman, vibrant and spirited, even in her steadiness. There was no doubt she would be the same in his bed. Strong, fiery, giving all of herself.

His body tightened at the image of Maggie, her hands clenching at the heather, head thrown back, glorious hair flowing over her shoulders and the worn cloak spread beneath her. He saw her bared skin flushed and glowing with passion, proud breasts and soft thighs straining upward for his touch.

Gabriel stopped in his tracks. It was too real, that image, and another moment of contemplating it would drive him mad. He stepped off the path, heather crunching beneath his feet, and turned his back to Maggie. He took a steadying breath, then another, silently cursing his body for behaving like that of an adolescent.

"Gabriel?"

"Tell me one of your tales," he commanded harshly.

"What?"

"One of your little bits of island lore. Ghosts, ancient hags . . ." Anything to divert his salacious thoughts.

"What has gotten into your head today?"

"You," was his simple reply. "Tell me more about your ghosts."

He thought she would refuse again. Instead, she came to stand by his side. "You know as much of their story as I can tell. He betrayed her, broke her heart. As the story goes, he'd made promises of forever and she'd lain with him. But as soon as he'd fulfilled his purpose here, he cast her aside. He was going home to England without her."

" 'Heaven has no rage like love to hatred turned,' " Gabriel murmured. " 'Nor hell a fury, like a woman scorned.' " He glanced down to find Maggie staring at him with a faint smile. "I have been known to read," he said mildly.

"You've the soul of a poet, Gabriel Loudon."

That fist clenched in his gut again. "I had the worst of Eton, actually."

She shrugged. "If it bothers you so, I'll keep my good opinions of you to myself."

"Few that they are?"

"I didn't say that."

"Mmm. So your island lass tipped her faithless swain over the edge and stabbed herself in a fit of remorse. . . ."

"Desolation, more likely. She'd pinned all her hopes on a man and I expect she felt she was left with nothing. They got their forever, 'tis said, but not together. Just here."

Gabriel pondered that. Then asked, "Why was the man here? Is that known?"

"Oh, aye. He was a soldier in His Majesty's Army, chasing Jacobites after Culloden. 'Twasn't a great secret that Prince Charles was fleeing this way with his supporters, nor was our Englishman the only one chasing him. He was merely one of the closest."

Now the fist turned into a chill knot inside Gabriel. "He was chasing traitors to the Crown."

"You would see it that way," Maggie remarked evenly. "But keep in mind that many Scots and not a few English came out in support of the prince when he arrived from the Continent with his claim to the throne. He was grandson to a king, after all."

"A deposed one. An unfit one."

"A Catholic one," was her sharp retort. "Had the Scots not been defeated at Culloden Field, we might have a Catholic king now."

"Of course. And look how well that worked for France," Gabriel said tersely.

" 'Tisn't about religion or royalty. I . . . Oh, I'm not

going to be drawn into this, Gabriel. There's no reason. 'Tis long past now. And I'd do well to remember that you're a Campbell. Campbells have always been loyal to the Hanoverian cause."

"I am not . . ." He didn't bother to complete the sentence. What difference would it make to insist that he was not a Campbell when, to a Scot, he was. "Keep this in mind, my dear: Should Napoleon have his way, we'll have a Catholic ruler again."

"You're comparing Charles Stuart to Napoleon?" she demanded, clearly incredulous.

"I am . . . I am getting us far off the subject of your ghosts. Have you seen them?"

He heard her take a breath. She was perfectly calm again, that resolute Maggie calm, when she replied, "Of course I haven't. 'Tis only a tale created from a bit of history, meant to keep young people off the cliffs and from throwing their hearts away on someone not meant for them."

"Does it work?"

"Nay. What does?" She pulled her cloak tightly around her shoulders. "Come along now. It will be dark soon."

Gabriel gave a last glance toward the cliffs before following. He would be back, in the dark, for his nightly vigil. He wouldn't think too much on Maggie's story. No doubt it changed with circumstance, just one more cautionary tale out of the thousands created throughout history.

They walked home in silence. There were lights in the kitchen as they approached, and the sound of laughter. Gabriel heard Tessa's voice, speaking Gaelic, and Jamie's. He didn't recognize the others.

Their identity was revealed soon enough. Lachlann MacDonald and Tearlach Beaton were seated at the kitchen table with Tessa and Jamie, mugs of tea and plates of Maggie's shortbread in front of them. They looked altogether too comfortable for Gabriel's taste. Both looked very much as if they belonged.

"See what I found," Jamie said with delight. "They followed me home, the pair of them."

Like stray curs, Gabriel thought. The behemoth MacDonald certainly looked ready to growl and snap. Beaton appeared the more genial of the two, rather like a floppy-eared retriever dog, but it was a matter of degrees. He didn't seem any more pleased to see Gabriel than his crony.

"*Sasunnach,*" he said in way of a greeting. MacDonald merely grunted.

"Sit down, sit down." Jamie waved at his daughter and guest, gesturing shakily to one empty chair. There was no doubt about his drunkenness. Gabriel assumed his shillings had paid for another bottle or two at MacAuley's.

"Gentlemen," he offered.

Tessa was bouncing in her seat. "Have you been out on the cliffs, then? Did you see them?"

Maggie hung her cloak on a waiting hook. "Isn't it your bedtime?"

Tessa rolled her eyes. "It's barely gone eight."

"And we're not living Town hours. Off with you. You can read with a candle if you like."

Clearly the girl didn't like, but she went, after shaking hands solemnly with both MacDonald and Beaton and giving her father a kiss atop his wild gray head. She paused as she passed Gabriel. "Well, were you? Did you?" she whispered.

"Yes and no."

"Maggie never sees them," Tessa confided quietly,

darting a glance at her sister, who was busy with a fresh pot of tea. "Because she won't believe. I'm going. I'm going," she muttered when Maggie looked up.

The room turned very quiet in the wake of her departure. Jamie stared dreamily into the fire. The other two men stared fixedly at Gabriel. He debated staying, just out of perversity—and the desire to keep Maggie from being alone with the pair. Jamie had taken on all the properties of a rock. But it would be more awkward than satisfying, sitting with two men who only spoke Gaelic. He imagined they'd insulted him thoroughly behind his back. He didn't care to have them do it to his face in a language he couldn't understand.

"If you will excuse me . . ."

Jamie didn't budge. MacDonald and Beaton merely blinked at him. Maggie barely spared him a glance. "Good night to you, my lord," she did say, hands busy and eyes on the teapot.

He stood for a long moment, waiting for anyone to say anything. Then, to stay longer would have made him look more than foolish. So he went. Once in his chamber, he took off his boots. He lay down on the bed fully dressed. He would still his thoughts, especially those of Maggie and what had happened between them, and he would sleep for several hours. He wasn't concerned about waking on time; that was one more talent he had honed in the military. By eleven, he would be on his way back to the cliffs, waiting for L'Écossais.

Downstairs, Maggie had poured more tea and was tidying the kitchen, ready to take her own bed. She wasn't feeling terribly sociable. She was weary and jittery at the same time, and certain she could still feel the heat of Gabriel's hands on her body.

"Sit down, lass. You're making my head spin with your pottering about."

She gave her father a tired glance. No doubt his head was spinning fast and furious. It was clear he'd imbibed more than his fair share at MacAuley's, though a fair share for Jamie was more than for most men. Chances were, he'd be sleeping on the parlor sofa unless Lachlann and Tearlach bundled him upstairs.

"I'm tired, Papa. I'll be off to bed as soon as I'm done here."

She'd slipped back into Gaelic as she always did around her friends. She saw their guests glance toward the door almost in unison, then back to her. So they didn't want her following Gabriel up the stairs. Well, she thought, Gabriel clearly hadn't wanted her staying here with them. Like little boys with a choice toy, all of them. She sighed.

"Bide with us for a cup, Mairghread," Lachlann suggested. Most of Lachlann's suggestions had a way of sounding like commands. She'd grown deft enough at ignoring them.

"Aye. Do." Tearlach patted the back of the chair beside him just as Lachlann pulled the seat at his side away from the table with a booted toe.

The pair were sitting across the table from each other, lifelong friends and sometime rivals—at such things as heaving cabers about and attracting giggling young women. They were solidly united now in their attitude toward the Englishman. Maggie had meant to hold her tongue on the matter, but she found she couldn't.

"Lord Rievaulx is a guest in this house," she said tersely, choosing to stand behind her father rather than choosing between the chairs. "And as such I'd ask you to be civil to him."

The pair blinked at her.

"I don't like him," Lachlann muttered.

Tearlach nodded. "I don't like him, either."

"You don't know him, either of you!"

"I don't have to—"

"I'll have none of that, Lachlann MacDonald." She shook a finger at him. "You cannot weight him with all the ill traits of a country. He's certainly never called you dense as an ox or penny-pinching."

"And what's wrong with a bit of good Scots frugality?" her friend demanded testily.

Maggie blew out an exasperated breath. It was like battering at a stone wall with a feather duster. She turned to Tearlach. He raised a hand and shook his head. "Don't you be looking to me, Maggie. I can't claim to know the man, either, but I can't believe there's anything there I'd care to know."

"If you would but—"

"What?" Tearlach demanded. "Mince and smile and trade snuff? What am I supposed to say to him or he to me? Hmm? I doubt his fancy schools taught him my language."

"Oh!" Defeated, Maggie threw up her hands. "Fine. I'm not your mother, Tearlach, nor yours, Lachlann, though I daresay neither would be pleased to hear what peevish creatures they've raised. Go ahead, then. Grunt and snarl, and may you enjoy it. Just remember these days should you ever find yourselves south of the borderlands with naught but a chill welcome at your arrival."

"Don't be daft. What would I be doing—"

"Oh, Lachlann. Even you might have call to visit England someday. Now, a good night to you all. I am going to bed." She added sternly, "And don't you be eating all the shortbread."

Lachlann and Tearlach shoved themselves to their feet in courtesy as she went. Her father tried, but succeeded only in nearly tipping himself over backward in his chair. Maggie's last glance was of the two younger men avoiding his flailing limbs as they tried to steady him.

She stopped on her way to bed to turn back her father's sheets, in case he actually made it upstairs one way or another. As she always did, she traced a finger over the little portrait of her mother that was the room's only decoration. Muire Gordon MacLeod had been as fiery-haired as Isobel, as fearless as Tessa, and as good-humored as Geordie and Rob. She had also been solid and resolute, a calm mountain in the midst of her lively brood. Her death of a fever seven years before had left an enormous, ragged hole in the fabric of the family, one Isobel and Maggie had struggled to darn as best they could.

Maggie missed her mother terribly—when she cooked with Muire's recipes, when Jamie or the boys needed tending, when Tessa took an occasional tumble from a tree. But most of all Maggie missed her mother on nights like these, when she so needed to empty her troubles into a welcoming lap and hear that everything would be fine in the end. With Isobel being so far away and Jamie, much as Maggie hated to admit it, being little help at anything, there was no lap available.

"There's something in him, Mama," she whispered to her mother's serene face. "Something behind the soldier and rake. It's drawing me, and I've no defenses against it."

Closing her eyes, she rested her head against the portrait, forehead to forehead with her mother. The old ballad came into her head yet again. *It's questions three you will ask of me. Savoury, sage, rosemary, and thyme.*

And it's questions three you must answer me. Before you are a true lover of mine.

The song was still playing in Maggie's mind when she slipped between her own sheets. The only question that came with it this time was a tearing one: *What would you lose, Mairghread?* The answer was worse still.

Everything.

10

So tell that young lady to buy me a new cambric shirt
And make it without needles or yet needles' work.
So sav'ry was said come marry in time,
And she shall be a true lover of mine.

So tell that young lady to wash it all out
And wash it all out in yonder well,
Where never was water nor rain never fell.
So sav'ry was said come marry in time,
And she shall be a true lover of mine.

Chack. An unseen finger cocked the pistol for that third shot, the one that would fell him as sharply and surely as it had the others.

Chack!

Gabriel woke, heart pounding, on his thirteenth day on Skye to find himself nearly eye to beady black eyes with a pair of jackdaws who were perched just outside the open window. "Chack," one chattered at him. "Chack, chack."

He dragged a heavy arm from the counterpane and the birds winged away. Little thieves; they had probably been eyeing the meager possessions Gabriel set on the bedside table each night: a handful of small coins; the watch, identical to nine others belonging to the rest of his military corps, that he used despite its being battered and not especially dependable. He rarely had to be anywhere at a specific time. And the worn gold signet ring bearing the Rievaulx crest that the last earl, his grandfather, had worn every day until he died.

Gabriel heaved himself up against the headboard and rubbed his palms hard over his face. He had a vicious ache behind his eyes and his heart was still beating a quick staccato. Damnable nightmares. They had haunted him for more than a year, always recurring just when he thought they might be gone for good. Naive of him, he knew. But the thought of spending the rest of his life with evil dreams was more than he was willing to contemplate on any given day.

In this dream, one of a dozen variations on a dismal theme, he was strolling down St. James's with Montgomerie and Brandon. Brandon had been dressed for milking, a byre apron over his homespun clothes. Montgomerie, son of a bishop and a discarded scullery maid, wore the absurdly patterned and colored dandy's garb he favored, his vividly green coat making him as conspicuous as a sitting mallard.

The pair, along with Gabriel, were just reaching their destination, Montgomerie's foot on the first step to Boodle's, when the shots rang out. Two shots, one just after the other. Montgomerie fell first, dead before he hit the ground, a lead ball in his back. But Brandon had time to turn, both hands clasped over the blooming red stain in the center of his apron, to meet Gabriel's eyes with his own astonished, pleading gaze. Gabriel reached out, his fingertips brushing Brandon's arm just as the younger man went down, head bouncing once, hard, like a cricket ball against the marble step.

"Chack, chack!" the jackdaws called sharply from a tree nearby.

Gabriel had never walked along St. James's with those men. He had already been on the Peninsula by the time Montgomerie had joined the corps. And Brandon had avoided Mayfair, saying the stiff-necked denizens of the clubs always made him feel as if he had bits of cow pats stuck to his boots. The truth, much to the amusement of the other members of the corps, was that he always did seem to have some muck on his shoes. With the un-concern of a farmer—or maybe the bad luck of a back-ward country boy—he had the uncanny ability to tread through any pile within a hundred yards of where he was walking. Had he ever been to Almack's, he would have managed to step in something there, too.

Gabriel had never seen Brandon in his milking apron. And he knew of Montgomerie's garish wardrobe only because the man himself had cheerfully described it over a campfire one night when, dressed as Portuguese peas-ants in rough homespun wool, they had shared the mid-night watch. So there was no truth in that part of the dream. Nor had the two fallen together. Their deaths had been hundreds of miles and months apart.

Gabriel had arrived in Badajoz a day after Mont-gomerie was felled by a French sniper's bullet. By the time he'd gotten to his comrade's side, the man had been laid out in a monk's cell by the good brothers who had found him. Garbed in rough brown robes, eyes closed, he looked as little like a merry-begotten dandy as anyone could.

Gabriel had been on time to meet Brandon, but ten steps too far away in the crowded Salamanca bazaar. The shot had scattered the crowd, leaving Brandon standing alone on the suddenly, eerily cleared steps of an ancient marketplace, halfway between a tumble of lush silk rugs, richly patterned, the top one a deep, sanguine red, and a row of knee-high ceramic milk urns. He had turned, hands clasped over the blossoming stain in the center of his chest. His eyes had met Gabriel's: wide, as-tonished, pleading. Then he had fallen. Gabriel, already running toward him, had reached out. His fingertips had brushed the dying man's sleeve as he fell, head bouncing once, hard, against the stone.

Gabriel had been the messenger of the corps, the one who relayed crucial intelligence across hostile lands. He'd gone back and forth across the Continent countless times, carrying broken codes, developing strategies, warnings. He had saved some lives, turned the tide of at least one battle. But he had failed completely in those final days.

He had let critical intelligence slip through his fingers, and in the most unforgivable of ways. Even now, more than a year later, he couldn't bear to think on it. As a result, comrades had died, and many more good men after them.

He had wandered like a ghost back through Portugal, Spain, and France, home at last to England. There, he hadn't even bothered to fight his demons. He'd swum his way through rivers of whiskey, sought out the shadiest games in the darkest gaming hells, and been so thorough at alienating those persons whose company he had shared through much of his life that it was an achievement in itself. Only Oriel had been persistent in his friendship. The rest of Society had responded with utter predictability. The ton had snubbed and shunned and whispered. And all for his lost refinement that, in reality, was nothing in comparison to what he'd so cravenly lost on the Continent.

Gabriel had never asked to be dubbed the Archangel by anyone. He'd fallen with a total lack of grace. And had even less idea of who he was once he'd landed.

The old earl, his grandfather, had imparted endless wisdom—real and dubious—during the nights they sat together by the fire in Scarborough House's drafty library. He'd had plenty to say on the subject of redemption. His grandson half listened, lulled into a pleasant torpor by the late hour and crackling fire. He had been so youthfully certain he would never need anything as mortal or ignoble as atonement. *Redemption is harder to find than horns on a snail*, the old earl had said, twisting the boy's hair into little cowlicky horns. Gabriel had never quite managed to forget that maxim, no matter how many bottles he downed. Now he found himself thinking how Brandon, master of the silly idiom, would have liked that one. But then, he doubted Brandon had ever spent much time in inner contemplation of atonement.

Climbing from the bed, Gabriel stalked across the creaking, wide-planked floor to the chair where he had left his coat the night before. He found his flask, shook it, cursed when not so much as a drop splashed inside. Tossing it down, he turned and gazed out the window. The chamber looked out over the tidy stone walk with its border of struggling marigolds, over rough, rocky earth that stretched away from the front of the cottage to slope gently down into an equally rocky glen. Hardy rowan trees dotted the earth where little other than heather grew.

It was MacLeod land, passed, Gabriel thought, through as many hands as his own estate. Jamie MacLeod, rumpled gentleman and charming drunkard, probably never gave any thought to losing it. He wouldn't know that one of his neighbors would gladly hand all of Skye, from plot to plow to shaggy red cow, over to the French. Gabriel wasn't so arrogant or stupid as to think the entire fate of Britain rested on his shoulders, but this was his domain now. His presence here mattered, no matter how little.

So far, he'd made little headway in his search. He had visited the cliffs at night for more than a sennight now and seen nothing other than the occasional flitting shadow. He'd bought countless bottles for the local men, who were perhaps slightly friendlier now, but neither welcoming nor helpful. He'd even tried to visit Edana

Malcolmson, only to find her gone and her brute of a butler unwilling to say where she might be.

He was going to have to do better. Time was running out, if it wasn't already too late. And he knew he couldn't stay with the MacLeods for much longer.

Maggie. Beautiful Maggie, with her glowing skin and shadowed eyes. He wanted to banish those shadows with his touch, with the heat of skin against skin.

As if he could grasp that chance. As if she would give it to him. She fed him, chatted with him, allowed him to follow her on the occasional errand. But for days now she hadn't met his eyes or stayed alone in a room with him for more than a few minutes. She hadn't gone anywhere near the cliffs in his company.

Now, as he listened to the sounds of morning activity from downstairs, Gabriel wondered if Maggie had any idea of the effect she was having on him, keeping him on edge during the day and awake at night. If she ever thought about him at all, even one fleeting thought of him for each damned hour that she refused to leave his head . . .

She had counted three dead apple trees in the tiny orchard, Isobel's rose bushes looked gnarled and hopeless, and the elder tree behind the cottage had suffered in winter. Maggie frowned as she surveyed its still-bare branches and wondered if perhaps the few buds would be its last. Lachlann had assured her there was still plenty of life left in the tree, but she suspected his pledge was more comfort than truth.

Maggie turned her eyes back to her task. She wasn't overly fond of doing the washing, but with Mòrag still away, it was left to her. She would gladly have handed over the task to Tessa, but heaven only knew what a hash the girl would make of it. Shirts would shrink, chemises would turn to balloons, and everything would come out of the water pink. Of course, Maggie thought wryly, she wasn't doing much better. She had caught herself not ten minutes earlier trying to lather one of her father's shirts with a rolled-up stocking. Well, it had felt like the soap in her hand. She checked again to make certain she was still going about it right.

The shirt she now held belonged to Gabriel. The soft strength of the linen spoke of Irish looms and London's best tailors. There was none nearly so fine to be found anywhere north of Edinburgh. Clodagh Norrie did well enough with her loom, but Maggie had lived long enough in England to know what could be found in the south. In London, one could buy Irish linen so smooth, it felt like silk. She had never been to London, but her brother-in-law's shirts had so awed the maid that she had been afraid to launder them during his visits, leaving the task to Maggie.

Her thoughts skipped easily from Nathan back to his friend. Gabriel was still asleep upstairs. Heeding no message her brain was sending, her eyes drifted to the second-floor windows. Not that she would be able to see anything. His room was at the front of the house. Chiding herself, she looked away. Some things were simply not to be contemplated. The Englishman out of his linen shirt and in a bed was one of them.

No good could possibly come of this quickening she felt when he was nearby. She had tried so hard to keep him at arm's length for the past few days. She'd learned that physical distance had little to do with ease of mind. It had been so very different with Peter. With Peter, even when he'd had his hands on her, she had filled her head with images of home and hearth and children underfoot.

She didn't see a gold wedding band when Gabriel was about. She saw tiny, licking flames and lush fields of wild thyme.

She had fallen for sweet words and a pleasant face once before and had her heart trampled for it. She wasn't about to suffer the same for a poet's mouth and brooding gaze.

Glancing down again, she saw she had tangled her hands in the linen. With a choked sigh, she dunked it firmly back under the water and held it there. As if she could drown her thoughts with such a silly act. She felt more than foolish now, and released the shirt. One cuff drifted upward, gave a languid wave, and settled.

"Maggie?"

She started, and got a mouthful of soap when one hand flew upward to stifle her cry. Cheeks flaming, she brushed ineffectually at her lips and looked up at Gabriel. Beneath tousled brown hair, his eyes flashed silver.

"*O Dia,*" she muttered, as much in prayer as curse.

"I startled you. I'm sorry."

"I was woolgathering. Is there something you need? I haven't anything on the stove, but there's tea in the pot and I'll put on some eggs if you'll but wait a moment."

She was babbling. Maggie sat back on her heels and resisted the urge to touch her cheeks. She was convinced they were a vivid pink. In truth, she felt as if she'd had something pressed hard against her from head to toe, leaving a faint pins-and-needles sensation in its wake. But that was nonsense, she scolded herself. She was merely goose-pimpled from having her arms in cooling water.

"Thank you," he said, "but I can wait for your father and sister."

Both were up and out already. Jamie was off fetching the weekly post, the only activity that was guaranteed to get him out of bed before noon, and that only because Isobel was always tucking money in with her letters. Maggie never let on that she knew, nor did she feel the need to mention that Mr. MacGruder hid Izzy's letters for her when he remembered. As for Tessa, she was with Edana Malcolmson, conjugating French verbs and bobbling teacups.

Maggie didn't tell Gabriel about either. It seemed safer somehow to at least pretend they weren't alone.

"If you're hungry now, I can make something for you," she insisted.

"Really, there is no need. Rest assured I will let you know when I become too ravenous to bear it any longer."

She was getting that warm sensation again. He stepped closer, then bent to crouch beside her. Maggie felt his hard thigh brushing against hers, felt the gentle tug as a fold of her loose apron was trapped between his leg and boot heel. She smelled the honey and sage of the soap she'd set out for him, scents far too familiar and comforting to be sending her heart pounding as it was.

"This," he announced, reaching into the tub to finger the sleeve of his shirt, "really should not be your job."

And he really shouldn't have been so close.

"I do what tasks need to be done, your shirt among them."

" 'Tell her to wash it in yonder well,' " he murmured.

Where water ne'er sprung nor a drop of rain fell. Yet again, Maggie thought of the ballad. Until so recently it had given her comfort, reminded her of her mother. Now it had become something quite different.

She stared at him for a long moment, then glanced

down at the washtub. "I'll try the well next time," she said, striving for levity. "This time, I needed the tub and washboard. I'll not ask what you did while wearing this shirt, but it appeared as if you'd been crawling about in the heather."

He was completely straight-faced when he replied, "I was crawling about in the heather."

Maggie found herself smiling slightly at his jest. "Well, I've nearly got the spots out."

"So you have. Not a mark in sight."

He hadn't meant anything by that. Maggie knew they were speaking only of a shirt. But the words pricked at her. There were stains invisible to the eye that could never be removed. Feeling her own like brands inside her, she pulled away. Her apron, still caught on his heel, tugged and held. She ended up half sitting, half kneeling on the ground.

Gabriel was on his feet in an instant. For a fleeting moment she was free, then he stretched one hand toward her. She knew better than to take it, knew it wasn't wise. But she did it anyway. His hand closed warmly around hers and he pulled gently. It seemed to take forever, the rise to her feet. Above her, his gaze held hers, hooded and dark and filled with a promise she could only half understand.

"Mairghread," he murmured.

A loud scuffling noise from beyond the gorse hedge made them both start. Maggie jerked out of Gabriel's grasp and nearly went down again when her shaky knees buckled. She recovered, however, and was standing reasonably steady when Tessa came bounding over the low garden wall.

The girl was wearing an old pair of their brother Rob's breeches, mud spattered to the knees, her hair a wild auburn tangle down her back. "Maggie, are we to have

dumplings with supper? I've a fierce taste for them today."
Oblivious to the tense scene, she grinned. "Ah, my lord,
have you been helping with the wash?"

Gabriel's eyes, fixed hotly only moments before on
Maggie's, slid away. "I . . . ah . . ."

"Better you than me," Tessa announced. "I loathe
washing. So, are we to have dumplings, Maggie?"

Maggie cursed the breathy edge to her voice as she
replied, "We are, as it happens."

"Grand. Is there any shortbread for now? I'm fam-
ished."

"Didn't Edana feed you?"

"Oh, all she ever has is fancy little bits that taste of
nothing and are impossible to eat. Besides, she wasn't
there."

"Truly?" Maggie demanded. Tessa nodded. For all
that the girl had a powerful imagination, she didn't lie.
"Well, then, you can help me."

"Shortbread . . . ?"

"After," Maggie said firmly. "And I'll need some fresh
Irish moss for the pudding. Since you've found yourself a
free hour, you can go to the strand to gather it." Tessa's
eyes brightened at the mention of collecting kelp. "Nay.
You'll not be taking the rock path. You'll go the long
way about."

"But it's so *long*!" the girl protested.

"Hence my use of the term *long way*." Maggie lifted
the shirt from the water. "Here," she said to her sister,
"wring this out for me and hang it to dry. Hold it away
from your muddy self, if you please."

Tessa's pert nose wrinkled, but she obeyed. "Feels like
a mass of Irish moss," she muttered. Then, "Just like that
about the ghostie's neck."

"Och, Tessa!" Maggie slapped one of her father's

stockings hard against the side of the washtub. "Will you stop with that, already? 'Tisn't a nice tale."

"I should say not! He with a hole in his head and all that seaweed wrapped round his throat . . ." The girl lifted Gabriel's shirt toward her own neck to demonstrate, but Maggie's quick glare had her draping it instead over the wash line. She bounded back toward Gabriel and demanded, "Wouldn't you like to see him, my lord? You being one of His Majesty's soldiers, too . . ."

"Tessa!" Maggie snatched the last stocking from the water. "Enough. Take yourself and your gruesome stories into the kitchen. There's shortbread and milk for you."

The only thing more guaranteed to get her sister moving than the threat of soap and water was the promise of food. Tessa grinned and loped off toward the cottage. Maggie added, "Wash your hands first! With soap!" for good measure. To Gabriel, she said, "Tessa has a penchant for that miserable tale. I suppose I found it romantic, too, when I was her age."

Gabriel found himself wondering what precisely she found romantic now. Minutes earlier, when she had been so close to his chest that he could feel her trembling, he might have demanded that she tell him. But the cool reserve was back, stiffening her spine and firming that lush mouth.

"People here seem to have an inordinate interest in things that don't exist."

He got a blood-stirring view of her rounded bottom when she removed the last of the wash from the water and tipped the tub away from them to drain. "True, perhaps," she replied, straightening. This time, he got a view of wash-dampened bodice that made his own mouth go dry. He lifted one hand, reaching for her, but she wasn't looking at him. "But it's hardly kind of you to be saying so. The tales are childish at times, foolish, but they're ours."

"You're right," he said simply. "I apologize."

He waved her back when she bent to retrieve the wooden washbasin and lifted it himself. "It goes there, in the shed," she informed him, gesturing to an ancient-looking pile of rocks and thatch. "And thank you. 'Tisn't your job, hefting my things about."

Ever polite, Gabriel thought with a tight smile. When she turned to go back into the cottage, he asked, "Why does it bother you so much that I think poorly of ghost stories and fairy tales? It isn't as if I'm shocking you with the truth that they don't exist."

She gave him a long look. "What vexes me," she replied calmly, "is how hard you try to keep yourself apart from where you are."

"And what am I supposed to make of that cryptic little statement?"

"You'll make whatever you will of it. What I see in you, Gabriel, is a need for something—something other than a dalliance with me," she added with a bluntness that surprised him. "But if it's here on Skye, you won't be finding it until you stop seeing yourself as one man against the rest. You've little patience and less acceptance in you."

"Do you really believe that?" he demanded.

"From the moment we met."

He stared at her. Her face was cool, resolute. "What is it you think I'm searching for, Maggie?"

She shrugged. "I've no idea, and I won't pry, though I suspect it has something to do with solace."

"And you believe I can find it here."

"You'll think this as foolish as our tales, but Skye has a

way of giving you whatever it is that you seek. But don't be holding your breath. You've closed your mind to so much. Now, I'll go put on some breakfast for you before Tessa and I go."

With that, she spun on her heel, presenting him with her graceful back and the tantalizing sight of her pale nape beneath the mass of autumn hair. "No," Gabriel muttered, his body damnably taut as he carried the wooden tub toward the tumbledown shed. "I won't be holding my breath."

He bumped both elbows and his head as he wrestled the basin into the crowded space. He emerged backward, cursing fluently, and thudded solidly into a stone-solid object. The epithets died on his lips when he discovered that the granite was, in fact, the towering Mr. MacDonald. God only knew how long he had been here and how much he had seen.

Some primal instinct had Gabriel immediately sizing up the man, making an assessment as to whether he could take him down. It would, he decided, be a good fight. MacDonald was a good four inches taller, outweighed him by at least two stone, and gave every appearance of possessing the devil's strength—and disposition. The brute strength was there, but the intelligence was debatable. At the moment, the man's rawly handsome face was drawn into a scowl and he had his tree-limb arms crossed over his chest.

"Good afternoon, Mr. MacDonald," Gabriel grunted, reluctantly unclenching his own fists. "I trust you are well."

It was like addressing a bull, and the problem of language was only part of the matter. MacDonald said nothing, merely stared down his impressive nose. He made no move to step aside, forcing Gabriel to walk either around or through him. In another time and place, Gabriel would have welcomed the fight. His own six-foot, decently muscled form had served him well against far worthier adversaries than this Skye peasant.

"Bloody hulking ox," Gabriel muttered under his breath as he stepped to the side. Then, louder, "I suppose Maggie will want to feed you." He gestured toward the cottage. MacDonald didn't budge. "As you wish. A good day to you, Mr. MacDonald."

He did not like the idea of turning his back on the man, but wasn't about to scuttle off like a crab. So, chin out, he strode off across the rough yard.

"Sasunnach!"

Gabriel halted, closed his eyes for a moment, then turned. He had a feeling that whatever Gaelic MacDonald was going to launch at him would be precisely along the line of the insults he himself had stifled. "Sir?"

"I've eaten, as it happens," MacDonald announced. "I brought this for the MacLeods' table, so I'd say Maggie will be feeding it to you. 'Tis a shame I can't be bothered to hunt crow." He tossed a rough sack at Gabriel's feet. A bloody wing that looked to be a pheasant's spilled from the top. "You're not half so clever as you fancy yourself."

With that, he insolently flicked the brim of his black leather hat and, vaulting easily over the stone wall, disappeared into the neighboring field. Gabriel closed his slack jaw with an audible click, then muttered, "We'll see, won't we?"

He was still staring over the field, thoughts roiling, when Tessa bounded from the house to tell him his food was on the table. She peered at the sack. "What's that?"

"MacDonald brought it."

"Ah. Dinner." Undaunted by the gore, she gathered the thing up. "Do you hunt?"

"Not birds," Gabriel replied tersely.

"Mmm. Well, you can come hunt kelp with me. 'Tisn't much of a fight, but it has its moments." She peered at MacDonald's receding form. "Lachlann doesn't much care for you, my lord."

That was hardly news to Gabriel. "Campbell and MacDonald?" he asked dryly.

"Not at all, unless you've been flapping your tongue about being a Campbell. Nay, I'd say it has more to do with the way Maggie looks at you."

His head snapped around. "And how is that?"

"With soft eyes," Tessa said absently, tucking a few feathers back into the sack she held. "She used to look at the Toad so."

"The Toad?"

"Aye. Oh." The girl looked up, smacked her forehead with her palm. "I wasn't ever going to speak of that. So, are you coming with me to gather seaweed?"

"You know," Gabriel said after a moment, "I believe I will."

⇥ 11 ⇤

Seaweed Oatcakes

Soak potful of fresh carrageen or dulse for several hours in cold water. Drain. Return to pot, cover with fresh water, and simmer for several more hours until it turns to jelly. Stir in a cup of butter, half a cup of honey, and mix well. Add ground clove, cinnamon, or ginger to taste. Stir in small amounts of oatmeal until stiff. Shape into small, flat cakes and fry.

Maggie left the postman's cottage with a letter from Isobel tucked safely in her pocket. She would wait until she got home to read it. Izzy's letters from England were among the best treats her sister could imagine, and needed to be savored with tea and a ginger biscuit in a quiet kitchen.

With Gabriel and Tessa collecting carrageen and Jamie off heaven only knew where, the house would be quiet. Thoughts on tea and what remained in the earthenware biscuit jar, Maggie didn't see Lachlann until she'd nearly bumped into him. He was standing in front of his sister's cottage, legs firmly planted, arms crossed, a handsome colossus blocking the little village road.

"You'll come to harm," he informed her when she faltered to a halt scant inches away, "walking about blindly so."

"So I will if I go bumping my head against you." She smiled. "Thank you for the birds."

"You're welcome. Be sure to feed the *Sasunnach* the bits with the shot in them."

She didn't scold this time. Instead, she invited him, "Come have supper with us tonight."

"I can't."

"Ah, Lachlann, he truly isn't so—"

"Nay, 'tisn't that, though I'll eat ground glass before I happily break bread with the English. I'm off to Glasgow tonight."

"Have you a buyer for your heifers?"

He shrugged. "We'll see. But it's more than that."

Something in his expression sent a warning chill through Maggie. "What is it?"

"I . . . Oh, Maggie Lil." He kicked at a stone with his booted toe. "I'm thinking of leaving the isle."

"For how long?"

His eyes, so fiercely blue, were solemn when they met hers. "For good."

"Oh, Lachlann. Nay!"

"I need to get away. There's naught for me here now. Best to move on while I can."

She'd known this man for most of her life. The loss of him would grieve her terribly. "Where would you go? Skye is your home, your place. What of your lands? Your family?"

He jerked his chin toward his sister's cottage. "Jeannie's husband will manage the land. 'Tis half theirs anyway. And they'll look after my mother."

"Where?" Maggie demanded again.

"The mainland, mayhaps. Or Ireland."

It might as well have been the end of the earth. "You're just feeling restless, Lachlann. 'Tis the curse of all men. You'll see to your business in Glasgow, then you'll come home. . . ."

Something there, in his eyes and the set of his jaw, told her he was already gone.

"When?" she asked quietly.

"Soon. Mayhaps as soon as I come back from Glasgow."

"Oh. Oh, Lachlann." Maggie stepped forward and rested her forehead against his chest. She fought against the tears that pricked behind her eyelids.

Lachlann stood still as stone for a long moment. Then he rested one heavy hand on her shoulder. "We've grown up, Maggie Lìl. And we've made our choices. As I don't care for some of yours, you'll be grieved by mine." He moved his hand to tip up her chin. "You know I'd not hurt you by choice."

"I do. I know that," she said shakily.

"Well, try to forgive me for the rest, then."

Maggie closed her eyes, took a deep breath. "You'll not go without saying good-bye?"

"Of course not," he answered. She wasn't sure he was telling her the truth. "Now, I have to go see to my cattle." He released her and tipped his hat. "A good day to you, Miss MacLeod."

"And to you, Mr. MacDonald."

She forced a smile, held it until he was out of her sight. Then she let her shoulders slump, nearly dropping her basket. She couldn't imagine not seeing Lachlann again, never seeing his long form striding over the heath. She'd never once considered that he might leave Skye, not even during his lengthy absences when he conducted business in Aberdeen and beyond. When other men had left the island to join the army, he'd scoffed and snorted, wanting no part of the king's concern. He'd never shown any wanderlust. And now he was leaving.

Heart heavy now, she continued on her way toward home. As she went she found herself composing a reply to Izzy's letter before she'd even read it.

Lachlann's leaving the island. I ought to have seen it coming with him gone so much and so often somber when he's here. . . .

Tessa's grown again. It's a race now to see if she outgrows her clothing before wearing it to bits. . . .

Your friend is still here, and I'm frightened of the things I think to do when he's nearby. . . .

She wouldn't be saying any such thing to Isobel. The distance between them since Isobel's marriage was so hard sometimes. She and Izzy had always been so close, had told each other everything. But there were things that just couldn't be said in a letter. And, sometimes now, things that weren't said at all.

Maggie had wanted so much to tell her sister about Peter, had needed Isobel for advice and fresh handkerchiefs and a steady embrace. But Maggie had been in Hertfordshire, Izzy in Town, and by the time they had seen each other—a fleeting visit that had left no time for intimate conversation—Maggie had already tucked her hurt and shame deeply away.

She hadn't told anyone about Peter while he was in her life and hadn't once spoken of him since he'd so abruptly left it.

She tucked a hand into her pocket and ran a fingertip around the edge of Isobel's letter. Good news, she hoped, with a few anecdotes of life amidst England's High Society told as only Izzy could, with her own brand of wit and a pinch of tart Scots' disdain for that society.

There was money sealed into the letter, too. Mr. Mac-Gruder, on seeing the special posting, had set it aside, and Maggie was grateful both to him and to her sister. Their father had been running through his monthly allowance far too quickly of late, no mean feat considering that they were on a relatively remote island and that

Nathan's settlement was more than generous. But Jamie wagered on anything with anyone, tended to buy all the ale on all the occasions, and was rarely left with more than a few shillings at the end of the month. Short of hiding money, which she frequently did, and scolding, which she loathed to do, Maggie had little recourse. Jamie was a grown man. His daughter knew better than to think she could change him, nor was it her job. So she economized as best she could, and was thankful for what Isobel sent.

The house was pleasantly quiet when Maggie reached it. She wasted no time in brewing her tea and settling herself at the kitchen table. She smiled at the unadorned wax seal. That meant Isobel had been alone when she had closed the letter. On those frequent occasions when Nathan's family was about, out came the large and intricate Oriel stamp. The Duke and Duchess of Abergele were perfectly lovely people, but they had never once in their lives erred on the side of informal.

Maggie broke the seal and unfolded the letter. She slipped the twenty-pound note under her saucer. It would go into the corner of her herb basket when she was done reading.

Maggie Lìl, the opening read, *you'll sit down now, please, if you're standing. You're to be an auntie come November.*

Maggie felt the tears springing to her eyes. "Oh, Isobel," she gasped aloud. "Oh, Izzy!"

She rose halfway to her feet, ready to shout the wonderful news to her father and sister. But of course they weren't there. Teary-eyed, grinning like a madwoman, Maggie sank back into her seat. *An auntie.* Little hands tangling in her skirts when they visited, a warm and sleepy little body in her lap in the evenings by the fire.

She wiped her eyes quickly with the back of her hand and kept reading. Isobel was, as she put it, sick as a dog and twice as quick to forget each bout. Nathan was trying to learn to pronounce *tha gradh agam ort*—I love you—properly and was practicing each night to his wife's belly. Maggie thought he would be a good father despite all his stern reserve. He was a good husband to Isobel, loved her fiercely. It would be the same for his child.

Her breath caught on a sudden sob. She ruthlessly swallowed it. There was no call to be crying over something she'd lost—when it wasn't something she'd ever truly had.

She would get some of the softest wool yarn from Clodagh Norrie. White, she thought, or perhaps pale yellow. She would begin now, in the evenings, and have a fine big blanket ready to swaddle Isobel's child in November.

"Oh, Izzy," she whispered again. "Marvelous, wonderful, lucky Izzy."

Her father and Tessa would be thrilled with the news. It called for a celebratory dinner. Jumping to her feet, Maggie went to the pantry. They would have spring onion soup before the pheasant, and a rich honey cake after. Jamie would gladly open a fine bottle of smuggled French wine gleaned from Nathan's cellars and Tessa could unwrap their mother's seldom used bone-china plates.

Maggie bustled around the kitchen, humming, planning, gathering the things she would need later. She cleaned the birds and did her best to remove all the shot. Lachlann might be amused by the image of Gabriel cracking his tooth on a little piece of lead; Maggie wasn't.

A good hour had passed before she replaced her now cold tea and sat again to finish Isobel's letter. She had a dozen tasks to see to and soon, but wanted to at least skim the last page. There were always greetings from Nathan, from their brothers. This time, there was more.

We're sending a dear friend of Nathan's to you and our fair island for a bit. He should be arriving on the heels of this letter, having seen to some pesty and thankless family business somewhere just south of the Highlands. Feed him well, darling—he doesn't eat as often as he should—and slip a few of your very best healing herbs into his wine, which he never declines. He has had a miserable year in England, a worse one before that on the Peninsula, trying to get home. He doesn't speak of it, but it marked him, like it did Nathan. Only this former soldier hasn't anyone at home for him.

Isobel followed with Gabriel's name and a description. *A handsome rogue,* she called him ultimately, *with all the pretty words necessary for any situation.*

That was true enough, Maggie thought. Her eyes paused on the following line, went back, and read it again.

Do be a bit on your guard, Mairghread. He has a fierce reputation here in Town, of chasing whom he shouldn't and not doing much of what he should. I daresay both are true. He does perhaps drink rather more than is seemly; I know Nathan has pulled him from more than one awful gaming hell. But Nathan loves him still, and the truth is that I know no real ill of him. I've seen as much good as not.

Be kind but firm, as I know you can be, and send
him back to Town with some color in his cheeks and
letters from each of you in his pockets.

Maggie folded the letter neatly and tucked it into her
apron pocket. She put the bank note with it. She gathered up her cup and plate with the remnants of a ginger
biscuit and set them aside.

She would think on Isobel's words. Later. Until then,
she would think of Isobel's baby, and how it would be
born already knowing the meaning of *tha gradh agam ort*.

Gabriel shaded his eyes from the rare sunshine and
stared across the water to the little island of Soay. A
handful of boats were just visible, bobbing in the waves.
Any could be waiting to transport a traitor. All could
merely be waiting for the next load of netted fish. Half a
mile down along the Skye shore, he could see the cliffs,
rising tall and severe from the sea. The drop appeared
just as dramatic from the bottom. A body would fall far
longer than a heartbeat before striking the rocks. The
land declined from the cliffs to the strand where he and
Tessa stood. At the end of the sandy crescent was a rocky
wall, nothing compared to the cliffs, but craggy and tall
enough that Gabriel had to tilt his head to see the top.

Ten feet away, knee-deep in salt water and seaweed,
Tessa was nattering away about rain and seals, or some
such nonsense. Only moments before, she had been re-
galing him with information on kangaroos. Not that she
had ever seen one. He had. Yes, he had agreed vaguely,
they did box with their forelegs. No, he'd explained, he
did not think the famous pugilist Gentleman Jackson
had ever sparred with one. No, he had admitted, he had
no idea if he himself could plant a kangaroo a facer.

They had taken the long way down, riding Gabriel's horse all the way to the far end of the strand, where the earth sloped gently enough to be walked. Tessa's disappointment at not being allowed to take the rather treacherous-looking path closer to the cliffs was muted by the opportunity to ride pillion. She had chatted all the way down, all the way along the strand, and was still chattering now as she slopped red seaweed into an oilskin-lined basket. She hadn't said a single word about any toad.

"We've dolphins sometimes," she informed Gabriel, "and sharks. Have you ever seen a shark, my lord?"

"I have. In the waters off Portugal."

Tessa's eyes brightened at the mention of the exotic land. "You were in Portugal? With Nathan, was it? Why didn't you say so? Why is it no one sees fit to include me in matters of a serious nature? I am not a child. Were you a spy?"

Gabriel lifted a brow. "You *are* a child, and I would guess no one discusses serious matters with you because you ask ridiculous questions."

"Rubbish." Unoffended and undaunted, Tessa pressed, "Did you fight with Wellington? Does he really have a nose the size of a shark fin? Nathan says no, but I think he's just being loyal. I've seen the prints in Papa's magazines and it looks like a grand, strapping fin to me."

Gabriel climbed over the sand and rocks, stopping above the tide pool in which she stood. "A shark fin, indeed." He crouched down carefully on the slippery rocks, wondering how he was going to steer the conversation gracefully from sharks to toads.

"You'd best stay where you are," Tessa announced, eyeing his Hoby boots with a mixture of admiration and scorn. "I don't expect you to help me."

"Generous of you," Gabriel murmured. He hadn't intended to, at least not at this point. He imagined he would be the one hefting the basket once it was full. "Tell me about Maggie's toad." Grace bedamned.

Tessa was back to rooting under the water. "Aye. His name was Peter, but I always called him the Toad. He looked like one, with his great, thrusting eyes. All the girls in our part of Hertfordshire thought him ever so handsome, but to me he was a toad. Pity, really. I've always thought toads rather fetching—in a homely way, to be sure. Don't you?"

"Toads. Certainly. But what did this Peter have to do with Maggie and your ghosts?"

"Just Maggie. Not the ghosts, except in how she looks at the tale now." Tessa glanced up and grinned. "She thinks I don't know. She thinks no one knows, not even our sister, Isobel, and they tell each other everything."

"Tessa . . ."

"You won't tell her, will you? That I know? I mean, it's all well and good for one to be recognized for one's cleverness, but I don't think Maggie would care for me speaking of it."

Gabriel's patience was a formidable thing, especially when it involved attaining something he wanted badly. "I won't breathe a word of it," he promised solemnly. "Now, the Toad . . . ?"

"Aye, the Toad. I think they were to be married and mashed lips. Ick."

"Mashed . . . *Married?*"

"Well, she used to sneak out of the house at night to meet him. I followed her once, to a clearing in the woods. They rushed forward, banged up against each other, and mashed lips. Ick." Tessa paused to lift a string of dripping seaweed and examine it carefully. Gabriel waited, one foot tapping against the earth. "I didn't stay, nor did I follow her again. Who wants to watch one's sister mashing lips with a toad? I didn't want to hear them talk of marriage, either, as I imagine they were."

The girl flicked the seaweed away and went on, "Not that it mattered in the end. After a month or so, she stopped sneaking out at night and turned very quiet and sad. Then, a few months after that, we came home to Skye. Can't say I was sorry for any of it, though I do hate to see Maggie sad. I didn't much fancy a toadly brother-in-law. Isobel's husband rather reminds me of a hawk sometimes, which is quite all right. I think hawks the most noble creatures. Don't you?"

Gabriel wasn't listening any longer. He was too busy imagining Maggie in the arms of a toadly creature, under moonlight and forest leaves. Had she expected the man to marry her? Had she been so sure of it, so in love, that she had given him more than warm kisses?

I understand quick heat and desire, better than you think, probably. You think me naive and perhaps I am. I've certainly none of your worldliness. But I know the human body, and I understand the urges within.

He hadn't been listening when she'd said those words. Not really. He'd been too caught up in his own heat and desire. Now he heard her. And he suddenly had a very good idea of just what had happened between Maggie and this Peter.

He betrayed her, broke her heart. As the story goes, he'd made promises of forever and she'd lain with him.

Was it possible? Yes, Gabriel thought. More than that, it was probable.

His angel, his Saint Maggie wasn't as inviolate as she seemed. She wasn't at all what he'd thought, what he'd come to desire. But God help him; he still wanted her. Perhaps more than before. And he had a feeling that his chances of getting what he wanted had just vastly improved.

"Here. You can help now."

Gabriel looked up just in time to see Tessa heaving the laden basket in his direction. He managed to get a hand on it before it tipped over, but was still graced with a long strand of seaweed slithering across his foot.

"Gathering wool while I'm gathering the food." Tessa grinned. "There's a man for you."

"That," Gabriel retorted, "is altogether too adult a sentiment for one of your age."

"And that stuffy little pronouncement was perfectly suited to someone of yours."

He couldn't help himself; he chuckled. "You will be dangerous in a few years, Miss Tessa."

"Aye, I know." She scrambled from the water onto the rocks, a cheeky bud destined to become a perfectly breathtaking rose. "And I won't be mashing lips with any toads, I'll tell you that now."

Gabriel shook his head wryly. "Someone needs to warn the boys in London."

"London? Pah. I've no need to go to London."

"I would imagine Isobel and Nathan are planning to give you a Season."

Tessa shrugged. "They'll learn otherwise. I am going to stay here and marry Tearlach Beaton."

"Does he know that?"

"Not yet. He still thinks he's going to marry Maggie. Or Sileas Wilkie. But he won't."

No, Gabriel mused. He won't. The Tearlach Beatons of the world didn't get the Maggie MacLeods.

"Well, come on, then. We've just enough time. I'll show you where the old *Sasunnach* fell."

One hand holding the heavy basket, the other searching for purchase as he followed the goat-nimble girl over the rocks, Gabriel demanded, "What on earth would make you think I want to see any such thing?"

Tessa, already a good twenty feet ahead, tossed him an incredulous look over her shoulder. "Who wouldn't want to—"

The loud crack silenced her. Gabriel started, then again as a small piece of rock from the wall above glanced sharply off his cheek.

"What—?" Tessa began.

There was another crack, followed by several echoes. More rock fell, a shard the size of an apple glancing off Gabriel's shoulder. He saw several smaller bits strike Tessa, watched as she struggled for balance on the slippery rocks. In an instant, he forgot the slick footing and his ill-suited boots. He dropped the basket, leapt over several small boulders and a tide pool, and grabbed the girl around her waist. Sheltering her with his body, he propelled them both forward, toward the narrow strip of sand that ran along the bottom of the rock wall.

"My lord—"

"Quiet!" he snapped, holding her upright by the elbow when she stumbled. He glanced up, eyes sliding along the top of the low wall to the south, trying to see anything. He thought he caught some movement, a human form in motion along the edge. He gave Tessa a quick push in the direction from which they'd come. "Run. Take my horse and go home."

"But—"

"Now!"

She went, with a single, frightened glance back. Just as she got out of range there was another shot, a lead ball slamming into the boulder just in front of Gabriel and sending up more sharp debris. As he threw himself flat onto the sand, cursing, he felt a warm trickle from his brow and caught a coppery whiff of his own blood. In the following moments as he lay waiting for the next blast, he heard hoofbeats pounding up the trail. The girl would be safe. He doubted she knew what had happened—she'd certainly never been shot at before— but she would send help. He could only hope it arrived before a shot found its target.

Whoever it was was on the slope some hundred yards down from the uppermost point of the cliffs, high enough to have a view of the whole beach and low enough to have a clear shot. Gabriel could only guess at the exact point. Judging by the angle of the first blasts, he had some cover. Not enough. Like a crab in a tide pool, he was safe only if he stayed right where he was, behind the low rocks. If he tried to follow Tessa, he became an easy target.

He took a chance and peered over his shelter. Almost immediately, a ball thudded into the sand a few feet away. A minute later, another knocked Tessa's basket several yards into a small pool, spraying pieces of dried reed and bloodred seaweed over the rocks. A large musket, Gabriel decided, French or Colonial, perhaps, probably intended for military use. A smaller gun, one of the sort a farmer would have, wouldn't have the distance or power.

For the moment, that distance was on his side. Unless the shooter chose to leave his own cover and make his way closer to the strand. Considering the fact that Gabriel had no weapon of his own, that wasn't an un-likely choice. On level ground, he was little more than a

sitting duck. L'Écossais—and Gabriel had no doubt that
it was L'Écossais—had him pinned.

It appeared the hunter had become the hunted.

Maggie was up to her elbows in flour, apples, and
honey at her side, waiting to be stirred into the cake
batter. Cinnamon was precious, but she'd added a good
pinch to the mix along with some ground cloves. She had
set out potatoes from last night's roast and some
sausages for the midday meal. They had only to be fried
up when Jamie, Tessa, and Gabriel wandered in.

*Feed him well, darling—he doesn't eat as often as he
should. . . .*

Maggie had grown used to seeing Gabriel at her table,
had grown accustomed to his satisfied smile when he'd
tucked away one of her dinners. Perhaps he had gone
glass-for-glass with Jamie early on, but he seemed to be
drinking less lately. It had been several days since Maggie
had seen the sleek silver flask go from his pocket to
his fist.

*Do be a bit on your guard, Mairghread. He has a fierce
reputation here in Town, of chasing whom he shouldn't
and not doing much of what he should.*

It was a warning to be heeded, certainly. Maggie
trusted Isobel implicitly, listened when she spoke. But
Isobel was hundreds of miles away, and had given
Maggie only a few lines in a letter. She hadn't watched
Gabriel with their drunken father, seen his simple kind-
nesses to a pesty Tessa.

She hadn't had his hands on her back or his lips on her
face. She hadn't felt a longing so strong that it threatened
to rend her in two.

"A bhoirionnaich gun chiall!" Maggie scolded herself
aloud and harshly for being a fool. The words wouldn't

come to her in English; the feelings were too strong. *"Air nàile—"*

She glanced out the window at the sound of hoofbeats. Someone was riding hell-for-leather into the yard. She quickly reached for a cloth to wipe the flour from her hands, but had barely begun when the outer door banged and Tessa came stumbling into the kitchen.

The girl's eyes were huge in a face that was ash pale beneath smudges of dirt. Her hair was a wild auburn tangle down her back. There was a large tear in her breeches and a frightening red smear on the collar of her white shirt. Flour forgotten, Maggie was across the flagstone floor in an instant, her sister's face cupped in her hands.

"What happened?" she demanded, searching for the source of the blood. "Where are you hurt? Where—"

"I'm fine. I'm fine. But Lord Rievaulx . . . The cliffs were falling . . . there was rock falling. . . . Oh, Maggie!"

Relieved in that instant that the girl was unharmed, Maggie gathered her close, stroking her hair and murmuring mindless reassurances. Moments later, heart beating a frightened tattoo, she asked, "Gabriel . . . Lord Rievaulx . . . Was he struck? Is he hurt?"

"I don't know." Tessa lifted a pale face. "He shoved me toward his horse, made me leave."

"Thank God for that." Maggie's mind was whirling, her knees shaking. "Are you well enough to ride for help?"

Tessa shuddered once, then drew herself resolutely upward. "Aye."

"Good girl. Go for Lachlann. Now."

She waited only until she heard the horse speeding away. Then she rushed into the pantry. Heedless of the jars and bottles she scattered, she seized her basket of healing supplies and riffled through the contents. Comfrey salve, nettle ointment, witch-hazel wash. Clean linen bandages. God only knew what she might need. God only knew how badly he was hurt.

O Dia. Gabriel.

Heart pounding, she ran from the house, leaving the door wide open behind her.

≈ 12 ≈

*Rosemary is carried at weddings
and at funerals.*

Maggie was out of breath and windblown by the time she crested the bluff above the beach. She was not the first one there. Several people stood at the edge. She saw Calum MacAuley and Tearlach among them. There was no sign of Tessa or Lachlann. Or Gabriel. Breath coming in quick gasps, pulse skittering, she ran the last twenty yards.

As she did, Calum stepped aside to reveal a familiar back clothed in an expensive coat. Only sheer force of will kept Maggie from dropping to her knees in relief. Gabriel turned to face her, eyes dark in a face smeared with dirt and streaks of blood. Then he lifted one hand from his side, briefly and no farther than waist level, but in her direction. And she had to clamp one fist hard over her mouth to keep the single, ragged sob from bursting out.

Seeing her, Tearlach called, "Your guest nearly had a cairn built atop him."

"What happened?" Maggie demanded, marching toward Gabriel on determinedly steady legs. "Tessa said—"

"Rock slide," came from Calum, in English. "I was strolling along and what should I see but this fellow climbing o'er the bluff, face bloody. Gave me a good

191

start, he did. I thought our walking *Sasunnach* from Scavaig Point was having a daylight ramble." Of Gabriel, he demanded, "Do you ken what a cairn is, lad?"

The oh-so-welcome sound of Gabriel's voice sent a new tremor through Maggie. "A mound of stones, so I gather."

"A burial mound." Calum nodded toward Maggie's basket. "You'll be right enough once Maggie slaps some salve onto your face. Someone's looking out for you above. You could have had the whole wall come tumbling down onto your head."

"Somehow," Gabriel murmured, "I don't think that was very likely. But I'll agree that I was fortunate this time." He demanded of Maggie, "How is Tessa?"

"Well enough to come flying home like the wind," she answered.

"Ah. Good." He flinched as she raised a trembling hand to his face, jaw going hard under her fingertips. "What are you doing?"

"Be still," she commanded, careful not to meet his eyes. "I need to see how bad this is."

"I've had far worse," he grunted, but allowed her to continue her gentle exploration.

After several minutes, she set her basket on the ground at his feet and began to dig through it. Wetting a bandage with rosemary wash, she set to cleaning away the grime and blood. What appeared were numerous nicks, one dangerously close to his eye, but the bleeding had all but stopped. There was nothing there that a thorough cleaning and some ointment wouldn't set aright.

"You'll be full bonny again by the time you get back to England." She ignored the twinge she felt in her chest at the thought of him going. "Now, this might sting a bit."

He didn't so much as twitch at the witch hazel, nor

when she gently dabbed comfrey salve into the wounds. He did give a slight intake of breath when she reached for his hand, intending to have him hold a bandage over the single cut on his brow that still bled sluggishly. Glancing down, she saw that his hands, just as grimy as his face had been, were covered with similar marks. One gash, snaking over the back of his hand between thumb and forefinger, was just deep enough to concern her.

She cleaned his hands as carefully as she could. "This might need stitching."

"Your job as well?"

"Aye. But never fear, I've been told I sew a decent enough seam."

" 'Tell her to make me a cambric shirt,' " he said, so quietly that only she could hear.

Another cry welled in her throat. She swallowed it. "I'll never be—" She was interrupted by the sound of an approaching horse. Expecting Tessa and Lachlann, she was surprised to hear, "A party alfresco, and no one thought to invite me?"

Maggie watched as Edana Malcolmson, neat as a pin in a heather gray riding habit, pulled her little Arab mare to a dainty halt. Both Calum and Tearlach stepped forward to help her dismount. Both were shoved back as the glowering MacGillechalum, an unlikely lady's groom with his wild beard and monster of a horse, moved in to do the task.

Once on the ground, Edana removed her sleek kid gloves, stepped in, and lifted Gabriel's chin with her bared fingertips. He let her. "I was on the road home when I saw this little congregation. You look like Prometheus after a bout with the sea serpent, my lord." She rested one hand fleetingly at Gabriel's waist. "Have you been left with all necessary bits intact?"

He grasped her hand, bowed briefly over it before letting it go. "I am quite well. Thank you. I was merely struck by some falling rock below."

Edana's golden brows went up beneath the delicate netting of her shako. "Did I not say from the beginning that you lead an exciting life?"

"Did you? On occasion I might be inclined to agree."

Behind them, Gabriel caught the butler's malevolent glare. The fellow had stepped back, as was his place, and was toying with a long pack tied across the back of his saddle, all the while keeping his eyes fixed on his mistress and the Englishman.

"Tessa was expecting to sit with you this morning, Edana." Maggie's voice was mild enough, melodic as always with its gentle lilt, but Gabriel detected the slightest edge to it. "She was sorry to have missed you."

The other woman's laugh rang out, light and practiced. "Why do I doubt that? We've been working on conjugating the more difficult French verbs." She turned her blithe smile on Maggie. "Unfortunately I was late returning from Loch Coruisk. My watercolors simply wouldn't dry."

Gabriel took a long look at the bundle attached to the butler's saddle. "I should very much like to see your work."

Edana waggled a finger near his chest. "A gentleman should wait for such things to be offered. And I cannot imagine why you would be thinking of a few splotches of color after what you have been through. No, I do not think I will show you anything just now. Let our Maggie finish with her tender ministrations. We'll all have a merry little gathering another time."

A large form came stalking over the heath just then. *Well, well,* Gabriel thought as Lachlann MacDonald approached, *we're having an interesting little gathering here already*. Most of the principle players seemed to be in attendance. It was all just a bit too coincidental for his taste.

He didn't know precisely why the shooting had stopped as suddenly as it had. He suspected someone had appeared along the cliff road. He'd heard MacAuley and Beaton speaking at almost the same time, Gaelic words he couldn't understand. Wisdom, and a suspicious nature born of far too much experience, had had him staying right where he was, belly pressed into the sand, until he heard a third voice, and a fourth. Then he'd made his way up the narrow and rocky path to the top.

A good little portion of the local population had met him there, all solicitous, all with perfectly feasible reasons why they were there. For the moment, Gabriel was simply happy to be in one piece. A careful examination of the events would wait.

He'd come far closer to dying on more than one occasion. But in the past, his urge to survive had been instinctive, all animal nature and roaring blood. This time, the force had been conscious. He'd thought of Maggie, of the fact that dying before he'd touched the depths of her was unbearable.

He could smell her now above the sea air and heather. The scent was sweetly familiar: clove and apple and more, and had worked its way inside his head. She was rummaging in her basket again, face hidden by rippling auburn hair set free by the wind. She wore no wrap, just a worn apron over her dress. Gabriel wondered if she'd come racing over the heath, forgetting something so basic as a shawl. She would be cold, and he found himself warmed by the the idea that she might have been so worried.

He started to remove his coat, ready to wrap her in it. She looked up, saw him tugging at the buttons with his battered hands, and gave a quick hiss. "You'll make it worse." Quickly, she returned to his side and made a tight bandage over the worst gash.

He didn't feel the cuts at all. The warmth of her fingers drifting over his was far too distracting.

MacDonald reached them then. "Where's Tessa?" Maggie demanded.

"I have no idea," was the reply. "Should I?"

"I sent her to find you. To help."

MacDonald's impressive brows drew into a scowl. "To help with what?"

It was Edana who answered. "Lord Rievaulx was nearly caught in a rock slide down below. He spent a rather unpleasant few minutes waiting for it to stop."

"He seems hale enough to me," MacDonald grunted.

The man's hands were shoved deep into the pockets of his rough trousers. He certainly wasn't carrying a gun. But then, Gabriel mused, there were endless crevices in which a rifle could be hidden, plenty of scrubby ground-cover for camouflage. He scanned the earth quickly. Yes, there between several tall stone masses. That was where the shooter must have been. There was a clear view of the beach, and of the village road. It would have been a matter of seconds to tuck the gun away at the approach of people and appear to simply be strolling by.

Gabriel wanted to cover those twenty-odd yards, to search the rocky furrows. But he knew it would be a futile act. He might find the gun, but he doubted its owner would jump forward to claim it. Whoever it was was clever enough to have realized Gabriel was not just a simple visitor. No doubt he was also clever enough to hide his own acts behind a very reasonable facade.

MacAuley? Beaton? MacDonald? Edana's beast of a manservant? It had to be one of them. Gabriel was certain, a bone-deep certainty, that he was in the presence of L'Écossais. Just as the Scot would be certain that he was in the presence of an agent of His Majesty's Army.

A swift thrill swept through Gabriel. It was fierce and familiar, the quickening of the blood that came with battles of might, battles of wit, and sex. This time, it was knowing that his foe stood not ten feet away, the secret of his identity only a matter of time, and very little time at that.

Gabriel's blood thrummed almost constantly when Maggie was nearby.

He felt a soft touch at his elbow and glanced down. She had a grip on his sleeve there. "Come along. I want to see to that hand and find my sister."

He nodded. "Let's go."

It took a few minutes to extricate himself from the altogether too cheerful attentions of Edana and the men, but at last he and Maggie were on their way back to her home. She was silent, face set in tense lines. He didn't intrude on her thoughts. She was worried for Tessa, he could tell, and there was nothing either of them could do until they'd reached the house and ascertained whether the girl was there.

Maggie did speak to him briefly several times, admonishing him to keep his hand elevated. He suspected she was working on instinct and habit, the innate attention of the born healer.

As it happened, they met Tessa at the rise above the cottage. She was still mounted on his horse; both looked a bit wild-eyed and breathless. On seeing her sister,

Maggie sagged ever so briefly against Gabriel's side in relief. On seeing the pair of them, Tessa cried out, slid from
the horse's back, and ran full-tilt toward them. Gabriel
was startled when she all but hurled herself against his
chest. But he managed to catch her with his good arm
and hold her for a moment while she stood in trembling,
uncustomary silence. Then Maggie was bustling them
into the house, once more her calm and efficient self.

"I went for Lachlann," Tessa said plaintively once
she'd been seated at the table with a steaming cup of tea.
"I went to fetch him, but he wasn't there."

"It's all right," Gabriel replied from his own seat
across from her. "I'm fine. You can see I'm fine. You did
well."

His hand had begun to throb, and he bit back a curse
as Maggie wrapped it in a hot cloth. "I'm sorry," she said
softly. "But I need to be certain it's clean before I decide
what to do about that cut."

She then tended to Tessa, tenderly cleaning the girl's
face with another cloth. Finding no injuries, she stroked
Tessa's hair for a minute, then disappeared into the
pantry. She came back with a plate of shortbread, which
brightened the girl's expression considerably, and a small
sewing basket that had Gabriel's mouth thinning. He'd
had numerous wounds stitched through the years and
knew what was to come.

"I'll be quick," she told him, eyes soft and steady,
"and I'll be gentle."

He felt almost nothing. Maggie rubbed a thick salve
into the wound. When the sting was gone, so was the
pain. Gabriel watched her as she worked on him. She'd
twisted her hair back into a neat, tight plait, leaving her
features free for his perusal. There was a faint flush to
her cheeks, a frown of concentration between her dark

brows. She was beautiful, and she was, in her serene, capable way, putting him back together.

Soon he was left with a tidy row of pale knots in his hand and a far larger knot in his gut. Had Tessa not been there, wide-eyed and silent, Gabriel would have hauled Maggie roughly into his lap and sated himself as best he could with her mouth. As it was, he could only mutter his thanks and hope he looked even a degree less desperate than he felt.

For her part, Maggie was well in control. She tidied the minimal mess she'd made, poured more tea, and turned from healer to housekeeper in the blink of an eye. As Gabriel watched, she deftly served a small repast of cold meat and bread from the night before and, not stopping to eat, went about shuffling bowls and pans. "Our supper," she informed him tersely. "It must go into the oven if it's to be ready in good time."

"Maggie—"

"I need to do this now. I'll leave the both of you to entertain yourselves for a bit."

There was no arguing. Gabriel could see she needed to work, to be left alone. So when Tessa, obviously recovered from her scare, offered to show him her grandfather's claymore, he accepted. She would prattle, he would be able to listen with half an ear, and he would have a very necessary distance from the beautiful fallen angel who was making the blood flame within his veins.

Maggie managed to get through the afternoon, through the evening meal which she barely tasted, without breaking. The tremors were there with the tears, teeming just beneath the surface, threatening to break out and turn her into a helpless wreck. The loss of her mother had been so very hard. She didn't think she would survive losing another member of her family. Her love for Tessa, for her siblings, was too deep.

And Gabriel. Gabriel. The image of him lying battered and bleeding on the sand had assailed her like a mace, sharp and heavy. She didn't know when his presence had become so much a part of her life that she couldn't imagine a day without him. It had. Oh, she knew she would have to face that day, and soon, perhaps. He would leave both her home and Skye. But she wasn't ready quite yet. She just wasn't ready.

Tessa had gone off to bed a half hour past, without so much as a whispered protest. Jamie, too, had tottered off, bottle in hand. He'd been spared the worst of the tale, taking only a mild interest in Gabriel's bandages and giving Tessa a quick pat on the head for being a brave lass. Her father, Maggie mused, was spared the worst of everything, and it was his daughters who saw to it. It wasn't fair, perhaps, having to parent the parent, but it was the way their family went on. It had always been the way their family went on.

So, still shaky inside, she had served the pheasant, sliced the cake, filled the cups. Isobel's news had been cheered and toasted. Jamie was still toasting it now in the parlor as Maggie put the last of the dishes away in the cupboard. She could go up to her room and hope for sleep. But she didn't think it would come. So, hanging her apron on its hook, she slipped out the back door. She needed to walk in the fresh, cool air, to clear her head of its sorry thoughts.

She saw him as she crested the little hill in front of the cottage, a dark outline against the night sky. And her heart thumped.

Gabriel heard her—or sensed her—and turned. "Maggie."

"Aye."

"What is this?" he demanded, voice deep and slightly rough.

Destiny, she thought, then noticed that he was pointing away from them.

The lights were pale in the sky, but still visible, rippling and dancing like water over pearls. " 'Tis the *Fir Chlis,*" she answered. "The Northern Lights."

"Ah. Of course. *Fir Chlis.*"

"That means 'the nimble men.' Whenever two chieftains fell in love with the same fairy woman, the nimble men would fight the battle in the skies."

She heard Gabriel give a faint chuckle. "You make it seem as if that's a frequent event: chieftains fighting over a fairy."

"Scoff if you will," she replied, matching his tone, "but there isn't a mortal man alive who can resist a woman of magic, a *bean sithiche.*"

"No. I know there is not." He was still facing the sky, but reached out his unbandaged hand. "Come walk with me and tell me about the lights, *bean sithiche.*"

She knew the choice was hers; she didn't have to take his hand. She could stay where she was, walk past him into the house, walk beside him without touching him at all. She could be safe, for the rest of her life if she chose to. And she knew she would be a wiser woman for it. But it had gone too far for that, to pay heed to sense. This was a matter of heart.

Gabriel was waiting, quietly, arm extended.

Maggie slipped her hand into his and closed her eyes for an instant with the resulting hot shiver. He drew her closer until her arm was pressed against his, their fingers twined together. They set off at an easy pace, following the slope of the hill down toward the hollow where the rowan grew.

Once there, Gabriel paused, then, as if he had a destination in mind, guided Maggie up again and over the rise. "I want to see everything clearly," he murmured.

They walked for a few minutes until they'd reached *Ailean MhicLeòid*, the small grassy knoll where Maggie's great-grandfather, so family legend told, had seen a fairy woman dancing in the moonlight. He'd met his wife, a newcomer to the area, the following day at market. It was a magical place always, and almost too appropriate in that moment.

Gabriel released her hand long enough to shuck his coat, which he spread on the ground. Then he held her again, and coaxed her down to sit beside him. She didn't resist when he twined their arms, pulling her snugly against his side. Lured by the place and by the man, she rested her cheek against his shoulder, breathed in the scent of her own heather soap and warm male skin.

Above, the Northern Lights swirled and glinted in layers of gold and pink and white—a pale, luminous glow that rippled like a curtain in a lazy breeze. "Tell me a story about the lights," Gabriel coaxed, and she did.

"A young Skyeman, a long-ago MacLeod, once met a woman on a lonely road on a black night. He could barely see her, but knew she was comely. She was lost, she said, blind in the darkness, and couldn't find her way back to her family. When he offered his assistance, she said she required the kiss of a mighty chieftain to regain her sight. Of course, the young man was more than happy to comply, though he was but a warrior among the chieftain's ranks. So he kissed her, softly, on her lips, which were surprisingly cool. And when he did, light flared in the sky, ripples of pearl and ruby, one atop and after the next. It took his breath away, as much as the woman growing soft and warm in his arms.

"The next thing he knew he was waking in the morning, and he was alone in the glen. There was no sign of the woman, nor did he ever see her again, but draped over him was a length of silken cloth, as tall as he and broad enough to wrap full round him. With it was a note, written on a large fig leaf from no tree he had ever seen, telling him the cloth was a gift, a flag to fly high above his castle, to always guide him home."

"A simple warrior, hmm?" Gabriel queried.

"The very next day the old chief was taken by a fit of the heart and the clan chose the young warrior as his successor. His first act was to build a castle with the tallest staff in the Highlands from which to hang the flag. He waited the rest of his life, and 'twas a long one lived happily, for another glimpse of the woman from the glen, but was never so graced." Maggie smiled into the night. "Would you like to see the flag?"

She felt Gabriel twitch. "You jest."

"I do not. It's but a remnant now, sheltered behind glass, but you can see it at Dunvegan, home of the Chief of Clan MacLeod. 'Tis called the Fairy Flag, and has protected the clan for hundreds of years from war and famine and disease."

"You are serious."

"I am indeed. Now, some might tell a different tale as to how we MacLeods came into possession of the flag, but it's real enough. I've seen it."

"Well." Gabriel sighed. There was a long pause where all Maggie could hear was his breath and the soft whisper of the breeze. "Considering what magic I have sitting beside me, I might as well believe your tale."

"Oh, Gabriel," Maggie began. Then, suddenly, she was crying, hot tears that soon turned into great wracking sobs that shook her hard.

She was crying for the tragedy that might so easily have occurred, crying out of the overwhelming relief that her sister and Gabriel had walked away virtually unscathed. It was all too much to keep in any longer, so she stopped trying.

His arms came around her, holding her close to his chest while she sobbed. "Shhh," he whispered against her hair. "Shhh." But he let her cry, making the whisper a comfort rather than a demand to stop.

Finally, the last sob subsided into a damp hiccup. She was spent. And calm. "I need . . . I think I need . . ." She fumbled for a handkerchief she soon realized wasn't there.

Gabriel covered her hand with one of his, then dried her cheeks with the soft cuff of his shirt. "Me. Please. Tell me that what you need just now is me."

"Oh, I . . . I do. I do—" She lost the words, and her breath, as his mouth found hers.

She saw pearly light and wasn't certain for a moment whether her eyes were open or closed. As sweet as the first kiss had been, this was sweeter, and warmer, and filled with a hunger that she felt in her very core. Gabriel's hands cupped her face at first, and she could feel the folds of the carefully tied bandage against her cheek. Then his touch slid along her neck, leaving a path of tiny sparks in its wake. Aching for more, she willed him to slide those warm palms lower. As if hearing her thoughts, he did, caressing her shoulders, her arms, her rib cage, coming to rest just beneath her breasts.

"Ach, Gabriel," she breathed against his mouth, then twined her arms around his neck, pulling him close, finally pulling him down with her until they lay on his coat, his weight a heated delight atop her.

She felt the imprint of his waistcoat buttons, knew he

was marking her, that she would bruise. She didn't care. When he deepened the kiss, his tongue sweeping against hers, she sighed with pleasure and wound her fingers in his thick hair, holding tight. They stayed just like that for what seemed an eternity, face-to-face, both breathing in quick gasps and sometimes not breathing at all. Then he pulled back ever so slightly and kissed her jaw, her cheekbones, her eyelids.

It was the gentlest touch, completely in contrast to the hard length of him pressed against her. *Magic,* she thought, then stopped thinking entirely when his hands covered her breasts. Sweet, wicked sensation rippled from where his fingers centered and teased, radiating to her cheeks and fingertips.

"*Ach, seadh,*" she gasped, head thrown back. He took advantage and pressed his lips to the point where her pulse thundered. "Ah, yes!"

One of his knees slid between hers, slow but persistent. She only held back for a heartbeat before allowing the intimacy. She wanted him close, as close as he could possibly get. Her foot, free of the simple leather shoe she'd donned for an evening in the house, slipped over his leg, up the length of his boot. They were well tangled now, her legs curved tightly around his. She pulled her hands from his hair, ran them across the breadth of his shoulders, down the length of his back to his waist. He was all hard planes and sleek muscle, so wonderful to the touch and so unlike anything she'd ever held that she reveled in the exploration.

He growled, a low, harsh sound. She might have let go, pulled away, but he was suddenly kissing her again, fiercely and hotly, and doing magical things with his fingers that took away most of her conscious will and all of her doubts.

"I . . . Oh, God. Maggie." He lifted his head, eyes glinting obsidian above her. "I want . . ."

"I know."

"More than I can control," he said, hands clenching for a hard, beautiful instant. "If you don't . . . If I can't, now, you must tell me. Now."

He propped himself up on his elbows. In the pale glow of the Northern Lights, Maggie could see the strain on his face. She could also see the hunger and, behind it, the desire she knew in her heart was there just for her, for all that she was and possessed. She knew, because it was roiling in her as well, a wanting for this man so deep that she wondered at it having come about so recently. It felt as if it had been a part of her for more years than she could count.

He would leave. She knew he would leave. Part of him was probably already gone, back in England and the High Society life he led. But the rest of him, most of him, was there with her, in the moment. And she knew she would regret not grasping that moment with him far more than she could ever possibly regret giving herself to him. Somehow she knew that a woman was incredibly fortunate to feel these things once in her lifetime. There wouldn't be a second chance.

He would leave and she knew she would be lost, left at the bottom of a long, long fall. It was all she'd feared and dreaded. Yet it was, too, what she wanted so desperately that she ached with the force of it.

"What is this?" she asked breathily. "This need that drowns out everything else?"

"Do you mind it so very much?"

"Nay," she replied. "I don't mind it at all."

"Then it's a grand passion," was his husky reply.

She reached up, traced the hard planes of his face with

her fingertips. "Ah. I was wondering how that felt. Can you make it even stronger for me?"

"Yes," he said. "I can do that."

"Good. I thought that you could." She touched his brow, his lips. Linked her fingers behind his head and drew him down. "Begin now, please."

Give me no diamonds, nor chains of gold,
No epistle nor pretty rhyme.
All I require is my true love's vow
and a bed of wild thyme.

Gabriel's hands shook slightly as he cupped them behind her shoulders. "Are you certain?"

God, how he needed to hear her accept him. It was, now, all he had to anticipate. There would be nothing for him once he left Skye. He was sending his last bridge to the man he once had been up in scorching flames. His last mission, his last friendship . . .

"Are you certain?" he repeated, harsh and desperate.

"I am," she replied softly. "Are you?"

He smiled then, unable to help himself, felt some of the ice inside him melt. "I have been dreaming of this very moment."

"Well, then."

"Well, then." He stared down into her night-shadowed face. Her skin glowed, pale and unblemished. He could see that she was smiling, too, but her eyes were wide. "Are you frightened?"

"Of course I am," was her immediate reply.

"Good Lord, why? Of what?" It was hardly new territory for her, he thought. If there were to be any surprises, he was determined they would be of the glorious sort. He wouldn't have it any other way.

"That we'll see each other differently come morning."

"You believe we will?"

"I don't see how we couldn't." She turned slightly in his arms. "Tell me again."

"Tell you . . ."

"How you've dreamed of this."

"Not just this. You. Every night," he said, pausing to kiss her once, "I've thought of you in your bed a mere twenty feet down the hall and imagined you in mine." He kissed her again. "Every morning . . ." And again. "I've thought of how it would be to watch your eyes open for the first time with the sun." And again. "When you wash the clothing, each separate item—"

"Och, Gabriel!"

"—I've imagined removing it from you, piece by piece. Your stockings." He skimmed a hand down her side, lifted her skirt and the single petticoat she wore, traced one finger up the outside of her leg, and felt her shiver through the sturdy cotton. He deftly tugged the garter free and pushed the stocking down. He did the same with the other. Both were soon on the grass nearby. He wanted to touch what he'd bared, to feel the silken length of her leg, but he resisted the urge.

"Your petticoat." Again, a quick tug freed the tapes. Maggie was still but for the faint fluttering of her fingertips on the back of his neck. He gently lifted her hips to pull the folds of muslin away and down. Again, he kept himself from exploring the luring expanse of warm skin. "Your dress . . ."

He turned her in his arms until her cheek rested against his shoulder. Here, at the first of the buttons running from her nape to her waist, his fingers faltered a bit. He had dreamed of this, so many times. He needed her reality to be as perfect as his imaginings. He undid the first button, then the next, and the next. When the fabric parted in a V, he pressed his lips to her nape, then lower to the gossamer-thin layer of her chemise.

"Oh, Mairghread." His voice was harsh, ragged to his ears.

She rolled onto her back. He could just see that she was regarding him solemnly, mouth unsmiling. Then, slowly, she placed one hand on his chest, pushing until he was sitting up. She followed. And curved her shoulders forward until the bodice of her dress slid down. With one hand, she pulled at the sleeve of the other arm, repeating the motions for the other side. In seconds, the dress was pooled at her waist.

Gabriel's mouth went dry. She was lovelier than he'd imagined. He could see the swell of her breasts, full and round against the chemise, see the dark thrust of her nipples. "Dear God," he murmured.

"Help me," she commanded.

He did, tugging at the dress until all that remained between them was the chemise. When he moved to undo the fastenings at the back, she stilled his hand. Without a word, she reached for the buttons of his waistcoat. Tongue caught charmingly between her teeth, she released them and parted the heavy silk. Gabriel shrugged the thing off and tossed it aside. His heart was pounding; he wondered that it wasn't visible against his shirt.

Then the shirt, too, was gone, added to the tumble of their clothing. Maggie sat back for a moment, staring at what she had unveiled. Then she lifted both hands, palms flat, and placed them on his chest. Gabriel's muscles leapt in response to her slow exploration. She paused at the scar, the enduring mark of the saber that had very nearly killed him in Portugal. It was hard and ugly and forever served to remind him of what he had once been.

"The war?"

"Yes," he replied.

"Ah."

He had no idea what Maggie was thinking, feeling, until she looked up with a smile that would have melted him had he not been a rigid mass, head to toe.

"You're a bonny creature, Gabriel Loudon," she murmured, then bent her head to feather her lips over the jagged mark. He hadn't realized he'd been holding his breath until he released it from his aching lungs. And he realized how grand the simple name sounded falling from her lips. No one in his life used his surname; no one ever had. There had always been a title to supersede it. But with Maggie MacLeod, he was simply a man, and that suddenly was too important to be ignored.

He wondered how many simple men and women had laid under the Northern Lights here, how many generations of Skye residents had crept away from their duties and concerns to make love in the open air. It was a wonderful, vital legacy, and here he was part of it.

His boots had never come off so easily; the placket of his breeches had never taken so long. But soon enough he was naked, exposed to the night and the woman he was so desperate to possess.

Her eyes, he noticed, were fixed on his groin. "Still bonny?" he jested somewhat painfully.

"Oh . . . Oh, aye." She reached out a hesitant finger to trace the length of him and he nearly came up off the earth. "Gabriel?"

"Do that again and I'll combust on the spot."

"I . . . I am sorry. . . ."

Grinning like a madman now, feeling more alive than ever before, he loomed over her, bearing her back onto his spread coat. "Do it again," he demanded, and closed his mouth hotly over hers.

He only let her explore for a minute. Then he did what he had been aching to do for what seemed forever and splayed a hand over the top of her thigh. As he'd dreamed, she was strong, silken, soft, a deadly combination. Ravenous, eager to taste every inch of her, he took her breast into his mouth, wetting the fine fabric of her chemise. He felt her arch against him, heard her response.

Maggie gasped with the pleasure of it. His teeth, his tongue—she wanted him to take more of her and now. He laved the other breast, deliciously chafing her skin with the dampened muslin. Her hands roamed restlessly over his torso, feeling the iron-beneath-velvet of his lean muscles, needing to feel the sprinkling of springy hair against her skin. She pushed at him, struggled to sit, tugged at the tapes of her chemise. He wasted no time in helping, and in moments they were chest to chest with nothing between them.

She felt no embarrassment, no hesitation, no shame. How could she? she thought, when she'd found something so precious as her feelings for this man.

When he began making a warm trail with his lips and tongue over her ribs, over the gentle swells of her belly and hips, she sighed. When that marvelous touch went lower, to the crease of her thigh, she hummed in delight. And when he gently coaxed her legs apart with deft fingers, pressing his lips to the soft inside of her thigh, she gasped.

"Gabriel!"

"Shhh. I need this. Let me."

"Why? I . . . *oh.*" Her eyes sprang wide at that first oh-so-intimate touch. *"O Dia . . ."* Little flames began licking at her, from the inside out. Hot, insistent, each built upon the last. She could feel Gabriel's warm breath on her thighs, feel the heat of his mouth. On and on the sensation swirled, too sweet to stop and too elusive to catch.

Then, suddenly, her very core went to flame.

Wave after wave of ruthless, glorious fire swept over her, making her cry out and tremble. She heard her own cry, heard Gabriel give a single, throaty laugh of pleasure and conquest. Then he was with her again, holding her close, his eyes locked fiercely on hers as she shook in his arms.

"Hold me, Mairghread," he commanded, and she did. "The devil call me a fool, but I'll ask once more." His voice was taut, tortured. "Are you certain of this? We can't go back once . . ."

She silenced him with a finger over his lips. "I can't go back even now."

"Nor can I."

She felt the hard press where his mouth had been, felt herself stretching as he thrust firmly, steadily into her. And she cried out at the sharp, quick pain. She'd known it would come, had readied her mind for it. Now she bit her lip against it.

"*Maggie!*" Gabriel pushed himself up, half away from her. "Oh, God," he growled. "Why . . . ? Ah, hell . . ."

Instinct had her arching again, drawing him deeper before he could withdraw and turn away. He groaned, a lost sound, then stroked once, twice, again. She clung to him, pressing hot kisses into the taut skin below his collarbone. She could give him this, this complete gift of herself, and she would. She twined her legs around his, matched the thrust of his hips with hers. And when at last he gave a final surge, falling against her with a shuddering sigh, she wrapped her arms around his back and held him tight.

They lay like that, breast to breast, two hearts thundering, for what seemed an eternity. Then Gabriel lifted himself again. He stared down at her, eyes soft but mouth hard.

"God, Maggie. I . . . am sorry. I didn't know. I thought . . ."

"What?"

He rolled onto his side, resting on one elbow. He ran the other hand, the unbandaged one, roughly through his hair. "I thought you had . . . done this before."

Something sharp and icy pricked around her heart. "Did you? Why?"

"I . . ." He paused, sighed. "Tessa told me about the man in Hertfordshire. She saw you together."

"Ah. Peter. And you thought I'd given myself to him."

"I'm sorry," he said again. "If I had known—"

"If you had known, you wouldn't have wanted me so?"

"No!" he replied sharply. "I don't think anything in heaven or earth could have stopped that. But I wouldn't have felt so free to . . . to pursue you."

"I see." Maggie struggled to sit up. She reached for her crumpled chemise and pressed it to her chest, covering what she could. "It makes so much of a difference, then."

He looked up at her through hooded eyes. "Of course. It was . . . I was your first."

"Aye, you were." Oh, Peter had tried. And she'd allowed him liberties she could never have imagined before that point. In the end, she'd been shamed, tormented by it, and it grieved her terribly now that Gabriel might leave her with the same shame. "I make my choices of my own free will," she told him. "You touched me, stirred me, from the beginning. So I chose you."

He was silent too long. She waited for him to speak, even to turn away, and it was an agonizing wait.

"Oh, Maggie." He lifted a hand and slowly, firmly turned her face toward his. "What did I do to deserve this?"

She felt new tears prickling behind her lids. "I never intended to burden you."

"Burden me?" Gabriel sat up, so suddenly that she flinched. "Is that what you think I meant?" He held her with both hands now, cupping her face with barely suppressed power. "You've given me something so precious, something I simply didn't deserve. I am not a worthy man."

"You are—"

"Debauched and cynical and sometimes cruel. That's mine to bear. And yours to live with now."

"And what does that mean?"

He released her, sat back. "You'll marry me, of course."

She realized she ought to have known he would ask. Or demand. That was just the sort of man Gabriel was. She ought to have known. And planned for it.

She shook her head. "Nay. I don't think so, but I thank you—"

"There's no choice here, Maggie. I won't be responsible for your ruin."

Pride stiffened her spine. "I am hardly ruined. I am whole and hearty and certainly able to make my own choices now as before."

"You might be carrying my child."

" 'Tisn't likely." Maggie closed her eyes for a weary moment. Aye, she might be. A seed that would grow into a

baby with earth-brown hair and a Cupid's bow mouth . . .
Weakened, she whispered, "You don't love me, Gabriel."

"Oh, Maggie—"

She pressed her fingertips to his lips. "Don't. Just tell
me what you do feel. Why you would bind me to you
with no more reason than a child we both know isn't
likely to come from this."

He grasped her hand, covering it completely with his.
"What of this?—I would kill any other man who
touched you."

It wasn't the sort of declaration of a girl's dreams. But
it was firm and fierce and she felt the truth of it in her
blood.

"We'll wait," she said, "and see."

"No. You'll answer me now."

She stared at him, at that hard, shadowed, beautiful
face. "You've asked me nothing, merely commanded.
And nay, I'm not demanding a pretty proposal. I am just
stating a fact."

He stared back for a long moment, elbows on his
bent knees, hands clasped loosely between them. Then,
"What's larger, Maggie—what we've just shared or what
we don't?"

How very clever he was, she thought. And how hard
the question.

"Why are you here?" she countered. "Truly."

"I've told you—"

"Aye, you've told us all. But I don't believe it any
longer, Gabriel. I can't tell you precisely why, but I don't.
There was something today above the beach, something
in your eyes, and it chilled me."

"Maggie—"

"Why?"

She heard him sigh. "Oriel asked me to come. To Scotland. A remnant from the war on the Peninsula needed to be retrieved. I can't tell you more than that."

"So there never was family business in Argyllshire."

"No."

"And you're done with the matter?" she asked.

"For now."

It pained her that he was lying. She could hear it, sense it. And something like fear pricked at her. There was something he still needed to do, she could tell, and it wasn't something she would like.

"Maggie." His hands were on her again, stroking the curls that had come loose from her plait back from her face. "Please. Do me the honor. Marry me."

She made up her mind in that instant. And firmly quashed the feeling that it might all be pretend. "Aye. I will. But on conditions."

"What are they?"

"I won't live in England the year through. I need to come home to this place."

He shrugged. "We'll spend part of summer here. Winter, too, if it pleases you. What else?"

"You'd planned to go home soon? . . ."

He dropped his hands, regarded her curiously. "I had. Within a sennight, most likely. That has changed. I'll tell your father—"

"You'll tell no one. Not until I'm ready."

"Maggie, why?"

She shook her head. "No questions. Not now. You'll have to accept me—my conditions—as they are."

"I don't understand."

"Aye, I know. But I don't mean for you to concern yourself over it. Just say aye or nay."

"And I'll have you in the end?"

"Aye." *Perhaps.* That, she feared, was up to him.

Gabriel leaned forward, a strange smile on his face. "Fine, then," he said softly. "Come here."

"Why?"

He reached for her, hands closing around her waist. When his thumbs flicked up to tease her breasts, she gasped. The desire rose so quickly within her that it completely stole her breath. It wasn't fair, she thought, that she could be so controlled by wanting him. Not fair, but, oh, the sensations were lovely. They certainly supplanted all else.

"A kiss to seal the bargain," he murmured, drawing her closer until she was seated in his lap, her bare skin sliding easily and warmly over his.

She fell into the kiss willingly. She reveled in the taste of him, in the touch of his hands, in the whisper of night air over her skin. She found herself smiling, feeling utterly feline, when he stirred and hardened beneath her. "Again?" she asked, surprised and delighted.

"And again and again," was his husky response. "Do you mind?"

"Not in the least." Her breath hitched as he turned her to straddle him and slipped inside her, all in one smooth move. "Ah, that's lovely."

He rocked her, setting a slow rhythm. She allowed her head to fall back, then leaned back farther at his coaxing, giving her own throaty laugh when he nuzzled at her breast. She could feel them again, the little licking flames. They came more slowly this time, rising with the rhythm of Gabriel's hips beneath hers.

"Wait for me," he said. "Wait."

Her hands grasped at the grass on either side. Gabriel was moving faster now, rolling her like waves in the Sound. This time, when the tremors began, they came from her knees, weakening her with their force as they swelled upward and out.

"Gabriel," she gasped. "Oh, don't let go!"

He held her, the slight roughness of his cheek brushing against her breast, as she shook. He pulled her upright and held her close as he thrust a last time and spilled himself within her. And he continued to hold her as he lowered them both to lie flat on his coat, still joined.

There was silence again. Then, "I will keep you," he whispered against her lips. "You do know that, don't you?"

She couldn't speak. Instead, she gave a single, jerky nod. She believed him in that moment. Whatever would happen later didn't matter.

She fell asleep with her fingers tangled in his hair. Gabriel gently pulled her hands free and settled them by her side. Then he raised himself to sit beside her. He wanted to watch her sleep, even if only for a few minutes.

She was breathtaking, displayed in all her glory. Hers was a form meant to be savored and a spirit meant to be joined. Their union had been all he expected: sweet, tantalizing, incendiary. He wanted her again. He wanted to lose himself inside her and let the fire consume them both. He wanted, too, just to hold her close. Unable to decide and not wanting to wake her, he watched her sleep.

He'd meant it when he'd said he would kill any man who tried to possess her. In fact, he was startled by the fervor with which he believed that. He also, as vowed, intended to keep her. Now that he'd had a complete taste of her, he wanted more. In the past, he'd wanted to try as much of life, as many women, as possible. Now he just wanted to sate himself with Maggie again and again and again.

For the first time, he was contemplating an attachment that would last longer than a week, a month, a season. He didn't want to think too far ahead; nothing lasted forever. Beyond that, he had no experience with marriage. He'd scarcely had a view of his parents'. What he had seen had been cool duty, politeness, and little attempt to hide infidelity. Then they were both gone and he'd grown to manhood in his widower grandfather's home and in school, surrounded by other men.

Gabriel supposed a day would come when he would tire of Maggie and she of him. He just couldn't conceive of the former, likely as it was. All the better, he thought. If his passion for this woman stretched as far as he could imagine, the end might not come so soon.

The question, of course, was how long she would feel the same for him. If it would even survive his time on Skye. For it had become clear that the man he sought, the Scottish traitor, was one of her neighbors, if not a lifelong friend. Gabriel was beginning to understand the connections and the loyalties of the Islanders. In another time and place, he would have been awed and perhaps even humbled. Now he was just concerned that no matter what he did, no matter how he completed his charge, those connections would bode ill for his future with one island woman. How, he wondered grimly, could it be otherwise?

Maggie stirred in her sleep. Gabriel smoothed a hand over her brow. Then he stretched out beside her and gathered her close in his arms. He would keep her warm. And he would hold the gremlins at bay, if only for a few hours.

"You've lifted me, Maggie MacLeod," he murmured.

As he closed his eyes he realized that the dancing lights had stopped. He had no idea when it had happened.

The first fingers of morning light were teasing the horizon by the time Gabriel and Maggie rose and, hand in hand, returned to the cottage. As they crept through the hall toward the stairs, they could hear Jamie's snores drifting from the parlor. Maggie said nothing, but Gabriel assumed his host had drunk himself to sleep. While he was relieved not to have to face an irate papa—doing damage to his prospective father-in-law might put something of a strain on the relationship, after all—he found himself cursing the man for being a decidedly poor parent. Maggie and her siblings deserved far better.

In that moment, as he watched her climb the stairs, splendid hips swaying with her steps, Gabriel imagined Maggie growing round and soft with his child. It wasn't something he had ever contemplated in his life and he vowed at that moment to be a far better father than hers, or his, whom he'd scarcely known even while the man was still alive. He couldn't foresee how satisfactory a husband he would be, but damned if he wouldn't try.

"Maggie."

She spun, finger to her lips. "*Cuist.* I don't want to wake Tessa."

He mounted the stairs, caught up with her at the landing. "Is that likely?"

"I suppose not." She smiled. "The girl sleeps like the dead once she's actually abed."

"Come with me." He captured her hand, coaxed her toward his chamber. He wanted to make love to her again. He would be content just to lie beside her.

She resisted, tugging until he was forced to release her. A good wrestle made for a pleasant activity, but it was neither the place nor time.

"I can't go climbing into your bed," she whispered. "Don't ask it of me."

He refrained from reminding her of what they'd spent the night doing. Instead, he gestured her toward her room. He would walk her to the door. He saw one of her expressive brows go up; her bedchamber was a mere few feet away. But he was determined. At the door he kissed her once, hard and quick.

"Dream of me."

"To be sure," she replied, brushing one hand down his cheek. Then she said, "You're a good man to the core, Gabriel. I see that."

As he climbed alone between sheets that smelled of heather, he wondered why she'd felt compelled to make that statement. He couldn't deny that it warmed him, bolstered him. But he still wondered why she'd said it. And how long it would take for her to realize she was wrong.

⊰ 14 ⊱

Wild Cherry and Thyme Infusion

For a cough, pour two cups boiling water over one teaspoon dried wild cherry bark and two teaspoons dried thyme.

Let steep for a quarter-hour. Take three times daily.

For the next four days it rained. And not the soft spring rain of Ireland, but the hard, pounding sort that lashed the Hebrides during much of the year. Jamie ventured out at least once every day to the pub, returning each time soaked to the skin and singing. Gabriel accompanied him on several occasions, returning earlier and somewhat drier. Tessa and Maggie, for the most part, stayed in the house, Tessa's restlessness a constant threat to the serenity her sister was working so hard to maintain.

Their one real outing was to church on the third day, Sunday, where, packed into a small space with the rest of the community, Maggie found little peace and less counsel. Her feelings for Gabriel, a heady combination of affection and desire, filled and distracted her. And it was all so uncertain, so terribly uncertain, that she couldn't help but question just where her good sense had gone.

For the third Sunday running, the Reverend Mr. Biggs read the banns for Elspeth MacDonald's betrothal to James Colson. The wedding would be the following Tuesday. As Maggie listened to that final reading, she'd caught herself imagining, as she always did when banns were read, that it was her name being called, her wedding being planned. She couldn't help it; she thought few women could. And now she had Gabriel's name to join with hers. A sweet thrill had coursed through her. She'd ignored the questions and doubts that nagged behind it.

It was possible. He'd asked—nay, demanded that she marry him. And she had accepted, unreal as the entire scene seemed days later. Unlikely as the pair of them seemed. But it was possible. Anything was possible.

She'd dared a quick glance in his direction then. He hadn't looked at her. Instead, he'd stared toward the pulpit, expression inscrutable, attention somewhere else entirely. He looked much the same now as he sat across the table from Jamie with the chessboard between them.

The rain had finally slackened, but the sun was nowhere to be seen. Maggie watched the muted firelight from the hearth play on Gabriel's hair, turning it a dusky bronze. He was bent over the chessboard, chin propped on his fist. From her vantage point in the doorway, she could not tell if he was contemplating his next move or dozing. Either was possible. Her father, as always, was considering all feasible checkmates for the next decade.

Jamie reached for his knight. Maggie saw Gabriel's shoulders twitch and his free hand start to lift. So he was awake. Jamie's fingers fluttered above the piece, then pulled back. Gabriel, rather than tearing at his hair and howling as most would have done, merely seemed to shrink a bit more into himself. It was no wonder. They had been playing for more than an hour and each had made only a half-dozen moves—his quick and confident, Jamie's with all the speed of sap in winter.

This was Gabriel's fourth game with her father. The others, played during the interminable rain, had no doubt been made less tedious by Tessa's presence. She had bounced at Gabriel's elbow, giving him advice on each move and asking him any number of silly questions. Why half the Englishmen she'd met had no chins. Where he'd learned to tie his cravat. Who would inherit the throne should the king's entire family die, leaving only the royal hounds.

He had answered every one, with patience and careful thought. But Tessa was gone now, having sprung from the house like an arrow from a bow the moment the rain had let up. She would return eventually, hungry and muddy and ready to pester their guest again. Maggie had cleared away the dishes from their luncheon and was more than ready for her own out-of-the-house activities. She had thought to inform her father and guest of her leaving, then slip out to have some time to herself. Each glance at Gabriel had weakened that resolve. She wanted to be with him, alone, even if it was in the middle of the village road.

"I'm off to see to some errands before the rain starts up again," she announced, raising her voice to be sure her father heard her through his glaze of deliberation. The eyes Gabriel lifted to her were sharp. And persuasive. "I'm thinking Gabriel should come with me, Papa."

Gabriel's quick, wicked smile was enough to make her bite back a laugh. Enough, too, to send her temperature up a notch.

"What was that?" Jamie queried. "Nay, Maggie, we're in the midst of a game now."

"And you'll not have chosen your move by the time we return." Knowing they would be there forever in discussion, she said firmly, "You'll come now, Gabriel. A bit of fresh air will do you good. No arguing. I'm resolved on the matter."

He rose far more slowly, she knew, than he was inclined, and offered her father a murmured apology. Jamie merely waved a hand at him and shot his daughter a vague scowl over his shoulder.

Satisfied, Maggie went for her wrap and basket. Gabriel was there suddenly, taking it from her hands. His fingers brushed hers and her pulse skittered.

"I don't suppose there is a bottle of fine wine and a few ripe peaches in there," he murmured into her ear, sending delicious shivers down her neck.

"I'm afraid not," she replied. "Why peaches?"

The smile he gave her was sly and seductive and made her want to press her lips hard to his. "To answer that would spoil a lovely surprise. I'll demonstrate for you another time. In summer, perhaps, when sun and fruit are at their peak."

Feeling rather too warm for a wrap, but heeding the weather outside, Maggie donned her cloak. Gabriel tipped his hat at a rakish angle and followed her out the door. The instant they were out of sight of the cottage, he seized her by the waist, pulled her flat up against his chest, and kissed her until she was breathless. She scarcely noticed when he let the basket, with its precious cargo, fall to the ground. She was too busy trying to slide her hands inside his lapels.

"God, I've been aching to do that," he groaned when they finally separated for air. "Four bloody days of not being able to touch you. Four bloody nights of staring at the ceiling which, I feel compelled to inform you, is in need of repair."

"Aye. I know."

"About the ceiling or the torment?"

"Both," she said tartly, and after going briefly onto her

toes to press a last kiss to the corner of his mouth, collected the basket from where it lay on its side. He took it again, and Maggie's hand. She tugged; he held fast.

"Ach, Gabriel. I can't be seen holding hands with you!"

"There's no one to see."

"Not just now, perhaps, but . . ."

He let her go with a faint growl. Then, setting a pace on his long legs that was a bit too fast for hers, he stalked toward the village. Maggie let him rush. His pride was smarting, she supposed. She'd spent her life among enough men to understand how they liked to make displays of possession. She knew, too, that the following day, when the romance of a wedding had every unmarried young lady gazing speculatively at every unmarried young man—especially those rare ones with the beautiful faces of fallen angels, she would want to cry out, *This one is mine!*

Gabriel finally paused as they crested *Binnean Storr*. It was fanciful, to be sure, calling the rise a little mountain, but Maggie's great-grandfather had been a fanciful man. The land had been his, purchased from a Mac-Donald, and he had delighted in putting names to each hillock and hollow. The view downward toward the village from *Lairig Mheic Leoid* was lovely. The rain had brought plenty of green to what it hadn't drowned in mud, dotted now with grazing cows and the occasional stone cottage.

"I could live here," Gabriel murmured, more, she thought, to himself than to her. "Perhaps. I could, perhaps."

The single word pained her although it didn't surprise her. He wasn't certain he could be happy in such a distant, rustic place. She had never been truly happy away from it.

Ask of me a shirt without seam.

The words came into her head suddenly and strongly.

Promise me a plot of land 'tween salt and sea.

She frowned, deliberately clearing her mind of the nonsense. It wasn't like her to dwell on something so silly as the words of an ancient ballad. It was even less like her to take the words and turn them into some sort of odd, inner conversation.

"Daft," she muttered.

"What was that?"

She sighed. "I've gone daft, and it's all your fault."

"Is that such a terrible thing?"

She looked into his eyes, tantalizing as the sheen of time-worn silver. "Nay. Not so terrible."

She allowed him to hold her hand then, at least until they reached the cliff road.

Minutes later, they entered the village. Old Mrs. Beaton was outside her cottage, giving the rain-battered rosebush there an encouraging talking-to. She looked up as they approached, smiled brightly, and greeted them in Gaelic. Maggie didn't need to translate. Gabriel had already doffed his hat and bowed charmingly enough to make Mrs. Beaton smile again like a young girl. She promptly chose a reasonably intact little spring bloom from the bush and plucked it. When she handed it to Gabriel, he tucked it into a buttonhole on his coat.

"Ah, you should be keeping this one, Mairghread Lìl," she commented. "I'd have sighed over him myself as a young lass."

"I'll tell him you said so." Maggie leaned in to kiss the parchment cheek. "How are you this fine day?"

"Oh, I'm right as rain." The old woman laughed at

her words. "Better lately to say right as sunshine, I suppose."

Maggie glanced at the gray sky. "Oh, the sun will come eventually. It always does. How is Mr. Beaton's chest?"

"Fairish. He's fine enough during daylight hours, but he coughs terribly most nights."

Maggie silently lamented the island's cool, damp nights. They were so hard on the aged and the ill. "I've as much hyssop put by as you need, and I can make a tincture of wild cherry and thyme. 'Tis good for a night cough."

"I'd be grateful for it. If it doesn't cure what ills Sim, I might go dipping into it myself. It sounds lovely."

Maggie grinned back. " 'Tisn't as sweet as it sounds, to tell you the truth, but we won't tell your husband just yet. Is he here?"

"Och, nay. He's off tippling and tossing the bones with Fen MacDonald."

"We'll dose him later, then."

Mrs. Beaton patted her cheek. "Bless you, Maggie. You're a dear thing. Now, will you bring your charming lad in for a cup of tea?"

"Thank you, Mrs. Beaton, but I've a bolt of cloth to collect from the Norries. 'Twould grieve my father fiercely not to have a new plaid for Elspeth's wedding. I'll bring the cherry and thyme mix by on the way to the church in the morning. Or you can send Tearlach to fetch it if you need it sooner."

"Tearlach's not here, love. He left straightaway after supper last night to see to his own farm."

"And you'll miss him, of course. 'Tis good of him to come help you here when he can."

"Aye." Mrs. Beaton nodded, her love for her family

shining in her eyes. "With Sim so poorly, I don't know what we'd have done without Tearlach."

Maggie could understand. The young man had left his own lands in the care of a neighbor to see to his father's farm. Of course he would want to go and be certain the place hadn't gone to pieces in his absence. "He'll miss the wedding, then?"

"Aye. 'Tis a shame, with James being such a friend. But I'm not expecting him back anytime soon. He has his own life. He needs to live it."

Maggie thought of Lachlann, another young man with a fierce need to live his own life. He hadn't been in church the day before and she had been too afraid to ask his sister about him, afraid to hear he had already gone.

Bidding Mrs. Beaton farewell, she and Gabriel made their way toward the Norries'. He remarked, "I'm surprised your swain didn't come bounding out to greet you."

Hiding her amusement at his silly male jealousy, Maggie replied, "Tearlach? He's gone, as it happens."

"Gone?" Gabriel demanded, his voice sharp. Maggie glanced at him curiously, but his face was impassive.

"For a bit, anyway," she said. "Doesn't that please you?"

"Infinitely," he replied. But it didn't. Gabriel cursed silently. If it was Beaton he was after, he might have just lost his quarry. "Although I have always preferred to know where the competition is."

"Tearlach's no competition at all. And he's only gone to check on his own lands. He comes and goes depending on his father's health."

"Ah. Convenient."

"Caring," Maggie retorted. "Have you no one at all to care for you?"

Gabriel thought of his grandfather, beloved and long gone. Then he thought of Oriel, of a friendship he had betrayed. "No. No one."

"I'm sorry." She rested a hand on his sleeve. "For what it's worth, you've been taken into the bosom of the MacLeods. Papa and Tessa are both quite in love with you, and Isobel says . . ."

She broke off, flushed, and Gabriel pressed, "So she did inform you of my impending arrival."

"Aye. In the letter I received last week."

"And she said . . ."

He was curious. Oriel had been his sole champion among his peers. Gabriel had decided some time ago that he would very much like to count Oriel's wife as another. Isobel was kind, clever, and, he thought, usually a very good judge of character.

"Izzy said kind things of you."

"She would. I imagine she is never unkind. But I also imagine she holds your welfare as dear as you do hers. So I can only assume there was a warning as well."

He watched Maggie's face as she considered her response. She wouldn't lie, he knew, but she might well soften the truth.

"She says you need to eat more. . . ."

"And drink less." Gabriel nodded, wryly amused. "True enough. What else?"

"That you've a blithe tongue and comely face."

"Mmm. A matter of opinion. I expect she also told you I am renowned, or should I say infamous, for some less than seemly behavior."

"I . . . Is that true as well?"

"Absolutely." He waited for her to take her hand from his arm. She didn't. "I haven't lived the best of lives, Maggie."

"Who has?" was her soft response.

You. Until I stomped into it. "If you're to share my life, you should know. I haven't much of a place in Society now."

To her surprise, she smiled. "Good. I've my own opinions of English Society, and few of them favorable. Is there anything else you think I ought to know?"

There was, but he had no idea how he could possibly tell her about his great fall. How he had all but delivered precious, irretrievable military intelligence right into the hands of the enemy. How sliding a blade between the ribs of one of her friends and neighbors seemed the only way to make it right. It sounded horrible even to himself when looked at that way. There might be no good way to look at it.

"I snore," he announced gruffly.

"I know," she said, and tugged at his sleeve to get him moving again.

He held her still, reached out to trace a finger along her jaw. She closed her eyes for a moment, turning her face into his touch like a cat. Then she pulled away.

"Where can we go?" he asked. "Someplace quiet, secluded. I need to touch more of you."

"I don't know. I don't know if—"

"Oh, Maggie. Live a bit." *Give me some of your grace,* he thought. *Please.*

She gazed thoughtfully past him, toward the low hills to the south. "It's going to rain again."

"I don't care."

"Well, then. We'll go back to the hollow. Where we were . . . that night."

His body tightened with the memory. "Lead on." But it was he who ended up leading. Somehow he knew exactly where he was going.

They made it only as far as the edge of the village. As they neared the familiar red door of the pub, Gabriel saw the lanky form of young Andy MacAuley appear from an outbuilding. The boy saw him, too, and waved excitedly. As far as messages went, it wasn't a subtle one.

"Andy? Is something amiss?" Maggie asked as the boy approached. She didn't seem to notice the fact that his eyes went a bit moonish as they settled on her. Gabriel decided she had probably long ago stopped noticing men tripping over their own jaws whenever she was nearby.

To add to the idiotic expression, young MacAuley blushed, and stammered, "I . . . er . . . nay. I've nothing to say to you. That is . . ."

Gabriel sighed and stepped in. "Did you wish to speak to me?" At Andy's nod, he informed Maggie, "We've become acquainted, Mr. MacAuley and I, during my time here. I've been telling him of—"

"Bloody battle!" the boy blurted.

"—Eton," Gabriel finished dryly. "If you will give us but a minute . . ." The boy was shaking his head with enough force to dislodge something within. "More than a minute?" Andy nodded with the same enthusiasm. It was only a momentary debate for Gabriel. As much as he wanted Maggie, he needed to hear what the boy had to say more. "Maggie . . ."

"Have your chat," she said. "I'll stop in to see Lachlann's sister. Then I'll go home."

She was gone, walking back the way they'd come, before he could stop her. "Well." Irked, knowing he didn't really have a right to be, Gabriel turned back to Andy. "Well?"

"I saw them again, sir. On the cliffs, last night."

"Saw whom?"

"Why, the ghosties, of course. A man and a woman,

walking apart." The boy didn't notice Gabriel's scowl.
Which smoothed somewhat when he continued, "I told
old Mr. Beaton, and he said you ought to know of it,
that it would matter to you."

"He said that? When?"

MacAuley jerked his head toward the pub. "Not half
an hour past. He's here still. . . ." He spun to follow as
Gabriel stalked toward the red door. "You'll be needing
me to translate."

"So I will. Come along."

He had no idea why the old man thought he would be
interested in a child's vivid imagination and a seventy-
year-old ghost story, but something told him to find out.
As promised, Mr. Beaton was still in the pub, tankard in
hand. Across from him, Fen MacDonald snored contentedly, head back and mouth wide. The elder MacAuley
stood behind the bar, wiping bottles clean with a dishcloth. He nodded in Gabriel's direction then raised a
whiskey bottle in question.

"Whatever the gentlemen are having," Gabriel said,
and took a seat next to Mr. Beaton.

The man let out a musical stream of Gaelic. "He says
'good day,' " Andy translated.

"That was all 'good day'?"

"Aye. Well, actually 'tis 'God and Mary bless you
and—' "

"Fine." Gabriel offered his own greetings, then commanded, "Ask him why I should be interested in your
ghosties."

The old man's eyes twinkled at the question. "He says
you're about making up for history," Andy explained
after Beaton had spoken, "and that you won't want to be
repeating it. What does that mean?"

"I have no idea," Gabriel muttered. But he did. Nor

was he terribly surprised that an elderly Skyeman would have understood him. Disturbed, but not surprised. He was beginning to take such things as a matter of fact. "Does he have any suggestions as to what I should do?"

This time, the response was short. "Take her and leave," MacAuley translated. Then, "Take who?"

Gabriel had no time to waste on making explanations to a besotted child. "Why?" he demanded of Beaton. "Dammit, why?"

Calum appeared with a pitcher of ale then, and a tankard for Gabriel. Gabriel absently pulled a coin from his pocket. Beaton smiled again and spoke. "He wants to know if you still have the crown."

"Of course. Does he want it back?" Gabriel started to dig for the coin he'd so reluctantly won from the old man. Beaton slapped his hand against the table, making the other men jump and waking Fen, who promptly announced, "The tide's in!" and gestured for Calum to hurry up with the jug.

"*An righ,*" Beaton said. "*Am fear as righ an Alba.*"

"The king—"

"Yes, yes, I know." Gabriel waved off Andy's explanation. "The king. He already showed me."

"But—"

"Ask him again—*why?*"

At the question, the old man rolled his eyes heavenward. Then, without responding, he drained his tankard and rose unsteadily to his feet. "Should I walk him home?" Gabriel asked.

After a brief consultation with Beaton, Andy nodded. "Aye, he'd appreciate that. If—" he added, and Gabriel paused halfway out of his seat "—you promise not to pester him with your questions until another day. He says they make no sense to him, and even if they did, you wouldn't understand the answers."

Gabriel was beginning to wonder if the old man wasn't the sharpest mind on the whole cursed island.

When your tasks are finished and done,
Whilst every grove rings with a merry antine,
O then I will marry thee under the sun,
And then thou shalt be a true love of mine.

Maggie and her family, Gabriel in tow, followed the
wedding procession from the church. Everyone was
there, dressed in Sunday best for this Tuesday celebration, ready to pass the time toasting and feasting and
dancing until dawn. The bride was lovely in her creamy
muslin and MacDonald colors, flowers in her hair. As
she went, the women around her showered her with
spring flower petals, a tradition so old that no one could
say when it had begun. Her new husband beamed,
visibly embarrassed at not being able to help himself. Elspeth's father beamed; the Reverend Mr. Biggs beamed.
Weddings were a splendid occasion in the Isles, and
everyone was thrilled to be attending one more.

Maggie allowed her arm to press for a long moment
against Gabriel's. He'd looked so bonny when he'd de-
scended the cottage stairs an hour past in his fawn
breeches and freshly brushed blue coat. He'd smiled
down at her from the landing, a quick, wicked flash of
white teeth and silvery eyes that made her lean for a moment against the door frame in which she stood. In her
eyes now, he outshone everyone present, including the
grinning groom.

A pair of pipers, startled by the abrupt end of the
service—Mr. Biggs appreciated a dram of whiskey and

haunch of mutton as much as any man and had hurried
through the sermon—had managed to scramble outside
and lift their pipes. Accompanied by rifle fire from
Calum MacAuley and Tavis Tolmey, the pipers led the
wedding party at a brisk march through the village to Elspeth's aunt's home, where the festivities would be held.
There, tables groaned under the weight of the food, the
canopy that had been raised in case of rain swayed gently
in the pleasant breeze, and music was already flowing
from the instrument of a lone MacDonald fiddler.

Lachlann should have been there, Maggie thought,
fiddle on his shoulder and loaded plate near to hand. But
he wasn't yet back from Glasgow. Either that, or he'd
simply gone, not wanting to endure the pain of good-byes.

Tessa trotted off immediately, no doubt to shuck her
shoes and climb a nearby tree with Andy MacAuley. And
Jamie, ever helpful, hurried to offer his services in
opening the whiskey and wine.

In a matter of minutes, the toasts had begun. After
that, plates laden and glasses full, the guests began to
celebrate in earnest. It was a large crowd, overflowing
the little house and yard, right into the neighbor's field.
The guests ate and toasted and danced in relay. The
whiskey and wine flowed unabated. Tavis Tolmey was
the first to slide off his chair, whiskey glass still gripped
tightly in his fist. No one bothered trying to right him.
His brother merely took a moment to toss a fold of
Tavis's plaid over his supine form for warmth and modesty's sake.

Fen MacDonald's beard ended up in his pudding plate.
The groom's brother had an unintentional swim in the
duck pond. The bride's sister soon disappeared with Mr.
Biggs's strapping son. And Sileas Wilkie, who had found
the silver ring in the tub used to wash the bride's feet the

night before—a tradition meant to foretell who the next would be to wed—was making her way through the revelers, hips and shoulders swaying, searching for the man who would someday join her at the kirk door. She smiled at Gabriel. He smiled back. Maggie, drinking in the sight of him as he lounged in a rough-hewn chair borrowed from someone's farm, plate and glass balanced on his knee, didn't mind.

He was hers. For now, at least. And she loved him.

She loved him. Simply. Sometimes desperately, it seemed. She had fallen so slowly and sneakily that she hadn't had time to welcome the giddy sensation—or steel herself against the landing. In truth, it was a wondrous thing, filling and warming her. But she was fast learning that even love didn't drown out doubt. That frightened her, almost as much as the thought that Gabriel's proposal might have been a matter of physical desire and a gentleman's sense of duty.

Gabriel hadn't finished what he had come to Skye to do. Maggie was as certain of that as she was of her love for him. What she couldn't see so clearly was whether he would stay—or whether they would be able to leave together—once he had.

The fiddlers finished their reel with a flourish. One by one, the dancers parted and drifted to the side. A single figure took their place, tiny and a bit bent, wearing an heirloom lace shawl so fine that it appeared to have been tatted by fairies. The guests leaned in, silent in anticipation. After a long moment, Mrs. Beaton took a deep breath and began to sing.

It was her alone; none of the musicians moved to accompany her. Her voice rose and fell, sped and slowed. She sang of love, of children, of home and hearth. Tune and verse alike were complicated, extensive, passed down from countless generations of Skyewomen from mother to daughter and daughter's daughter. Cait MacKenzie, the Beatons' only daughter, mouthed the words where she stood. And the little girl on her hip would do the same someday.

Beside her, Maggie heard Gabriel give a low, impressed whistle.

" 'Tis *puirt-a-beul*," she told him quietly. "Mouth music. 'Twas begun by women long ago while they were weaving, to pass the day. This one was probably sung first by a mother as her daughter prepared to be married."

"I've never heard anything quite like it."

"Nay." She smiled. "You wouldn't have. Ach, *Sasunnach*," she said lightly, "how did you ever get on before coming to Skye?"

"I don't know," was his simple reply.

Propelled by a firm push from her husband, Cait stepped forward and joined her mother. When they'd finished the song and the cheering had stopped, Lachtna Norrie and Anna Wilkie joined them, and the quartet launched into the most familiar local *puirt-a-beul* wedding song, *"Cia Mor Do Shaoibhreas"*—"How Great Is Your Richness." Maggie watched her friends and neighbors smiling, swaying, tapping their feet to the music, and felt a quick, sudden surge of well-being that was almost painful.

What she had missed so much during her time away was the color of the Skyefolk, as much a part of the people as their blood. The music, the mingling of language and tartans, the pink of sunset. Mr. MacGruder, Glaswegian to the core, stood prim and tidy in his cutaway coat and dark pantaloons beside old Mr. Beaton, who was draped in the traditional twelve yards of the green, red, and blue tartan that he wore as a sept of Clan

MacDonald, a sprig of heather tucked into the brim of his black bonnet. Calum MacDonald took a dirk from its place inside his Highland coat to pick his teeth; Maggie's father reached inside his own coat for the flask that he had no doubt filled and refilled from the endless celebratory bottles. Some of the younger men wore their clan plaid in the form of little kilts, wrapped and pleated around their waists in the fashion of the military. Others wore breeches in English style.

Maggie wound her fingers in the soft wool of the MacLeod tartan sash she'd pinned to her shoulder over a simple, full-sleeved white dress. It was Lachtna Norrie's work, each alternating black and gold square woven with love and skill. It was the first time she'd donned the sash since leaving for England three years before. She'd wrapped herself in one of her father's old plaids once for warmth before sneaking out to meet Peter. The young man had fingered the wool in distaste, teased her for being a rustic, then proceeded to spread the plaid on the damp earth in hopes of coaxing her down onto it.

But Gabriel's eyes had sparked at the sight of her that morning, much as hers had for him. She'd promptly gone weak-kneed and light-headed. She was light-headed now, warmed with wine and the tartan draped over her shoulders, and the simple, solid presence of the man beside her.

Night was falling slowly, daylight replaced by one shimmering lamp and torch after another. " 'Tis the gloaming," Maggie said softly. "My favorite time of day."

Gabriel hadn't known that. He was beginning to realize that there were countless details about Maggie he didn't know. He meant to change that, one shimmering fragment after another.

"Come away with me," he murmured.

Her face was luminous in the torchlight. "Where?"

Anywhere, he thought. *Scarborough, Venice, Xanadu.* "Some shadowy glen, perhaps?"

She dropped her head, long lashes brushing her cheeks. " 'Twould be improper, departing before the bride and groom."

"I have lived improper, Maggie MacLeod, and found some great pleasure in doing so."

He allowed his hand to skim slowly over hers, a very private touch in the midst of a very public place. He heard her catch her breath. She jerkily pulled her hand away, linking it with the other in her lap. "I promised my cousin Iain a dance. And I need to be sure Tessa and Papa—"

"Go. Dance with Iain, tend to your family. I'll be here, waiting for you."

He watched her slip into the crowd. She reappeared a minute later with a squat, red-haired man with legs like tree stumps and a grinning moon face. Iain, Gabriel mused, and decided he quite liked the fellow. They were a quaint pair, the cousins, and they looked to be having a grand time. Iain, amazingly sprightly for his size, swung Maggie into the rollicking reel. Her laugh carried over the music, a bright sound that made Gabriel smile.

In the past hours, while the merriest party he'd ever attended whirled around him, he'd almost been able to forget why he was there. Women had smiled at him, some with the dreamy eyes of the young and unmarried. More than one man had tipped a measure from their bottle into his glass. Sweet Mrs. Beaton had winked at him as she passed. And Maggie had never strayed out of sight, a lush beauty in her Highland garb, a cluster of tiny white flowers in her fire-touched hair.

He'd almost been able to forget that he wasn't just another guest at a springtime celebration. Almost. He had been altogether too aware of MacDonald's absence, and Beaton's. He had watched Calum MacAuley closely. And not been able to shake the sensation that someone was watching him just as carefully.

"You aren't dancing." Edana Malcolmson slipped into the seat beside him. She'd chosen a garnet dress, not appropriate for a wedding, perhaps, but it made for a very attractive picture indeed.

"Nor are you, it seems."

She shook her sleek head with a smile. "I seldom exert myself on something so strenuous as a Highland fling. I find so much effort positively exhausting."

Gabriel studied the crowd of dancers. "They seem to be enjoying themselves."

"It's a simple life here, Lord Rievaulx. We're happily roused by the simple things. Music, love, a good fight."

"Interesting combination."

"Isn't it?" Edana toyed gracefully with a lace fan that should have looked out of place in such a gathering, but in her hand somehow didn't. "Some would call our little corner of the world an idyll."

"And you? What would you call it?"

She tilted her head, gazed at him thoughtfully. "You really think me out of place here, don't you?"

"Surprisingly, I don't."

"Mmm. Clever man. I've spent so much of my adult life away, but when one is born to a place like Skye, one never loses it. When I am in London, I am an Island Scot. When I am in Moscow, I am an Island Scot. In Paris . . ."

"An Island Scot?"

Edana laughed. "No. In Paris, I suppose I am something quite different. But who isn't?"

"The Stuarts," Gabriel said dryly.

"Have you ever met a Stuart?" the lady asked mildly.

"Not to my knowledge. I was rather under the impression the line had died out."

"Silly man. Of course it hasn't." Edana waved at the assembled revelers. "You've probably rubbed elbows with a dozen people who proudly claim royal blood, if illegitimate and likely not there at all."

Gabriel's eyes traveled over familiar faces. Gnomelike Jamie MacLeod with his brilliantly red nose; Calum MacAuley, rough and ruddy and reminiscent of nothing so much as an oversized goat; old Mrs. Beaton of the gnarled hands and plain, gently lined face. "I suppose we all have our dreams."

"Ah, but there could well be a smidge of truth to this one. Our Bonny Prince Charlie was a lusty lad. He was certainly rumored to have cuddled Flora MacDonald during his time in the Isles."

"And you believe that?" Gabriel demanded, amused.

"No. I don't. Flora was long gone by the time I was born, but her reputation as a woman of unbreakable principles still survives."

"You admire her."

"Of course I do." Edana appeared surprised by his remark. "How could I do otherwise? She did Scotland a great service, spiriting the prince to Skye right under his pursuers' noses. And she did it at great risk, I might add. She will have a special place in history and she well deserves it."

"It sounds as if you might have your own dose of Stuart blood," Gabriel commented, enjoying the banter. Skyewomen, he'd come to learn, were an extraordinary breed. A man could count himself fortunate—and count on a lifetime of fiery exchanges—when joined with one.

"Not a drop." Edana waved to someone nearby. "My pedigree is clear, if humble. I am merely one more romantic Highland heart among thousands. So is Maggie, though I daresay you know that already."

Gabriel's eyes slid to Maggie. She was laughing, skipping with the music, and looking altogether too beautiful to be of this world. His body tightened in desire and an odd wistfulness that surprised him.

"Different worlds," he said gruffly.

"Absolutely. Though sadly, most people learn that too late," Edana murmured. "You know, it's rather a shame that you are who you are, my lord."

"Oh? And why is that?"

Gathering fan and gossamer shawl, the lady rose gracefully to her feet. Gabriel stood with her. "Given time, Lord Rievaulx, I believe you could be made into a marvelous Highlander. You certainly have the intelligence. And the eyes. But there's never enough time, is there? Pity. Now, I am off to do Highland things. Don't follow me." Tapping his cheek with her fan, an act so familiar among the ton and so delightfully absent here, she glided off into the crowd.

Maggie was back by his side several minutes later, cheeks flushed and some hairpins lost. "Elspeth and James are leaving."

"Good. So can we."

She smiled, shook her head. "There's a bit more to the celebration."

Scanning the happy gathering, Gabriel returned, "I was under the impression that the bit more of the celebration will go on all night."

"Oh, aye, the drinking and dancing. But I meant for the bride and groom."

"If they are fortunate, they will go on all night as well."

Her blush deepened charmingly. "You shouldn't speak of such things."

"You are quite correct," he agreed. "I would much rather do them. Come along." He rose and pulled her to her feet. She wouldn't let him hold her hand.

" 'Tis tradition to escort Elspeth to her new home."

" 'Tis torture to make me burn for you like this," he shot back in a fair imitation of the local brogue. "Come make love with me, Maggie, lass."

He saw her eyes and mouth go soft. "Oh. Aye. I will."

Grinning, he tucked one hand under the trailing wool of her sash, flattening it against the small of her back, feeling the warmth of her skin there. He guided her away from the revelry, back toward the village.

"Not that way." She turned up a tiny path. "I'll take you to the castle."

"I thought that was well north of here."

"Not Dunvegan. This is Dunogol." They crested a hillock and she took his hand as they continued up a gentle slope toward what appeared to be a small forest. " 'Tis a special place."

She could be guiding him to the mouth of hell for all he cared at the moment.

The trees came more suddenly than he'd expected, dense and dark. "I was hoping for some moonlight," he jested, and she shushed him.

"Wait." She walked with the confidence of someone born to a place, slipping surely through the foliage and around hip-high stones. Hand tight around hers, Gabriel let her lead. After a few minutes, she slowed, then stopped. "Here."

She had given him moonlight. As abruptly as the forest

had begun, it cleared, leaving a circle perhaps ten yards across. Gabriel felt lush grass beneath his feet, saw the rounded outlines of more rocks curving around the clearing.

He didn't question that it was a special place. There was a stillness to the air, and a warmth to the light breeze that was at odds with the landscape they had just left. "Well," he said, turning her to face him, "you've convinced me. But where is the castle?"

She laughed softly. "You're standing in the center of it."

Gabriel glanced around, saw nothing to make him believe he was standing in any sort of edifice at all. "Is this another tale of fairies, by chance?"

"It might be," she teased, then, "No one knows who built the walls. They are there, only fallen." She waved to one of the rocky mounds. " 'Twas before the Vikings, even. As far back as Skye has recorded history it has been here, called the fort of the stranger, *Dun a'ghoill.* They say magic was done here when there was still magic to be found in everyday living."

"Who says that?"

"Everyone who believes." Maggie lifted his hand and placed it over her heart, which was skipping merrily. "I daresay even a hardened skeptic like you can feel it."

When his palm slid down to cup her breast, she sighed with the pleasure of it.

"Oh, I feel it," he replied, low and gruff, against her mouth. "I feel it."

He tasted of MacAsgaill whiskey, sweet and spicy and unique. Maggie slid her hands up over his lapels to grip his shoulders. She pressed herself as close to him as she could, feeling as if she could become as light as the mist and slip easily through his clothing. His fingers were working their magic, caressing her so expertly through the fabric of her bodice that she felt it all the way to her toes.

"Lie down with me," he whispered. "Please."

"I will. Of course I will."

As he unbuttoned his coat, Maggie crouched to test the grass for damp. It was cool but dry, springy beneath her palms. She smelled celandine and wood sorrel and, behind them, the teasing scent of wild thyme. Delighted, she reached up and got a grip on Gabriel's waistcoat.

"Hurry," she commanded, and tugged.

Later she would realize that her impatience might well have saved his life. In the moment, she only jumped at the crack of something hard against rock. Even when Gabriel, already leaning, came down hard on top of her, she hadn't an inkling that anything was wrong. Then a clod of grass and dirt flew up, not a foot from Gabriel's shoulder. Maggie heard him curse. Then he was rolling, taking her with him. More grass showered over them.

"What—" she managed.

"Shh!" He came up into a low crouch. Maggie saw his head turning quickly back and forth as he searched for something in the darkness. It was then that she caught a whiff of gunpowder and understood.

Someone had shot at them.

"Gabriel—"

He pulled her to her knees. Then, tucking her safely against his chest, he half dragged and half pushed her outside the castle circle and behind a taller section of fallen wall. Just as he did, a stone behind them shattered. Maggie bit back a cry. There was a moment of silence, followed by the unmistakable if faint sound of someone stalking through the ankle-high vegetation of the forest.

"Listen to me," Gabriel hissed into her ear. "We need

a way out of here other than the one we took to get in.
Do you know of one?"

"Aye." She raised a shaky hand and pointed west.
"There's a hunting path there."

"Anything else?"

She thought. "We can go down the other side of the
hill. There's a stream at the bottom. If we follow it, we'll
come to the brae below the cottage."

"That will do. Be as quiet as you can. I'll follow."
Gabriel reached past her and picked up several stones.
With several whipping flicks of his wrist, he sent them
expertly in the direction of the hunting path. The footsteps stopped, then continued more quickly in that direction. "Now."

Maggie gathered up her skirts and slipped into the
trees. She did her best to move quietly, staying low to
avoid hanging branches. She could just hear Gabriel
behind her, heard him grunt as he encountered some
obstacle.

"Gabriel—"

"Shh. Don't talk. Move."

So she moved, weaving in and out between the oaks
and spiny holly bushes. Then the ground cleared and she
heard the quiet burble of the burn, slowed just in time to
keep from sliding from the mossy bank and into the
water. Gabriel's hand fisted in her sash, holding her
steady.

"Can you jump it?" he asked.

She judged the distance in the dark. "I think so." She
tensed, ready to spring, but he held her back.

He stepped around her, spanned the stream with an
easy leap. Then he reached back. She jumped, felt his
arms close around her. He held her for a heartbeat, then
shoved her in front of him again, and they were off. It

wasn't easy going; the banks broke and sloped at ir-regular intervals. More than once Maggie nearly went down, only to have Gabriel, moving like lightning, steady her.

It was almost a mile later that Maggie, footsore and breathless, stopped. "There," she said, pointing up the slope to their left. "There's the cottage."

Gabriel placed a finger lightly over her lips. They stood, listening. But the only sounds were their quick-ened breathing, the rushing of the burn, and the call of a lone owl in the distance.

"I don't think he followed us."

Maggie was still struggling to catch her breath. "Did you see who—"

"No."

She shivered, recalling how close several of the shots had been. "Someone from the wedding, drunk. I suppose we must have looked like deer—"

"Maggie." He grasped her chin almost roughly, tilting her face toward his. The mist was coming in, and she could only just make out his features. They looked hard as granite. "You don't really believe that."

"Why wouldn't I?" she demanded, desperate for any explanation other than the one that kept hammering its way into her head. "Why wouldn't I? Why would anyone want to . . . do that . . . to us on purpose?"

"Not us," came the grim retort. "Me. He was shooting at me. And nearly got you in the process. May he rot in hell for that." The final words were a growl that sent new chills down Maggie's spine.

"Why, Gabriel? Why would . . . Dear God, *why* are you here?"

And he told her, simply and coldly. "I am here chasing a traitor, a supporter of Napoleon's cause. A Skyeman who is responsible for the deaths of more than a hundred of His Majesty's soldiers."

"Impossible," Maggie snapped immediately, incredulous. "I know everyone you've met. I know . . ."

"You know him. Make no mistake about it. And I need you to help me now."

She felt dizzy suddenly and groped behind her for support. There was nothing there. Gabriel reached out and once again kept her on her feet. "Nay," she whispered. "You're wrong, and I can't be a part of it. I can't."

"Maggie." She heard him sigh, then curse quietly. "We can't stay here discussing the matter. Come along. Even if he hurried, we should still be here first."

Hand firm but gentle on her arm, he led her up the slope. Once at the cottage, he made her stay outside, sheltered by the garden shed, while he checked inside. Mind whirling, she sank to her heels against the stone outbuilding.

A traitor . . . responsible for the deaths of more than a hundred . . . A Skyeman . . .

"It's clear. I'm assuming your father and sister are still in the village."

She looked up, startled, to see Gabriel looming over her. "You're mistaken, you know," she said shakily. "About your traitor. You must be."

"I wish I were." He helped her to her feet, kept an arm around her as they walked through the mudroom and into the kitchen. "You need to sit."

"Aye." She sank slowly into a chair, vaguely aware of him clanging the kettle lid, stoking the fire.

"Is there a gun in the house?"

"Hmm?" she looked up, blinked at him.

"A gun. Does your father own one?"

"Oh. Aye. There." She pointed to a recess above the door. " 'Tisn't loaded. We've learned not to . . ."

She didn't bother finishing the sentence. Gabriel would know how dangerous her father would be with ale in his gut and a rifle in his hands.

"In the pantry. There's an earthenware jar," she told him, "a large one. You'll find what you need there."

Minutes later, her grandfather's old musket lay on the table in front of her. "Do you know how to shoot?" Gabriel demanded.

"Aye. But I—"

"The gun should be cleaned, but I don't want to take the time. It will do its job if it has to. Now, I am going upstairs for a minute. I'll be back. If anyone other than your father or Tessa comes through that door, I want you to point the barrel at their forehead and put your finger on the trigger. Do you understand?"

"Aye."

He fixed her with a steely gaze. "I mean it, Maggie. Anyone."

"Aye, aye. Go."

He was barely out of the room when she heard the shout outside. She was on her feet in an instant, hurrying to the window. The gun lay right where Gabriel had left it on the table.

She had her hand on the latch when he was suddenly beside her, shoving her aside. "Dammit, Maggie!"

"Maggie!" came from outside. "Maggie, are you there?"

" 'Tis Andy MacAuley," she said sharply, ducking under Gabriel's arm. She reached the back door and opened it just as the boy came barreling up the step. He was coatless, hatless, his hair standing up in wild licks about his head.

"Andy?"

"Come quick!" he panted. "You've got to come quick."

"What's happened?" she demanded, feeling the cold weight of bad news already.

" 'Tis old Sim Beaton. His wife says he's dying."

⊰ 16 ⊱

This Nightshade bears a very bad character. . . .
—Culpeper's Complete Herbal

The old man looked awful. His deeply seamed face was ashen, pale as the sheets against which he lay. Across the room, his wife didn't look much better. Her white hair was wild about her drawn face, eyes frightened. As the man she'd loved for fifty years labored to breathe, Mrs. Beaton wrung her hands. She was still in her best dress, a filigree brooch at her neck and little pearls at her ears. But the lace shawl had been discarded and now lay crumpled at the foot of the bed.

"When did this happen?" Maggie asked as she bent over Mr. Beaton. "He seemed well at the wedding."

"Aye, fit as a fiddle and wanting to dance. We came home, had our tea, and were sitting by the fire when suddenly he started gasping. 'Twas a terrifying sound." The old woman's voice shook. "By the time I'd gotten up from my chair and across to him, he'd gone over onto the floor. I couldn't lift him . . . I couldn't." She began crying now, fragile shoulders shaking.

Leaving the bed, Maggie gently guided Mrs. Beaton to a chair, urged her into it. "Rest a moment. Cait will be here soon. Let me make you some tea." There was little she could do for Mr. Beaton at the moment, but she could see to his wife.

Apparently Calum and Andy MacAuley had been

254

heading home from the wedding celebration when they'd heard the old woman's cries. Always quick of mind, Calum had sent his son running for Maggie. He himself had lifted Mr. Beaton from the floor and carried him into the bedchamber before hurrying back to the MacDonald holding for the Beatons' daughter.

At first, Gabriel had tried to keep Maggie from leaving the house. She had argued, appalled by the very idea of ignoring a plea for help. There had been a quick, heated exchange before she'd simply snatched up a wrap and her herb basket and hurried past him out the door. He'd followed and, muttering all the while, helped Andy to saddle Jamie's gelding. Then he'd hoisted the pair of them up and sent them off.

"I don't like this," he'd said grimly as he checked the girth. "But you'll be fine as long as I'm not with you. Stay on the village road."

Maggie had looked back once as she and Andy rode away. Gabriel had stood tall and silent, silhouetted in the doorway. She'd offered a quick prayer for him. For them both.

The scene that had met her at the Beatons' cottage had her praying anew. The old man was motionless, colorless. His wife wasn't much better.

Maggie glanced up now as Cait MacKenzie came bursting into the room. *"Màthair."* She dropped to her knees beside her mother and gathered the fragile form into her arms. *"Ciod?"* she asked of Maggie.

"I don't know. I don't know what it is."

She bent over the unconscious man again, felt his forehead. It was cool, clammy to the touch. Then she placed a hand on his chest. His breathing was labored, but his heartbeat was regular, if not very strong. Mr. Beaton was an old man; his health had been indifferent for a long time. Maggie wouldn't have expected a robust beat.

Perhaps it was just age. Perhaps it was just his time. . . . But something didn't seem right somehow. Something small and elusive and . . .

She sniffed. And again. Pressing her face close to his, she breathed in. *"Dia is Muire."*

"What?" Cait demanded. "What, Maggie?"

Doubting her nose, doubting her presence of mind even more, she shook her head. "I thought I smelled henbane."

"Henbane?" Mrs. Beaton lifted her tear-streaked face. "But there's none near the house, certainly none in it."

"Nay, I'm sure there isn't. 'Twas something else, then." But Maggie recognized the odor. Even when untouched, the plant smelled foul. It grew in sandy spots near the sea and was a familiar sight along the coast. In the earth it was a smelly nuisance. If consumed, it could be deadly. Was usually deadly.

"Do you think it was the excitement of the wedding?" Cait asked. "He would be skipping here and there, all but dancing, even with *Màthair* and me telling him to sit and enjoy the music."

Maggie wasn't certain she would have called it skipping, but she had seen Mr. Beaton on his feet more than once. At one point she had even thought he was on his way over to where she and Gabriel were sitting. He'd smiled and waved as he approached. But Cait's husband, Alan, had waylaid him, urging him into a seat with a plate of food and a cup of something. Then Maggie had gone off to dance with Iain and she hadn't seen the old man again.

"Has someone gone for Tearlach?" she asked Cait quietly.

"Aye. Alan set off as soon as Calum found us. He'll ride as fast as he can, but they won't be here until tomorrow at best, more likely Thursday. By then . . ." She glanced at her failing father and gave a choked sob.

Maggie squeezed her shoulder. "We'll keep him comfortable. Where's Mairi?" Cait and Alan's two-year-old daughter didn't need to see her beloved grandfather this way.

"She's with Jeannie MacDonald. She'll be fine there."

"Aye. She will. Now, let's get you a cup of tea. I was just going to brew some for your mother."

Cait's eyes darted back to the bed and the woman sitting beside it. "I don't want to leave them."

"You don't have to," Maggie answered. "Stay here. I'll see to it."

"What can I do for him?"

"I don't know," she replied sadly. "Mayhaps nothing. I'll bring some broth and a spoon. It might help if we can get some liquid in him. Beyond that, all we can do is stay with him and wait."

Cait nodded. "Thank you, Maggie. We're indebted to you."

"Ach, nonsense." She watched as the young woman went to sit next to her mother. They were so alike, this pair, different only in age and its effects. Someday Cait's round face would bear the lines of hard work and laughter. And Mrs. Beaton's hair had once been the same rich gold of her daughter's. Longing for her own mother swept through Maggie, sharp and poignant. Then she gave silent thanks that her father was still there, and went for Cait's tea.

She walked into the cottage's main room. It was kitchen and living area all in one, scattered with Mrs. Beaton's knitting, old copies of the Gaelic newspaper from Portree, and the wooden toys Mr. Beaton had carved for his own children and which had been taken out, probably that very morning, for the pleasure of Cait's daughter. Maggie lifted a wheeled horse, fitted with leather tack and a real horsehair mane and tail, from the middle of the floor. It was worn perfectly smooth by years of loving little hands, and the string for pulling it had no doubt been replaced several times. But it would survive young Mairi MacKenzie, and probably her children as well.

Maggie set the horse on the large table. Then she scanned the room, her eyes falling on the Beatons' discarded tea mugs. Mr. Beaton's lay at the foot of his old chair. If he'd swallowed something evil, it might have been that recent. She hurried across the floor, scooped up the mug, and held it to her nose.

It smelled of strong tea and nothing more.

Then she saw a very familiar bottle standing empty on a side table. It was one of hers, the distinctive blue glass she favored, left days before. She'd filled it with hyssop tonic for Mr. Beaton's cough. He'd wrinkled his craggy nose, teasing her with the accusation that she must have a grudge against him to be pouring such strong-tasting medicines down his gullet. She'd teased back, telling him he'd best beware the ingredients she was *hiding* behind the hyssop's powerful taste.

Heart in her throat, she reached for the bottle.

Gabriel had finally climbed the stairs to his bedchamber when the parlor clock struck three times. Tessa and Jamie had wandered in several hours earlier, daughter supporting father, and the three had sat together in the kitchen, listening to Jamie groan and wheeze his bagpipe tune. Eventually, the wheezing had turned into loud snores. Gabriel had carried the little man up to bed. Tessa had followed.

Gabriel had gone back down to the kitchen and retrieved the gun from where he'd hidden it behind the door. Then he'd settled himself in one of the hard wooden chairs, rifle across his lap, and waited for whatever might come. At three, he'd laid down atop his bed, his own pistol taken from deep in his valise and placed beneath his pillow, and waited.

He wasn't worried for Maggie. Or at least he wasn't concerned for her safety. L'Écossais wanted him, not the MacLeods. He did know, however, that both the earlier gunfire and his revelation had tipped her world off its familiar axis. It would be difficult for her to believe that one of her neighbors was a traitor and murderer. It would be even harder for her to accept the truth when L'Écossais turned out to be a friend.

It might be impossible for her to even be in Gabriel's presence when his job was done.

For a fleeting second, he found himself wondering if it was worth taking the chance, if he couldn't just carry Maggie back to Scarborough and let L'Écossais slip away. The answer came hard and fast. No. He had undertaken a task for his king, for his friend. For himself. It had to be done, consequences bedamned. The fact that he had come to admire and even like some of the local Skyefolk, with their fierce loyalty to each other and their history, was unfortunate. It was a shame that he'd come to feel almost at home in a place where he should only have been on his guard. And it was a cruel twist of fate that he was going to break Maggie's soft heart. It was unavoidable.

He heard the tread of footsteps in the hall. In an

instant, he was crouched beside the bed, pistol in hand. The door creaked quietly as it swung inward.

In the glow of the candle she held, Maggie was perhaps the most beautiful sight he had ever beheld. Her hair was loose, illuminated by the soft light. It framed her pale face and white-clad shoulders like an aura, a burnished halo. She'd removed her tartan sash and wore only the white dress. It was loose-sleeved, flowing, and brought angels to the mind of one man who'd never believed in any such thing.

He slipped the gun beneath the bed before she could see it and rose to his feet. "Maggie."

"I shouldn't be here." She set the candle on the washstand and crossed the room on bare feet. "But I couldn't stay away."

Gabriel opened his arms and she came into them, soft and warm and smelling of autumn. He couldn't stop himself from closing his eyes and resting his cheek on the silk of her hair. "That's good."

She sighed against his chest, a small, forlorn sound that tugged at his heart. " 'Twas such a magical day at the beginning."

He could feel the sorrow and weariness emanating from her. He would have taken all of it if he could, absorbed her burden. But all he could do just then was hold her close. "Tell me what you need."

"This," she said softly, and tangled her fingers in his hair. With a gentle tug she tilted his head down, then pressed her parted lips to his. He didn't need further encouragement. She didn't need to be caressed into excitement. Her kiss was hungry and demanding, a heady mixture of desire and need.

"Take me to bed," she whispered against his mouth. "Now, before I think better of it."

Gabriel wasn't going to let that happen. Nor, apparently, was she. She made quick work of the shirt and breeches he'd kept on after coming upstairs, tugging at the fabric until she could run her hands over the planes of his chest, down to the long muscles of his thighs. Her touch burned him, a glorious trail of sparks, and he was hard, ready in an instant.

She held him at the hips, her fingers pressing into his flesh. "Help me."

She tilted her head and rested her forehead against his chest, giving him free access to the tiny buttons at her back. Gabriel drew a deep breath, forced himself to unfasten each one, rather than scattering them with a single, violent tug. Then the last came free and she was lifting her arms, helping him to rid her of the layers of virginal white.

His hands were on her breasts before the chemise hit the floor, filling themselves with her warmth and softness. She fit perfectly, from her breasts in his cupped hands, to the way she cradled him with her supple thighs.

"Now," she commanded.

He lifted her easily and laid her on the bed. Her hair spilled over her shoulders and the sheets, a river of dark fire in the candlelight. Gabriel reverently stroked the length of it as he came down on top of her, carefully taking his weight on his arms. He parted her knees with his, felt the damp heat of her beckoning, welcoming him.

It was all he could do to keep from surging forward, sheathing himself as fast and forcefully as his passion demanded. But one glance into her face, heartbreakingly beautiful in its trust and desire, and he was in control again. He eased into her slowly, gently, and felt her close around him so tightly that he had the fleeting conviction that they'd been made together for just this moment, two parts of a seamless whole.

Then she lifted her knees, feet flat against the sheets, and began to rock her hips in a rhythm old as time. Gabriel felt her hands grasping his shoulders on the outside and her muscles clasping him within. It was, without question, one of the sweetest moments of his misspent life.

Murmuring her name again and again, he rocked with her. And when at last she convulsed around him with a sighing, shuddering laugh, he smiled with her, lips pressed into the curve of her throat. He hovered for one long, incomparable moment at what he realized was heaven's gate. Then he spilled himself into her with a growl that sounded and felt much more like a sob.

Gabriel had no idea how much time passed before he felt her tenderly running her fingertips through the overlong hair at his nape. "Am I crushing you?" he asked lazily.

"Aye, but I rather like it."

Smiling, he rolled onto his side, taking her with him. "We'll try this for a bit."

"Mmm." She tucked her sleek head beneath his jaw and nuzzled at his neck. "Thank you."

"For what?"

"For giving me a magical end to the day."

"Ah. It was my pleasure." He knew he had to ask the question, and discovered he cared about the answer. "How is Mr. Beaton?"

"He lives, but I haven't much hope for him."

"He's an old man, Maggie." Beaton's bright eyes and kind smile flashed into his mind. "He can't live forever."

"He was poisoned."

"What?" Gabriel couldn't believe he'd heard her correctly.

"With henbane. And it might have been in one of my bottles." She was crying now, silently, tears sliding down her cheeks. Gabriel could feel them on his skin. "I couldn't tell. It had been washed clean, but he would have taken anything I gave him, no matter how vile the taste. . . . He would have. Oh, God. I could have pulled a leaf, added it by mistake."

Gabriel swore harshly. Then, "Nonsense. You would fly before you'd make a mistake like that."

She lifted her tearstained face. "I've been so scattered of late. Almost since coming home. Certainly since . . ."

He waited for her to finish. She didn't. She just huddled in his embrace. Gabriel didn't know how to comfort her; he'd never felt easy with others' emotions. But he knew the value of cold logic. "Have you ever confused this henbane with another plant?"

"Nay," she sniffed.

"Could it be easily confused?"

"Not by one who knows herbs. It has an awful smell and the flowers are purple-veined. 'Tis distinctive, like so many poisonous plants."

He nodded. "And what was meant to be in the bottle?"

"Hyssop tonic . . ." Maggie sniffed again and swiped at her damp cheeks. "I've been over the day I filled the bottle again and again. I don't know how I could have gone wrong."

"You didn't." Gabriel's mind was working furiously. Had he in his compete ignorance of Gaelic missed a message the old man had been giving him? Had someone else heard it—or suspected? "Is there much of this plant on the island? Is it simple to find?"

"Simple enough. It grows on waste ground and at the edge of sandy strands."

"And it's well known to be deadly?"

"Oh, aye. 'Tis a nightshade, like belladonna. Long ago it was used to bring sedation, but 'tis too hard to dose, and too many people died." She propped herself up on an elbow, shoving the curtain of hair behind her shoulder. "Why?"

He shook his head. "Bear with me a moment. How was it consumed when it was used?"

"As an oil or tincture, I suppose, mixed with something else. I'd think it tastes just as vile as it smells."

"So it would have to be given in something equally strong-tasting."

She shuddered. "My hyssop tonic."

"Or raw whiskey?"

He felt her stiffen. "Dear God. You think it was deliberate. You think someone poisoned him deliberately."

Gabriel saw the anguish in her eyes. It was stronger than the disbelief, even if she didn't know it yet. "Can you honestly find another sensible explanation?"

"He's a dear old man. Why would anyone . . . ? Ach, Gabriel, he's grandfather to the village. He's seen three generations of family and friends born on Skye."

"I think we can safely assume he's seen more than that and it might have killed him." Gabriel was startled when Maggie turned and swung her legs over the edge of the bed. "What are you doing?"

She found her dress and dragged it haphazardly over her head. She scooped the rest of her clothing into an untidy bundle and clasped it close to her chest. "I'm going to my own bed."

"Maggie—"

"I need to think on this, Gabriel," she said, her voice faint but hard. "I need to think on all of it."

He knew he couldn't stop her, much as he wanted to. "I'm sorry," he offered.

"For . . . ?"

He ran one hand roughly through his hair. "For bringing this all to light. For perhaps putting Beaton at risk by not listening well enough. For allowing you to be dragged into it."

She stood by the bed, waving him jerkily back when he started to rise. "Tell me this before I go," she commanded. "If you hadn't come to Skye, hadn't come here chasing your shadowy sinner, what would have happened?"

"He would have gone free. To Ireland, perhaps, or more likely France."

"I see. And what if he's gone already?"

Gabriel scowled. "We know he hasn't. Tonight, at the ruin—"

" 'Tis easy enough to get off the island as long as the waves are favorable. So what if he's gone already?"

He didn't know what she expected him to say. "As I speculated, he'll go to—"

"Aye, Ireland. Or France. And you? Will that be the end of it? Will you be done with the matter, or will you chase him?"

"I don't know." He hadn't contemplated that possibility. He'd been so sure, so determined to catch L'Écossais on Skye. "I don't know."

"And if he's here, if you catch him, what will you do?"

"Whatever is necessary," he answered, the violent truth unspoken but there like a grim echo.

Maggie nodded once, firmly. "Well, then. I'll bid you a good night."

"Maggie."

"Aye?"

"Can you accept it now, what I have to do? After what has happened to Mr. Beaton?"

"Do you mean vengeance, Gabriel? Are you asking if I condone it?" Her face was composed, pale and beautiful as a marble statue.

"Yes," he said quietly. "That is exactly what I am asking."

She took a long moment to reply. Then, calmly, " 'Tisn't mine to demand, this revenge. But I am angry. And heartsick."

"Then . . ."

She bent and kissed him, quick and hard. "Good night, Gabriel."

She took the candle with her, leaving the room in dark and shadows.

Maggie was at the Beaton cottage soon after daybreak. Cait met her at the door, hollow-eyed and wan. "He's no better," she announced.

Maggie hurried into the room where the old man lay. He was much the same as he'd been when she had left, still just as waxy and wasted-looking, struggling to breathe.

Mrs. Beaton, who had been asleep in a chair beside the bed, came awake with a start. She saw Maggie and managed a pale shadow of her usual smile. "Bless you for coming, Mairghread. I think he's a bit better this morning." She ran a trembling hand lovingly over her husband's ashen brow. "Don't you think so?"

"He's certainly no worse," Maggie offered, trying to give some hope, even if there was little. "Has he awakened at all?"

"Nay," the old woman replied, "but he twitched a bit when the rooster crowed. 'Tis a good sign, isn't it?"

"We'll hope and pray so."

Bending over her basket, Maggie bit her lip to still its trembling. She'd seen farm animals who'd eaten poisonous plants, lacking the intelligence or instinct to avoid them. It wasn't uncommon for a sudden noise to send them into tremors, muscles contracting, legs pedaling. After that, they usually died.

"Have you been trying to get liquids into him?" she asked.

Both women nodded, and Mrs. Beaton lifted the spoon she'd been clenching in her lap. "I think he took some broth from Cait."

"Aye," her daughter said. "Just a wee bit that I spooned into him, but he swallowed."

"And I've a bowl of well water here," Mrs. Beaton said.

Maggie felt the old man's forehead. It was cool and perhaps, just perhaps, less clammy. "Come back to us," she whispered. " 'Tisn't your time yet."

She heard Mrs. Beaton muffle a sob. "He would see this war through, he said, every time we had news of our Skye lads on the Continent. He'd been born just as the last Scots lost their fight and would see these home victorious. And he would bounce Cait's next on his knee. . . ."

Cait hurried over, one hand pressed to her still-flat stomach, the other wrapping around her mother's shaking shoulders. Maggie's heart ached for them, for all of them. She couldn't believe—wouldn't—that someone would strike against this beautiful family. They were so dear, to each other and to all around them. It wasn't right. It was too horrendous a thought.

The three took turns at Mr. Beaton's bedside through the morning. They gently spooned water and broth into his mouth, wiping away what he didn't swallow and trying again. Maggie urged the others to lie down, to try to sleep. Cait finally went into the bedroom she'd occupied until her marriage. Mrs. Beaton refused to leave, but eventually dozed fitfully in her chair.

As noon approached, neighbors began arriving. One by one they crept in, offering their prayers and silent moments of respect to the beloved man who lay motionless in his bed. Many brought gifts. Elspeth Colson, more somber than a new bride should be, arrived with her husband and siblings, carrying platters and baskets of savory food left from the wedding. Calum MacAuley brought a bottle of Mr. Beaton's favorite MacAsgaill whiskey, placing it reverently on the bedside table.

"So it'll be near to hand," he murmured. Fen Mac-Donald set a glass beside it.

Edana Malcolmson shook her head with a wry smile as she proferred her own gift of fine French claret. "I can't compete with Calum and his Skye whiskey." Then she tapped Maggie's arm. "Come with me," she commanded. They slipped into the corner of the main room, which was filling fast with well-wishing neighbors. "Where is he?"

"Who?"

"Who? Oh, Maggie, please. Lord Rievaulx."

"I've no idea." Maggie's voice was sharper than she'd intended.

Edana shook her head and sighed. "Pity. Ah, well—"

"Maggie!"

She looked up and her heart did a glad little skip. Lachlann was there, pushing his way through the crowd toward her.

"I'm going now, but I should like to have a word with the earl, Maggie," Edana insisted.

"I'll be sure to pass that on." She was already moving toward Lachlann, hands extended. He caught them in his massive fists. "I thought you'd gone without saying good-bye."

He shook his head. "I've only just come back from Glasgow. There's been no ferry between the mainland and the isle for three days. Ach, *Dia is Muire,* Maggie Lìl"—he jerked his chin toward the Beatons' bedroom—"did I hear true? Is he dying?"

"I don't know," she said sadly. "He might be."

She wanted so much to tell him about the henbane. He would understand. He'd jested often enough about feeding her the stuff when he'd been an adolescent and she'd been a few years younger, pestily trailing after him like an unwelcome little sister. But she held her tongue. Until she was absolutely certain how it had happened, and she didn't know how she ever would be, she wouldn't mention poison.

"Where's Tearlach?" Lachlann asked. "He'll be needing a friend."

"Cait's husband has gone for him. He's certain to be here as soon as he can manage it. Go speak with Mrs. Beaton. She'll be glad to have you nearby."

He nodded. "I've certainly been in and out of this cottage through the years as if it were my own."

"Aye, so you have. I wish you'd brought Peadar home with you from Glasgow."

Lachlann and the Beatons' elder son had been of an age, boon companions until Peadar had left Skye for the lure of the Highlands' biggest town. Maggie had always felt that Lachlann's presence was a joy to the Beatons with all of their children away from home.

"If I'd known . . ." Lachlann lamented.

"You couldn't have, darling. But go now, give her your shoulder if she needs it."

"I will." He lifted a hand, cupped her face with it. "But first, tell me how you are. You're still beautiful, Mairghread Lìl, but you look as if you've had a terrible time of it since I've been gone."

She placed a hand over his. "I'm fine. Tired. Sad. But fine. I missed you while you were gone."

"Did you?" Something flitted through the blue eyes, gone before she could recognize it. "I'm sorry for that."

"Aye, well, I'll just have to grow used to it, won't I?"

He sighed. "You think leaving won't grieve me, too?"

"So don't go."

"Och, Maggie. You're not helping matters here."

She stared at him, this friend of her childhood, and realized she didn't know the man he'd become nearly as well as she'd thought. The three years she had been gone had changed them both. It was something that couldn't be helped and likely shouldn't be.

"Go on, then," she said quietly.

"Aye." He started to turn. "Maggie . . ."

"Hmm?"

"You'll know when I leave."

She nodded. Then watched as he threaded his way through the crowd to find Mrs. Beaton. She raised a weary hand to her brow, closed her eyes for a moment. When she opened them, she saw Gabriel.

There was no telling when he'd come in. He was standing across the room, not far from the door, alone, imposing and handsome in his London garb. Just looking at him sent warmth curling through her stomach. Then she saw his eyes. Even from the distance, she could see that they were hard, dark in his face.

"Maggie." Cait appeared at her side, eyes bright with

hope. "My mother is asking for you. She thinks *Athair* blinked."

"I'll come now." When she looked again, Gabriel was gone.

17

O once I had thyme of my own
And in my own garden it grew;
I used to know the place where my thyme it did grow,
But now it is cover'd with rue,
But now it is cover'd with rue.

—Lancashire ballad

Gabriel stretched as best he could and shifted his position on the damp ground. He had been lying on the hill above the Beaton cottage for the better part of the night, watching and waiting. Now, as the morning light rose, he debated whether or not he should stay. He needed to bathe and exchange his clothing for a dry set. The Skye mist had a way of slipping through even the warmest of wool garments.

He thought it would be safe to abandon his post. The occupants of the house had begun moving about a quarter hour past. Gabriel had seen smoke coming from the chimney, then the Beatons' daughter had come into the yard and drawn water from the well. The old man was still alive. Gabriel knew he would have heard the keening of the women otherwise.

Beaton hadn't awakened the day before, but apparently he had become restless, tossing in the bed and muttering aloud. Gabriel had no idea what the man had said, but Mrs. Beaton had given him an odd look in one of the brief periods when she had left her husband's side. It had been awkward at times, standing among the Beatons' friends in their home. He was so much the outsider, in his London clothing and lack of Gaelic. But no one had made him feel unwelcome. Instead, he'd had a plate of food pressed into his hands at one point, mugs of tea and ale at others.

The little community was gathered out of love and respect for one of their own, and they accepted the Englishman's presence with quiet goodwill. Gabriel found himself in the middle of more than one knot of people telling tales of Sim Beaton. In each one, the fond words had either been spoken in English for his benefit or someone had translated for him. He'd caught himself smiling more than once, both in genuine amusement and in appreciative sadness.

Still, he hadn't been able to forget the reason he was there.

And he'd taken this position above the cottage in the middle of the night not out of caring, but because he was convinced that L'Écossais would be back. There was no doubt in Gabriel's mind that Beaton had been deliberately poisoned by a traitorous Scot who feared what he might say. Whether out of carelessness on the part of L'Écossais or the old man's strong will to live—and Gabriel knew L'Écossais was seldom if ever careless—the job hadn't been completed. Beaton struggled to stay alive and seemed to be winning the fight. It was certain that L'Écossais would try again.

Not now, with the day beginning and people starting to go about their tasks. L'Écossais would have to wait until the visits started before he could enter the cottage unobtrusively. Gabriel had no idea how he could prevent the man from slipping Beaton more poison; he'd already managed it once. But as long as it was light and the house was busy, there would be no chance of the blackguard slipping in and finishing what he'd begun, with a knife between Beaton's ribs or a pillow over his face.

Maggie had been there most of the day before, and

Gabriel assumed she would be there today as well. She would be alert, watching the people who came to pay their respects—even if she didn't realize she was doing it.

Unfortunately, Gabriel feared she wouldn't be watching certain persons closely enough. MacDonald had returned from God knows where. And Maggie had been so cozy with him, her face glowing as they spoke. Gabriel's jaw hardened at the memory. Others, too, came and went from the house with the ease of family. It was a damnable situation and it could only get worse.

Time was running out; Gabriel could feel it.

Maggie entered the kitchen to find her father with his nose buried in a southern racing report. More were spread over the table. He was clearly happy as a cow in clover. Maggie smiled as she dropped a kiss on the top of his head.

"You're up early, Papa."

"Morning, darlin'," he greeted her. "How's old Sim?"

"I'm off to see him now, as soon as I've put the porridge on. You'll see to serving yourself?"

"No need, lass. I've had my breakfast already." Jamie waved to the sideboard.

Maggie sighed as she surveyed the remnants of the cold meat pie she'd meant to serve for luncheon. "Oh, Papa. Well, I'll do the porridge anyway. Tessa and Gabriel will have it when they come down." She gestured to the pile of papers. "Where did all this come from?"

"Cousin Henry sent them from Edinburgh. They came with Tuesday's post." Jamie tapped the top of one sheet with a grin. "And scarcely a week out of date. The mail's running fast these days."

Maggie peered over his shoulder. "Faster than you

think, at that. Mr. MacGruder must have gotten his lot last week and held it for some reason. There was no ferry Monday or Tuesday. Lachlann said so."

"Rubbish. Either the lad is having you on, or he's been walking into door frames again and muddling his head. I can't say about the post, but Calum had a new batch of port in from Aberdeen. It would have come over Monday."

Monday. But why, Maggie wondered, would Lachlann lie? . . . A cold knot formed in her stomach. "Oh, nay," she whispered. "Please, not him."

"What was that?"

"Nothing, just muttering to myself." She patted her father's shoulder. "Will I make a fresh pot of tea? 'Tis a wonder you don't choke on the stuff in your cup."

Jamie glanced at his black and leafy effort and shrugged. " 'Tisn't so bad, but, aye, if you're so inclined . . ."

Maggie emptied the sludge from the pot and hurried to brew a fresh one. She stirred oats into hot water and set them on the stove to cook. She wanted to get to the Beatons' as soon as possible.

In the end, it was nearly an hour later when she finally left the house. Tessa had bounded into the kitchen, begging for eggs and sausages. Seeing his younger daughter happily tucking in, Jamie had of course decided he was ready for his second meal of the young day. Gabriel hadn't appeared at all. With decidedly foolish optimism, Maggie had left her sister to the washing up and had made her own escape.

Mr. Beaton had been restless through the previous afternoon and evening. Not awake, but Maggie had sensed an improvement. His movements had seemed more to her like those of a man with a fever than one twitching in a death dance, but again, that might have been mostly wishful thinking on her part. She quickened her pace as she approached the Beaton cottage, hoping for the best, doing her best to steel herself for the worst.

Cait answered the door. She looked exhausted, the dark smudges beneath her eyes testifying to two days with very little sleep. But she was smiling.

"He's better," she announced, then pulled Maggie into a quick embrace. "He's resting now, but he took a cup of broth at dawn and spoke to my mother."

Maggie nearly sagged in relief. "Thank God. Oh, thank God." Then, "You won't be needing me. I'll leave you all to each other; I'll come back later."

"When did you eat last?" Cait demanded.

"Oh, I don't know. It doesn't matter—"

"Come inside." The other woman all but hauled her through the door and into a chair. "I've bacon frying and we have more bannocks and honey from the wedding than I know what to do with. Here." She shoved a mug of steaming chocolate into Maggie's hands. "From Edana. I've just poured it. I'll go get another. She sent some of that god-awful India tea, too, for Papa, and some fresh-shot venison. With all that's been brought since yesterday morn, the larder is full to the rafters."

Maggie sipped at the chocolate, resisting the urge to dart into the next room and have a good long look at the sleeping Mr. Beaton. Instead, she shared a meal with Cait and Mrs. Beaton, who was still pale but clearly over-joyed. The first of the day's visitors began to arrive, bearing more food and drink, and there was soon a quiet celebration going on in the little cottage and spilling onto the flagstone walk.

When she was finally able to see Mr. Beaton, Maggie nearly wept. He was weak, fragile-looking, but he was alive and awake, smiling his familiar smile at her. He reached for her hand and she took it, settling herself in the narrow chair beside the bed. "My wife and daughter tell me you've all but moved in with us," he said.

"I was a wee bit concerned about you."

"Oh, rot. Anyone can see I'm fit as a fiddle." His eyes twinkled in his drawn face. "Now, if you're to have one of our spare rooms, we'll have to discuss charging you bed and board. . . . Ach, lass," he murmured when tears came to her eyes, "I'm going to be just fine. Don't cry. Everything will be just fine. And I thank you for the care you've given me."

She nodded, then started to rise. "I'll leave you to rest."

His grip was weak but insistent. "Sit, please." She did. "I need to speak to you, about that young man of yours."

"Lord Rievaulx?"

"As if there's another. Aye, that one. You must send him away, Maggie."

"I . . . why?"

The old man turned his head toward the bedside table. "I'd best have some water if I'm to talk. My throat feels as if I've been swallowing sand."

The little jug was empty. "I'll fetch some." Maggie hurried out of the room. And was almost flattened by a surge of brown wool. "Tearlach."

Her friend managed a faint smile. "I need to see him."

"Of course." She rested a hand on his sleeve. "Calm yourself, darling. He is much better."

"Truly?"

"Truly. Here," she reached up, removed his cap, smoothed his ruffled fair hair. Then she handed him the dishcloth she'd tucked into her apron. "You've grease on your face."

He sighed and wiped at the smudges. "I was working on my plow when Alan arrived yesterday."

"And you didn't stop to wash before riding hell-for-leather to get back here. Am I right?" She patted his somewhat cleaner cheek. "Better. Go see him now."

"You're an angel, Maggie MacLeod," he announced, and disappeared into the bedroom. Maggie fetched the water and sent it in with Cait. The family deserved a bit of time to themselves.

The morning stretched into afternoon. She served food alongside Cait and her mother, tidied up after the steady stream of visitors, took a precious hour to play with Cait's little girl and the collection of wooden toys—then another hour just holding the child as she slept in her lap. She wanted to speak to Mr. Beaton again. He'd been so adamant that she should hear what he had to say. But he needed the time with his family, and rest. So she waited. She did slip in to see him once, for a minute. He was sleeping, his breath easier and more even than it had been the day before, his skin dry and showing a bit of color. Smiling, she tucked the coverlet under his whiskery chin and went back to give a good report to his assembled well-wishers.

Late in the afternoon, she went outside. She would grab a few good breaths of fresh air and fetch some fresh water from the well. There was a kettle going constantly on the hearth and a steady supply of plates to be washed. So, pail in tow, she headed across the yard. As she did, Lachlann came striding across the neighboring field.

"How is he?" he asked as he swung easily over the low stone wall.

"Better." Maggie set the pail down and studied his face carefully, looking for the boy she'd grown up with, the one who had teased and taunted, and pulled her plaits. She realized she couldn't find him at all in the man standing in front of her. "I need to ask you something, Lachlann, and I need you to give me the truth. Will you promise me that?"

He raised a dark brow. "This sounds serious."

"Aye. It is. Will you promise?"

"The truth. Of course."

" 'Tis about Mr. Beaton."

"Aye?"

She took a deep breath. "You care for him, don't you?"

Now Lachlann frowned. "What sort of question is that? Of course I care for him. Everyone does."

"And wouldn't harm . . ." Maggie bit her lip. She couldn't do it. She couldn't even say the words aloud. It couldn't be Lachlann. He would never harm the old man who'd been so good to him through the years. She made her decision, hard as it was. "You must go."

"What? Why?"

"Oh, Lachlann." She shook her head sadly. "He's after you. Gabriel. Lord Rievaulx. And he won't leave until he's brought you down."

"Maggie—"

"I know you believe the choices you've made are for the best and I wish I could say I do, too. But all that matters now is that you leave here before he does you ill. You're strong, Lachlann, and able, but he's being driven by something I don't understand, and it's larger than all of us. Will you heed me now? Will you go?"

Lachlann stood for a long moment, staring down at her. Then he glanced to the cottage and back. "You don't know what you've gotten yourself involved with, Maggie Lìl," he said gruffly.

"Does that really matter?" She touched his hand, lightly. "Go."

He nodded once, then stepped back and turned sharply on his heel. Without a word, he vaulted over the wall and strode away without a single glance back. Maggie watched him go, heart in her throat. She'd done the right thing, she told herself. She'd done the only thing she could.

A sound behind her caught her attention. She turned to find Gabriel standing at the corner of the cottage wall. She didn't know if he'd heard, but his eyes and jaw were hard.

"Gabriel."

"What did you tell him?"

She just shook her head, knowing there was nothing she could say to make him understand.

"You told him to run, didn't you?" he demanded. *"Didn't you?"*

"Aye."

"After what I told you."

"Aye."

"And after all you've seen."

She lifted her chin, squared her shoulders, and took a step toward him. She felt it like a slap when he shook his head sharply, freezing her with his gaze.

"Why can't you let this go?" she pleaded. "Let him go? You can't possibly understand how we are here— *who* we are. . . ."

"I won't argue the issues of ties with you, Maggie," he growled, "but I will remind you of a night in a fallen castle and something called henbane."

"That wasn't Lachlann. I know it wasn't."

She cringed at his snarl. "You would absolve him of anything, wouldn't you?"

"Absolution isn't mine to give. 'Tis between ourselves and God."

She'd never seen anything as cold as his eyes in that moment.

"So speaks Saint Maggie. Do you have any idea," he asked, voice low and deadly, "what it is like to commit an act so heinous that there's no chance of redemption?"

"I . . ."

"To betray not only your friends and comrades, but your very principles as well . . ." He paused, fists clenching and unclenching at his sides. "And hundreds, maybe thousands of people you've never met, but whose very lives depend upon you *not* committing such a mistake?"

When she didn't answer—couldn't answer—he bared his teeth in a hard, frightening smile. "Of course you haven't. How could you? You've spent your life in a place like this." He swept an arm in a cutting arc, encompassing the rough, simple yard and rocky fields beyond. "A place where connections and loyalties are astoundingly strong, but never tested. Until now. And you chose that bloody, infernal loyalty over logic. Over what was *right*, dammit! And over me."

"Gabriel—"

"I should have known. I certainly shouldn't be surprised. At the heart of it all, you're only one of them." This time, he jerked his chin toward the cottage and the people within. "Believing in fairies and ghosties and things that go bump in the night. They—you and I are different to the core. It's all so simple, isn't it, Maggie? Living so comfortably with magical things that don't exist. You couldn't possibly be expected to understand what life in the earthly realm can make you do."

He stared hard at her, cursed. "Christ. Your only crime has been to look like you do, your only mistake to lie with the enemy. With me." Suddenly he stopped, blinked, then gave a short, harsh laugh that chilled her to the core. "Well. Perhaps we're not so different, after all. Do you want to know what it was that I did, Maggie? The transgression so great that it cost the lives of countless good, noble men? *Do you?*"

She was shaking, desperate to hold him and soothe him, just as desperate to run away. And she was so tired, suddenly, that it was an effort to simply draw air into her lungs. "You're going to tell me, whether I wish it or not."

"Damned right I am. My irrevocable act was this simple: I bedded a whore."

"Gabriel, don't. You don't have to—"

"A Spanish whore. Beautiful, although not," he hissed, "half as beautiful as you. Agile—she danced for me in a tavern. And eager to please. God knows I'd gone months without a woman's touch. Without any *ordinary* human contact at all. I should have known—of course I should have known that she was too convenient, too bloody perfect to be who she appeared to be, but I'd been tracking through the Pyrenees, back and forth between Spain and France with my communiqués for so long. . . ."

He laughed again. "But there I go, making excuses when there are none. All that matters is that I took a whore to my room upstairs, and when I awoke the following day, she had taken every last shred of army intelligence I carried. A dozen weeks of reconnaissance. Names and locations and codes. I found her, but it was too late. She had already passed the information into the hands of the men who'd trained her."

"What did you do when you found her?" Maggie asked, not certain she wanted to know.

"I buried her," Gabriel said flatly. "The same men decided she was expendable, apparently. I buried her. No one did the same for the first corps of English soldiers who died in the Portuguese hills a fortnight later as a result of my carelessness."

There was raw pain in his voice and in his eyes. It tore at Maggie. In that moment, she understood him, completely. And she ached for him.

"Oh, Gabriel. Oh, *mo grádh*." She reached out to him again, and this time wouldn't be held off by his glare. She touched his chest, his hard face. He stood silent and stony, hands still clenched at his sides. "You've taken the weight of the world on your shoulders, and broad as they are, 'tis too much."

"Did you hear a word I said?" he growled.

"I did. Of course I did. And it's an awful tale. But I've said it before to you: God didn't make you an angel. You're but a man."

"I was a soldier in His Majesty's Army, entrusted to deliver critical information."

"So you were. And I'm guessing Nathan was part of the same corps." When he neither affirmed nor denied what she already felt to be true, she pressed. "Along with others. How many?"

"Ten," was the heavy response. "There were once ten of us."

"Ten of you together, and ten more under another command, I'm sure, and another and another. You weren't alone, and you weren't expected to win or lose a war on your own."

"You have no idea what was expected of me."

Maggie stroked his shoulders, feeling the bunched muscles beneath the fine dark wool of his coat. "I am beginning to understand what you've expected of yourself. I can't make you forgive yourself for falls real or imagined. And we can't change the past, Gabriel, no matter how much we wish it. All we can do is live with what has been and try to keep the worst mistakes from happening again."

At long last, his hands came up, closing tightly around her shoulders, tightly enough to leave a mark. "Are you telling me you regret betraying me to MacDonald?"

In that moment, Maggie fully comprehended for the first time why it was called heartbreak. She could actually feel a pain in her breast, real and sharp and steady, just as if her heart were being rent in two.

She met his eyes. "Nay," she replied. "I can't tell you that."

"But you wouldn't do it again, knowing what you do."

There was a shout from the cottage, followed by laughter. Maggie thought of the people within, of love and good cheer and roots deeper than the well behind her. "I would do just the same again, Gabriel. I've been careless with my heart, handing it over so easily to you; that's my cross to bear. There is so little I wouldn't do for you, who've stirred me, made me feel things I could never have imagined. I'll hold all that dear when you've gone." She touched him a last time, stroking her palm down his cheek. "But there's nothing I wouldn't do for the people who've loved me all my life without reserve or demands or deception."

His hands dropped away. "You don't think Mac-Donald has lied to you? God, Maggie. You're not stupid. You don't think he has lied to you, and to others, and very likely had at least a few of the people you care for so much lie for him?"

"That falls on his shoulders if so, not mine." She pressed one hand over the steady ache in her chest. "What will you do now?"

He didn't answer. Instead, he demanded, "Tell me where he lives."

"Oh, Gabriel."

"You did your part. I let him walk away just now, but don't think I won't go after him. Tell me where he lives."

She shook her head, fighting to keep the tears from falling. "I won't."

"I'll find out anyway."

"Aye, you probably will."

There was an endless, cold minute of silence. So cold. Maggie shivered just looking into his eyes.

"I trusted you," he said at last, harshly.

She shook her head again. "Nay," she replied softly, "you didn't."

He laughed, another sharp, bitter sound. "Well, there's another similarity between us, then. You didn't trust me, either."

Maggie was stunned, wounded that he would think so. "I made love with you. I fell . . . I fell in love with you."

"But you never once believed I intended to spend the rest of my life with you, did you? You thought I would leave without you. Oh, hell, Maggie. I'm not your bloody dead *Sasunnach* on the cliff."

She felt his fury like a blade in her breast. "You can't believe we would have had a happily ever after," she said sadly.

"Well, we'll never know now, will we?" And he was gone, striding away over the hard earth.

Maggie managed to stand as she was until he was out of sight. Then she sank slowly to her knees and let the tears fall.

*   *   *

Gabriel resolutely ignored the fact that his chest ached like fire and that it had become harder and harder to draw a full breath. He kept his pace steady and his mind clear of everything except his goal as he headed for the MacLeod house.

Tessa met him at the top of the path, mud up to her knees and a wide grin on her face. "Have you heard? Mr. Beaton is awake! I've just met Andy at the burn and he told me."

"I know already," Gabriel said shortly, and watched as the girl's smile faded.

She tilted her head and regarded him questioningly, rather like a puppy who has suddenly been swatted. " 'Tis happy news."

"Yes. It is."

He knew he should talk to her, make some sort of effort to bring the smile back to her face. But he was already steeling himself against the loss of her. He'd never had a sister and, although had someone ever bothered to ask him if he would have liked one he certainly wouldn't have chosen a pesty firebrand with too much intelligence and too little self-control, he had grown to care for Tessa. To care what became of her. He supposed Isobel would keep him informed—if a report from Maggie didn't have her spurning him.

He realized that since that heartrending night more than fifteen years ago when he'd sat at his dying grandfather's bedside, holding the old man's hand, he had not said a good-bye to anyone. He'd chosen instead to simply walk away.

He kept walking now. Tessa stood where he'd left her for a moment, then hurried to catch up. "You're leaving, aren't you?" she asked, voice small.

He stopped in his tracks, closed his eyes for a second

before facing her. He debated lying. It would be so much easier to reassure her then slip away. "Yes," he heard himself saying. "I am."

"When?"

"Soon. Tonight, probably."

"Why?" she asked, then shook her untidy head. "Nay, don't tell me. I don't think I want to know."

It was the first time Gabriel had ever heard her refrain from demanding any information. The girl picked the damnedest time to become adult on him, when he was realizing how much he would miss the child. He opted against platitudes and continued into the cottage.

She followed him up the stairs, leaning hesitantly in his doorway while he shoved his meager belongings into his valise: clothing, boots, his empty flask. "There's a shirt of yours on the line in back," she informed him, hope lighting the face that was so much like Maggie's.

"I'll get it on my way out."

"And another waiting to be washed. You won't want to leave without it."

"Would you fetch it for me?"

That clearly hadn't been her plan and she studied her feet, no doubt looking for an excuse not to do as he asked. Then she nodded and, eyes still downcast, crept from the room.

Gabriel gathered the last of his clothing, stuffing it atop the rest. He almost failed to notice the lace-edged handkerchief that didn't belong there. He drew it out and, before he could stop himself, lifted it to his face. It smelled of rosemary and cloves. It must have tumbled from a pocket when Maggie came to him—a night that seemed years ago.

He folded the little linen square carefully and packed it in his valise.

By the time Tessa had dragged herself back up the stairs, he had emptied the room of his presence. His bag was next to the door, waiting only for that last item, his hat and greatcoat draped over the newel post at the top of the stairway. He took the shirt from Tessa, stowed it away, and closed up the valise. He would leave it in the stable. Once he had finished what he'd come to do, there wouldn't be any need to come back into the house.

"Where is your father?" he asked the girl. The least he could do was offer the man thanks for his hospitality.

"He's not here." Tessa's eyes brightened suddenly. "Come downstairs and wait. He's bound to be home soon."

Not with the pub door open and the quiet celebration going on at the Beatons', Gabriel thought. "Where does MacDonald live?"

Tessa tilted her head and pursed her lips. "Which? There's Fen and David and Mòrag and Elspeth, but she isn't a MacDonald any longer, but a Colson—though I suppose one must consider the fact that Colsons are a sept of the MacDonalds. Then, of course, there's Tormoid and Angus—"

"Tessa."

She wilted. "You mean Lachlann."

"I do."

She beckoned and he followed her dragging footsteps to the window. "Do you see where the road curves down into the glen?" He nodded. "Follow it. You'll come to Lachlann's holding after two miles."

He rested a hand on her shoulder. For a precious minute, Tessa leaned against him, face pressed to his side. Then he stepped away and went out the door.

He saddled his horse and took the road in the direction she had indicated. When he spied the stone house and outbuildings in the distance, he dismounted and tied the animal to a hardy rowan tree. He needed as much of an element of surprise as he could get.

In the end, it didn't matter. There was no sign of Mac-Donald anywhere. Gabriel carefully checked the nearby fields full of shaggy Highland cattle and the farm buildings. Pistol in hand, he let himself silently into the cool, still cottage. An ancient herding dog lay on a thick rug by the hearth. It lifted its graying head, tail thumping a slow welcome. Then it closed its eyes again and went back to sleep.

Resisting the urge to go upstairs and riffle through the man's belongings, Gabriel left. He didn't expect to find anything of use. It was MacDonald he wanted.

Cursing the slowly waning light, he collected his horse and set off again. There was far too much ground to cover, and limited daylight. Eyes sharp, he scanned the fields as he rode west. He knew MacDonald had a large holding. He didn't know where it ended and someone else's land began. After more than an hour of fruitless search, he turned back toward the MacLeods'.

It took him longer than he expected. And the place was uncustomarily silent when he reached it. Tessa had gone again; Jamie had probably not been back. And Maggie wasn't where she could usually be found: standing in the kitchen in a tidy apron, up to the wrists in bread dough or fragrant herbs. Gabriel could smell her, though, in the air, and hurried out of the house before she filled his senses entirely.

In the end, he decided to go to the pub. He didn't think he could face entering the Beaton household. He would leave that until he absolutely had to. As he cantered along the cliff road he saw a hulking figure walking in the distance, and pulled his mount to a shuddering stop.

MacDonald. Then a smaller figure, decidedly feminine, appeared behind the other. Edana Malcolmson and her brute of a servant. Not MacDonald after all. Grim, eyes on the rising mist that hadn't seemed to vanish at all that day, Gabriel resumed his ride.

MacAuley looked up as he pushed through the red door. There was no one else inside. "Drink?" he offered gruffly, holding a dark bottle aloft. "I've a bottle of my homemade blackberry wine here. 'Tis a bit strong, but might suit you."

Gabriel glanced briefly at what looked to be leaves floating in the depths. "A whiskey, if you would." He had time for a quick, burning shot. He could well use one.

The door thumped behind him. He turned.

"*Sasunnach.*" Lachlann MacDonald stood in the doorway, long-barreled hunting rifle in hand. "I think it would be best if you were to come with me now."

18

He learned too late, our lad,
that the sea is full of fallen angels,
thyme and rue tangled in their dampen'd wings.
                              —Dubhgall MacIain MacLeòid

Maggie picked her way carefully over the sharp rocks to the edge of the cliffs. She'd passed the last quarter hour on the village road, bidding a good night to friends and neighbors as they left the Beaton house or passed by on their way to their own. Then she'd sat quietly, sheltered by the outcropping of boulders some hundred feet away from where she stood now, making certain she would be alone. She didn't feel like company, was weary of so many hours spent in the midst of a cheerful crowd when what she needed was time to herself.

The mist that had never really dissipated during the day was rising again as darkness fell. Maggie could hear the waves crashing and hissing below. It would be a cold, damp night, especially here on the cliff edge, not suited for being out and about. Maggie didn't plan to stay long, just long enough to clear her mind and glean some comfort from this place that had brought her so much solace through the years.

She didn't know if Gabriel would be gone by the time she returned home. She didn't know if he had found Lachlann. She had contemplated running all the way to her friend's holding to find him, but she'd already warned him once. And no matter how fast she went, she knew Gabriel would have found a way to be there first.

The loss of Gabriel already felt like a bleeding inside, a quietly steady pulse that had thundered with her steps as she walked over the moorland to the cliffs. She would learn to live without him. She knew that. She'd managed for the twenty-two years before he'd slipped into her life; she would go for many more once he had slipped out of it.

She just didn't know where she was going to put the wrenching pain.

"What happened to you, lass?" she asked herself softly. The answer came so quickly and clearly that it could have been someone else's. *Thuit mi ann am gaol air.*

I fell in love with him.

It was that simple and that profound. Maggie closed her eyes and wondered why, simple or profound, it had to be so *hard*. Why the one true love of her life had left her feeling battered and broken. And yearning, desperately.

She turned her face into the wind and tucked her hands into the pocket of her cloak. She fingered the sprig of wild thyme she had plucked while sitting among the rocks nearby. It was a misunderstood herb, she'd always thought, its strongest association being with violence and death. But women through the centuries had given their lovers sprigs of thyme as a symbol of remembrance. Men had gone off to the Crusades, Agincourt, Culloden, with these tokens of love and faithfulness in their pockets.

Maggie withdrew the sprig and brought it to her nose, inhaling the pungent scent. Then, with a choked sob, she cast it over the edge. *Savoury, sage, rosemary, and thyme.* Gabriel was, once and always, the true love of her life. She knew she wouldn't stop loving him; she could sooner find land between sand and sea. She would simply go on loving him, wherever he might be.

She heard the crunch of a heavy foot behind her. Heart leaping with hope, she turned. And tried to maintain a pleasant smile even when that hope was dashed.

"I wouldn't expect to find you out here now," she remarked. "Were you looking for me? Am I needed?"

Then she saw the knife blade.

Gabriel walked ahead of MacDonald. He didn't have a choice, really. The man had a gun in his hands. Gabriel's own weapon was tucked into the waistband of his breeches. By the time he reached it under his coat and waistcoat, the other man could put a hole the size of a cannonball through his chest. So he walked, and waited for his chance to turn the tables.

Surprisingly, MacDonald wasn't leading him away from the village. On the contrary, they were going right along the central road. They passed a handful of people, all of whom waved or nodded, either not seeing anything odd in the armed Skyeman walking along a step behind the visiting *Sasunnach*—or perhaps just not caring.

"Turn here," came the gruff command several minutes later.

Gabriel found himself walking up the path to the Beaton cottage. Anger and curiosity rising together, he demanded, "Why in the hell have you brought me here?"

"You'll see, won't you?" MacDonald reached around him and rapped at the door. When Mrs. Beaton opened it, he addressed her with a short stream of Gaelic. Her brows went up at the sight of the gun, but she smiled and ushered them inside.

The place was empty but for a small girl playing in the middle of the floor. At the sight of MacDonald, she giggled and waved what looked to be a wooden duck in his direction. *"Hallo, a Mhairi,"* he said, bending to chuck her under her plump chin. To Gabriel, he commanded, "In there," indicating the bedchamber.

Mr. Beaton was propped up against the pillows, looking drawn, but hardly like a man who had been at death's door a day earlier. At the sight of Gabriel, he grinned and waved cheerfully toward a chair. Gabriel took it, MacDonald coming in after a moment to settle his long form in another nearby.

The two Skyemen had a quick, sober conversation in Gaelic. Then MacDonald turned to Gabriel. "He wanted me to bring you here and says now it's time for you to hear what he has to say."

"Fine."

The old man spoke; MacDonald translated. "He wants to know if he's right, if you've come to Skye in search of a man who has acted against the king."

Gabriel nodded. Then, slowly, to MacDonald. "It isn't you." Not a question, but a certainty.

The man snorted. "I'd be pleased to show the Hanover lot the hard side of my fists, but nay, I've never done anything to serve them ill."

"Tell me the old man knows who it is."

MacDonald spoke to Beaton, who nodded. "He believes so."

"Someone in the community," Gabriel announced, and again received an affirmative nod. "And he's going to tell me who? Why would he do that?"

After a brief consultation, MacDonald replied, "Because it's gone too far, from principle to madness. He's afraid good, innocent people are going to be hurt, probably badly and certainly needlessly."

"Scores of good, innocent people have already died, needlessly."

"He wasn't certain, but he thought as much. It grieves him." There was another quick stream of Gaelic. "He asks you for two things, though, before he tells you all he knows."

Gabriel leaned forward, eyes narrowed. "That will depend on what he asks—and tells."

"He wants you to listen to a little bit of history first. And to remember it when you face your quarry."

Gabriel had an idea how very hard it was for this noble old man to betray a neighbor, how much of a struggle the decision must have been. "Agreed. I won't promise leniency, but I will promise to keep whatever he tells me in mind."

MacDonald translated. Beaton took a deep breath, then nodded once more. "Agreed." The old man leaned back against the pillows, eyes taking on a sad, faraway look, and started speaking.

"It all began sixty-six years ago," came his story, "when Prince Charles Edward Stuart, fleeing the English army after his defeat at Culloden, was rowed across the water from South Uist to Skye. . . ."

Some ten minutes later, Gabriel and his unlikely ally were hurrying through the door. Mrs. Beaton, settled by the fire with her knitting in her lap and her granddaughter at her feet, looked up as they entered. "Ask her if she knows where Maggie is," Gabriel commanded, the knot in his gut tightening like a fist.

MacDonald did. "She says Maggie left nearly an hour ago and started off on the cliff road."

"Alone?"

"Aye, as far as she knows."

With a quick thanks, the two men left the cottage and headed for the cliffs.

*　　*　　*

Maggie had carefully backed as far away from the knife as she could, but there was no room left behind her, only a foot or two of earth and the empty air beyond. "Will you put that away?" she managed calmly. "And we'll talk."

"I don't think so." Tearlach Beaton twirled the blade in a lazy circle. "I've found I like the feel of it. But we can talk all you want until your *Sasunnach* arrives. Would you care to sit?"

Maggie debated for an instant. Her legs felt like jelly, but she knew she needed to stay on her feet. Given a chance, she would be able to run—or fight. "Nay, thank you."

Tearlach nodded, then looked past her into the mist. "A grand night for this sort of thing, don't you think?"

"What sort of thing?" She could see the crazed sheen in his eyes even in the rapidly descending dark.

"Repeating history. Creating it. You'll be a part of both, Mairghread MacLeod, as well you should be."

"I don't understand."

He tapped the knife against his thigh. "And I don't suppose that really matters."

"You shot at us."

"I did. I will say this for your Englishman, he's quick."

"But you'd gone back to Glenelg before the wedding. Cait's husband—"

"Arrived on my land mere hours after I had. Oh, I'd meant to go earlier, right after eliminating an English thorn in my side. But there was no ferry, so I had to wait. And a good thing, too. Now I've done almost all I need to do here. By tomorrow I'll be sailing happily away to France. I suppose I might be bumping into your unfortunate lover again then, quite literally. Depends on where the tides carry his body."

Maggie swallowed, did her best to calm her pulse. "Harming him won't bring you any glory, Tearlach."

"Mmm. I wouldn't be certain of that. The French delight in the demise of English soldiers, especially the elite ones. And killing him will bring me a good deal of pleasure. Another *Sasunnach* who thought to topple the Stuarts goes over the cliff. History repeating."

A ghastly thought flashed into Maggie's head. "You want me to push him?" she gasped, stunned.

"Not especially, although 'twould be interesting to watch. Nay, I intend to stay with history." Tearlach chuckled. "But then, you still believe the woman did the shoving. Amazing how well that story took hold. Your great-grandfather had a way with telling tales."

"M-my great-grandfather?"

"Of course. He was there that night, perhaps gave the fatal push himself. He might even have thrust the dirk into the woman's breast, although I've always suspected that was Calum MacAuley's grandfather. He was the one who was betrothed to her. But 'twas Dubhgall MacIain MacLeòid who created the story of betrayal and jealousy. And he who wrote the ballad. You ought to know it."

And she did, although to her it had always been a fanciful story created by her fanciful ancestor. " ' 'Tis said he bore the scent of wild thyme, our lad,' " she whispered, " 'as he made his way through lands where angels fell.' " It made no sense to her. "Why would he kill a stranger and then create such a tale around it?"

"Amazing what your fool of a father never knew," Tearlach remarked with a grin. "The Englishman was chasing the rightful prince through a land of Jacobites. And he managed to seduce your great-grandfather's sister Saraid on top of it. 'Twas a dishonor no righteous

Scot could bear. My father thinks the fellow had chosen her over his quest and that she was ready to send him off out of loyalty to her people, but I expect that's just the notions of another romantic fool. God knows we can't let our women go giving themselves to English swine."

Maggie's mind was whirling. "Your father . . . What has he to do with this? He wasn't even born—"

"Until the following year. Ah, Maggie. Are you beginning to understand, finally? My father is the son of Charles Edward Stuart. Illegitimate, to be sure, but no less a son of the rightful king of England, Ireland, Scotland, and beyond. When he dies, that right falls to me."

"O Dia." Horror gripped her like an icy fist. "Tearlach, your *father*. You tried to kill him. And for what? A crown you can't possibly think to wear?"

"I'm not daft, Maggie. I don't expect to rule the Isles. I'll leave that to Bonaparte. But I will take the recognition as a male descendant of the royal Stuarts, and I will take the recognition for having been part, at last, of the downfall of the Hanovers. My father, sadly, never understood. And he was ready to betray me."

"You're responsible for the deaths of hundreds of innocent men," she said shakily, recalling Gabriel's words.

"War, my lass," he replied cheerfully, "is a dirty business. And no one is innocent in it. Ah. I believe I hear the soon-to-be-fallen warrior approaching. Now I'd best be making my decision, hadn't I?"

"What decision?" Maggie needed to keep him talking while she made her own.

"Whether to make the Englishman watch you die"— he brandished the knife—"or the other way about."

In that instant, Maggie saw the dark outline of a man appear from the road. She knew what she had to do.

"Gabriel, stay back!" she cried, and threw herself at Tearlach.

He heard her. And saw her throw herself forward. He saw, too, the glint of metal in Beaton's hand. Gabriel was already running hard when Maggie cried out again, this time in pain. He covered the ground in long, furious strides, but he was still precious yards away.

They were so close to the cliff. Maggie had propelled Beaton back, so they were no longer right on the edge, but they were still close, far too close. As he sprinted those last yards, Gabriel heard the man grunt, saw him thrust Maggie away—shoving her hard toward the precipice.

"No!" he bellowed, and launched himself toward them.

His weight knocked Beaton aside and to his knees. The knife bounced once, near Gabriel's ear, then plummeted past Maggie where she clung to the edge. He reached out desperately and somehow got a hand on her arm. He closed it tight, felt her fingers scrabbling for purchase then tightening on his sleeve.

"Don't let go," he commanded through clenched teeth. "For God's sake, don't let go."

Lying flat on his belly, he dug his toes into the hard earth, got a grip on Maggie's other arm. He could hear the waves crashing below, felt the ice of wind and fear sliding along his back. Inch by desperate inch, he moved backward, pulling her with him.

"Rievaulx!"

He heard MacDonald's shout an instant before Beaton's boot connected with his side. He grunted with the pain, but held on. Then the second blow came, to his head this time. It rolled him violently onto his side. Lights exploded behind his eyes. When the next struck him hard in the chest, flipping him onto his back, he felt his arms jerk, felt Maggie's hands sliding away.

A fourth strike sent fire screaming along his ribs, rolled him another several feet along the edge. But he barely noticed. He heard MacDonald shout, "I've got her!" and felt a surge of power. Fueled by rage unlike anything he'd ever known, he heaved himself up and tangled his fists in Beaton's coat. The man came down on top of him, fists flailing. But the fight was even now.

Gabriel swung as best he could and his fist connected with Beaton's jaw, rocking his head back. But anticipated triumph and madness had given the other man reinforcement. He struck back, thumping an elbow down onto Gabriel's already battered ribs. Gabriel gasped, twisted, and managed to thrust Beaton off his chest. They rolled once, then again. The edge of the cliffs loomed.

Beaton snarled and writhed, scratching at Gabriel's face. Then his hands closed around Gabriel's throat with bone-crushing force. Eyes wild, spittle flying from his mouth, he made it to his knees, never loosening his grip.

"How does it feel," he mocked—in English, "knowing she is going to die, too?"

Gabriel saw black at the edge of his vision, heard the man's shrill laugh as if from a great distance. Then he heard Maggie shout his name.

In that instant, he knew he wouldn't die. He was going to live a very long time with this woman by his side.

Bracing his wrists between Beaton's arms, he slowly pushed them apart, breaking the hold on his throat. As soon as he could draw a breath, he declared, "You are not a Stuart."

Beaton froze.

Gabriel fisted his hands together and drove them into

the man's breastbone, shoving him backward. Beaton windmilled his arms, managed to right himself into a crouch.

"Your father is not Charles's illegitimate son," Gabriel continued, biting out each word, one arm clamped over his ribs to contain the pain. "He wasn't illegitimate at all. As desperately as you've always believed otherwise, your grandfather was Georàs Beaton. A servant to Lord Clanranald, keeper of Clanranald's swine."

"Liar!" Tearlach's lips pulled back over his teeth. Hissing, he rose slowly to his feet and pulled one leg back for another vicious kick. "You will die," he said coldly.

Then his head jerked around and his mouth opened in a soundless scream. "No," he whispered. "Stay away from me." He took a step back, eyes fixed on a spot in the mist, hands raised as if to ward off a blow from no hand Gabriel could see. *"Noooo!"*

He stepped backward into empty air.

Maggie fought her way free of Lachlann's arms just in time to see a figure go tumbling over the edge, arms flailing, scream guttering into a faint splash. She was too far away, the mist was too thick. She couldn't tell which man it had been. She could just see another form slowly rising from the ground. Gasping, numb, she stumbled toward it. She heard Lachlann shouting behind her, heard the rasping click of his gun. She didn't stop.

When Gabriel came limping toward her through the mist, she nearly went to her knees. But she managed to get to him, to throw herself into his arms, ignoring his grunt of pain and the screaming of her own wound. All that mattered was that he was pressing her tightly to his chest, and she could feel the beat of his heart, strong and steady, beneath her cheek.

"You could have died," he said hoarsely. "For me.

God, Maggie, would you really have died for me?"
When she gave a firm nod, he rested his chin on top of
her head. "You can ask the same of me, you know."

"I don't have to. I know you would. But I've something else to ask of you."

"Anything."

"Will you buy an acre of land—"

"Between the sea and sand." He gave an anguished
sigh. "You know I can't do that. If I could, my love, I
would. I would—"

She silenced him with a hand over his lips, allowed all
of her love for him to show in her eyes as she looked into
his face. "An acre of land," she repeated, "somewhere
between my father's holdings and the sea. So we'll have a
home of our own here when we want it. Will you do
that?"

He answered her with a fiery kiss.

Lachlann pounded up to them then. "Christ, man," he
muttered. "I nearly shot you."

"Why?" Gabriel demanded wearily.

"I thought . . . Good God, what is that?"

Maggie turned in Gabriel's arms in time to see a slight,
cloaked figure fading into the mist, followed by a much
larger one.

"Edana?" she whispered. "With MacGillechalum?"
There was a roaring in her ears suddenly, like the waves,
but so close. " 'Tis a spot for lovers, this. . . ." The pain
of her wound swelled; the mist seemed to be growing at
the edges of her vision.

Just as her knees failed her, she felt Gabriel lifting her,
cradling her against his chest. "You keep me aloft, my
love. You will not leave me," he said slowly, his voice
low and ragged at the edges. It was the same desperate
roughness that had coaxed, driven away doubt, and

called out her name as they lay together at night. "You will not. . . ."

"Nay." She raised a hand, rested it against his cheek. "I'll not ever be doing that."

19

Now I have answered your questions three,
Parsley, sage, rosemary, and thyme;
And you have answered as many for me,
Thou art now and always a true love of mine.

Scarborough, the following May

Gabriel winced as hard wood smacked solidly into his chin. "Careful, darling," he murmured. "If you keep on like this I will be forced to grow a beard, and I cannot think that would be a popular decision."

In his lap, his four-month-old daughter gurgled happily and waved the little carved seal Sim Beaton had made for her. It was new, this talent of holding on to an object long enough to smack her father with it, and Lady Saraid Elizabeth Loudon was perfectly delighted with herself. She had the MacLeod green eyes and the beginnings of MacLeod red curls, and Gabriel's heart swelled at the very sight of her.

She swung again, this time nearly flipping his fork from his plate to the floor. Maggie glanced up from her reading and smiled. "Will I take her now and let you finish your breakfast?"

"No." Gabriel wasn't about to hand over just yet one of the two most precious creatures he'd ever held—certainly not while she was dry and still in possession of her last feeding. "Is that a new dress you're wearing?"

Maggie glanced down at the leaf-green muslin. "It is,

of course. 'Tis always a new dress after Isobel pays a visit."

She absently ran a fingertip over the scar from Beaton's knife that was just visible over the bodice's lace trim. Unlike most women would have done, she never tried to hide the mark, but instead wore it with pride. It was only fitting, she said, that she'd gotten a dirk in the breast for love of an Englishman, and on the cliffs no less.

"You look very fetching." And she did, all rose-touched skin and fire-touched hair. She took his breath away.

"Thank you. And you look as if you'll need a new coat."

He glanced down, sighed resignedly as he reached for a napkin to wipe away the large milky splotch his tooth-lessly grinning daughter had just left on his lapel. "So, has Skye fallen into the sea in our absence?"

Maggie studied the few scrawled lines from her father. "I've no idea, but the racing track at Edinburgh has been terribly muddy these past few weeks." She read on, drummed her fingers against the tablecloth. Gave her own sigh. "Will you do something for me?"

"Anything," he replied, and Maggie knew he meant it. He'd been proving it for a year now, day after day, night after glorious night.

"Send my father some money."

"Anything but that," Gabriel grunted, but she didn't listen. She knew he would arrange for a generous amount to make its way into Jamie's pocket. As would Nathan and Isobel, who had no doubt received a similar woeful missive.

She read Tessa's contribution. It was rather longer than their sire's but certainly no neater. "Elspeth Colson has a new son. According to Tessa, he looks like a stoat. Lachtna Norrie is in an orange mood and is apparently quite upset that Mr. Biggs refuses to use the new altar cloth she gave the church. And Edana is still in Italy with MacGillechallum. Apparently the Italians think they make a perfect pair. She writes regularly, including Italian lessons in her letters. Tessa is presently working on translating a book that Lord MacDonald's son left in MacAuley's pub when he passed through the village. She's finding many of the words a bit obscure."

Maggie looked up, asked, "Do you know what 'spogliami' means?"

"Yes," Gabriel replied dryly. "I do."

"Well?"

"It means 'undress me.' "

"Oh, dear. I don't suppose I'll be sending that tidbit back to Tessa. I wonder if I ought to write and ask Papa to sneak away the book. . . ."

Maggie shook her head as she went back to reading. " 'I am very sad to report that the ghosties seem truly to have gone, and before I could get a good look at his head. Andy and I go in search of them at Scavaig Point as often as we can—' Oh, I do wish she wouldn't go climbing around the cliffs at night. 'Tisn't safe. '—but there's been no sign of them since last spring.'

"And no wonder," Maggie remarked, "as Edana and her fellow aren't around to be walking the cliffs."

Gabriel smiled as he removed his watch fob from Saraid's mouth. He had a very good idea why no one had seen the ghost lovers at Scavaig Point in such a long time. And he knew Maggie believed the same. They seldom spoke of that night on the cliffs. He'd never told anyone what he'd seen in those moments before Beaton had gone over the cliff edge. No one would have believed him, believed them—that they'd seen a pair of figures melting into the mist as if they'd been no more than the air itself.

" 'I very much enjoyed my time with Nathan and Isobel in Town,' " Maggie read on, " 'although I loathe having to *always* be wearing shoes and dresses. Little Edward is crawling and I did so wish Isobel would have let me take him to Hyde Park more often. I cannot be nearly so entertaining an auntie in the great museum of a place they call their townhouse. Most of the people I met were dull as duck teeth—Isn't that a marvelous expression? I . . .' "

Gabriel had leaned forward, his eyes wavering from his daughter at the last line, and was rewarded by a small fist landing in his plate, spraying them both with bits of egg and mushroom. "Go on."

Maggie rolled her eyes as he mopped at Saraid's head with his napkin, but complied. " '. . . dull as duck teeth—Isn't that a marvelous expression? I learned it from a perfectly splendid friend of Nathan's, called St. Wulfstan. He has a terrible scar on his face and sometimes speaks with an Irish brogue that Nathan's mother calls atrocious and Isobel says is deliberate. I overheard him tell Nathan he was thinking of taking a cyprian called Nell to Ireland—' Oh, why can men never watch their tongues when there is a child nearby? '—which made Isobel ever so cross. I cannot imagine why. People sail on boats with silly women's names all the time. . . .'

"It has just occurred to me that I ought to feel very sorry for the young men who will be kicking up their heels in London when Tessa makes her debut, should she choose to," Maggie commented. She bent over and plucked a mushroom from Gabriel's sleeve, then stroked a finger down the cheek of her now dozing baby's cheek. "She will terrify each and every one of them."

"Good for her," was Gabriel's reply.

"Mmm. Isn't it?" Maggie tilted her head and studied the portrait before her. Gabriel didn't see past the MacLeod eyes and hair, but Saraid had his patrician brow and that poetic mouth that turned his starkly handsome face into something much more. "Ach, but you're bonny, the pair of you. I think I'll be keeping you."

Gabriel gently jiggled the baby in his arms, then raised a wicked brow. "She's asleep."

"So she is."

"Are you having the same thought I am, beloved wife?"

Maggie grinned. "Oh, aye."

"You're not too tired? If I recall correctly, you didn't sate yourself with my humble person until dawn this morning."

Maggie's eyes sparked in memory and mischief. "I can manage it if you can." She set the letter aside and eagerly rose to her feet.

"Well. Let's go, then."

After two stops: the first a quick one to leave Saraid with her nurse, and the second a rather longer one in their own bedchamber, the Earl and Countess of Rievalux slipped out of the castle and wandered hand in hand across their Yorkshire fields to join in the long-awaited spring festivities of the Scarborough Fair.

So there you have it, then. A happy ending. Of course, when one door closes, a window opens. There's another pair waiting to find their happiness across a sea. Cupla bliain ó shinin Éirinn . . . *Ah, but that's Gaelic* again, if from a different land. So I'll begin again. Some years ago in Ireland, there was a boy and there was a girl.

And that is a different story. . . .

AUTHOR'S NOTE

The ballad "Scarbro Fair" is but one of many versions of an ancient song that appears in the form of "The Elfin Knight" in England and "My Plaid Awa' " in Scotland. By the mid-eighteenth century, the refrain of "Savory, sage, rosemary, and thyme"—or something similar—was common, as was a variant of "For once he/she was a true lover of mine." I owe a debt of gratitude to Francis Child (1825–1896) for collecting fifty-five versions of this wonderful song in his *English and Scottish Popular Ballads*. Boston-born, fiercely patriotic, Child might seem an odd choice to be the man who would save thousands of English and Scottish ballads from disappearing forever. But he did it, and I thank him. I am just as grateful to my mother for giving me complete access to her turntable and LPs from the moment I was old enough to reach the record needle, and to Paul Simon and Art Garfunkel for being the voices on one of those records.

On sale now!

In Regency England, there is a very thin line between
love and hate and betrayal . . .

ENTWINED
by Emma Jensen

Nathan Paget, Marquess of Oriel, returns to London
society a great military hero of the Peninsular Campaign
and a most eligible bachelor. Unbeknownst to the rest of
the world, Nathan has been blinded and has only one
goal in mind—to uncover the traitor responsible for the
death of his comrades and for his injury. He shares his
secret with only one person, the headstrong and beautiful
Isobel MacLeod, who agrees to serve as his "eyes" and help
him unmask the traitor in their midst. This unlikely duo
can barely stand each other's company—or so they
think—until they find themselves falling deeply in love,
a love threatened by an unknown enemy with murder
and betrayal in his heart.

Published by Ballantine Books.
Available in your local bookstore.

Now in mass market for the first time!

THE INNOCENT
by Bertrice Small

Deceptively fragile-looking, Eleanore of Ashlin had promised her life to God . . . until fate intervened. With her brother's untimely death, Eleanore—known as Elf to those who love her—becomes the heiress to an estate vital to England's defenses. She is ordered by royal command to wed one of the king's knights rather than take her final vows. With a resistant heart, but obedient to King Stephen's will, she complies.

Sir Ranulf de Glandeville is all too aware that his innocent bride wants no man; yet his patience, gentle hand, and growing love for his spirited young wife soon awaken Eleanore to passions she never knew, or desired . . . until now.

But their love is not secure from the wicked schemes of an evil woman who hates Eleanore with all her heart—and who seeks to destroy the innocent in a depraved plot that will put Eleanore's life in jeopardy and her faith in love to its greatest test. . . .

Published by Ballantine Books.
Available in bookstores everywhere.